T0271510

The Many Lies
of
Veronica Hawkins

The Many Lies

of

Veronica Hawkins

Kristina Pérez

CONSTABLE

CONSTABLE

First published in Great Britain in 2024 by Constable

A CIP catalogue record for this book
is available from the British Library.

ISBN: 978-1-40871-901-5 (hardback)
ISBN: 978-1-40871-902-2 (trade paperback)

Typeset in Bembo by Initial Typesetting Services, Edinburgh
Printed and bound in Great Britain by Clays Ltd, Elcograf S.p.A

Papers used by Constable are from well-managed forests
and other responsible sources

Constable
An imprint of
Little, Brown Book Group
Carmelite House
50 Victoria Embankment
London EC4Y 0DZ

An Hachette UK Company
www.hachette.co.uk

www.littlebrown.co.uk

To the women who made me who I am

Part i

Hungry Ghosts:
Life and Death
on the Peak

Martina Torres

Camden Press

Uncorrected proof. First edition: June 2015

ADVANCED READER'S EDITION

When Martina Torres arrived in the glamorous and vibrant metropolis of Hong Kong newly married to her high-school sweetheart, the world seemed to be her oyster. But looks can be deceiving. Adrift in a foreign city, with no job and no friends, Martina chafed in her new role as Expat Wife.

Everything changed the day she met Veronica Hawkins.

Veronica was the epitome of old Hong Kong — the last surviving member of a British mercantile dynasty that built the city during its colonial heyday — gorgeous, filthy rich, the Gloria Vanderbilt of Hong Kong. Martina never expected to be taken under Veronica's wing. She certainly didn't expect Veronica's fierce kindness, unswerving loyalty, or the many things Veronica would teach Martina about herself.

The last thing she could ever have expected was Veronica's mysterious and tragic death. *What really happened to Veronica Hawkins?* asked tabloid headlines around the globe.

It's the wrong question.

Who really was Veronica Hawkins? That's the right one. In Martina's words, 'She was my best friend.'

Based on Martina's viral BuzzFeed article, '10 Things You Learn When Your Best Friend Dies', *Hungry Ghosts: Life and Death on the Peak* is an unflinching account of the complex nature of grief, the meaning of belonging, and the transformative power of friendship.

Major Marketing & Publicity Campaign

- National Print Review Campaign
- Multi-city Author Book Tour
- Consumer & Trade Advertising
- Trade Show Marketing
- Book Club Marketing
- Comprehensive Awards Campaign

Media Inquiries: publicity@camdenpress

Agent: Jamie Jackson with JJ Literary

Prologue

The End of the Beginning

My mother always told me no relationship ends well. Either you break up or somebody dies.

I didn't believe her at the time. I was ten or eleven, watching her tweeze her eyebrows to within an inch of their lives (a seventies hangover, I presume). She caught my gaze in the mirror on her vanity and held it the way she did when I was in trouble. I can still smell her Cartier perfume – the one with the panther perched atop the bottle stopper: pepper and narcissus that made me sneeze.

I didn't believe her because I assumed she meant messy kissing relationships with boys who picked their noses and other body parts. I was still several years away from being interested in those. Now I know better.

But there's no word for a woman who loses her best friend. I can't call myself a widow or an orphan, although I often feel like both. Friendless isn't quite right, either, because I can still feel her close to me.

I became intoxicated with Hong Kong and Veronica Hawkins all at once. The charged scent in the air right before a black rainstorm strikes will forever mean Hong Kong and Veronica to me. No doubt you've seen the headlines surrounding the mysterious and tragic death that has captivated tabloids around the globe. Some say it was an accident, others suicide, still others murder.

Without incontrovertible proof, the police case is closed, but the public speculation will remain cocktail-party chitchat forever. Veronica Hawkins's death has already become legend: joining the ranks of Natalie Wood, Marilyn Monroe, Princess Diana.

The world loves a beautiful dead white woman.

And yet none of the blind items, whispers or innuendo captures the Veronica I knew, the Veronica who drew me out of my shell and helped me find the Martina I was meant to be.

I'm the last person I'd ever have suspected would write a memoir. It's happened mostly by accident. My entire childhood, and most of my adult life, has been about polishing myself until my skin was so buffed it bled. Admitting I have any weaknesses or imperfections an impossibility. I became a journalist to write about other people, to prevent anyone from looking too closely at me – from finding me wanting.

When Veronica vanished one sultry night, my heart shattered. Broke wide open. At the depths of my grief, fuelled by a few too many glasses of Sauvignon Blanc, I poured my heart into words to try to make sense of a world without Veronica in it. If I'd never met her, I'd never have had the guts to send my ramblings to an editor at BuzzFeed. My friendship with Veronica altered me on a cellular level – she believed in me enough for both of us.

The response to my article was overwhelming and unexpected. I started by writing about Veronica and discovered I was really writing about myself, writing my way back to myself: someone new whom I still don't always recognise. I thought I'd said everything I'd needed to say, told the world the ten things I'd learned when my best friend died.

Some of the comments on my article (note: never read the comments) made me realise how much Veronica would have hated how her death became more grist for the mill. I needed to tell the whole story, the unvarnished truth of our friendship, of Veronica's final days, even if it meant revealing my own pain, letting the sun stream in through a magnifying glass. I owed it to Veronica. It was the only thing I had left to give her.

If you've picked up this book looking for a whodunnit or a true-crime exposé, apologies in advance, you're going to be disappointed.

This is a love story.

Veronica taught me to love her hometown the way she did, showed me a Hong Kong I never would have seen without her. This is a love letter to my best friend and to the city where we met. Both are gems made more precious by their flaws.

It's fitting that I should be writing this on Qingming of all days. Tomb-sweeping Day, when families across Hong Kong tidy the tombstones or cremation urns on the terraced hills of the city's columbaria, the air filled with the sandalwood smoke of burning joss sticks and silvered spirit money to honour their ancestors. Some offer villas and Lamborghinis so they can live out their afterlife in style.

Veronica once took me to the old colonial cemetery in Happy Valley to sweep the grave of her first ancestor, who set foot on the island when it was still considered nothing more than a desolate rock. She never felt like she belonged in Britain, she told me. She thought of herself as a Hongkonger. It's where she was born.

It's where she died.

This memoir is my attempt to sweep up the rubbish and scandal surrounding her death and to celebrate her life. It's the story of us. We're inextricably bound now, Veronica and me, Veronica and the woman she believed I could be. When I feel that self slipping from my grasp, being pulled out to sea, feeling out of my depth, I remember that Veronica was there for me, and she always will be there – somewhere out there – watching over me.

I'm not sure what comes next but, tonight, I'll be burning a papier-mâché bottle of Dom Pérignon in Veronica's honour.

Wherever she is, I'm sure she's the life of the party.

Heiress goes overboard at charity gala on luxury junk

Asearch is underway for Veronica Hawkins, 35, scion of the Hawkins family and CEO of Hawkins Pacific Limited, who disappeared from a luxury cruise in Victoria Harbour last night.

The Fire Services Department received a report at 1.15 a.m. from the captain of the *Tin Hau 8* that a woman had fallen overboard. In a press briefing at around 6 a.m. this morning, the department's marine and diving division commander Cheung Pak Hei said that they were coordinating with helicopter pilots from the Government Flying Service to scour the waters near the West Kowloon Cultural District.

Ms Hawkins was a guest at the Lifting Hope charity fundraiser gala to benefit orphans in Cambodia.

The event was organised by Cressida Wong, daughter of shipping tycoon Donald Wong and wife of Jack Zhang, founder of the Beijing-based SinoTop, the leading Chinese defence and security firm.

The boat departed from the Royal Hong Kong Yacht Club around 7.30 p.m. in the evening, carrying a veritable who's who of the city's elite, including film star Venus Lam.

Jean-Pierre Renard, 54, artist and husband to Ms Hawkins, was also in attendance.

Guests at the party told the *South China Daily* on the condition of anonymity that the missing heiress appeared intoxicated and disoriented shortly before her absence was noticed.

This is a developing story.

Chapter 1

An American in Hong Kong

*Y*ou already know how this story ends. What you don't
know is how it started. My life in Hong Kong truly began
the day I met Veronica Hawkins.

The humidity was thick enough to chew as I battled my way
down the steep, narrow streets of Central. I'd arrived in the Fragrant
Harbour, as it's known, the month before and hadn't yet learned to
keep a collapsible umbrella in my Longchamp tote bag at all times.
Or the futility of wearing kitten heels on the jigsaw of tiles and
pockmarked pavements.

A growl of thunder reverberated between the skyscrapers of the
business district that nearly made me believe in the dragons sup-
posedly dwelling beneath the serpentine Nine Hills of Kowloon
across the filmy green strait. Fat raindrops fell on my raw-silk blouse
and perspiration dampened the nape of my neck as I hustled down
Queen's Road. Perfect, just perfect. I was late and I'd be a wet,
sweaty mess by the time I reached the gallery to interview a notoriously formidable heiress. My heart sank. The article for *HK City
Chic* was my first professional gig since arriving.

It took no time after landing in town to hear Veronica's name
whispered at expat events with a mixture of envy and fear. Her family business, Hawkins Pacific, was one of the last remaining British
hongs, or foreign-owned trading houses, and had been instrumental
in transforming Hong Kong from a collection of fishing villages

to the Pearl of the Orient. Veronica lived her life in regional and international society pages – especially following the tragic boating accident that orphaned her as a teenager.

I'd been primed to detest Veronica: obscenely wealthy and cloaked with elegant grief, practically a Gothic heroine. Which was why I'd been surprised when her PA had agreed so readily to an in-person interview without any pre-specified no-go topics.

Another crack of thunder resounded overhead. You'd think growing up in New York City, loud noises wouldn't set my teeth on edge, but there's something about a coming storm that unnerves me.

Skittering as fast as I could in my kitten heels, my gaze skimmed the expertly coiffed women, foreign and local, brandishing Harvey Nichols shopping bags like shields against downward mobility as they queued for red-and-white taxis outside the Landmark Mandarin Oriental. *Tai tais*, I would learn to call them: ladies who lunch. That had always been my mother's greatest ambition for me, why my parents insisted on sending me to a Manhattan private school we could barely afford. Status was the hit they craved.

I accosted a hotel bellboy, soggy map of Central in hand. 'I'm looking for the Gallery de Ladrones? Duddell Street?'

Rain pelting the golden fan logo on his cap, the bellboy flung an arm towards the busy road, an artery gushing through the island, while hoisting a suit bag over his shoulder that looked like it weighed more than he did.

'Across the street, turn right.'

Everyone knew the Gallery de Ladrones. Founded by Veronica's mother, it quickly became known for showing the most avant-garde Mainland artists. After Tiananmen, with fears of the implications for the Handover agreement in 1997 swirling, the gallery's gutsy stance held a certain cachet. On the eve of the gallery's twenty-fifth anniversary, the same fears were once again starting to swirl. Nearly losing an eye to a rogue umbrella spoke as I crossed the road, I found Duddell Street at last.

Still the most romantic street in Hong Kong, a flight of impos-
ing granite stairs at the far end was dotted by Victorian gas lamps.
Sprawling tree roots climbed the stone walls that supported Ice
House Street above, lush green foliage shimmering in the hazy light,
like the last gasp of empire. Sometimes it seemed the British had
colonised Hong Kong not for its deep-water harbour but because
the opaque white light and constant mist reminded them of home.

Boom!

My shoulders stiffened and my eyes widened as a waterfall began
to gush from the top of the steps. Squinting, I made out the gallery
logo – the distinctive red sail of a junk ship: curved, almost triangu-
lar, with bamboo battens for support like the ridges on the shell of a
prehistoric crustacean.

The heel of my strappy, open-toed Jimmy Choo caught on a
loose tile just outside the entrance. My ankle turned and I went splat.
Pushing myself up from the pavement, I glanced around like a startled animal. I wanted – no, *needed* – to make the right first impression.

Grabbing the tattered map from the ground, I shoved it into my
tote, and caught my reflection in the small mirror dangling above
the door (a feng shui trick to ward off evil spirits). *Fuck.* I rearranged
my dark caramel-streaked chignon and forced myself to unclench
my jaw, pale cheeks neon pink. So much for casually chic.

A laughing figure approached me from inside.

The man who blasted me with a welcome polar vortex of aircon
was a silver fox par excellence. His skin was a tanned brown that
showed a complete disregard for SPF and yet it looked supple. It
was almost impossible to resist smoothing the crow's feet around his
eyes. He was slim, but not runner gaunt, in his early fifties. The cool
blue of his linen suit contrasted with the warmth of his skin.

He looked nothing like my husband.

Spencer is blond and preppy. When we arrived in Hong Kong,
Spence had just turned thirty-two and I was twenty-eight but his
baby face made him look younger.

'*Bienvenue*,' the gentleman said breezily. He seemed like a gentleman, his wine-dark eyes glinting with amusement. 'Veronica is inside,' he added in a thick French accent; he said it in an offhand way, clearly on his way out, as if no one ever came to the gallery looking for him, which I found hard to believe.

The door swished shut behind me and the gallery went still. Only the sound of the whining A/C unit remained. I shivered as another arctic gust blew down my spine. I had also not yet learned to carry a cardigan with my umbrella at all times.

Sometime later, Veronica confessed she'd married a Frenchman because she'd wanted to fall in love with the same abandon her father had with her mother. A talented photojournalist, the much younger Geneviève Varenne had moved to Hong Kong from the remnants of French Indochina. She met Arthur Hawkins at the Foreign Correspondents' Club bar where many confessions have been made and even more confidences betrayed, and they eloped a week later.

I'd never wanted to fall in love like that, not truthfully, but Veronica was inherently braver than me. She lived boldly, and that's not me airbrushing her for posterity.

Surveying the teak floors and sparsely hung walls of the gallery, I noted two black leather Barcelona chairs on either side of an antique lacquer coffee table inlaid with mother-of-pearl flowers and adorned with a voluptuous orchid plant. Feeling as if I were being watched, my eyes were drawn back to a small oil painting just inside the door.

A young Chinese woman with an arresting stare commanded the canvas. Swathed in a diaphanous red robe, she floated above a seascape, her hands outstretched: a fish clasped in her right fist; a toy junk ship in the left. A flat-topped cap was positioned at a jaunty angle like a beret, her head held with imperial grace, red beads dripping from either side. I could almost hear them clacking in the wind.

'Tin Hau,' said a cultured British voice, throatier than I'd expected.

'Who is she?' I asked, not removing my eyes from the painting.

'Goddess of the sea. Patron saint of fishermen. Empress of heaven. Take your pick.' Veronica paused. 'She was just a girl, at the start. She died trying to save her father and brother when their boat sank in a storm. So they made her a goddess.'

From the corner of my eye, my focus snagged on a signature: *Varenne, '78*.

'I didn't realise your mother also painted.'

I felt more than saw a shrug. The shrug of someone unsurprised a total stranger knew who her mother was. 'This is her only portrait. She painted it for my father the year I was born.' An adoring expression softened Veronica's features. 'He was a keen sailor. The Hawkins empire was built on the sea, he never failed to remind me. The company always sponsors a dragon dance for Tin Hau's birthday.'

Neither of us spoke. We were both thinking the same thing. The goddess had failed to save Veronica's family.

And, in the end, she didn't come for Veronica, either.

At that moment, I heard what sounded like a slap. My eyes darted back to the gallery entrance where a wall of white water pounded the glass. The rest of the city had disappeared as if we were encased in a raincloud.

I must have seemed spooked because a gentle hand landed on my wet silk blouse.

'Black rain,' said Veronica. 'Your first storm?' I nodded. 'We have amber, red and black rainstorms here,' she explained and it sounded biblical. 'You don't have far to travel home?'

'Mid-Levels.'

'Ah, the domain of soulless condos.'

Which had been precisely my feeling about the tiny apartments that spackled the hills above Central and boasted ridiculous monthly price tags.

'It's just temporary,' I said, kicking myself for my knee-jerk defensiveness. 'The bank put us in a serviced apartment while we find something permanent.'

Veronica nodded. 'Fresh off the boat.' I heard the tease in her voice. 'In my father's time, bored colonials would still greet new arrivals at the port. Tell your relocation coordinator to look for places on the Peak, above the fog line.'

'Our housing allowance barely covers a shoebox.' A nervy laugh escaped me. 'And I thought property in New York was bananas.'

I already knew that Veronica had been born on the Peak, which in Hong Kong is both literal and figurative. The lofty summit from which the former colonial governors looked down on their subjects and the container-ship-strewn South China Sea beyond, where the Chinese inhabitants were forbidden to live until after the Second World War, is still home to the most prestigious villas – if the most mould prone. There's also the chill of damp that never quite leaves your skin.

With a commiserating sigh, Veronica told me, 'Expat packages aren't what they used to be before the financial crisis. More like half-pat.'

'Half-pat – that's me.' In-between was how I'd always felt and it seemed that Hong Kong would be no different. I was certain Veronica would treat me like the wildly privileged girls at The Buxton School who'd tormented me because Papi spoke the door-man's language and I didn't summer in the south of France or at my family's compound in St Barths or even – most pedestrian of all – at a shingled summer house in Quogue.

'You came with your husband. Three-year contract, I suppose,' Veronica said and it was as if she could see the DEPENDENT stamped on my new Hong Kong Identity Card.

The HKD 800 fee I was making for the profile piece barely covered lunch in Central but I didn't care because it was a job. I'd been working at magazines since grad school and I didn't know what else I wanted to do. Plus, I was lonely.

Desperation tasted metallic and I choked it down. Shifting my shoulders as if preparing to look at an eclipse, I allowed my gaze to land fully on Veronica Hawkins for the first time.

The pinlights glittered on the gold dust sprinkled across her black T-shirt spelling out '14K'. She had paired it with linen capri pants and Chanel espadrille wedges with the ribbons laced as if she were about to hop en pointe and pirouette.

Curving my lips into my most arch smile, I nodded at the '14K' and said, 'I would have expected at least twenty-four carats.'

Veronica laughed and it was smoky, rich. Her porcelain skin was also sun-touched, emphasising her unusual hazel eyes. Smooth waves of auburn, not quite crimson hair swept around her shoulders.

'It's a joke,' she said. '14K is one of the biggest Triad groups.' I'd vaguely heard of the Triads operating in Chinatown back in New York and knew only that they were Chinese mafia.

Tracing the outline of the 'K', Veronica mused, 'The British taipans were the first gangsters in Hongkers, of course.' She spoke without judgement, unapologetic.

Hawkins Pacific Limited had been founded in the north of England at the beginning of the nineteenth century by Alistair Hawkins, an ambitious young Scotsman, opening an office in Shanghai before a second location in Hong Kong. Like the other heads of the hongs, Veronica's ancestor was on the wrong side of history regarding the Opium War, running armed clipper ships up the Pearl River, making a fortune bolstered by British gunships. Alistair soon multiplied his initial packet by building railways in China and investing in telecommunications.

Standing there covered in gold dust, Veronica embodied the spirit of the taipans who had come before her, helming all of the Hawkins Pacific holdings since the age of nineteen.

'I'm Martina Torres,' I said abruptly, realising I hadn't introduced myself. 'From HK City Chic.' Veronica lifted an eyebrow in confirmation of what she'd presumed. 'My friends call me Marty,' I offered. (Actually, I'd hated the nickname in elementary school but it stuck, and it made me sound WASPy, so I kept it. With the exception of our wedding vows, Spence has never called me Martina.)

I extended my hand but Veronica didn't shake it. Frowning, she took my hand and flipped it over to expose the palm. 'You're bleeding.'

A flush spread down my chest like a rash. Veronica reached for the other hand, the furrow on the bridge of her nose deepening. Both palms were grazed.

'I slipped,' I said and pointed at one of the guilty Jimmy Choos. 'On the tile.'

'I've been meaning to get that fixed. You're not going to sue me, are you? Isn't that what you Americans do?'

Fighting my flush, I countered, 'I think I'll invest in flats.'

Veronica lifted one of her feet, circling the espadrille at the end of her dainty ankle. 'They're knock-offs, but they're dead comfortable. Stanley Market.'

I bit the inside of my cheek because I hadn't noticed they weren't real Chanel. Before I married Spencer, living in Manhattan on a publishing salary, hamstrung by Ivy League debt, my only high-end designer goods were found at sample sales. Yes, I have class anxiety, but I came by it honestly.

'Nice,' I complimented her. 'Thanks for the tip.'

'Come, let's get you cleaned up.'

Veronica started walking towards the back of the gallery and I followed. The gallery was larger than it initially appeared, a wrought-iron staircase twisting its way towards a mezzanine that served as the offices. Sat pertly at a desk in a royal blue Marc Jacobs dress (which in a few months I'd assume to be a Shenzhen copy rather than original), a visibly annoyed Chinese woman yelled into her handset. 'That's Apple,' said Veronica. 'My PA. She's wrangling a missing sculpture for the anniversary exhibition.'

Veronica turned the handle on a door that blended seamlessly into the wall, discreetly revealing a washroom. 'I'll make tea,' she said, leaving me to it.

A strange feeling settled over me, as if I were on a film set of a gallery in Hong Kong and not really here at all. When I re-emerged, Veronica had ensconced herself on one of the Barcelona chairs, a ceramic teapot and two round cups the colour of jade set upon the table.

'Better?' she said, glancing at my hands. Before I could reply, she went on, 'Jasmine. I hope that suits.'

'Perfect.' I seated myself in the chair opposite hers as she poured the tea. Thanking her, I raised the steaming cup to my mouth, hoping the leaves didn't get stuck between my teeth. The jasmine smelled sharp and clean, like the rain that continued to beat the pavement.

Veronica pushed a crystal dish in my direction with a flick of the wrist. 'You must try some ginger with the tea. Even Queen Victoria was a fan of Hong Kong's preserved ginger – after my great-great sold it to her. No fashionable table in London would be without it.'

I looked at the sparkling candied ginger in a new light. *Great-great*, I would discover, was how Veronica referred to any of her illustrious lineage older than her grandfather.

At my hesitation, she said, 'Don't tell me you're doing keto,' like it was a dare.

I chose the plumpest piece I could find and popped it into my mouth.

Veronica spread her lips in a satisfied smile and I realised there were a lot of things I would do, that anybody would do, for that Cheshire cat smile.

'I'm curious,' she said. 'How did you get on Evelyn's radar?'

Evelyn Ho was the editor-in-chief of *HK City Chic* but no relation to Stanley Ho, the billionaire who controls a huge swathe of the Macau gambling industry – at least not as far as I'm aware, although billionaires tend to be discreet.

'Through a friend of a friend in New York,' I said. The opportunity had come up in a roundabout way from one of my college friends' friend at business school who was Evelyn's cousin.

Veronica sipped her tea demurely, gaze sharp, listening to the spaces between the words.

'Six degrees of separation makes the world go round,' she said after a few moments. 'You'll fit in here, Marty.' Coming from Veronica, I found myself suddenly liking the nickname; in her British accent the long 'ah' made it sound sophisticated rather than Long Island. But I'd never fit in anywhere, of that I was convinced.

The rain continued to pummel the windows. I swallowed the ginger, warmth spreading down my gullet as if it were an ember. Jasmine and ginger and black rain: a Hong Kong afternoon. There would be more, many more, before there would be none.

'Let's get to the interview,' Veronica said, leaning forward. 'Although I'd much rather hear about you. I know all about me, and it's not nearly so interesting as people like to think.'

I smiled, fidgeting a small piece of ginger with my tongue, as if I believed her.

I wanted to believe her.

With a resigned sigh, she said, 'But that's not why you're here. I know, I know.' Her eyes suddenly shone very bright. 'You're here for my hungry ghosts.'

My lips parted.

'I'll let you in on a secret. It's not just the living who want. The Chinese are right about hell – we all go on wanting when we're dead.'

Chapter 2

Fishbowl Princess

*V*eronica was always full of surprises. She gave me my first the very next day when she called me up herself – no PA intermediary – and invited me to lunch at the Hong Kong Club, barely giving me enough time to blow dry my hair. Veronica lived in the moment, as if she knew the value of every second and didn't want to waste a single one. At the time, I thought it was the product of losing her family to the capricious sea.

After what happened to her, I can't help but wonder if she always knew, somehow, that she was running out of time.

If Hong Kong is a fishbowl and Central is the castle at its heart, then the Hong Kong Club is its throne room. Established a few years after the Qing emperor ceded the island to the British, the club provided a place for the heads of the largest hongs to meet and Veronica's great-great was among the founding members. Colonial governors would come and go, but the true rulers here were the taipans. The city runs on *guanxi* – relationships, influence, soft power – and the Hawkins name opened every door.

I strolled into the Red Room of the Hong Kong Club, hiding my apprehension while surreptitiously giving my lightweight turquoise knit Missoni dress and Ferragamo pumps a once-over. Although I'd quickly Googled the club's dress code, I almost expected a white-gloved hand to tap me on the shoulder and tell me to vacate the premises. Spence's family had been members of the right Manhattan clubs for generations but I was only accepted with their sponsorship, and they didn't pretend otherwise.

The walls of the dining room were lined with Constable-esque landscapes in gilded frames and, appropriately enough, painted a deep red. If it were a nail polish, the muted colour would be called '9-to-5' and worn by female executives. Scanning the room, I'd hoped to be shown to a secluded corner by the hostess. A table from which I could fade into the scenery.

More fool me.

Seated at the most prominent table, with the perfect vantage point to observe whether anyone notable was entering or exiting, Veronica's posture was relaxed as she lifted her gaze to mine and smiled. This wasn't the Cheshire cat smile from the day before. Veronica possessed many types of smiles but she reserved this one – the unguarded one that crinkled her eyes – for a very select few.

That afternoon she was wearing an emerald-green cocktail frock that brought out the golden flecks of her eyes, and she'd traded her comfy espadrilles for patent leather platforms with tell-tale red soles. She radiated life. This is how I still think of her, even after the photos of her bloated corpse were leaked to the *Sun*.

'Marty,' she said, almost breathing it in, as I reached her. 'You found me.'

Veronica's voice was undeniably Oxonian, yet it was also deep for a woman, like a modern Marlene Dietrich – altogether disarming. Again I was struck by how different my nickname felt coming from Veronica, how differently she was already making me feel about myself.

She stood to give me a kiss on either cheek, very Continental. The brief intimacy took me aback. A few curious glances sideswiped me, openly wondering who Veronica Hawkins was greeting like a long-lost friend. And, strangely, it did feel inconceivable that we'd only met the day before. She'd been so gregarious during the interview, a far cry from the ice princess I'd anticipated, affably rehashing her life story for what must have been the umpteenth time. Almost as if she'd been needing to talk to someone – anyone.

'Thanks so much for the invitation,' I said as she motioned for me to be seated in the chair next to hers at a table meant for four.

'Of course,' Veronica replied. 'It's hard to be new in town.' She plucked the wedge of lime from the highball glass in front of her, squeezed it, and tossed it into the blue-tinted ice. 'Sun's over the yard arm. Arthur considered G&Ts mother's milk – best way to keep malaria away. Quinine in the tonic.'

Another thing I noticed early on was that Veronica called her father Arthur and her mother Maman, without any real affection. The real affection was reserved for Lulu, the baby sister lost to the waves.

'Mad dogs and Englishmen,' she said with an insouciant shrug, and when the waiter asked what I'd like to drink, I ordered a G&T too.

Tipping her cut-crystal glass at the English pastoral scenes, 'You'd be forgiven for forgetting we lost the empire,' Veronica told me with a wink.

'It reminds me of *Jane Eyre*,' I blurted, and she went still, glass paused mid-air, waiting for me to dig myself deeper. 'The red room where Jane's aunt locks her in as punishment.' I wanted to bite my tongue in the worst way – did Veronica think I was insulting her? After she'd been so gracious? 'You know, the room Jane thinks is haunted.'

Veronica inhaled deeply.

'Aren't we all?' she said. She took a healthy sip of her drink and let out a full-throated laugh. 'Here I was thinking you were about to point out that red is a lucky colour. But you're not the typical trailing spouse, Marty.'

Her eyes lit with approval. Yet somehow she knew I was flailing, a fish out of water, not so much in a new city as in something much bigger. In those early days, Veronica saw me more clearly than I saw myself.

Setting her glass back on the fine linen tablecloth, Veronica stee-pled her fingers. 'We've already talked about my ghosts. Now it's my turn to interview you.'

My mouth went dry, wishing the waiter would hurry up with my drink.

'Let's see. Martina Torres: a born-and-bred New Yorker, nearly perfect SATs.' Veronica began to rattle off my CV, which she must have gotten from Editor Evelyn. 'Bachelor's in art history from Columbia, master's from the Other Place – on a Gates Scholarship, no less.'

Inwardly, I squirmed. You might think I'd bask in my accomplishments but it was just the opposite. When The Buxton School doled out As and Bs among my classmates, Papi pulled me aside and told me I was an A-student. I couldn't afford to be a C-student. Not least because of my last name. We made a bargain that first day of fifth grade, Papi and me, and you don't welch on a deal with my father.

'Lastly,' Veronica added after a beat, 'features writer at Hearst.' She didn't point out that line on my CV came to an unceremonious end several months after Lehman collapsed, and I'd been scrounging freelance gigs ever since. Although I'd harboured ambitions of bylines in the *Atlantic* or *Vanity Fair* (like every other pretentious college grad), I settled for writing pieces about the different flavours of liquid Xanax available for cockapoos. (Chicken, beef and bubble-gum, if you were wondering.)

Veronica leaned closer. 'And now you've come here, to my little island.'

'So it would seem.' And it was hers, indeed.

'I hope we'll be able to keep you entertained,' she said. 'It must have been difficult to leave the glamorous world of New York publishing.'

Eating Cup O'Noodles in my cubicle when I was still fortunate enough to have a cubicle was the antithesis of glamour but I parroted the same response I'd given my girlfriends at Pilates class and that I'd come to hear parroted back at me from other transplanted wives with Marry Well degrees.

'It was a fantastic opportunity for my husband. We couldn't turn it down.'

Truth be told, it was a godsend. Spence was about to get downsized when a headhunter friend of his from Brown recruited him into the Multinational Relationship Management team of an American investment bank expanding into Mainland China. Asia was the only place banks were still jazzed up about after the crisis, so we took a yellow cab straight to JFK.

'Torres isn't your married name, though,' Veronica said, and I wondered if she had called Evelyn to vet me. The thought was both disquieting and thrilling.

'No, it isn't. My father's from Argentina. I didn't want to change it.'

Much to the chagrin of my mother-in-law. *Don't you want to be one of us?* she'd said, and I knew that she didn't just mean a Merton. Spence liked to call me *mamacita*, fancied himself a gaucho in the bedroom, and once endearingly surprised me with incredibly high-end Japanese matcha tea because he'd confused it with the *maté* I'd learned to love during summers in the foothills of the Andes. But he was trying. Sybil Merton, on the other hand, was a dyed-in-the-wool Daughter of the American Revolution who didn't want a grandchild with a tainted pedigree.

'Ah, Argentina,' Veronica said. 'One of my great-greats invested in the railroads. We Brits did get around.' She had a way of relaying history that made it seem less like a guidebook and more hush-hush. Another laugh. 'But you and Spencer are high-school sweethearts – that's delicious.'

'Well, not exactly.' I coughed. 'We went to the same school but Spence was several years ahead,' I said, thinking back to how he used to swan around the hallways in his Varsity jacket, completely oblivious to the freshman girls lining up to give him their virginity. Well, *almost* completely oblivious. He took the adulation as his due, but, unlike some of the Buxton boys, he didn't have a cruel streak.

Occasionally our eyes would meet across the cafeteria or the chapel and he'd smile, sending my heart racing, but 'He didn't know I existed,' I confessed. 'I was in his sister's class.' Sometimes I still couldn't believe we'd ended up together.

Gratefully, I accepted my G&T from the waiter who had covertly reappeared. He took our orders for lunch. Again, I followed Veronica's lead and selected the crab and mango salad.

'You and your sister-in-law must be close,' mused Veronica, twirling the swizzle stick of her G&T idly. 'Elsie wanted me to marry her brother so we could really be sisters.' She wrinkled her nose. 'I'd rather kiss my own toes.'

'Elsie?'

'Oh, of course you haven't met. I'll have to introduce you.' A fleeting look of devotion passed over her face. 'Elsie Barron. You'll love her. The Barrons have been in Hong Kong almost as long as the Hawkins and they practically adopted me after . . .'

After. Secretly I'd wondered what it would be like to have a life so dramatically interrupted, divided into discrete parts.

Now that I know, I wish I didn't.

'Elsie's father passed away four or five years ago,' Veronica went on. 'The last of that generation. During the Japanese occupation, Rupert Barron and Arthur were in the Stanley internment camp together as boys.'

I'd skimmed the company history on the Hawkins Pacific website and gleaned that her grandfather had been one of the elderly taipans who'd defended the North Point power station against the invasion.

'The British governor surrendered on Christmas Day, didn't he?' I offered.

'An Eton man. Never trust an Eton man.' Veronica's shoulders lifted as she sighed. 'Arthur and Rupert didn't speak about the camp, but it forged a bond stronger than steel. They were heirs to rival hongs and yet they were always brothers first. Uncle Rupert was my godfather. He showed me the ropes, mentored me when I returned from Oxford with less than half a degree.'

'He sounds like a great man.'

'He was.' Clinking the ice in her glass, Veronica said, 'Gin makes me sentimental.'

The waiter's timing was note perfect as he returned with crystal dishes of crabmeat layered between wafer-thin slices of mango.

'Let's tuck in,' Veronica encouraged me.

I'd skipped breakfast and my stomach rumbled as I enthusiastically speared a large slice and began to chew with what I hoped wasn't too much gusto. Veronica laughed a little at my expense as she indicated a dab of crab stippling my upper lip.

Cheeks heating, I swiped at it with the napkin. 'It's divine,' I said, laughing along. I soothed my pride with a gulp of my G&T.

At that moment, someone caught Veronica's attention and she lifted her hand in a small wave. I followed her gaze towards the entrance and saw a broad smile part the lips of a Chinese man in his late fifties. His black hair was shot through with white and wrinkles gathered at the corners of his round, deep-set eyes.

He started walking towards us. I noted his Church's brogues, the conservative navy tie and the fine cut of his handcrafted suit, most likely made by a Shanghainese tailor, who are considered the best.

Extending his hand, 'Veronica,' he said. 'I haven't seen you at the club in an age.' He spoke with an unplaceable accent, neither entirely British nor American. Later, I learned to recognise it as the international timbre of elite Hongkongers who had gone to boarding school in England, followed by university on the East Coast – or vice versa.

'I know, Edwin,' replied Veronica as she shook his hand. 'I'm trying to impress my new friend, Martina. She's just moved here from New York. She's a very important journalist and she's writing a profile of me – so don't say anything bad.'

Edwin chuckled while giving me an assessing look. 'Oh, I wouldn't dare,' he said and slanted his shoulders towards me, shaking my proffered hand. 'I'm Edwin Leung, delighted to meet you.' The name rang a bell but I couldn't place it.

'Martina Torres.'

'That does sound like a journalist. Who do you write for?'

'Everyone who matters,' Veronica answered for me, and he nodded, not pressing the issue. 'Martina did a master's at Cambridge – although we won't hold that against her.'

'Which college?' he asked.

'Peterhouse.'

Renewed interest showed in his eyes. 'My brother is a Tab too, read Economics at Peterhouse. Before they let in women.' He released another chuckle.

I conjured a smile. 'A dark day.'

Touching my elbow, Veronica said, 'I've known Edwin forever. He started his career working for Arthur at Hawkins Pacific. He caught me sneaking champagne at one of Fat Pang's parties.' Fat Pang being what some locals jovially called Chris Patten, the last governor of Hong Kong.

'Be sure to put that in your article,' Edwin told me. He twiddled the silk-knot cufflink in his left cuff. 'Work brings you to Hong Kong, then?'

Veronica spoke before I could open my mouth.

'As a matter of fact, that would be you, Edwin.'

His eyebrows, also going white, lifted sky high and I felt like I was having an out-of-body experience.

'Marty's husband just started at Hutton Brothers. He joined the Multinational Relationship Management team. Isn't that yours?' she said.

My blood went cold. How had Veronica known that? I was fairly certain I'd never mentioned Spence's team to Editor Evelyn. Like a lightning bolt I remembered him mentioning that Edwin Leung was the head of the entire division. He was my husband's boss's boss's boss's . . . I couldn't even count how many rungs up the ladder he was.

After I'd known Veronica for a while, I understood why she had to be so careful about the people she allowed into her sphere.

Everyone wanted something from Veronica Hawkins.

Edwin coughed, frowning slightly. 'Torres?' he asked me.

'My husband's name is Spencer Merton,' I said, barely resisting the urge to add *Sir*, as if I'd suddenly found myself in the principal's office for a prank I hadn't played.

'Oh, yes,' he replied politely. 'The new transfer.' Edwin had no idea who Spence was – why would he?

'I hear you have Marty and her husband on one of those half-pat packages,' Veronica said to Edwin. Beneath the table, I dug my fingernails into my thigh. 'They're going to end up living in the New Territories on the housing allowance you've given them and that simply isn't on. It's not the way we do things at Hawkins Pacific.'

The challenge in her voice was unmistakable.

'Americans have different priorities.' Edwin's voice was smooth and he managed a smile, but his shoulders drew back.

'That's true,' I said quickly. 'We're very happy to be here. It's a wonderful opp—'

Looking at me hard, Veronica interrupted, 'Do you have kids?' although I was sure she knew the answer.

'No.' It was a small word.

Veronica beamed at Edwin. 'See, they're not even costing you school fees. I'm sure it wouldn't be too *mah fan* for you to at least increase their housing allowance? I want Martina to feel welcome in my city.'

They locked eyes and some kind of understanding passed between them.

'It's not necessary . . .' I trailed off because neither of them was listening.

Edwin took a breath. 'I'm late for my lunch,' he said, eyes darting towards the back of the dining room, 'but I'll look into the issue when I get back to the office.'

'Thank you, Edwin. I hope you'll stop by the opening tonight.'

'My wife has been looking forward to it.'

'Wonderful.'

To me, Edwin said, 'Lovely to meet you, Martina. Welcome to Hong Kong.'

When he walked away, Veronica returned to her salad. I'd lost my appetite. I imagined Spence and me being put on the next Cathay Pacific flight to New York – this time in coach.

Mustering all of my courage, I told Veronica, 'You didn't need to do that.'

She looked up, confused. 'It was nothing. Arthur gave him a job when he was rebelling against joining his family's business. It's how the city works. Favours and grudges.'

'But you barely know me,' I protested.

Veronica set down her fork. 'I know we're going to be friends,' she said. 'True friends.'

'I'd like that.'

Even if I was in awe of her, even if she intimidated me, I wanted that. Veronica was a whirlpool, her inexorable pull drawing me in, along with a feeling that whatever she was about to offer me was more thrilling than anything I'd ever dreamed of.

'Did you know there's no future tense in Mandarin?' Veronica said. I shook my head. 'My *amah* was from Beijing,' she explained. 'I spent more time with her than Arthur or Maman when I was a girl. She taught me one of the most important lessons I've ever learned. In Mandarin, you express desire to do something as a way of making it future tense. That's my philosophy.'

'What is?'

'I *want* to do something and so I *will* do something. I don't rely on the future to just happen of its own accord. I will it to be so – and so should you.'

After that day, I did.

I do.

Chapter 3

Double Happiness

*M*orning, Marty,' Spencer said, waking me up with a spearmint-tinged kiss, and I groaned, trying to hide from the light of day, my head pounding from too much champers at Veronica's gallery opening the night before. A Bloomberg anchor droned on about the daily market report from the flat screen and I covered my ears.

Spence smiled down at me, already dressed for work, a Brooks Brothers catalogue incarnate, and touched the ticklish spot behind my ear. He laughed as I emitted a very undignified squeal. 'Last night was fun,' he said, meaning in more ways than one.

First he'd run out of business cards at the opening, then Edwin Leung's wife told us we must come to brunch at the Shangri-La, their treat – I couldn't help revelling in the fact that he was my plus one for once. When we'd arrived home, Spence unzipped my cocktail-party dress with his teeth and we'd had the best sex we'd had since leaving Manhattan. Spence seemed fully energised, back to his usual horse-powered self and – I can't help but brag – extremely generous, eager to please. Cliché as it is, we communicated most candidly in the bedroom and I was enormously relieved things were back to normal in that department.

Patting me on the bottom, 'Don't sleep all day,' my husband teased, and strode from the serviced apartment to the International Finance Centre, the IFC, an eighty-eight-storey skyscraper that dominates the harbour skyline. From Spence's desk he could see the South China Sea stretching towards Macau, a seemingly infinite expanse. At the best of times, bankers in Manhattan can see New Jersey.

I resisted full consciousness for another half-hour. Another hour. There were so many hours in the day to fill now. I had no harrowing commute or job waiting for me. I could get a manicure or a massage or just lie in the bathtub until mid-afternoon.

Nobody would notice. Nobody cared.

What was I doing here? Who *was* I in Hong Kong?

A sudden tide of despair rushed over me. Then I remembered I had an article to file.

Finally throwing back the covers, I strolled towards the window and drew a zigzag in the condensation. The day was a soupy grey. Down below, a group of elderly Chinese women practised tai chi in the courtyard of the building across the street. Their movements were achingly slow. Deft. They looked serene.

Work, Martina. Just focus on the work. It had always been my lifeline.

Stretching my arms above my head, I wandered into the living room in search of coffee. The morning passed in a blur of caffeine and moving commas around the page and before I knew it my cell phone was vibrating across the beige Formica countertop. Everything in the serviced apartment was a shade of brown, like a Whistler paint-ing gone horribly wrong: *A Nightmare in Russet.*

'Marty?'

The excitement in Spence's voice was tangible. I sat up straight.

'I just got off the horn with HR and it seems they made a mistake with our housing allowance. We're in a higher category and there's a place the relocation agent wants us to see asap.'

The corners of my mouth turned upward. Veronica had worked her magic in less than twenty-four hours. 'Is it on the Peak?' I asked.

'No. A penthouse in Wan Chai.'

There was a noise behind him and Spence told me, 'Gotta go.

Meet me in an hour. Tell the cabbie Starscape on Star Street. I'll wait outside.'

Immediately, obediently, I slipped into linen pants and a bright Lilly Pulitzer print blazer. Dress for the job you want is good advice but in my experience you also have to dress for the apartment you want. *Your clothing is your costume*, my mother reminded me every time I complained about my hideous maroon-and-hunter-green plaid school uniform. If only I played pretend hard enough, one day I'd be a real girl. Now I'd swapped tartan for Day-Glo resort wear.

The finishing touch was a pair of black Tahitian pearl earrings that were a wedding gift from Bitsy, my only real friend at The Buxton School (yes, the 'The' is very much capitalised). Bitsy Butterfield had the bloodlines to rule Buxton but she committed the cardinal sin of being chubby – it was a shame her last name lent itself so easily to the nickname Butterball. By second grade, we'd found each other because neither of us belonged.

When I returned to New York after graduate school, Bitsy couldn't bear the thought of me becoming part of the Bridge & Tunnel brigade so she invited me to move into the co-op apartment her parents had given her for her twenty-first birthday. At 'friend price', of course, which to Bitsy meant that I paid for cable and the occasional takeout. Strictly speaking, sublets aren't allowed in co-op buildings but none of the neighbours dared to come out and ask whether we were romantically involved.

I've always liked to walk, I don't feel trapped when I'm in motion, so I headed to the Mid-Levels escalator – the longest covered escalator in the world – and down the nearly five hundred feet towards Central. Maps are next to useless in Hong Kong because they would need to be 3D. Some roads can only be accessed by taking an elevator in a random office complex or descending into a subterranean shopping mall. Literally building a city on a hill has its disadvantages.

During my first few months, getting around Hongkers was akin to navigating an elaborate game of *Super Mario Bros.*, but I knew real pride the day I could walk from the Star Ferry terminal by the IFC to Admiralty without getting lost. All residents think they know the quickest route through an unknown service stairwell to get any-where. As I made my way through the elegant Landmark building to the MTR below, hordes of office workers swarmed around me to buy their *yuenyeung* (a coffee and milk tea concoction) and a variety of *bao*, or buns, from the bakeries in the basement.

Being a New Yorker, my self-preservation instinct recoiled at the notion of purchasing food in the subway but the stations of Hong Kong's MTR are spotless, definitely cleaner than my college dorm room. The trains also run on time 99.9 per cent of the time, which made a nice change. The little girl in me delighted in swiping my Hello Kitty-themed Octopus card at the turnstile as well as using it to buy the bottled sweet green tea to which I was becoming addicted.

Glancing around the train car, I realised that I was again the only Westerner, something that soon became the norm to me, something I stopped noticing. But on that day, the side of my mouth kicked up in a quarter-smile. In Hong Kong, I was a foreigner. I wasn't sup-posed to look like everyone else. It was freeing.

At Buxton, in New York, I was never white enough. Here the boxes I did or didn't tick on the US census form were irrelevant. Hongkongers paid absolutely no attention to me, busy with their own lives, dismissing me as part of the expat community in their city. You might think I liked getting a taste of unfettered white privilege. But that's not how I saw it, why I felt giddy in the middle of the train car.

For the first time, I could just be Martina Torres – whoever the hell she was supposed to be. It definitely is a privilege, of course, to fly across the world and decide to be the Other, rather than being othered at home, and it's a wholly different experience.

Home. A word that was quickly shifting meaning for me.

When the MTR stopped at Admiralty station, my gut told me this was my stop, where the buck stopped for me: in Hong Kong.

Fidgeting the black pearl in my right ear, I slalomed my way through the crowds in the upscale Pacific Place mall towards signs for Star Street. I could practically hear Bitsy taking credit for bringing Spence and me together to anyone who would listen at our wedding reception. And it was true.

I'd had zero intention of attending our fifth high-school reunion – or paying $200 a head for an evening in the newly refurbished Buxton gym – but Bitsy didn't want to go alone and she insisted on covering my ticket. Spence dropped by at the end of the night to escort his sister, Merritt, to some pseudo-speakeasy in the Meatpacking District and see how the frosh had grown up. Well, apparently, in my case.

The connection between us that night was electric. I was on cloud nine that Spencer Merton was giving me his undivided attention, especially since Merritt sulked into her Sidecar. I knew better than to invite him home, though. When I'd visit my cousins in northern Argentina as a teenager, I couldn't even go to a movie with a boy without at least two female chaperones. I didn't take things that far, of course, but I did make Spencer work for it.

He went whole hog on the old-fashioned courtship: sending me flowers just because, picking me up for our dates, rifling through my CDs for the bands I liked and surprising me with tickets. The first time we slept together was on the three-month anniversary of our first official date – and he'd whisked me away to the Breakers in Palm Beach. Bitsy had been sent to investment camp at the Breakers for a week in middle school and I'd been green with envy. I couldn't understand why my family didn't have a family office since everyone else's family seemed to.

My quarter-life crisis never reared its ugly head because I started dating Spencer. Overnight I was being invited to all the right parties, weekend trips to Canyon Ranch with Merritt and her friends who'd studiously ignored me in our K-12 days. I got everything a private school girl could want: a gift registry at Bergdorf Goodman, heavyweight monogrammed stationery, a wedding reception at the Pierre (the Mertons footed the bill), a goddamned trousseau.

I didn't question whether it would make me happy.

Why would I? I was the pumpkin who turned into a coach.

Ascending several more escalators and another hill, I passed through the lobby of one of the many office buildings owned by the Swires – a rival *hong* to Veronica's family – and emerged into a gust of humid air on Star Street. Bentleys, Hummers and taxis encircled a large pool of water outside in which the two towers of Starscape, my soon-to-be new home, were reflected. Around the corner was a hot coffin of a laundry that stank permanently of industrial chemicals and charged by the kilo, but here drivers with white gloves opened doors for executives sporting a different Piaget for every day of the week.

My gaze was drawn to a huge red screen, about thirty feet tall, suspended in the air above the alley between the apartment building and a French bistro where, if you were so inclined, you could pair your *crème brûlée* with a magnum of vintage Château d'Yquem. Veronica did once just because it was so ridiculous. A Sauternes never tasted as sweet.

Directly in front of the enormous red screen was a freestanding shrine. A bearded Earth God smiled at offerings of incense, oranges, bean curd and *yuan bao* – shoe-shaped gold ingots. Personally, I would have preferred Louboutins. Even so, I got this uncanny feeling. I was about to hear my first Hong Kong ghost story.

'Torres!'

Spence's voice shook me from my reverie, his preppy-jock tone endearing. He waved at me from beneath the portico of the left-hand tower.

Waving back, I crossed the narrow street towards where Spence stood with Sherry, our Hutton Brothers relocation manager, and an early-twenties Chinese man who introduced himself as Maxwell, the landlord's agent. A doorman and a concierge gave us a perfunctory greeting as Maxwell showed us into the building. We weren't yet worth too much effort. Instead of Christmas bonuses, staff in Hong Kong receive *lai see* – red envelopes filled with cash – during Chinese New Year and that had just passed.

Sherry was a no-nonsense middle-aged Hongkonger with a page-boy haircut and an efficient manner. She smiled a lot more at Spencer than she ever did at me.

'Wan Chai is very trendy these days,' she was telling my husband. 'Not like it used to be. No more Suzie Wong. Lots of fashionable restaurants.'

As Sherry called the elevator, my eyebrows lifted at a sign informing passengers that the buttons were sanitised each hour. The legacy of SARS was to be found in the details of everyday life and the strange becomes normal faster than you'd expect.

We stepped inside and Sherry shifted her tote from her shoulder to her hands. A Goyard. Nothing so cliché as LV for Sherry. She probably went a year without lunch to afford the HKD 25,000 bag and I respected that.

Sherry pressed the button for the penthouse. A digital screen displayed the Typhoon signal from the Hong Kong Observatory beside the floor number. Anything above an eight and the city shuts down. No school. No work.

'There's no thirteenth floor?' I commented.

Sherry showed me a patient smile, shaking her head. 'That's the British influence. Nothing with a four in it, either. The number four in Cantonese sounds like the word for death.' She exchanged a look with Maxwell who nervously pushed his glasses up the bridge of his nose.

The doors swished open on a vestibule embellished with a regal purple bauhinia plant, the floral emblem of Hong Kong. Being inducted into the Order of the Bauhinia Star is the most coveted accolade for those hoping to gloss over their origins with philanthropy.

Maxwell led the way down the corridor. At the end was a single mahogany door. Above a lion's head knocker, someone had taped a poster made from thin red paper inlaid with two golden characters. 'That should have been removed,' said the agent, irritated, not wanting to put off the Westerners.

I tilted my head at him. 'What does it mean?'

'Double happiness.'

'I like it.' I wanted to be happy, so much. Double happiness. What could be better than that?

Maxwell turned the key in the lock, plainly relieved. He stood aside and motioned for Spence and me to enter first.

Floor-to-ceiling windows washed the lacquered parquet in pearly light. Grandiose brass chandeliers dangled from the high ceilings but otherwise the vast space was barren.

'Unfurnished?' Sherry said, nose wrinkled, stating the obvious.

Maxwell swallowed. 'Unfurnished.'

'I wasn't aware of that when you quoted me the asking price.'

'I—' He started but didn't get more than a syllable before Sherry silenced him with a glare. Spence bristled beside me. WASPs have an aversion to discussing money.

'It will have to be lowered,' she said and Maxwell nodded like a spanked schoolboy. 'Let's see the rest.'

I maintained a neutral expression as we were shown three bedrooms that faced the rolling green hills above, three bathrooms, a study, a generous kitchen, a dining room and a living room with stunning views of the harbour.

'This is a palace,' Spence whispered in my ear. In no world was this the apartment befitting someone at his level in the company.

Pointing at an oddly large closet beside the kitchen, I asked Maxwell, 'Is that the pantry?'

'That's the maid's room,' Sherry replied.

My lips parted. 'It doesn't seem like it would fit a bed.' She shrugged.

Sherry glanced at Maxwell and he grew stiff. 'There is something I must ask you,' he said soberly, looking from me to Spence.

'Yes?' my husband responded, an edge to his voice.

'Are you afraid of ghosts?'

Spence bellowed. 'Are we afraid of ghosts?' Another chortle. 'You had me going there, buddy.'

For some reason, I couldn't laugh.

'He's serious,' said Sherry. 'By Hong Kong law, we must inform you that there was a murder in the apartment below.'

'What happened?' I found myself asking with a slight quaver to my words.

Maxwell cleared his throat. 'A man stabbed his elderly mother to death.' Afterwards, I looked it up. He stabbed her 151 times.

'Well,' said Spence, 'I might do the same if I still lived with my mom. Marty definitely would.' He flashed me a grin. Spence brought my mom a bouquet of hyacinths, her favourite, every time he visited, and she definitely preferred him to me.

'I presume the bad *qi* has been cleared by a feng shui master,' Sherry said to Maxwell in a stern tone.

'Of course.' Feng shui masters in Hong Kong bless everything from new hotels to traffic crossings. It can be quite the grift.

I asked the agents, 'The giant red screen beside the building – is that also feng shui?'

Maxwell swallowed again. 'The hill behind was a bomb shelter. Prisoners of war were kept there. The shrine appeases their restless spirits.'

'Oh Marty, I'll keep you safe,' said Spencer, a twinkle in his eye.

'Why don't we give you a few minutes to explore the apartment alone?' suggested Sherry.

'That would be lovely,' I said.

Maxwell followed at her heels towards the entrance.

'You're not scared, are you?' Spence said once they were out of earshot.

'No. Yes. I don't kn—'

The Mets fight song resounded off the walls, interrupting me.

Checking his phone, 'It's Sidekick,' Spence told me, meaning his sister, Merritt.

'Isn't it one a.m. in New York?'

'She's on the West Coast for work.' He stared at the screen another second. As an only child, I found it rather disconcerting how much in each other's pockets the Merton siblings were. Sometimes I felt like a third wheel in my own marriage. Lifting a shoulder, he said, 'I'll call her back.'

'Take it if you want.'

'Come here.' He extended his hand and walked me back into the living room. The sun was just starting to peek out from behind the clouds, tipping the choppy waves with silver.

Spence folded his hand over mine, stroking the princess-cut diamond of my engagement ring, an unconscious habit of his. The design of the setting (a hollow space beneath the diamond) gave me a persistent bacterial infection.

'Look at this, Marty. The city at our feet.'

I came to stand beside him, pressing my nose against the glass. My mother would turn green when she saw this place. She'd always resented living in a condo rather than a co-op.

'I'm so glad we took the plunge,' he went on. 'My career is going places here. Edwin Leung sees something in me.'

Cocking my head, I said, 'We may have Veronica Hawkins to thank for this view.'

Spence furrowed his brow. 'What are you talking about?'

'Yesterday, when Veronica invited me to her club for lunch. She told Edwin that we needed a better housing allowance.'

'Are you serious?' Dropping my hand, he raked his fingers through his blond curls anxiously. 'You *complained* to Edwin?'

'No, no, not at all. It didn't happen like that. Veronica brought it up – it was all very smooth. She knows how to operate.'

Spence planted his feet, widening his stance. 'Who's Veronica to him, then?'

'She's Hong Kong's answer to Mrs Astor. She said Edwin owed her a favour.'

He was quiet for what seemed like forever. Then he nodded slowly.

'And now it seems *we* owe her one.' Spence exhaled a resigned breath. Veronica started transforming my life from the day we met, my husband's too, but his gratitude was overshadowed by scorekeeping. It wasn't his fault. It was how he was raised.

Spence moved behind me, placing his hands lightly on my hips and drawing me back against him. I felt his erection beneath his trousers. He smelled of sweat and vetiver and aspiration – a heady combination.

Nipping my earlobe, catching the pearl, he said, 'How do you feel about sleeping with ghosts?'

Heat flooded me, desire pooling between my thighs; I pressed myself more firmly against his crotch.

'I think I'll be scaring away the ghosts with all my screaming.'

I wanted him, I wanted this city. Our new life. Recklessness surged through me.

'Challenged accepted,' Spence taunted, growling a bit for effect.

Expertly, he manoeuvred a hand beneath the front of my pants. His fingers stroked along my lace thong to the bare skin he preferred.

Spence had proposed to me at Turtle Pond in Central Park, under the willow that had been my refuge since childhood, in the shadow of Belvedere Castle, making my high-school dreams come true.

You're not like the other women I know. You really appreciate things, he'd said.

Spence had wanted someone grateful to be with him – and I was.

I looked down on Hong Kong, and I screamed.

Search for missing heiress called off

The rescue mission for Veronica Hawkins, 35, taipan of Hawkins Pacific, was suspended early this morning according to Cheung Pak Hei, commander of the Fire Services Department's marine and diving division.

For two weeks, Hongkongers have been gripped by the search operation for the missing heiress. Unnamed sources disclosed to the *South China Daily* that by the third day the divers were conducting body recovery but none has been found.

Reports that Ms Hawkins appeared to be intoxicated before falling overboard have been corroborated by evidence found on the luxury junk, *Tin Hau 8*. The Hong Kong Police Force discovered a Martini glass containing both Ms Hawkins's fingerprints and traces of a 'club drug' called GHB (gamma-hydroxybutyrate) that impairs inhibitions.

Police Commissioner Raymond Kwan would not confirm whether Veronica Hawkins's death was being treated as an accident or a homicide.

Speaking exclusively to our paper, socialite and lifelong friend, Elsie Barron, was distraught when she said by telephone, 'I can't believe she's gone. The last of the Hawkins dynasty. And to drown in the same manner as her family, it makes me heartsick. Veronica had nightmares about her sister Lulu sinking beneath the waves. Fate can be so cruel.'

Arthur Hawkins, his wife, Geneviève Varenne, and their twelve-year-old daughter, Lourdes Hawkins, perished when their pleasure boat suffered an electrical fire and capsized in May 1997.

Without a body, Ms Hawkins's husband, Jean-Pierre Renard, 54, refuses to plan a funeral. All of Hong Kong's elite shares his shock and his grief, supporting one of the island's oldest families in their time of need.

Chapter 4

The Dark Side

A sultry breeze tickled my brow as I leaned out the window of the Star Ferry. Looking back at Hong Kong Island from the iconic green-and-white boat, the towers of glass reflected the corals and tangerines of sunset. It was blinding but I couldn't look away.

Veronica was like that too.

The ferry chugged through the waters of the ever-narrowing harbour towards TST on Kowloon or, as locals call it, the Dark Side. Traces of the once lawless Hak Nam – City of Darkness, never fully under colonial rule – could still be found in the mettle of its residents. Spence was running late at the office, so he was going to hop on the MTR and meet me at the Peninsula Hotel where we had invited Veronica and her husband, Jean-Pierre, for dinner.

I hadn't met Jean-Pierre except in passing on my first visit to Gallery de Ladrones for Veronica's interview but I'd subsequently heard around town that he was a sought-after portrait painter. In the month since my profile piece had appeared in *HK City Chic*, I'd been about town quite a bit: interviewing a singer revitalising Cantopop, a local heartthrob who'd recently made his Hollywood film debut, and an Austrian installation artist whose exhibition entitled *Freud* at the artists' village in a former slaughterhouse consisted of sculptures made from faecal matter.

All in all, an eventful few weeks.

Editor Evelyn quipped that all of my interviewees had requested

'Veronica's friend'. I much preferred that sobriquet to Dependent Spouse. Nevertheless, in between assignments, I'd found time to browse the homewares at Lane Crawford, the Harrods of Hong Kong, as well as the tchotchke stalls lining either side of the treacherously steep and slippery Ladder Street.

My nesting instincts had kicked into overdrive and I was determined to create a real home for Spence and me on Star Street. I'd purchased yards of silk at the Western Market in Sheung Wan for a fraction of what an interior decorator would have charged at the D&D Building and commissioned draperies that would make any Park Avenue matron jealous.

The hues of the draperies matched the blossoms from my wedding bouquet. Bitsy had been my maid of honour, of course, and she was a romantic at heart, obsessed with anything and everything Victorian from Penhaligon's perfume to the language of flowers. Bitsy insisted we craft a message with my bouquet: orange roses for desire, delicate white myrtle for love, ivy for fidelity, and I was committed to filling our home with all of those things. Spencer's hand had trembled when he slid the ring on to my finger and I'd been glad he was nervous too, that we'd jumped out of the plane together, that we could figure out what being married meant one day at a time.

Making my way from the ferry terminal through throngs of commuters, I meandered along the Avenue of Stars in the direction of the Peninsula. With its trademark fleet of green Rolls-Royces standing like sentries before the stone facade, a helipad on its roof for guests who simply can't stand traffic on the way to the airport, the hotel is part of Hong Kong history. When the Japanese invaded, the erstwhile governor – that Eton man Veronica said not to trust – signed the surrender agreement at the Peninsula and was promptly imprisoned within one of its suites.

The hotel's signature restaurant, Felix, seemed like an appropriate place to take Veronica as a thank you for her intervention with Edwin Leung.

I shared the elevator to the twenty-eighth floor with an impeccably dressed woman in a pink mink jacket. If the temperature drops below sixty, the city issues a cold-weather warning. Not an exaggeration. Hong Kong is the fur-buying capital of the world – also not an exaggeration.

Spence tapped his watch as soon as he spotted me. He leaned against the circular marble bar, single malt in hand. I ignored his chiding glance, enamoured by the panorama of rolling hills and sky-scrapers behind him. The light had faded to mood indigo.

The island's dramatic vistas are an architect's best friend and Hong Kong is a city of glass houses. Not that it stops the denizens from casting stones.

'How can you be late when you left before me?' Spencer teased.

'Female prerogative,' I snapped right back.

Spence laughed. 'Good thing you're hot.' He ordered a bottle of Dom Pérignon from the dapper barman.

Dry yet creamy, I welcomed the first hit of bubbles. My eye-lids drooped just for a moment as downtempo electronica pulsed through me.

'Lightweight,' chided my husband, a hint of older brother in his tone.

I took another sip, cold and exquisite, as my attention was drawn back in the direction of the elevator banks. From the corner of my eye, I spied Veronica and Jean-Pierre. They stared at each other intently; anger tightened Veronica's brow. Jean-Pierre's shoulders lifted in a dramatic inhale, and I could practically feel the steam rising from his nostrils.

This was one of those married-life moments not meant to be witnessed, a hint at the rollercoaster of their relationship Veronica would eventually divulge to me. How she lived for the moment right before the plummet. Quickly, I gazed down at my drink.

Spence lifted his hand and waved them over.

When I angled my shoulders to greet them, Veronica and

Jean-Pierre were all smiles. The storm had passed. They glowed. King and Queen of the Prom.

Veronica wore a bronze sheath dress that only flatters the naturally gamine, while Jean-Pierre sported one of his many linen suits. He was a man born to lounge on verandas, swirling a long drink. Or perhaps frolic in the Tuileries by lantern light – the *on-dit* being that Jean-Pierre descended from a mostly headless French aristocratic family.

'So good to see you, darling,' Veronica told me, giving me a kiss on either cheek. 'Spencer.' His name was clipped although her tone was honeyed. She gave him one peck. 'This is my husband, Jean-Pierre.'

Spencer thrust out his hand. 'Nice to meet you, JP.' The men shook. A faint, wry chuckle escaped Jean-Pierre. 'This is my wife, Marty.'

'Americans love their nicknames, *non*?' Appraising me, he said, 'You don't look like a Marty.'

'Martina, actually.'

Jean-Pierre held me with his dark eyes. 'Yes.' One word made me feel like we shared a secret. I didn't know if he was just being French or if he was trying to needle his wife. Or my husband. Probably all of the above.

Spence placed his palm on the base of my spine. 'In school we called her Marty McFly. You know, like *Back to the Future*.'

'Very droll.'

My entire body stiffened. By unspoken agreement we'd never discussed our relative places in the Buxton pecking order. 'I didn't think you knew about that.'

Spence kissed my cheek. 'Don't sweat it,' he said. 'You were always *guapa*.' Spence's accent was terrible but the fact he tried to speak the odd word of Spanish earned him a peck in return.

He signalled to the bartender for more glasses.

'I took the liberty of ordering some Dom,' he said to our guests.

'A Frenchman never refuses champagne,' replied Jean-Pierre. He flirted as easily as breathing.

My husband looked from Jean-Pierre to Veronica. 'A thank you for all of your help. Tonight is on us. To new friends!'

Flutes filled to the brim, the four of us toasted.

And it was the beginning of something new. Something fresh. A place where I could become Martina rather than Marty.

When Veronica removed the glass from her lips, the rim was stained a deep cerise, like ruby port. It was her signature colour. I couldn't have known then how important that detail would become. How I would mention it to the police.

'I'm happy to help smooth your transition in any small way,' Veronica demurred, aiming a mischievous smile at Spencer. 'How are you both finding Auntie Heung, then?'

Seeing my quizzical expression, she explained, 'She was a pirate. Some people claim Hong Kong gets its name from her.'

'If anyone knows about female pirates, *c'est ma femme.*' Jean-Pierre winked, first at me, then at his wife.

She arched a brow at him but affection infused her gaze.

'We're loving it,' Spence jumped in. 'And such a great launchpad to explore the rest of Asia. We went to Phuket over Easter. Visited the beach from *The Beach* . . .'

I cringed as Spencer recounted with relish our long weekend to the most unoriginal vacation spot we could have picked. Every white Westerner who moves to Asia goes to Phuket for their first long weekend. Spence relived his fraternity glory days doing shrooms he'd bought from the pool boy whereas I preferred a hot stone massage and bottomless cocktails.

'Veronica!'

Spence's monologue about snorkelling off the Phi Phi Islands was blessedly cut short by an enthusiastic woman's voice.

Veronica's jaw tightened microscopically. The owner of the voice was a Chinese woman in her mid-thirties, swathed in a black silk-crêpe Prada number I'd been salivating over, and clutching a limited edition Miu Miu purse.

'Cressida!' Veronica exclaimed as the woman joined us. She afforded the newcomer what could only be described as a shit-eating grin. 'Lovely!'

'I'm just on my way home from afternoon tea. What luck running into you. I've been meaning to talk to you about my Lifting Hope fundraiser and I haven't seen you since the BritCham gala.'

BritCham – the British Chamber of Commerce – would become part of my expat vocabulary. As would AmCham, AusCham and the like. The chambers of commerce were an endless source of networking drinks and kept the business ties in the city well lubricated even when political tensions flared.

'Lucky for me indeed,' said Veronica.

Cressida gave Jean-Pierre a kiss hello. *'Bonsoir.'* She looked expectantly from me and Spencer to Veronica.

'This is my good friend, Martina Torres,' Veronica obliged her, somewhat reluctantly. 'She's just moved here from New York. She's a very important journalist – I'm sure you've read her work.'

Prickly heat spread beneath my leopard-print wrap dress. We both knew I wasn't winning a Pulitzer anytime soon. But Veronica's word was better than truth.

'Of course,' said Cressida. 'Delighted to meet you.' We shook hands.

'Cressida and I went to boarding school together. In Somerset,' Veronica went on, which accounted for the other woman's mostly British accent. 'And this is Spencer Merton. Martina's husband.'

Spence's Adam's apple bobbed. I don't think he'd ever been introduced that way before.

'Would you like a glass of Dom?' he offered.

'I'm afraid I can't stay long. What are you celebrating?'

'Martina and Spencer have just moved into Starscape,' Veronica told her.

'A prestigious address. Congratulations.' The sentiment was sincere. Frank. It was the first but not the last time I would be congratulated on my address. Hongkongers can be forthright in a way WASPs never are. No bullshit.

Straightaway, I warmed to Cressida.

'Has your container arrived yet?' she asked me. Complaints about the delayed arrival of container ships were commonplace at the American Women's Association. What I didn't know was that Cressida's father was a shipping magnate who could have expedited pretty much anything.

'It has. Spence and I didn't have much in it, though.'

'All the better. You can get excellent custom-made furniture on Queen's Road East for less than IKEA.' Cressida beamed at me as if I believed she frequented the Nordic labyrinth. 'I'd be happy to take you to the best shops. Do you have a card?'

Veronica finished her champagne. 'I need a refresh.'

The catch of my Birkin bag made a satisfying click as it opened. An engagement present from my sister-in-law. I extracted my business card holder. Editor Evelyn had rush printed them on Gough Street.

MARTINA TORRES, WRITER-AT-LARGE was engraved beneath the magazine logo.

I presented it to Cressida one-handed; later, I would learn to use two.

'Looks great,' Spence said beside me. Then he added, *sotto voce*, 'Perfect for an important New York journalist.'

I was standing close enough to accidentally step on his foot with my stiletto. In Manhattan, Spence took advantage of the fact that my journo perks included the inside track on the hottest new tables and bars. I wasn't Woodward or Bernstein, but he'd never belittled me before. I decided to dismiss it as a jock joke that didn't land.

Gripping the card, Cressida said, 'Fabulous. I'll give you a ring.' Another round of kisses and she was gone.

As the maître d' showed us to our table through a maze of Philippe Starck Ghost Chairs and diners in five-thousand-dollar suits, Veronica said to Spencer, 'You simply must visit the gents. The urinals have one of the best views in the city. All glass. Swinging dicks just love to piss all over the city.'

Then she caught my eye and gave me her special smile.

Sometimes knights in shining armour also wear Louboutins.

Chapter 5

Portrait of a Lady

We were seated at a prime window table – Veronica was on a first-name basis with the Peninsula's GM – and Victoria Harbour rippled with flashy greens, turquoises and magentas as the daily laser show played out behind us.

The sun may set but the lights never go out in Hong Kong. Clouds are eerily bright, incandescent yet menacing, even in the middle of the night. I felt them like a spectral presence lurking on the hillside above my apartment building. Watching.

We slid oysters down our throats and Spence ordered another bottle of Dom.

When the blue lobster was served, the head chef came with it. He exchanged a flurry of French with Veronica and Jean-Pierre. The fawning was primarily directed at Veronica. Jean-Pierre's gaze darted to his phone, the screen illuminating at regular intervals atop the table. He huffed a breath and gave a Gallic shrug.

The chef wished us 'Bon appétit' and Veronica returned her attention to her husband, eyes narrowing.

'Don't mind Jean-Pierre,' she said to me and Spence. 'He's always like this on Wednesdays.' Her tone was breezy; her smile pained.

'What happens on Wednesdays?' asked my husband. He popped a truffle frite into his mouth.

'Race day,' replied Jean-Pierre. 'Désolé.' He didn't sound sorry at all but he did turn his phone screen down on the tablecloth.

Fiddling with the stem of my champagne flute, I chimed in, 'Oh, that's right. A woman from my yoga class says she always goes to Happy Valley on Wednesdays.'

The racecourse is considered hugely lucky in feng shui terms. Basically a big bowl of money. It does wonders for the property value of the surrounding skyscrapers.

'Horse racing is the only legal gambling in Hong Kong, dates back to my great-great's arrival,' said Veronica. 'Besides stock trading.'

'That's why God invented Macau,' Jean-Pierre retorted, casting a sidelong glance at his wife. Veronica's hand stilled on her fork and, as if he hadn't spoken, she looked directly at Spencer and said, 'All of the clubs have their own sections of the stands at Happy Valley. The racecourse is nearly as old as the colony. Weren't you given a membership to the American Club as part of your package?'

Spencer chewed his truffle frite slowly. Very slowly.

'Half-pat, remember?' I said with a laugh.

'Oh.' Veronica pursed her lips. 'Well, my family helped found the Jockey Club. Hawkins Pacific always sponsors a big fete for St Andrew's Day. You'll just have to come as my guests. We'll have a grand 'ole time, as you Yanks say.'

'Sounds wonderful.' I tipped my glass at her. 'I'm starting to think you're my fairy godmother.' We clinked flutes.

Coughing into his hand, Spencer said, 'Next time you're in New York, I'll have to return the favour. The University Club has the best guestrooms in the city.'

I blanched at my husband's attempt at one-upmanship, staring at my oyster fork. He wasn't accustomed to being outclassed, whereas I'd learned my place while still in diapers.

Veronica drained her flute. 'Delightful.'

'So, Jean-Pierre, tell me how you and Veronica met,' I said. His eyes flipped up from the back of his phone. 'I'm sure it was terribly romantic.'

'It was,' said Veronica instantly.

A small snort from the Frenchman. 'She fell in love with my painting – of her.'

His tepid agreement smacked of one of those comedy bits performed by couples that was growing stale with age.

'Do tell,' I urged.

Jean-Pierre tugged at his earlobe, shifting in his chair. '*Alors*, this was about seven, eight years ago. I had a show at a gallery on the Rue de Seine. Veronica was in Paris on business. Always business with my wife.'

'Business keeps the lights on, husband.' She smiled at Jean-Pierre indulgently, then shifted her gaze to me. 'He's forgetting to tell you the best bits.'

'You're the master at telling stories, *ma puce*.'

'Indeed. You see, Marty, there was something rough, almost savage about the brushwork. Thrilling. I was intrigued.' She skimmed her husband's profile with her gaze. He took a long pull of champagne. Suddenly I felt like a voyeur.

'I wasn't in Paris to buy any art,' Veronica went on, 'and usually the galleries in the sixth are filled with derivative drivel but Jean-Pierre's landscapes stopped me in my tracks. I marched into the gallery and demanded to know where I could find the artist.'

'Fortunately for me, I wasn't far,' Jean-Pierre broke in. 'Most afternoons I could be found sketching at La Palette around the corner.'

'With pastis in hand,' said Veronica.

I made the appropriate *oohs* and *ahhs* of an engaged spectator. Spencer was less convincing. 'Was it love at first sight?' I wanted to know.

'First,' began Jean-Pierre, 'I had to pass a test. She asked me to do a portrait of her.'

Veronica brushed the back of her hand gently against his cheek. 'I asked him to do a portrait because it's the mark of a truly great artist.'

'How's that?' Spence asked.

'A *truly* great artist can reveal something about you in a portrait that even you don't know.'

Not quite under his breath, Jean-Pierre said, 'Or don't want to know.'

Veronica glanced at her husband. 'In any event, I offered him a show to lure him to Hong Kong.'

'And here I am.' He lifted Veronica's hand and grazed her knuckles with a kiss.

'See, I knew it would be a romantic story,' I told them.

'You and I are alike, Martina,' said Jean-Pierre. 'You paint your portraits with words. We both must examine our subjects, peer below the surface.'

Throat itchy, 'I suppose that's true,' I said, part of me flattered that he might consider me an artist, the other part convinced I'd become embroiled in some tit-for-tat he was having with his wife.

'Don't be modest,' he told me. 'I didn't know about the Polaroids until I read it in your article. A very insightful detail. Veronica doesn't speak much about her mother.'

Spence furrowed his brow. 'What's this about Polaroids?'

Jean-Pierre shifted his gaze to my husband. 'Didn't you read Martina's piece?' he said and it was clear from Spence's blank expression that he hadn't.

'Work has been busy,' he mumbled into his Dom.

'Oh, I'll put you out of your misery,' Veronica said with a smirk. 'When I was a little girl I told Maman that I wanted to be a photographer like her, so she gave me a Polaroid camera. I used the entire ten-pack taking pictures of light on the water off our boat.'

There was a weighted pause. Jean-Pierre and I exchanged a look. It was the same boat that would capsize and take Veronica's family with it a decade later.

'I liked the contrasts,' she said. 'Light shines more brightly the darker the water is.'

How could I have known that night that she would soon be

following her family into the sea? Veronica was a conflagration of driftwood, salt burning green and blue.

'You see,' said Jean-Pierre, resting his case, 'it takes a true talent to get my wife to open up. *Félicitations.*'

Uncomfortable with the praise, I changed the subject. 'What are you working on at the moment?'

'Jean-Pierre has portrait commissions lined up for the next two years,' Veronica answered for him.

I skewered a pearl onion on my plate. 'No more landscapes?'

'Portraits keep the lights on,' Jean-Pierre replied. He plucked his phone from the table and slipped it into the inside pocket of his jacket.

'Do you golf, JP?' Spence said, an odd challenge in his voice. He poured the last dribble of champagne into his flute and signalled for another bottle.

As I mentally tallied what we were spending, I tried not to hyperventilate. When I signed our prenup, I waived any rights to Spencer's trust fund so I just had to assume he could afford it. Papi negotiated the prenup on my behalf, taking his role as paterfamilias very seriously, and concluded that on the whole our family had received an appropriate number of cows.

These types will never give you access to their trust. Only for blood, Papi had said. *The real money is in grandchildren.*

'I've never understood the obsession with using a stick to flick a ball into a hole,' Jean-Pierre told my husband. I chortled softly.

'It's not that at all, JP. It's a mental game. All about precision. Acuity,' Spence said like a true zealot. I preferred to quaff Arnold Palmers at the clubhouse with the other golf widows. 'I took a client to the Hong Kong Golf Club in Fanling this week. Terrific course. I had to let him win, of course.' Spence's laugh was too loud.

Veronica's mouth twitched. 'My great-greats used to hunt civet cats and red foxes in Fanling – can you imagine it? Horses and hounds tromping all over the New Territories in full hunting regalia?' She paused for the appropriate laughter. 'There's a mothy old taxidermy fox in our house on Lamma that always gives me the creeps.' Looking at Jean-Pierre, she said, 'Please don't stuff me when I die.'

'But you'd make such a *belle* corpse.'

Thinking about it now, the exchange makes me shudder. Veronica's corpse was anything but *belle* after weeks in the water.

The waiter picked an opportune moment to clear our dishes and refill our glasses before a Baked Alaska was presented with compliments of the house.

'Speaking of corpses,' Spence began, digging into his ice cream with a fork. 'Did you know our apartment is haunted?'

'*Vraiment?*' Jean-Pierre's sceptically raised eyebrow required no translation.

'No, not really,' I said. 'The murder was in the apartment below.'

'Yes, that's right. I'd forgotten. The Starscape murder.' Veronica got a distant look in her eye. 'The landlords were furious. No Hongkongers will rent or buy anywhere near a murder.' Zeroing in on Spencer, she said, 'If memory serves, Edwin owns a few apartments in Starscape. *Hmm.*'

I had new admiration for Edwin Leung. In doing a favour for Veronica, he'd done himself a favour too. *Guanxi* all around. From the look on my husband's face, he didn't see it that way. If I didn't know him, if I didn't love him, I would have said he was acting like a spoiled child who wanted to be King for the Day every day.

But I did love Spence. I squeezed his knee beneath the table in solidarity, savouring the Grand Marnier liqueur and meringue on my tongue.

When we'd finished our desserts and the third bottle, Spence asked our guests, 'Another?'

'No, thank you. I have an early morning,' Veronica answered.

'Early bird catches the worm,' said my husband. He asked the waiter for the bill and a few minutes later the maître d' appeared.

'You have all enjoyed your meal, I trust?' he enquired. The

maître d' was a handsome Chinese man in this thirties whose broad shoulders were emphasised by his finely crafted suit, and he knew it.

'Absolutely delicious,' I enthused. The others were a chorus of praise.

'Wonderful. We're always honoured to have you dine with us, Madame Hawkins. Monsieur Hawkins,' said the maître d', and Jean-Pierre grimaced. 'The bill has been settled. A token of appreciation. After the success of the Hawkins Pacific Christmas dinner.'

'That is so kind, Anson,' said Veronica. 'I'm sure we'll be seeing you again soon.'

Spence's cheeks were rosy. This had not gone as he'd intended. He didn't like being on the back foot.

Recovering quickly, he said, 'It seems we're in your debt again. Thank you.'

'Nonsense.' Veronica's smile was dazzling. 'It's the company that counts.' She reached across the table and squeezed my hand. 'Real friends are hard to find.'

'They are,' I said.

'Do be careful of the ghosts, though. They can attach themselves to the living.'

Veronica was right. It's all too easy for the dead to find purchase. Especially when the living don't want to let them go.

We said our goodbyes in the hotel lobby as Veronica and Jean-Pierre disappeared into her chauffeured Bentley. Spence and I waited for the doorman to find us a cab.

As the red-and-white stop-started along Salisbury Road towards the Cross-Harbour Tunnel, my cell vibrated in my Birkin. One corner of my mouth lifted as I read the text: *Lovely to meet you. Free for lunch Mon at China Club? Cress*

'Your lover?' Spence jested.

'Veronica. Thanking us for a wonderful evening.'

He crinkled his forehead. 'We should have paid.'

'Next time.'

I can't say why I lied. Perhaps because I didn't want Spencer to be jealous I had more new friends than he did.

I rolled down the window – literally cranked it down – and stuck my head out for a lungful of languid, gasoline-flavoured air.

'Looks like somebody had too much Dom.'

'It's not that.'

A hand encircled my knee, the pads of his fingers tight against my skin. 'You're not . . .'

Whipping my gaze back to his, 'I'm not,' I assured him.

We didn't speak of the morning I woke up in a pool of blood. The child I didn't know I was carrying. The child neither of us had expected. The child that was no longer our problem.

It was as if it hadn't happened.

It happened three weeks before we boarded the flight to Hong Kong.

Cranking the window down further, I stuck my upper body out of the window until the cabbie complained. *Gweilo*, I heard him gripe.

Night air is heavy, stagnant in this part of the world. Swollen. Fecund. Half an hour later when I threw up on Spencer's loafers, I did blame the Dom.

I giggled until the tunnel devoured us whole.

Chapter 6

Tai Tai Life

unch with Cressida Wong required back-to-back hot yoga classes in preparation. There are over thirty thousand eating places, many unlicensed, in Hong Kong, and some of the most in-vogue chefs in town cater to supper clubs that move around and to which you must be invited. It's hardly shocking that locals greet each other with *Nei sik jo fan mei a?* – 'Have you eaten?'

Dripping with sweat, panting for breath, I mentally patted myself on the back as I stared at myself in the mirror of the yoga studio. I admired the tendons in my neck.

Don't judge me. Every girl I grew up with had at least experimented with bulimia by seventh grade. My mother bought me an exercise bike for my tenth birthday and I had to ride for at least thirty minutes a day if I wanted my allowance. *Less is more, Martina,* she explained.

A slavish devotee of jazzercise and the thighmaster, Anette Torres ate half a grapefruit every morning and nothing but cabbage soup for weeks at a time. Despite the fact she was lissome and Viking-statured at nearly five foot eleven, with a shock of white-blonde hair that hung past her shoulders. I, on the other hand, spent my allowances on illicit chipwiches bought from the bodega around the corner. Bitsy and I had that in common.

Nobody had told me the story of Sisyphus yet.

I grabbed a quick shower, styled my hair in the women's locker room and burned some extra calories dodging the minibuses on Des Voeux Road. Minibus drivers all seem to be intent on breaking the sound barrier and one trip was enough for me.

My destination that afternoon was the Old Bank of China headquarters in the heart of Central, now overshadowed by the sleek Bank of China Tower designed by I. M. Pei (the same starchitect who put a pyramid in the Louvre). The tower's knifelike edges are generally accepted to disrupt the good *qi* of the vicinity, deliberately designed to strike at the heart of the bank's rivals, and were held responsible for sundry financial and political troubles during its construction.

A pair of stone lions flanked the bank's entrance on the ground floor while an equally formidable hostess greeted guests to the club in the sky. Strictly no polo shirts allowed.

The dining room evoked the glamour of 1930s Shanghai: intricately carved mahogany chairs and screens set against white walls lined with period photographs and scrolls of Chinese calligraphy. Huge fans dangled from the ceiling, rotating mostly for show. Red draperies and fabric lanterns punctuated the sumptuous interior.

I ordered a G&T and waited for Cressida. There's something soothing about the hubbub of a restaurant, I've always found, and I enjoyed sifting the English from the Cantonese. Hongkongers switch between the two mid-sentence or mid-word like Papi's family does English and Spanish. Covetously, I watched as fragrant steam billowed from beneath the lid of a bamboo basket on the table kitty corner to mine. I withdrew my new iPhone from my tote and began scrolling through my emails to distract myself from the delicate, pale green dumplings.

'Martina, Martina, Martina!' exclaimed Cressida as she rushed in, twenty minutes late. She had donned a buttercup-yellow Céline dress that paired perfectly with ballet flats. 'I'm so sorry! I hope you haven't been waiting long.'

'Just arrived.'

Cressida leaned down to give me a greeting kiss and I was hit by a wall of ambery perfume. Taking her seat, she spoke rapid-fire

Cantonese to the *qipao*-clad waitress. The form-fitting dress would never stretch over my Latin hips, as my mother invariably complained.

'How was your weekend?' I asked, sliding my index finger through the condensation on my highball glass.

'My mother-in-law is in town,' Cressida said. 'It's why I was late.' I released a groan of commiseration. 'Yesterday we all had to *yum cha* with my parents.'

'*Yum cha*?'

'Ah, yes, you're new. *Yum cha* means to drink tea but it's short-hand for going for dim sum. Sunday is family day in Hong Kong.' Glancing at the bamboo-basket-laden tables around us, she said, 'I hope you like dim sum?'

'I'm a New Yorker. I pretty much grew up on Chinese takeout.'

Cressida screwed her lips together and I worried I'd offended her. Then she laughed. 'You are funny, Martina. The dim sum here is better than in New York, I guarantee. Finding the best *yum cha* is a matter of honour.'

I smiled as the gin went down smoothly.

The waitress in the electric blue *qipao* reappeared and placed a porcelain teapot on the table. 'You should also try Jumbo in Aberdeen – it's on a boat and great for out-of-towners,' Cressida continued as the waitress poured oolong tea into her cup. 'City Hall is popular too. Lei Garden. Or Crystal Palace.'

'If I'm not careful I think I could spend all my time eating.'

'Probably a lot of it.' Another solicitous laugh. She raised her teacup in a toast, touching my glass halfway down. In time I would learn the position of a glass in a toast is a sign of respect.

The waitress asked if we were ready to order. 'I'll follow your lead,' I told Cressida. 'I'm an omnivore.'

Her smile was bright and surprised. I trusted Cressida to pick the best dishes and I knew it would endear me to her. After several nods, the waitress left.

'How long is your mother-in-law in town?' I asked.

'Too long.' We both laughed. 'She goes back to Chongqing on Friday. But don't worry, it still gives her time to buy all the Vuitton at the Landmark. Her friends each made an order – you never know if what you get on the Mainland is real.'

'That's where your husband is from?' Generally, I wasn't a big fan of the get-to-know-you dance but so far everyone I'd met in Hong Kong had a much more interesting backstory than Hoboken to a Seven Sisters college to Manhattan.

Cressida paused with her teacup at her lips. Again I got the impression I'd said the wrong thing.

Sipping her tea, she said, 'Jack is self-made. His father died when he was young. He studied at Beijing Normal University – which is very hard to do if you are not from Beijing. He founded SinoTop when he was twenty-five. In fifteen years it has become China's leading security firm.'

'Very impressive.'

'Yes, yes it is.' The corners of her mouth relaxed, her face beaming with pride. Of all the women I'd met in Hong Kong so far, Cressida seemed to like her husband the best. Then she lowered her voice, leaning across the table, and said, 'Hongkongers can be the worst snobs in the world when it comes to Mainlanders.'

'Oh. I didn't realise.' Although it didn't take long before I discerned that certain Hongkongers viewed people across the border the way Manhattanites do the Jersey crowd.

'Jack loves *Top Gun*,' she said. 'He named his company after it.' Cressida rolled her eyes. 'He has a great talent for negotiating tense situations between Western businessmen and local party officials.'

I was desperate to know what those tense situations might include but I was afraid to ask and certain I wouldn't get an answer.

'In fact,' Cressida continued, 'it's one of his new ventures that I wanted to talk to you about.'

'I'm intrigued.' Astounded was more like it. What kind of

opportunity could Cressida possibly have to offer me, who she knew so little about?

'SinoTop is branching out into private jet services that offer the utmost security,' she said. 'I'm heading up the marketing, as well as concierge packages.'

'Sounds exciting.'

She held my gaze. 'We're going to have an in-flight magazine. I want to call it *852* – after the Hong Kong area code. I'd like you to be its editor. *Managing* editor.'

The gin burned my throat. 'I'm flattered.' And I was, but a tiny alarm bell sounded at the back of my mind. There had been something off between Cressida and Veronica the other night, something I didn't understand yet.

'I've read your work. It's well written.' Cressida refilled her tea-cup, her eyes sharp. 'Evelyn won't be leaving *HK City Chic* anytime soon.'

'I'm still finding my feet after the move,' I started to dissemble but Cressida raised a hand. 'Just think about it,' she said as several baskets of dim sum were laid on the table. Spring rolls, *siu mai*, sesame prawn toast. I tried not to drool.

The sweet pork of the *char siu bao* melted in my mouth and I vowed to do another two hot yoga classes while I reached for another bun. Make that three classes.

Spooning a minuscule amount of rice into her bowl, Cressida said, 'Have you joined any of the American women's groups yet?'

'I'm not that into groups.'

Without Veronica the highlight of my social life would have been the bottomless brunches at Zuma or alumni society parties on trams slithering along the north side of the island from Kennedy Town to Quarry Bay. Maybe the champagne tent at the Rugby Sevens (tacky costume required – what Brits call 'fancy dress') or the annual Ivy Ball. Filling my days with Chinese calligraphy classes and jewellery-making at the American Women's Association, playing tennis with other silently seething *tai tais*, tagging along on trips to Sri Lanka with the sole purpose of buying revenge sapphires to punish spouses for indiscretions, and quietly losing my mind.

Veronica saved me from my head-in-the-oven moment.

'No, me neither.' Cressida took a small bite of rice. 'I do chair a charity committee. You should join. They're all good women, I promise. Friendly.'

'What's the charity?' I asked, although I was fairly certain I already knew.

'Lifting Hope. We're helping orphans in Cambodia. We have a big benefit this autumn.'

'That's a worthy cause.'

'Besides, you can't be a true *tai tai* if you're not on a zillion committees.'

I laughed. 'You're probably right.' *But I don't want to be a* tai tai *at all*, I nearly let slip.

'You'll join us, then?'

'Count me in.'

Cressida clapped her hands. 'We'll have so much fun,' she said. Spence would be pleased. His mother was a docent at several museums and organised disease-of-the-week fundraisers in her sleep.

I dipped the end of my spring roll in strong black vinegar. The fried dough crunched between my teeth.

'I'm so glad we ran into each other at Felix. It's always nice to meet likeminded people,' I told her. *Crunch, crunch.*

'I feel the same way,' she agreed. 'How long have you known Veronica?'

A tingle shot through me. 'Not nearly as long as you,' I assured her. Women could get very territorial about being someone's oldest friend.

'No, I didn't think so.' Cressida's eyes did a circuit of the dining room. She inched her chair closer to mine. 'I had debated whether to say anything,' she began, 'but I like you, Martina.' She paused.

'Veronica is the reason I don't like groups. She's also the reason I don't drink. Not in public.'

'What do you mean?'

'We're both from Hong Kong, our parents did business together – I thought it would make us friends at St Edith's.'

I held my breath, waiting for what she would say next. Veronica would be a tough act to follow at any age, let alone in high school. Cressida had a pretty, open face, but Veronica had innate mystique. Jealousy would be par for the course.

'The other girls called me Watercress as soon as I arrived, which wasn't so bad,' said Cressida although it evidently still irked her. 'Veronica was two years older and I'd hoped she'd defend me.' She shrugged.

'Girls can be cruel,' I said. The memory of how ecstatic I'd been to be invited to Tinsley Palmer's slumber party only to be turned away by the doorman, sleeping bag under my arm, the elderly Irishman apologising that there'd been a misunderstanding, still gave me a bellyache.

A nod. Sadness touched Cressida's eyes. 'Ching-chong Wong was worse.'

'Oh God. I'm sorry.'

I could relate more than I was willing to admit. At least at Buxton I could pass for white, mostly. Still, if I hadn't had Bitsy . . . not worth thinking about. Bitsy petitioned her mother's friends to get me accepted to the Junior League and invited me to come out as a debutante at the Thanksgiving Eve Ball. The first Latina to hold the honour. 'Thankfully' I didn't look the part, according to one of the fan boys (yes, that's a thing – they distribute the green ostrich plume feather fans to the debs).

Cressida sighed. 'I thought bragging about my family's fortune would make the other girls like me.'

'Not so much,' I inferred.

'Not so much.' She tucked a loose hair behind her ear. 'Which was why I was thrilled beyond belief when I was invited to join the secret society known as the Saints.'

My stomach pinched. 'You don't have to tell me . . .' I trailed off, afraid of where this story was going.

'There was an initiation, of course. A joint initiation with the Sinners from our brother school, St Dunstan's, on the other side of town.'

The remnants of spring roll turned sour on my tongue.

'I'd never had more than a sip of champagne for a toast before that night.' Cressida spoke with false detachment. 'Brits love their drink and I wanted so much to fit in. Veronica poured me glass after glass of Buck's Fizz. It was the nineties, after all.'

I gave a small laugh, growing increasingly queasy.

'I lost all track of time,' Cressida continued. 'I felt floaty and wonderful.'

Leaning in, I said, 'Was the drink spiked?'

'I don't know.' She eyed my G&T. 'There was a boy. I had a huge crush on him. Veronica knew it. She said he liked me too. What I didn't know was that he was her boyfriend.'

'Oh, shit.'

'Yes. Oh, shit.'

Goosebumps pricked my arms picturing the scene. This was not the Veronica I knew. This was not the Veronica who had shown me nothing but kindness. How could I reconcile these two very different versions of her?

Holding my gaze, Cressida said, 'I confessed my crush when I thought we were alone. I tried to kiss him and he pushed me away. "Good God, Ching-chong Wong! You taste like the cream of some young guy, get off me!"' She hammed up her posh British accent and a wash of sympathy flooded me.

'Veronica and the others were watching,' she said. 'It was all a big joke.'

'That's terrible,' I said. 'What a racist prick!' I didn't want to believe Cressida, but I sensed she was telling the truth, and I realised how much I didn't know about my new best friend.

'They laughed even harder when I threw up all over myself.'

'I'm so sorry. You and Veronica seem friendly now, though?'

'It's better to be Veronica's friend than her enemy,' Cressida replied. Regret stained her face. I opened and closed my mouth several times.

Silence stretched between us. The ice cracked in my glass.

'Just be careful, Martina.' She stared me straight in the eyes. 'Veronica only needs you as long as she needs you.'

But I was the one who needed her.

The apartment was too quiet when I got back from lunch around 5 p.m. Spence was taking a client out to dinner that night and I had no plans. I certainly wasn't going to eat. Maybe ever again. My afternoon with Cressida had stirred up insecurities and the worst of my schoolgirl memories. I pushed Cressida and my childhood from my mind and changed into a one-piece, punishing myself with a hundred laps in Starscape's outdoor pool.

It was unheated but the humidity was enough to make it refreshing. I started with crawl, then flipped over to backstroke, watching the sun set over the lush hills and looming skyscrapers. My ears cocooned beneath my bathing cap, the dull roar of the city muffled, I propelled myself through the water as if in a trance.

Time passed. The floodlights came on, illuminating the otherwise empty pool, but still I kicked. The temperature of the water grew from pleasantly brisk to chilly, but still I kicked. When people asked me my favourite animal, my standard answer was a swan because it's elegant above the water, paddling like hell beneath it. A Hollywood starlet said that in an interview I read once. I knew it was a lie. I was a duck, plain and simple. I was amazed people didn't notice how hard I was trying to look poised, as if I had it all figured out.

Maybe what drew me instinctually to Veronica was the fact she knew I was a duck, right from the start. She knew I was a duck and she befriended me anyway.

Sometimes to make your life your own, you have to unmake it first, she told me a few months later. Befriending Veronica was the first step in my unmaking – and my remaking.

When I couldn't stand the cold any more, I towelled off and headed upstairs. The effects of the G&T from lunch had long since diminished and I decided to remedy the situation. I unscrewed the cap on the half-full bottle of Bombay Sapphire, sniggering at the lowball glass that I'd swiped from my parents' apartment before leaving New York. A gold hexagonal pattern covered the heavy glass. It was one of a set of six, leaving a mismatched pair that would drive my mother nuts – which, juvenile as it was, greatly enhanced its appeal.

Dropping ice into the tumbler, I poured in two fat fingers of gin. Papi's clients would often come over for drinks before they headed out for the evening and I was expected to play Cute Little Girl, serving them in these same gold-patterned glasses. I understood the difference between 'neat' and 'on the rocks' by my sixth birthday, and I used to think when I could drink from one of these glasses, I'd be a sophisticated adult with all the answers too.

Wrapped in a bathrobe, I ensconced myself on the sofa and stared out at the lights of other people's apartments sprinkling the hills on Kowloon side. The floor-to-ceiling windows felt bare without the draperies I'd ordered but apparently there was a backlog at the factory in Shenzhen. Pressing the glass to my lips, I wondered how many times my mom sat alone waiting for my dad?

I suppressed a sudden yearning to call her. Confiding in her rarely ended well. The key turned in the lock and my head swivelled towards the sound.

'Spence?' I called out. How long had I been swimming? Surely it was too early for him to be home. His keys jangled as they hit the table in the hallway, followed by the thud of his briefcase on the floor.

Spencer stumbled into the living room. His suit jacket was crumpled, slung over his arm. Bankers in Hong Kong didn't generally wear ties, too hot, but I noticed several of his shirt buttons were also undone, and there was a stain of some kind on its monogrammed pocket.

Squinting at me, he said, 'You look like you're celebrating.'

Did I? I suppose I should have been celebrating Cressida's offer, rather than ruminating on how miserable I used to be in middle school. I couldn't talk about Buxton with Spence. He wouldn't understand, and he wouldn't believe that Merritt, his very own Sidekick, had been one of my chief tormentors.

Sitting up straighter, I forced a smile. 'I got offered a job today. An editor job – something permanent.' The longer I forced the smile, the more real it became. 'Isn't that great? I'll have something to do here too.'

Spencer hung his head, raking a hand through his sweaty locks. 'Great, Marty. That's just great.' But he didn't make it sound great.

'Shouldn't you be at dinner?' I asked.

'Didn't happen,' he mumbled to his feet.

'Right.' I waited a beat. 'So where have you been?'

Spence swayed. 'Out with Andy and some other guys from the office.'

'Getting trashed,' I said.

His scoff was harsh, practically a bark. 'Everybody's a critic.'

'What are you talking about?' I pushed to standing, growing more concerned, my grip tightening around the glass.

When my husband raised his eyes to meet mine, I saw his were glassy. A tendril of fear coiled in my chest. In all the time I'd known him, I had yet to see him cry.

'Oh, Spence. Did somebody die?' I said, low. 'Is it your mom?'

He barked another chortle. 'You *wish*, Marty.' Spence shook his head. 'No, nobody died. But my career is on life support.'

I didn't bother denying that the next thirty to forty years would be a lot less stressful if my mother-in-law was pushing up daisies. Instead, I set down my glass and walked to where Spence continued to sway. 'Come here,' I said, wrapping my arms around him, and he dropped his chin onto my shoulder.

'Are you naked under there, Torres?' He was aiming for sexy, I think, but it came out slurred.

I gave a laugh. 'Things can't be too bad if you're thinking about me naked.'

'I'm always thinking about you naked, but things are shit.'

Pulling back so I could read his face, 'What happened?' I asked him, and the emotion that crossed his features was guilt.

'The bank lost the big BMW deal today. They'd been working on it for the last year, long before my ass landed in Hong Kong – but somehow it's my fault.'

'That doesn't sound fair.'

'It's not fair but I'm nobody out here and the head of structuring decided to make me the fucking sacrificial lamb!' Spence exploded, his breath reeking of whisky.

Lifting my hand to his face, I stroked his jaw the way he liked, but he bristled. Disguising my hurt, I said, 'What did your boss do?'

'He said politics are shitty. Take one for the team. People will forget.' Spence rubbed his eyes. 'Better me than him is what he meant.'

'I'm sorry, Spence, but he's probably right. You only just got here and people will forget.' Although I doubted Edwin Leung ever forgot anything.

'This never would have happened in New York,' he said and it sounded distinctly like a sulk. He tugged at the belt of my bathrobe, loosening the knot.

'I know,' I told him because he was right. In New York, some other nobody would have been thrown under the bus. Spence expected to win at life because he always had and he didn't seem to realise it was because he'd been playing a rigged game. I didn't have the heart to tell him.

Spence drew me into his chest. 'You smell of chlorine.'

'You smell like happy hour.'

He laughed at that. 'I don't want you to worry, Marty.'

'I'm not,' I lied.

When I'd finished college, Papi took me aside and told me that I should go to med school or law school because I was too attractive to be taken seriously in finance and I'd been raised to expect a standard of living few professions afforded. The other option was to marry a banker or Old Money but to watch out for the third generation rule. Spence was the fifth generation of fully loaded Mertons so I'd figured I was safe.

Spence chucked me under the chin. 'You're not a very good liar, Marty.' He kissed me and I tasted the whisky sour. 'But I mean it. You don't have to take the editor job. None of the other bankers' wives work.'

'I've always worked. That's what I do. Merritt has a high-flying job.'

'Hey, Marty, I'm not a caveman.' He chuckled, yanking at the belt of my bathrobe until it fell open. 'What we *should* be working on, though, is starting a family . . .' He slipped his hand inside the robe, caressing the line of my hip, and tingles followed his fingers.

Not allowing myself to be distracted, 'We agreed to wait until I turned thirty,' I reminded him. 'And that's a couple of years away.'

His hand stilled at my waist. 'So you're glad you miscarried?'

I sucked in a breath, feeling as if I'd been slapped. 'No, of course not!'

'Then what are you saying?'

'I don't know. Maybe it was a sign that we should wait?'

'Jeez, Marty, I didn't think you were *that* Catholic.'

'I'm not. You know I'm not.' I stepped out of his reach. 'My *abuela* is spinning in her grave because I got married in an Episcopal church to please *your* grandmother.'

Spence scrubbed a hand over his face. 'I'm sorry, Marty. That was a dick thing to say.'

'Yeah, Spence.' I crossed my arms. 'It was a dick thing to say.'

'I know, it's just . . . you're my *wife*, Marty. Don't you think I can take care of you?'

The look he gave me was so pained that it stopped the torrent of angry words from leaving my lips. I took several deep breaths in and out.

'Can't we take care of each other?' I said softly.

Spence bit his lips together. His nostrils flared. Finally, he said, 'That's not how my parents operate.'

'No offence, but I don't want to be your parents,' I told my husband. 'I definitely don't want to be mine.' I caught his eye, showing him the glimmer of a smile. 'I just want to be us: Marty and Spence.'

'Marty and Spence, huh?'

'Yeah.'

'That sounds good to me.'

A surge of tenderness lifted me on to the balls of my feet, pressing a kiss to Spencer's lips, forcing them open with my tongue, no longer caring about his whisky breath. This was good, he was being vulnerable for once, and despite the circumstances I was glad we were connecting. He drove his hands through my wet tangles as I lightly scratched the back of his neck with my pristinely manicured nails. He groaned into my mouth and I started to wriggle out of my bathrobe, not caring if we gave all of Victoria Harbour a show.

'Hold that thought,' said Spence, and drew the bathrobe back over my shoulders. 'I want to get Dad's advice.'

'*Now?*'

'He'll be at the club later and they don't even let POTUS take calls inside.' At my stupefied look, Spence promised, 'It'll take thirty minutes tops. I need to know how to play it at the office tomorrow. I'll make it up to you very, very soon . . .'

I stared after my husband as he disappeared into the bedroom.

How did Spencer think he was ready to be a father when he still couldn't make a move without consulting his? I loved him, almost too much, but I wanted to tell him to grow the hell up.

After the father–daughter dance at our wedding, Mr Merton had cut in. He'd told me to call him Tucker (not Dad, thank God) but it still seemed too familiar. Mr Merton was exceptionally tall – nearly six foot four – especially in my husband's mind, and he led me around the ballroom with compelling force.

'Spence showed some spine in marrying you,' Mr Merton told me. 'We both know you're not who Sybil would have picked for him.' My smile brittle, I nodded. 'But I'm hoping you're a good influence.' Twirl. 'You're a hustler, Marty. I like that about you.' We box-stepped together. 'My wife doesn't, naturally, but you'll get the hang of doing it more subtly,' he said, twirling me again. 'And maybe your grit will rub off on my boy.'

Mr Merton had established his expectations and it would be clear when Spencer phoned home that night I wasn't meeting them.

Picking up my gin, I took a large drink and decided to get my own weekly call with my mother over with.

Reader, I regretted it.

Chapter 7

Games of Chance

*V*eronica was not a planner. She'd text last minute with the most exciting and glorious invitation to an exclusive designer preview at Joyce, the boutique most à la mode, or a pre-Cannes screening by Hong Kong's latest It director. When she told me to pack a carry-on and meet her at the Shun Tak Centre for a girls' trip to Macau, I cleared my schedule (an interview with an ikebana master and a lesson from my infinitely patient tennis pro).

I'd be lying if I said I wasn't apprehensive about the trip after Cressida's chronicling of Veronica's career as a merciless Queen Bee, yet I also couldn't resist the chance for more alone time with her. Something in me was attracted to Veronica in a primal way – I don't mean sexually, or even something as trite as a moth to a flame. Despite the chasm between us, or perhaps because of it, my soul recognised a kindred soul in her.

Could she be as callous as Cressida alleged? Or was she misunderstood?

Given my own bullying at Buxton, my inclination was to support #TeamCressida but a good journalist gets both sides of the story. I resolved to remain an objective, unbiased observer on our jaunt to Macau. And, more than that, if Cressida Wong, who wielded a fair amount of her own influence, didn't want to antagonise Veronica, then neither did I.

The beginning of the typhoon season had brought with it a

ferocious new assault of humidity, making my tongue stick to the roof of my mouth, and it was only May. Grateful for the cool air of the terminal, I wandered up and down four floors of fast-food joints and grotty travel agencies before finding my way to the TurboJET kiosk in the ferry concourse.

The subterranean holding pen teemed with tourists and locals of all ages waiting to board the hydrofoils that run several times an hour, all day and all night, every day of the year – typhoon permitting. Macau is the playground for anyone with a buck in their pocket or a *kwai*, a Hong Kong dollar, a Macanese *pataca*. The Hungry Tigers (slot machines), the *fan-tan* tables (a game of chance similar to roulette), the bouncing dice of *dai siu* care for the heart of no man – or woman. They gobble up aspirations and last chances indiscriminately.

Departure announcements blared through the hall in Mandarin, Cantonese and English. My eyes were drawn to the ubiquitous red-blue-white bags of heavyweight plastic, woven almost like a snakeskin, that are often used instead of regular suitcases and sturdy enough to transport a body. Transparent thermoses of tea dangled from the wristbands of middle-aged Chinese women, the green leaves bobbing inside as they scolded their restless children.

As I idled my rollboard back and forth on the linoleum, it was her voice that reached me first.

'I need a night away like you wouldn't believe,' Veronica said as she strolled towards me and I knew my face had lit up the way it did whenever she appeared. 'You packed light,' she noted. 'Excellent.'

Veronica had what looked like a vintage LV keepall over her shoulder.

'I didn't expect it to be so busy,' I said.

She shrugged. 'Buddha's Birthday. We get both the Chinese and British holidays in Hong Kong.' As time went on, I came to appreciate how having a holiday every month gives life a hopeful rhythm – something new and different just within reach.

'Usually I take the helicopter,' said Veronica, 'but I wanted you to have the full Macau experience.' She winked.

'Can't wait.' Biting my lip, I said, 'Speaking of which . . . Evelyn wants me to do a travel feature on Macau – *your* Macau.'

When I'd cancelled the ikebana master interview, Editor Evelyn had pouted down the line but said I could make it up to her by filing a piece on Veronica Hawkins's guide to the Monte Carlo of the Orient.

Veronica drew in a breath. 'She never misses an angle.' A resigned laugh. 'Well, why not? I'll show you something to write home about.'

I wasn't totally reassured. 'It's no trouble if you'd rather not . . .'

Another tinny boarding announcement rattled my eardrums.

'That's us, Marty. I've got the tickets.'

The sea of passengers didn't quite part for Veronica but she moved with a confidence that would intimidate heads of state. Hongkongers are in a perpetual rush, even more so than New Yorkers, and it took me only about a week to realise that if I didn't barge my way into an elevator or out of an MTR carriage that I'd never get anywhere. Old ladies will happily stare you in the eye while they press the door closed button. It's not personal. Time is money.

Following in Veronica's wake, I caught up to her on the gangway where we were directed to the Premier Grand Class cabin. The black leather seats were ample, reclining just enough to irritate the person behind you.

As the hydrofoil began to speed away from Hong Kong Island, Veronica turned to me. 'I hope Spencer doesn't mind me stealing you for the night.'

'I doubt he'll notice.' It came out more bitter than I'd intended.

'Trouble in paradise?'

'No, no. I think the job is just more challenging than he expected.'

I wasn't yet prepared to confide how Spencer had re-emerged from the bedroom after his call with his father with sunken cheeks and shoulders curled forward, no longer in the mood for fooling around, and tossed back an enormous tumbler of whisky before passing out in the middle of the bed, snoring like a bandsaw.

He was now pressing the flesh every night, coming home later and later. Without his network of private school, Ivy League and Union Club buddies, Spence needed to work harder than ever before to retain the bank's clients. When he wasn't demanding a command performance from me as The Charming Wife, he was growing increasingly withdrawn.

I did my best. I wanted to help him succeed – to be a team. Somehow I kept missing the mark. A constant pressure in my chest refused to go away.

The engines rumbled beneath us and I realised I'd been quiet far too long.

Veronica simply nodded. 'Edwin runs a tight ship. My father always liked that about him,' she said, and I was grateful she didn't pry further.

A harried woman in a navy-blue uniform stopped at our seats and proffered two glasses of slightly warm Prosecco. It was only 10.30 a.m., but who was I to refuse?

'Cheers, darling,' said Veronica. 'To us.'

'To us.'

Aside from taxi rides to the airport, I hadn't yet explored much of the archipelago that comprises Hong Kong. My jaw slackened as the platinum-jade sea opened in front of us. Our catamaran soared through the shipping lanes around all vessels great and small. Low-lying mountains were shrouded in a dull haze as the Mainland coast scudded by.

From the captain's seat, I might have glimpsed the nineteenth-century Guia Hill lighthouse gleaming white on the highest point of the Macau Peninsula. I'd been to Atlantic City, another seaside town propped up by the gambling industry, so I thought I knew what to expect in Macau. I was wrong. The powers-that-be had reclaimed what's known as the Cotai Strip from the tides, joining the islands of Coloane and Taipa at the behest of the Las Vegas Sands Corporation. Once one of the jewels in the crown of the Portuguese empire, Macau's gaming revenue had far eclipsed that of Vegas, overflowing with high-rollers from across Asia.

'You know, it's funny,' Veronica said, pulling my gaze back from the sea. 'Macau's and Hong Kong's fortunes have always been entwined.'

'How's that?'

'When my great-greats got thrown out of Guangzhou – Canton as was – for selling opium, they wanted to settle in Macau but the Portuguese didn't want to piss off the Chinese emperor. The Portuguese didn't have the firepower to hold their colony by force.' A sigh. 'The British won the Opium War, of course, took Hong Kong with its deeper harbour and the rest is history. Hong Kong had the money but didn't want to sully its streets with casinos – what would the Queen say? Macau was cash poor but had few qualms about vice.'

Listening to Veronica, it seemed banal, inevitable, the way empires rise and fall.

And so, Macau became Hong Kong's degenerate little brother.

Before the jetfoil came to a complete stop, the passengers were out of their seats and bustling towards the exits. Front and centre after immigration, a square-shouldered Macanese man in a three-piece suit festooned with gold epaulettes held up a placard from the Lusitano Palace.

SENHORA HAWKINS was scrawled across it.

Veronica gave him a small wave and I could see the awe register on his face. Even wearing a simple linen dress, her auburn hair swept into a nonchalant up-do, she appeared utterly majestic. He hurried to take our bags, steadfastly ignoring the rivulet of sweat running down one side of his face as he showed us to a limousine with tinted windows.

Hovering above the terminal, I heard the whir of helicopters but I was glad we'd come by sea. More fitting, more romantic.

Veronica exchanged a few words in Cantonese with the driver.

'Marty, if you don't mind not changing for lunch, there's someplace special I want to show you. The driver will take our bags to the hotel – I keep a suite.'

Considering my Moschino T-shirt and Bermuda shorts, I said, 'Am I up to scratch?'

She released her patented throaty laugh. 'You're with me.' And that made me happier than I'd been for a long time. Just being in her presence for a couple of hours had already lessened the weight between my breasts.

As the limo traversed the narrow streets, I was captivated by the cheerful blues, yellows and pinks of the neo-classical architecture that wouldn't be out of place in Lisbon or Madrid. Plazas lined with swirling black-and-white mosaics reflecting the city's maritime heritage – dolphins, seashells, tall ships – dazzle the eye. Threadlike alleyways promise mischief or something more lurid. The Moorish Barracks with their Mughal-inspired arches remind the onlooker that Macau was originally part of a vast trading network that began in Goa and Malacca, providing a convenient waystation for ships en route to Nagasaki where the Portuguese traded Chinese silk for Japanese silver.

A half-moon smile appeared on Veronica's face as the car stopped. She stepped out onto the monochrome cobblestones.

Tourists milled in front of a Chinese temple larger than any I had yet visited in Hong Kong. Built on a leafy hill, cherry-tomato-tinted paint peeled from the exterior walls in places, almost shabby chic. Ornate carvings bedecked the green-tiled roof, its edges upturned and foreboding, and I spied two enormous ceramic fish guarding a granite gate.

Veronica was pensive as I came to stand beside her. Redolent smoke permeated the air, drifting towards us on the breeze from a circular portal in the temple wall.

'Joss,' she said. She pointed at thin ribbons of burning incense fashioned in a conical shape and suspended from the ceiling inside. 'It's a Cantonese word – but it comes from the Portuguese *deus*: God. Macau is the original melting pot.'

Veronica took in a deep breath. 'Lulu always loved it here. Especially the egg tarts. *Pastéis de nata*. When she was a toddler, she'd demand *Natas, natas* and cry bloody murder until she got them.'

This was the first time she had mentioned her younger sister to me directly. There was something about Macau that made Veronica drop her guard.

She took my hand, almost uncomfortably tight.

'This temple is older than the colony itself,' she said. 'Fishermen have come here to pray to A-Ma since the Ming dynasty.' Veronica raised an eyebrow. 'In Hong Kong, we call the goddess Tin Hau.' The penetrating stare of the girl in her mother's painting flashed through my mind. She'd died rescuing her family from the ravenous tide.

Tugging me forward like a kid at a carnival, we dodged and weaved through tourists with dueling selfie sticks. The inhabitants of South China are a seafaring people and they have various names for the girl they hope will save them from the waves. I can't blame them. I can't help but hate her, either, because she didn't save my best friend.

But that came later.

On this day, the sun broke out from behind the clouds as we followed the staircase up Barra Hill. Veronica stopped beside a huge rock on which a ship had been carved. 'Maman loved this.' She traced the outline of the mast. 'It's a *lorcha* – the junk boat that brought Tin Hau to Macau. This carving is over four hundred years old. Maman sketched the logo for the gallery based on this one.'

Staring down the hill towards the water, it was easy to imagine the shore lined with junks, sampans with their oars lilting in the sea, and galleons packed with silk.

'Maman named it Gallery de Ladrones because that's what the Portuguese called Hong Kong back then – the islands of pirates: *ladrones*.'

I laughed. 'It's the same in Spanish. Each of us has a little bit of pirate inside us.'

She nodded, quiet for another long beat. Then, out of nowhere, 'I blamed myself for Lulu,' Veronica said aloud, in a hush, the murmurs of the tourists fading to nothing. 'I should have been there – not her. I deserved it more.' She sucked in a breath. 'I avoided boats after the accident. Water. Air. It took a horse tranquilliser to get me on the plane from Oxford back home for the funerals.'

Veronica snort-laughed. A sound I came to recognise as presaging real emotion.

'I was numb for years after they died. All of them in one fell swoop. As if they'd angered some god we didn't know existed.'

She gazed at the horizon. 'One day, Marty, you have to face your fears. I faced mine here.'

Veronica wanted to paint the town red, and that we did. We started with dinner at Joël Robuchon's outpost perched atop the Grand Lisboa Hotel. Only three Michelin stars for Veronica. Most people would book months in advance for a window table beneath the vaulted glass dome, views stretching across the city and the surrounding waters. I was glad I'd packed my brand-new Vivienne Tam cocktail dress, a gauzy sheath finely embroidered with peonies over a blue silk slip.

Pan-fried Hokkaido scallops melted in my mouth, light and divine, followed by chilled pineapple for dessert. We shared a bottle of vintage champagne from the 450,000 varieties of wine available. Slightly tipsy, we roamed the gaming halls downstairs, which were packed to the gills with men in khakis and knock-off Ralph Lauren, fanny packs crammed with thousands of dollars slung around their hips. Higher-ups from the factories that delivered iPhones to the world. They sipped Hennessy XO mixed with sweet, bottled Lipton tea while playing Texas hold 'em.

Next stop were the VIP tables of the Paiza Club at the Venetian, taking its name from the tablet Mongolian nobles carried to signify their authority. I don't play the lottery and I don't have a poker face, so forking over the eye-watering minimum bet didn't appeal.

'You can't come to Macau and not gamble,' Veronica teased me, pulling me towards a roulette table near an ersatz canal. She opened her sparkly purple Judith Leiber clutch and withdrew a HKD 1,000 note, nicknamed the Gold Cow, and exchanged it for a chip. 'When's your birthday, Marty?'

'April twenty-third.'

'St George's Day. I'll have to call you Dragon Slayer.' She smirked and placed the chip on red 23. The croupier called time and set the wheel in motion.

My heart sped up, a tingly feeling starting at the tip of my head and raising the tiny hairs on my arms. I didn't think I had an addictive personality. Maybe it was the night. Maybe it was Veronica.

Against all the odds, the ball stopped on red 23. I squealed. Veronica squealed. I was seeing the girl beneath the sophisticate. It made me feel so much closer to her, made me want to give her a hug.

'It's yours,' she declared. She'd won HKD 35,000. 'Too bad Jean-Pierre doesn't have my luck.' Being called Monsieur Hawkins by the maître d' at Felix had obviously rankled and their sniping about his portrait commissions had been awkward. Male egos being what they are, Jean-Pierre's resentment about Veronica having the upper hand financially would only continue to grow.

Was it enough to make him do something unspeakable?

The croupier laid the chips before Veronica and she scooped up her winnings from the table. 'Open your purse,' she told me.

'No, Veronica. It's too much. That's your money.'

'But I don't need it. Come on, Marty. Be a good girl and open wide.' I did as she bade me. The red-and-white-striped chips rattled as they tumbled inside. 'Now you have a slush fund Spencer doesn't need to know about.'

Veronica held my gaze and I realised she'd deduced something I tried not to think about too closely. I felt seen in a way I never had before. I'd never had as much money as my peers at Buxton and I'd expected to sign a prenup when I married into the Merton clan, but it still chafed.

'No, Spencer doesn't need to know,' I agreed.

'Back to Vasco's to celebrate!' She smiled triumphantly.

Vasco's is the high-rollers' lounge at the Lusitano Palace but you won't find it in any guidebook. The original structure of the hotel was painstakingly restored to its full colonial glory before adding several elegant modern buildings, all very understated for Macau.

'*Boa noite*, Senhora Hawkins,' the lounge manager greeted Veronica.

'Nice to see you, João.'

The man was in his late thirties. Around his throat was fastened a silk paisley Ascot, which he wore with panache. His maternal grandfather was from Lisbon, I learned, and he'd studied at the university there. His other grandparents were Macanese Chinese. João spoke Cantonese, Portuguese, English, Mandarin and a bit of Russian, which comes in handy in a casino. He said this with a wink, preternaturally self-possessed.

'I'm delighted you could stop by,' João told Veronica as we followed him to a plush velvet booth. 'I missed you when Jean-Pierre was here earlier in the week.'

Veronica stopped short. 'When was my husband here?'

'Tuesday, I believe,' he replied without hesitation.

'Thank you, João. Jean-Pierre is painting tonight.'

'Of course. I'll bring you a Cohiba.'

'Make that two,' she told him. 'And two glasses of port. Taylor's 1863.'

'*Sim*, Senhora.'

A jazz trio played a mellow riff on 'My Favourite Things' in the corner, the walking bass line working its way under my skin.

'Is Jean-Pierre really painting tonight?' I asked Veronica in a concerned voice.

'Could be. He's not gambling anyhow.' She leaned back against the velvet. 'The trouble with husbands is you can't kill them and you can't sell them for profit.'

I touched a hand to her shoulder. 'Do you want to talk about it?'

'No, I really don't. We're two women in our prime. We have more interesting things to talk about.' She summoned a smile as João returned with two Cuban cigars and a pair of Riedel port glasses, the ruby liquid nearly jet in the low lighting.

A guillotine cutter was laid on the silver tray beside the cigars.

'Compliments of Ao Wing,' João told Veronica blandly, then dematerialised effortlessly.

To my quirked eyebrow, Veronica replied, 'Ao Wing owns the Lusitano Palace, among other things. His friends call him Vasco, after Vasco da Gama. My father told me I could always trust him in a pinch.'

Veronica snipped off the cap of her Cohiba. 'Remember how I mentioned facing your fears at the temple?' That sly smile overtook her face again. 'After my family's funeral, Vasco took me to the black sand beach in Coloane. He threw me in the ocean. He made me swim against the current until I wasn't afraid any more.'

I inhaled a shocked breath.

Later, when I was fact-checking my travel feature, I discovered that Ao Wing had managed to procure one of a very few casino-operating licences from the Macau government despite – or perhaps because of – his rumoured ties to the Triads. With billions of dollars of gambling revenue on the line, it's not surprising gangland violence erupted in Macau that rivalled Chicago during Prohibition. It was only about a decade since judges in the city had to worry about car bombs. There's no sign of anything but opulence now. At least not in plain view.

Veronica took my Cohiba and snipped off its cap too. 'Here,' she said. 'You looked like you needed help with that.' She handed it back to me. 'Have you smoked a cigar before?' I shook my head. 'A virgin, then,' she said, laughing. 'Jean-Pierre doesn't like it when I smoke. Such a hypocrite. He smokes a pack of Gitanes a day.' Veronica wrinkled her nose. 'He thinks cigars are unladylike. Fuck the boys' club.'

Veronica lit my cigar first. She watched as I inhaled, savoured the aroma. Satisfied, she lit her own, took a long drag.

'Fuck the boys' club,' I echoed.

She smiled and smoke filled my eyes.

I picked up the glass and swirled the port. I'm no connoisseur but it went down very smoothly indeed after aging one hundred and fifty years.

'I'd promised myself I wouldn't marry an artist because my mother was so dramatic,' said Veronica. 'But I'm my father's daughter.'

'What was it you saw in the portrait Jean-Pierre did of you that made you fall in love with him?' I asked, my curiosity getting the better of me.

One corner of her mouth edged up, wistful. 'It was the eyes. He captured my fear. My childish hope. He saw the girl who'd lost everything – not the mask I show the world.' Veronica's bottom lip quivered. 'In the middle of the night, when I can't sleep, I'm still that girl. Part of me will always be nineteen. An orphan.'

Setting down my glass, I covered her hand with mine. 'You're not alone, Veronica.'

She stared down at our hands. 'You make me almost believe it,' she said. There was a rough quality to her words, a barely muzzled despair.

Trying to lighten the mood, I told Veronica, 'Spence says my eyes are the colour of mud.'

She snorted. 'What?'

'When we were first dating, he'd say how beautiful my eyes were. One night I asked him how he would describe them – big mistake. He stared at me like a deer in the headlights and then said, "Mud?"' I snickered at my own expense. 'I stopped trying to get him to be poetic after that.'

'Oh, Marty,' said Veronica, shaking her head, but at least she cracked a smile. 'We're quite the pair. And somehow we've ended up talking about the men.'

She knocked back the rest of her port. 'Did you ever meet up with Cressida Wong?'

Her tone was blithe, the query innocuous. I'm not a talented liar and Veronica had a finely honed bullshit detector.

'We had lunch a few weeks ago,' I admitted, mimicking her off-hand manner, took another puff of the cigar.

'She hates me, you know,' Veronica murmured. A jittery spark zipped down my spine. 'I'm sure she told you. Cress can't resist the opportunity to poor-mouth me.'

Sidestepping the statement, I said, 'It was more of a business meeting. She offered me a job.'

'Watercress is a canny one.' Veronica released a low laugh. She angled her face to meet my gaze. 'Full disclosure: I was a bitch at boarding school. Oxford, too. Nothing like losing your entire family to put things in perspective.' She caught João's eye and ordered another round. 'Whatever Cressida told you is probably true – I was an immature mess, and I had a mean streak. But that was half my lifetime ago. She needs to get over it.'

'Some people never get over high school.' I was proof positive of that. If I'd never left Manhattan, I probably wouldn't have, either. I would have played by those rules forever.

'I suppose.' Veronica tucked a strand of hair behind her ear. There was a hint of genuine hurt in her eyes. 'I did try to make amends when she moved back to Hong Kong after her MBA. She'd rather smile to my face and stab me in the back than accept my apology.'

'I'm sorry.'

'I'm not making excuses, but when Watercress arrived at St Edith's I was going through a bad patch with Arthur. We were fighting about which A levels I should take, what I should study at uni.' Veronica blew a smoke ring. 'He asked me to look after Watercress because of his business relationship with her father – so, of course, I did the opposite. To spite him.' Her jaw tensed. 'If I ever went to therapy, I'm sure they'd say I hurt Cressida to hurt Arthur. But it didn't work. I don't think she ever told Donnie Wong how miserable she was at school.'

Regret was etched into the fine lines around Veronica's mouth. I didn't know whether my tormentors at Buxton had come to regret their actions but Veronica clearly did. She was big enough to admit she'd been wrong.

'We could all use a lot of therapy,' I said.

João silently slipped fresh drinks in front of us.

'Cheers to that, darling,' said Veronica, lifting her port. 'These days I think Cress is mostly sore that Hawkins Pacific declined to give her husband's security firm our business. He's bought a fleet of planes and I hear he's leveraged to the hilt. If she's not careful, she'll have to ask her daddy for the cash to bail them out.'

'Oh,' I said, swallowing the word. 'Cressida did mention something about private jets.'

'What was the job she offered you?' Veronica's gaze grew wary.

'She's thinking of starting an in-flight magazine for her clients. She asked if I'd like to run it.' *Managing editor* did have a nice ring to it.

'Well, of course she did,' said Veronica. 'You'd be brilliant. Are you considering it?'

I held my breath. My answer would forever alter our relationship, I could tell. Veronica Hawkins, who was the definition of aplomb, vibrated with nervous energy.

'She put me on the spot,' I hedged. 'I told her I'd consider it – just to be polite. I didn't get a great vibe off her and I don't have the risk appetite needed for a start-up anyway.'

Veronica's brow softened and she showed me an airy smile. 'You're a quick study. You can do better than Cressida Wong.'

'I'd like to think so but, to be perfectly honest, I'm not sure who I am or what I'm doing in Hong Kong. I gave up my job in New York to follow Spencer out here and lately it's as if . . . well, they say the first year of marriage is the hardest, right?' My breath hitched as I suddenly found myself fighting back tears. It must have been the second glass of port that magically appeared in my hand that made my doubts flow out of me.

'What if I made a mistake?' I said. 'What if I've been wrong . . . about *everything*?'

'It's not you, Martina. You're whip smart. Anyone can see it. It takes a strong man to be married to a smart woman. Maybe Spencer isn't up to the challenge?'

I wanted Veronica to be right and I didn't want her to be right all at the same time. Pride swelled at her assessment. 'He used to call me Brainiac affectionately,' I said.

'You both need to find your feet out here. Then you can decide if you still want to be walking in the same direction.'

I looked away so Veronica wouldn't see the sheen to my eyes.

'You're not alone either, Marty,' she said, and for the first time since moving to Hong Kong, I knew I'd found a real friend. 'Remember that.' I blinked back my tears.

Veronica demanded my gaze with her own as she told me, 'I feel like I can trust you, you know that? And I don't trust most people. I *can't* – including Cressida. It's not in me. Do you understand?'

I did understand. I had to choose. This was the moment. I had to pick a side.

As much as I wanted a career of my own, I didn't want it more than the acceptance, the belief Veronica had in me. Taking Cressida's job offer would antagonise my husband, which I didn't want to do, but I would have done it under other circumstances. Losing Veronica was already unthinkable. Her friendship was quickly becoming the most honest thing in my life.

'You can trust me, Veronica,' I said. 'Always.'

And she did. Until the end.

Body found on Discovery Bay beach

A decomposing corpse was found on Tai Pak Beach in Discovery Bay early yesterday morning by members of the Bauhinia Boat Club.

Two members of the sailing crew immediately rushed to alert policemen stationed at the Discovery Bay Police Post at the south end of the beach.

The Criminal Investigation Team of North Lantau Police District was called to the scene and a small cordon has been erected around the boat club while preliminary investigations are carried out.

Witnesses contacted by the *South China Daily* believed the body may belong to that of missing heiress Veronica Hawkins because of the colour of dress she wore on the night she disappeared. Police Commissioner Raymond Kwan would not 'engage in any speculation' and would only confirm the body to be female.

Ms Hawkins, 35, was last seen aboard a luxury junk in Victoria Harbour five weeks ago in the company of her husband, Jean-Pierre Renard, 54, a notable artist and high-society playboy.

When reached by telephone, Mr Renard's frustration with the police investigation was clear. 'I don't know if it's her,' he said. 'The police don't tell me anything. I only heard about the body because a friend called me from the sailing club. I am living a nightmare. I can't wake up.'

Family friend and member of the Bauhinia Boat Club, Quentin Turner, told this paper, 'I've never seen a man more in love with his wife. Jean-Pierre and Veronica were like something out of an old-timey film. I hope to God it's not her.'

Chapter 8

Silent Auction

I dream of the sea. Some nights, I wake up in a cold sweat. I don't feel as if I'm choking; I watch as Veronica collects stars like pebbles from the midnight currents toing and froing around Hong Kong Island.

In my unconscious, she is luminous. A newly minted goddess. She swims through the places of my mind I never want exposed to the light of day.

I can't help but wonder if it didn't all start at the Foreign Correspondents' Club's annual gala. Hawkins Pacific traditionally bought several tables since Veronica's parents met at the FCC bar. They had a long-standing corporate membership and Veronica sponsored me for a journalist membership based on my work for *HK City Chic*. The joining dues only took a small portion of my Macau slush fund and it promised to bear other assignments now that I'd politely turned down Cressida's offer.

Veronica and I had been nearly inseparable since our trip to Macau and I felt most anchored, most content by her side.

That year the ball was taking place at the Hong Kong Convention and Exhibition Centre on 1 July to coincide with the anniversary of the Handover: Hong Kong Special Administrative Region Establishment Day. The morning of the event, she treated me to a spa day at the W Hotel. As we prepared for our ginger-root body polishes, changing into fluffy robes, Veronica noticed my gaze catch on the thin red strings that encircled several of the Chinese women's abdomens.

'It's to ward off misfortune,' she explained. 'When it's your Chinese zodiac year, every twelve years, you're more prone to bad luck – wearing red mitigates it. Next year I'll wear one too.'

But Veronica never made it to thirty-six.

Did the first of a long and twisty string of dominoes fall that evening? Initially my husband bucked at being hosted by Veronica once again until he learned that the FCC gala held a certain cachet among the clients with whom he was trying to cement relationships. More than a tad sheepish, Spence asked me to procure a couple invitations for his clients who thought journos threw the best piss-ups.

They weren't wrong.

Men need one finely tailored tuxedo and they're set; perhaps two, if you include tails. How I envy them. Mid-foil, my colourist let me in on an open secret: a designer outlet mall called Horizon Plaza on Ap Lei Chau, a small island off the south side of Hong Kong next to Aberdeen Harbour. Once a small fishing village, it's now the third mostly densely populated island in the world. Horizon Plaza is an ugly twenty-five-storey concrete high-rise where instead of Rapunzel, it's the designer clothiers letting down their hair.

From Paul Smith to Salvatore Ferragamo, they all have warehouses here, as well as local brands like I. T. and Shanghai Tang. Lane Crawford and Joyce, too, and my other favourite local designer emporium the Swank, whose displays at their Landmark shop I admired like a teen girl having her first sexual awakening.

I was to be Veronica's guest at the ball and I wanted to do her proud. When I found a heavily discounted Balmain evening dress, I nearly stroked out. My mother worshipped his vintage couture gowns, beloved of Gertrude Stein and Wallis Simpson, the American divorcée who seduced a king out of his crown. Anette Torres (née Olson) boarded a Greyhound with big dreams of becoming a buyer for Bergdorf Goodman. No one in New York City cared what a hick from northern Minnesota thought about fashion. She got a job as a secretary at an insurance firm and then one day she became my father's secretary.

When they got engaged, she fielded calls from the Midwest and the Old Country asking if Benjamin – not Benjamín – Torres was white. Of course, she said.

The Balmain dress called to me from the rack, knowing my mother would be proud and jealous. It fit – *just*. The zipper screamed. I promised myself to do a hot yoga class every day. And to cut down on the G&Ts. Maybe.

I spent pretty much the rest of my Macau winnings on the bronze silk-satin gown with a plunging neckline and a sky-high slit in the skirt that blossomed around me as if I were Circe herself. *Poof!* I made myself an island. Why not? Veronica would.

As I strutted into the ballroom on Spencer's arm, I was confident the Balmain was worth every penny. He didn't ask if it was new.

The Convention Centre lies on Victoria Harbour, within walking distance of Star Street, but I didn't want to risk getting dark pits in the July heat. The building's glass-curtain design is reminiscent of the Sydney Opera House, only less impressive and more eighties. The interior has the same soulless feel as airports the world over. Even so, the convention hall had been transformed with undulating gold draperies and tablecloths in keeping with the theme 'All That Glitters' – halfway between a wedding and a prom – and I felt as if my life in Hong Kong had suddenly been touched by Midas.

Photographers from all the local tabloids wended their way through the thousand or so guests, taking snaps for the society pages and rearranging the clusters of women according to a one to ten rating – discreetly edging anyone deemed less than a eight to the outside so they could be cropped out more easily. I smiled until my teeth ached as the photographer from *HK City Chic* asked Spence and me to pose.

We made chitchat with Spence's clients during the cocktail hour.

The ache in my teeth spread to my jaw as a Swiss mergers and acquisitions manager for a German bank went on at length about how he had his live-in Filipina helper cut the crusts off the sandwiches for his packed lunch every day. He was a forty-year-old single man. Would I come to find that normal?

I drained my champagne flute.

Excusing myself to search out the ladies room, I milled between the long gilded tables of the silent auction items outside the ballroom. The gala was a fundraiser, of course. Getting trashed for charity is just so much more socially responsible. On offer were weekends at the Four Seasons in Koh Samui, cooking classes with Michelin-starred chefs, works of art from galleries in Tokyo and Beijing, and several conspicuously large pieces of jewellery. My eye was drawn to a simple jade bangle.

MINIMUM BID: HKD 10,000.

Several bids were already scrawled beneath it. Oh well.

'There you are, Marty. You've been hiding.' I jumped as Veronica appeared at my shoulder. She plucked the bracelet from the table. Examining it, she said, 'Good quality. Feel: ice-cold. Anything else is junk.'

Veronica slipped the bracelet over my wrist. The chill provoked a frisson like snow on your tongue.

'I think it's meant for you,' she said.

'I don't need it.'

Impulsively, I tugged it off, almost afraid I might steal it. Veronica laughed as if she could divine my thoughts. 'You need to worry less about what you need, Marty, and more about what you *want*.'

She was right, probably, but I couldn't tell her so — it made me too ashamed.

'Good evening, V.'

A deep, posh British voice with the hint of a brogue rumbled through me. I spun on my heel. Veronica turned around far more slowly, shoulders stiff.

'Quentin.' The two syllables were sharp; her lip curled as she spoke them.

He smiled, a dimple appearing on his chin. His blue eyes sparkled but there was an emptiness to them. Boyish brown curls framed his face. Thrusting his hand in my direction, 'Quentin Turner, at your service,' he said.

I had no choice but to shake, the pads of his palm rough and callused. I must have flinched because he explained, 'Sorry, Dragon Boat season just finished.'

But he kept hold of my hand.

'Oh, right,' I said. 'Veronica took me to watch the festival.'

Dragon-headed boats have raced in southern China for thousands of years, similar to an eight but with a crew of twenty paddlers plus a steerer at the helm and a drummer at the front of the boat. The rhythm pulses through the crowd as well as the crew.

Quentin tilted his head at Veronica. 'And you didn't come say hello, V? You know I always row for Bauhinia. I'm hurt.'

'Must have slipped my mind,' she replied.

'And who are you?' he asked me, squeezing my hand. I could feel the sweat between our palms.

'Too good for you,' Veronica said before I could answer.

Quentin threw back his head and a laugh wracked his extremely tall and muscular body. He wore a green-and-navy tartan kilt with his tuxedo jacket.

'Of that I have no doubt, V.'

He dropped my hand.

'Aren't you hot in that?' I said.

'I think that's more a judgement for your discerning eye, Mysterious Lady. But like my Scottish ancestors, I prefer nothing but air beneath my kilt.'

Veronica clucked her tongue. 'That's quite enough of that.'

'You used to be so much more fun.'

Glancing over Quentin's shoulder, Veronica declared, 'Oh look,

Marty's husband is coming this way.' Quentin's smiled broadened.

Spence and the anti-crust fascist joined us. Veronica begrudgingly made introductions. 'Don't you think this bracelet would look gorgeous on your wife?' Veronica said to Spencer.

'My wife always looks gorgeous,' he replied smoothly.

'I think you should bid on it.'

Spencer's grin locked in place. 'Do you like it, Marty?'

I looked between Veronica and my husband. 'It's pretty.'

He leaned over the bid sheet. 'It better be more than pretty with that price tag.'

'Oh, go on.' Veronica elbowed me. 'You're an independent woman. You can bid for it yourself.'

Veronica had a way of simultaneously laying down the gauntlet and knowing what I wanted despite myself. I couldn't fault her for that, not really. Acid churned in my stomach as I picked up the pen and made a bid. I was sure I'd be outbid soon enough.

'That's my girl.' Veronica winked at me. 'Ah, there's Elsie,' she said, looking towards the ballroom doors. 'Marty, I need to introduce you. We'll see you gentlemen at dinner.'

She dragged me away from the men before I could protest or assuage Spence's bruised ego.

'Apologies for Quentin,' Veronica said as we walked into the ballroom at a brisk clip. 'We were at Oxford together.'

'No need. He seemed like a harmless flirt.'

'He's the definition of filth.'

'Filth?

'Failed In London Try Hong Kong.'

'Ha.' I giggled. 'Sounds like the title for my next column.'

'Whatever you do, don't get talked into investing with his wealth management firm. I mean it.'

'I won't.' I had no wealth to invest. Not my own anyhow.

At dinner, I was seated between Jean-Pierre and Elsie Barron. Spence and his clients were seated (or perhaps exiled) at the adjoining table. Veronica had arranged the place settings so that she was on the other side of the round table between Iain Barron, Elsie's younger brother, and her surrogate mother, Philippa, the Barron clan matriarch. I resisted the urge to curtsy as I shook Philippa's hand.

'You must be the new American friend of Veronica's I've heard so much about,' the older woman said, neither approving nor disapproving. She held herself with august stillness, her smile practised, her gaze laser-focused on me as I replied, 'It's an honour to meet you,' and she simply nodded. Nevertheless, I was deeply touched that Veronica had chosen to include me at what was clearly her family table and which was prominently situated at the edge of the dancefloor. Occasionally eyes swept my face as other revellers came to pay homage to Veronica and the Barrons, wondering what I was doing there.

'I've been dying to meet you, Martina,' said Elsie as we were served our smoked salmon starters. Her voice was plummy yet devoid of the whisky burn that Veronica's held.

'Likewise,' I agreed. 'I know you and Veronica are basically sisters.'

'I'd always wanted a sister.' She smiled, sliced into her salmon. 'I got Veronica. Sometimes fate is cruel – it took such a tragedy to bring us together.'

Elsie was close to Veronica's age, perhaps a year or two older, but the grooves around her eyes were deeper and I sensed a tiredness in her. A well of sadness. She and her brother Iain possessed the same red-sand hair, a strong resemblance in the shape of their jaws. Philippa had silvering blonde hair and finer features; the siblings must take after their father.

'I'm so grateful Veronica took me under her wing,' I said with total sincerity.

'She's one of a kind. Since we were girls.'

The corners of my mouth turned upwards. 'That she is. You were at St Edith's together?'

'Oh no, my father wanted both me and Iain to reconnect with

our Scottish roots so we were shipped off to Fettes College in Edinburgh – that's the James Bond school.' Elsie waited for me to laugh along, and I did. 'When I was a right wee lassie,' she added in an exaggerated Scottish brogue.

I snorted. 'What brought you back to Hong Kong?' I peered at her inquisitively as my knife slid through the oily fish.

'Iain and I both stayed at Edinburgh for uni. He studied medicine although he knew he'd give in to our father and come back to run Barron Industries eventually. No one was as stubborn as Rupert Barron. Not even Arthur Hawkins.'

She heaved a small sigh and signalled for a waitress to refill her white wine glass.

'I was always more interested in the family business,' Elsie continued. 'But I'm not the firstborn son, am I? I travelled around Europe for a year or so and then Mum got sick.'

Her eyes flitted to the refined and stylish woman across the table. Philippa's cheeks were flushed from the crowd and the wine, but she looked the picture of health for a sexagenarian. No hint of weakness of any kind — a true English rose.

'The big C,' Elsie divulged. 'Made a full recovery.'

'Thank goodness.' I took a bite of salmon.

'Auspicious timing, I suppose. All four of us Barrons were in Hong Kong when Veronica's family died.'

'She's told me she wouldn't have been able to cope without you. All of you.'

Elsie leaned back in her chair. 'We were happy to take her in. They call the Hawkins and the Barrons the Montagues and the Capulets, but it's utter, utter rubbish. We're two of the last legacy hongs left standing; a little infighting is to be expected.'

Surreptitiously, the waiting staff bussed the oil-coated plates, now distinctly unappetising, and began serving the beef Wellington or squash Wellington, depending on your proclivities. A nice light Marlborough Pinot Noir was poured all around.

'Enough ancient history,' Elsie said, drawing a line under the topic. She and Veronica had that in common. 'How are you finding our fair city?'

'It's more than I ever expected.'

'More what?'

'More *everything.*'

A dark chuckle. 'I think I understand.' Lifting her red wine glass, Elsie asked, 'Where are you living? Have you found a helper yet?'

'Not far from here – at Starscape.' I bit into the tender meat. 'We don't have a helper. I'm not sure I'd feel comfortable having someone knowing our every move. And the room the estate agent said was for the maid is more like a broom closet. I doubt it will fit a bed.'

'The helpers do see everything but they're discreet. The best ones.' Elsie finished the white wine before switching back to the red. 'You can use an agency or I can invite you to a Facebook group where wives swap helper referrals. Generally the helpers list their height on their advertisements because they know they'll need to fit into small rooms.'

'You're not serious.'

Elsie watched me a moment. 'Completely. Believe me, they're grateful for the jobs here. Much better money than the Philippines or Indonesia, much safer than working in Saudi or the UAE. If their employer gets handsy there, well . . .'

I swallowed the beef hard, stomach turning. 'I guess you have a point.'

'If you have kids, you might want a helper who's a trained nurse. The Philippines has excellent nurses but they can earn more here as helpers.'

'No, no kids.' Strangely, I didn't feel a pang. The miscarriage had happened in another life, a different timeline. Did I even want children now? A child would be an anchor, something tying me and Spencer together forever.

Realising I'd let the silence lapse too long, 'How about you?' I asked. 'Any kids?'

A half smile touched Elsie's lips. 'Two cheeky little monkeys. Maggie is six and Rupert is four. I named him for my father. He died a month before Rupes was born.'

'I can only imagine how hard that must have been.'

Elsie shifted her shoulders towards me. 'You're easy to talk to, Martina. I see what Veronica sees in you.'

Blushing, 'Thank you,' I mumbled.

'Anyway, do think about a helper. Tala and Malaya are absolute godsends. Without them to look after my monkeys, I'd never be able to leave the house.'

'What about your husband? Not one for childcare?'

Elsie scoffed. 'Dex?' She scoffed again. 'He's in Singapore half the time. BP has their regional hub there. All the oil giants do. I married a Texan – Dex the Texan – can you believe?'

Leaning in, she said, 'Texans don't just have big hats.'

I nearly spluttered my Pinot all over her. 'Elsie, you're a naughty one.'

'Sometimes.' For the first time I saw a twinkle in her eye. Then her reserve descended.

A tap came on my shoulder from my other dinner partner.

Jean-Pierre's salt-and-pepper hair was slicked back. His craggy face extra tanned. Veronica complained that he sunned himself like a lizard in their garden on the Peak.

'Would you care to dance?' he asked me. The band was doing a cover of 'My Way'. I cast a glance back at Elsie.

'Go, have fun,' she told me. I wanted to stay and get to know her better but I couldn't turn down my host's husband.

'I'd be delighted,' I told the Frenchman. He helped me from my seat and proffered his arm.

Scanning the dancefloor, my eyes alighted on Spencer dancing with the strikingly beautiful wife of another of his clients. Veronica danced with Iain, their bodies moving with an intimacy born of long acquaintance. Perhaps not always platonic.

Jean-Pierre studied my face as he led me to the centre of the faux parquet. Expertly, he slid his arm around my waist. He did not grope or graze anything he shouldn't.

The band slowed their tempo and transitioned into the melancholic melody of 'My Funny Valentine'.

'They are good at what they do,' Jean-Pierre said, his French accent thicker, I supposed, with drink.

'Pardon?' I took a step back as he led me towards the stage.

'Our spouses. Your husband. My wife.' He tipped his head in the direction of Spencer as he twirled his dance partner. 'They are good at what they do – charming people, selling things, smiling while lying.'

My husband was smiling at the other woman with his classic Date Rape Ken square jaw – he knows I call it that. We used to laugh about it.

Watching them together, 'You could put it that way,' I told Jean-Pierre.

'They love it. The hunt.' Veronica's husband pressed me into a twirl. 'The fish wiggling on the line.'

Our eyes met. 'The thrill of the chase.'

Jean-Pierre's hand was clammy on the small of my back, yet I knew this flirtation was fleeting. Flattering, but nothing more. Of all the many things I came to think of Jean-Pierre later, there was no doubt he adored his wife, worshipped her. Maybe too much, even. Veronica was the only woman who existed for him.

'Is there a thrill in being caught?' he asked me.

The room spun as he twirled me again. 'I think there is,' I said, and I still believed it. I had wanted to be caught. I was no good at being a lone wolf.

'Ah, *ma puce* is a romantic.' Jean-Pierre tapped my nose. 'Don't change. *Viens*.'

He pulled me towards the exit. Others were following. I heard animated murmurings of 'fireworks' among the frolicking partygoers.

I broke away from Jean-Pierre as the masses flooded towards the waterfront. The results of the silent auction had been gnawing at the back of my mind.

As I approached the table, I didn't know which outcome I wanted.

The jade bangle gleamed before me. A security guard hovered nearby.

My eyes scrolled down the bid sheet. My bid was gone. Blacked out with ballpoint pen.

I fought a few stinging tears, clenching my fists.

'Torres! Torres!' My husband was calling me, slightly slurred, with jock-enthusiasm. 'You're going to miss the show!'

My face was stone when I met his gaze. 'You had no right.'

Spence stopped, rubbing a hand over his chin. His classic stalling-for-time move.

'It's expensive, Marty.'

'If you're going to scratch out my bid, at least have a *conversation* with me about it. Would you ever do that to Merritt or your mother?'

'That's not the same.' There was a whine in his voice. 'Besides, do you even want that bracelet? Or did you just bid on it to impress your new best friend?' he asked with a sneer.

My hands flew to my hips. 'So this is about Veronica now? You're here as her *guest*. Thanks to *her* you're the one impressing your clients. I think you're jealous.'

'Don't be crazy. Why would I be jealous?'

'Because you're not the top dog in this town and you can't stand it.'

Spencer winced. 'You know what I think? Bitsy would never egg you on like this. Veronica *wanted* us to have a fight. She's a manipulator, Marty.'

'You don't know what you're talking about. At least *she* pays attention to me.'

He groaned. 'Are you drunk?'

'I'm not drunk. I'm an adult and if I want to bid on this goddamn bracelet then that's what I'm going to goddamn do.'

Spencer took a step forward, lowering his voice and saying, 'Look, I'm not the asshole here. All I'm saying is you need to consult me on big purchases since I'm the only one depositing a steady pay cheque into our joint account.'

I drew in a deep breath, knowing he wasn't entirely wrong – I didn't need a bracelet that cost more than our rent, and yet, 'Whose fault is that?' I charged. 'I gave up my income to follow you here. I turned down Cressida's job offer because you wanted me to!'

Something had changed in Spence the night he'd lost the BMW account. For the first time, he was a small fish in a big, unfamiliar pond. I didn't know who he was becoming and that terrified me, but it was easier to get angry.

Grabbing the pen beside the bid sheet, I wrote HKD 100,000 in frenzied chicken scratch.

Spencer's jaw dropped. 'Fine, Marty. But you're having the time of your life,' he said, shaking his head. 'Don't even try to deny it.'

'And you hate that, don't you? You like me being totally dependent on you.'

'Or maybe you only like me when I *am* top dog.' He drew back. 'I'm going to see the fucking fireworks.'

A solitary tear welled as I watched my husband storm towards the harbour.

What had just happened? I couldn't feel my face; my heart pounded. This wasn't me and Spence – was it? He hadn't always been so closed off. I thought about the Saturday afternoon just before we got engaged when he'd asked me to give him my personal tour of the Museum of Modern Art, show him the paintings that meant the most to me. He had been interested in what I had to say then, hung on my every word.

We'd stopped in front of an image that had always haunted me.

'*Time is a River without Banks*,' I said. 'Marc Chagall.' A fish with wings carried a grandfather clock above a midnight blue river, lovers canoodling on its banks, all while playing a violin. I could hear its fraught melody, feel it in my bones.

'Why do you like it?' Spencer had asked me, eyes intent.

'It's . . . it makes you feel the past, how the past bleeds through you . . . how you're never done with it – or it's never done with you,' I stammered, cheeks smarting.

'You're cute when you ramble,' he said. 'But I think I get it. Family, tradition – it always has its hooks in you.'

Dull cheers echoed from outside the Hong Kong Convention Centre along with *pop, pop, pop*s.

That afternoon at MoMA, I'd thought Spencer understood the constant clawing of the past, that maybe he also wanted to break away from the expectations with which we'd both been raised. But standing in the middle of the ball, abandoned by my prince, trying to hold on to the fleeting glimpses of the real Spencer was becoming harder and harder – like grasping at shards of glass. You can't blame the jagged edges for cutting you if you're the one who won't let go.

From the corner of my eye, I saw an attendant in a simple black frock collecting the bid sheets from in front of the silent auction prizes.

'Have you made your final bid?' she asked, extending her hand for the sheet.

'No. *Wait*.' I took a couple big breaths. 'Yes. OK.'

The woman screwed up her nose as she took the sheet. Regret rushed through me as she disappeared into a service entrance. I wanted to take it back. I couldn't take it back. I didn't want to take it back.

Wiping away the tear, I pulled my spine erect. I walked out to the harbour front.

The sky exploded in turquoise, red, lavender, myriad clouds of stars. *Pop, pop, pop.*

'Marty.' Veronica found me by the railing. 'You've been hiding again.'

'Sorry.' I couldn't conceal the frog in my throat.

'What's wrong?'

'Spence and I had a fight. About the stupid bracelet. He thinks it's too pricey since he's the one with a salary.'

Veronica draped her arm loosely around my shoulders. 'Men can be so pig-headed. What about your Macau slush fund?'

'You're looking at it.' I motioned up and down my silhouette.

'Well, your gown *is* glorious, darling. But don't fret, I'll loan you the money.'

My breath caught. I'd been treading a very fine line with Veronica for a while now. 'I appreciate the offer but I have to decline. I'm your friend, Veronica. Not your charity case.'

She looked at me for several beats until it became uncomfortable.

'You really are my friend, Marty. I don't want you to think otherwise. I'll talk to the committee and tell them your bid was a mistake.'

'Thank you.' I gave her a friendly peck on the cheek.

'Chin up. Hong Kong is giving you its best show.'

Pop, pop, pop.

Veronica was right. Hong Kong was everything I never knew I'd ever wanted.

A couple of days later, a courier delivered a box for me to the *HK City Chic* offices.

Inside lay the jade bangle. Frosty to the touch, it warmed my heart.

To celebrate our friendship. Don't worry, I outbid you fair and square.

Chapter 9

Two to Tango

*F*riday night in August and it was hot enough to fry an egg on the terrace of the trendy Isola bar on the first floor of the IFC where I waited for Spence to finish up work. Sunset shimmered on the skyscrapers of Kowloon across the water and I sipped a glass of Cloudy Bay Sauvignon Blanc. Being vaguely close to the equator, there was only about an hour's variation in sunlight between the longest and shortest days of the year. Something I found oddly comforting, dependable when so much else about my life here was in flux.

Down below were the Central ferry piers. I watched the wakes of the boats crisscross each other as commuters headed home to the outlying islands for the weekend. White churned slate blue as evening fell.

Spence and I both pretended the blow up at the FCC Ball hadn't happened. We'd never had an eruption like that before and neither of us knew how to discuss it — or maybe we were just cowards. Things were tensely polite for a few days before falling back into our usual pattern. Part of me knew I was lying to myself, that a seismic shift had occurred in our relationship, but angry sex had its perks.

Spencer's work had also grown even busier as he followed up on leads he'd made at the gala and the upside was that he studiously avoided asking me about the jade bracelet that now graced my wrist. That evening we were invited to a pool party at Quentin Turner's house in Discovery Bay. I hadn't forgotten Veronica's warning not to invest with him but Spencer thought it would be a good networking opportunity. They'd hit it off at the ball, and Quentin had taken him for drinks at the exclusive KEE Club on Wellington Street. I wasn't in the mood but it wasn't worth the fight.

If meeting Quentin Turner was the first domino, the pool party was the second.

Spencer startled me as I gazed out from the terrace. 'Starting early, aren't we?' my husband teased, skimming my cheek with a kiss, then took a gulp of my wine.

'TGIF.'

He laughed and the orange-hued light caught him just right. For a millisecond, I was that insecure ninth grader who thought he hung the moon again. I won't claim I was an ingenue when I married Spencer, and yet I wasn't nearly as sophisticated as I pretended, either. The freshman in me yearned for the Hallmark ending.

My fingers slid around the jade bangle. It had become my talisman. Hong Kong has a way of holding up a mirror and showing you the truth about yourself.

So did Veronica. She believed better things awaited me and she made me believe it too. I didn't know how I'd do it just yet but I was determined to make a place for myself in Hong Kong that had nothing to do with being Spencer's wife.

'You've got our suits?' he asked.

I tapped the monogrammed canvas tote bag. WASPs have yet to meet an inanimate object they don't want to monogram. 'Never fear, Iris packed your Vineyard Vines.'

'Cute, Marty. I'll pay your tab.'

After the Swiss banker had extolled the virtues of helpers to Spencer, I'd relented and had Elsie add me to the 'Mother's Little Helper – Hong Kong' group on Facebook. My husband had grown up with a live-in nanny so he didn't have the same qualms as me. I'd done some research and exporting foreign labour had been a vital part of the Philippines's economy since Imelda Marcos first indulged her shoe fetish. I reassured myself that I was providing gainful employment to someone who needed it. Win-win.

A week later, Iris arrived on our doorstep with hearty endorsements from Elsie and a few other Southside ladies. In her mid-forties, Iris was originally from Manila but had been working in Hong Kong for over twenty years. Her daughter was only a few years younger than me and worked as a tour guide on the resort island of Boracay.

I thought having a stranger live with us would be like having a permanent houseguest you had to entertain but Iris knew how to make herself scarce. Sometimes I had to remind myself she was there at all.

Spencer took my hand as we descended the escalator in the centre of the shopping mall. Ginormous hearts dangled from the ceiling of the atrium for the Qixi Festival, billed as Chinese Valentine's Day. Celebrated since the Han dynasty, Qixi is dedicated to a forbidden love between a cowherd and weaver girl. My husband wasn't usually a hand-holder so I took it as a sign that our cold war was thawing.

'Andy and Eden will be at Quentin's too,' he said as we strolled through the marble-tiled palace of capitalism and back out into the heat of the walkways leading to the piers. 'Andy says Quentin's parties are wild. They're regulars.'

'Terrific.'

I marshalled a cheery smile. Andy was an Australian colleague at Hutton Brothers. He was technically on the same rung of the ladder as Spencer but he was considerably older, pushing fifty. Eden and I hadn't exactly hit it off. She seemed nice enough but mostly talked about how homesick she was for her family farm in Queensland.

My gaze drifted down to one of the beggars on the walkway and my stomach lurched. Most of the begging in Hong Kong is organised by Mainland gangs and they often maim the poor souls who get caught up in their rings. Far more hardcore than Fagin.

Opening my purse, I dropped HKD 20 in the young man's cup.

I knew he probably wouldn't be able to keep it but it made me feel better.

'Such a softie,' Spence said, but there was affection in his tone.

With a swipe of the Octopus card, we boarded the ferry for Discovery Bay. I soon discovered why some expats call it Stepford Bay. Expat families move to DB when they 'need more space for the kiddies', trading the frantic pace and microscopic apartments of Hong Kong Island for McMansions that come with golf carts to get around, both on and off the course. Located a thirty-minute ferry ride from Central, it's essentially like taking the Metro-North from Grand Central to Greenwich.

Looking around me, I saw mostly white faces. Not surprisingly this cookie-cutter community of only twenty thousand is more than half foreign. If Noël Coward had still been alive and kicking in Hong Kong when the development on Lantau Island was purpose built over the 1980s and 1990s, he would have penned a wickedly satirical song about it.

The uniformly drab high- and low-rises are afforded sea views and aspirational names such as Amalfi, Siena and Chianti. Almost all the properties come with a debenture to one of the four private members clubs that are often resold in a secondary market – Hongkongers never fail to make their assets work for them. It's as if someone decided to bring all the worst aspects of suburbia to a previously unspoilt landscape of rockpools and jungle valleys.

As we disembarked again into the ferry terminal, I spied a bratty boy of about seven throw his ice-cream cone at his helper.

'What are we doing here?' I whispered to Spencer.

'Look, there's Tai Pak Beach. Quentin said his house is just behind the boat club. He said he'd take us sailing. Wouldn't that be great?' Spence gave me an excited grin. 'We haven't been since last summer on Nantucket.'

'You know I get seasick.'

He pinched my cheek. 'Let's have fun tonight.'

Quentin's house sat on a lane that adjoined a private beach. Outside, a Hummer was parked that boasted a HOLE-IN-1 licence plate.

Pointing it out to Spencer, I said, 'It's missing the "Ass" at the front.'

'We're here to make friends, Marty.' He threaded his fingers through mine.

'I have friends.'

'Besides Veronica?' Spence raised an eyebrow.

I refused to take the bait. He was jealous of Veronica and it wasn't a good look. Spencer liked Bitsy because she fawned over him the way he was accustomed to. In my darkest moments since Veronica died, I've let myself ruminate on just how deep my husband's animosity ran.

Instead of replying, I squeezed our intertwined hands. 'Let the fun begin,' I said.

We could hear chill-out music drifting on the torrid breeze as we approached the entrance. The door was wide open.

Following the din led us to the swimming pool around which the house had been designed. A small, manicured garden opened out onto the beach. Flames from tiki torches fluttered against the deep sapphire sky. Guests in a wide array of attire from semi-formal to board shorts flocked to the bar on the far side of the pool. My nose detected grilling hot dogs and hamburgers.

'Ah, mate, you made it,' Andy said, walking towards us, gripping a can of Foster's. He was barrel-chested but toned, clearly working out regularly to mitigate his short man's syndrome. 'Wasn't sure you would.' He looked between me and Spence. 'The lovely Marty. Looking particularly lovely this evening.'

'Thank you,' I mumbled. 'Is Eden here?'

He thrust out a finger towards the bar. Eden was at least a head taller than her husband and as svelte in her silver bikini as any twenty-two-year-old had the right to be. Her long blonde hair hung in a thick braid along her spine.

Spencer lifted the canvas tote bag. 'Where can we change?' he asked Andy, and the other man indicated a cabana at the edge of the garden. 'All of the other rooms have their function labelled on the door,' Andy explained. 'Make sure to follow the rules.'

Spence nodded. 'Um . . . OK,' I said. 'I'll change later. I'm going to go say hi to Eden.' Boy, I needed a drink already.

I felt eyes on me as I trod along the circumference of the pool. The guests were brazenly checking me out. There were at least thirty people here, mostly couples. I half smiled out of instinct, the same survival instinct that makes a woman carry on a conversation with a weirdo on public transportation; better to keep smiling than to get a knife in the jugular. Something was off here.

'Hey, Marty,' Eden greeted me as I reached the bar. Her pupils were a tad dilated. 'Andy and I had a bet that you guys wouldn't make it.'

'Why not?'

'Oh, you know. Quentin's parties aren't everyone's thing.'

'Huh. You never know unless you try, right?'

A surprised yet knowing smile parted her lips. 'That's the spirit.'

'Speaking of which, who do I need to murder to get a cocktail?'

'No need to be so drastic.' She giggled. 'I like the Cosmos.' A fit man in Speedos waved at Eden from a few feet away. 'That could be fun. Catch you later, Marty.'

Scrunching up my nose, I watched Eden skip away. When the barman got to me, I ordered a neat vodka.

Spencer reappeared in his cartoonish lobster-covered trunks, no shirt. To give credit where credit's due, my husband's abs were a thing of beauty. I wished we were back at our apartment for some more hair-pulling sex rather than at a Pod People pool party.

I touched the cool jade at my wrist and it calmed me.

Spence was utterly in his element, schmoozing potential clients and having women ogle his physique. All of the men were Westerners; the wives were a mix of white expats, Mainlanders,

Hong Kong Chinese or from South-East Asian countries. The less appealing the man, generally speaking, the fewer economic choices the woman had in her country of origin. God bless the patriarchy. I didn't judge the women for improving their circumstances – had I done anything different by marrying Spencer? I could have spouted a dozen flimsy self-justifications, of course, but the truth troubled me.

The first time I had sex I was fifteen; he was twenty-two. Ford Davenport was the best friend of Bitsy's older brother, Cortland. They'd been ahead of us at Buxton, now both about to graduate from Harvard, and had been roped into attending Bitsy's Sweet Sixteen at the Water Club. Ford had been a big cheese at Buxton – valedictorian, captain of the swim team, and comfortable enough with his masculinity to star in the school musical.

I hadn't thought he'd noticed me in my crushed purple velvet dress with Juliet sleeves. I didn't bother trying to flirt with him like all the other girls in my class – he was so out of my league that I refused to humiliate myself. But as the party guests jump-jumped along with Kris Kross for the last time, Ford found me at the edge of the dancefloor and asked me to go for a drink at Dorrian's. Famously the last place Robert Chambers, aka the Preppy Killer, was seen with his victim, the bar remains an Upper East Side institution teeming with blue blazers.

'Bitsy's basically my kid sister,' said Ford. 'But you're not. You seem much more mature.'

I called my mother from a payphone and told her I'd be sleeping over at the Butterfields'. As I left, Bitsy whispered, 'Are you sure you know what you're doing?' I didn't, not really, but I knew how all of the other girls were staring at me now. Covetously. Indignantly. Ford Davenport had chosen me. I'd been anointed. At least for the night.

High on the envy of my peers, after he regaled me with a blow-by-blow of the Harvard–Yale game, we retired to his empty penthouse. Ford's parents were on two different continents.

I'll spare you the rest of the details. Suffice it to say, the earth did not move, and yet I still felt like I'd won something, something I couldn't quite name. I didn't see Ford again but my female class-mates treated me with a new begrudging respect. If Ford Davenport thought I was worth his time, then maybe I was worth theirs too. Invitations to other Sweet Sixteens arrived in the mail, much to my mother's delight.

Glancing at Spencer across the patio, I was unable to shake the tingling feeling on the back of my neck. There were giant pieces missing in my parents' marriage, which had always made me feel untethered, and maybe what happened next that night was partially my fault. When I would come home in floods of tears from being bullied at Buxton, Papi would tell me that I must always play the game but never take it seriously, never become too invested in any of the players. By age twelve I knew my father practised what he preached and that his philosophy extended to me too.

Perhaps my own husband intuited there was a part of me I held back that he could never reach. A Martina I kept all to myself. Intimacy was not something I'd learned how to do.

Maybe that's why Spencer did what he did?

Yet no one had ever reached the real Martina – except Veronica. I decided to slip away with my vodka to the beach.

Lying back in the sand, I looked up at the light pollution, listened to the lapping waves. On impulse, I arced my arms and legs, the gran-ules soft, still warm from the sun. I repeated the motion several times.

'Do I need to call security?' asked a shadow with a British accent, his frame backlit. 'This is my beach.'

'All of it?'

'I like to think so. May I join you?'

'Well, it is *your* beach.'

Quentin Turner lowered himself into the sand beside me. He was also bare-chested. I noticed a few errant white hairs in the dim light. He elongated his legs purposefully in the sand and crossed his ankles.

'So, why are you skulking out here all on your lonesome? You make me feel like a neglectful host.'

'I wasn't skulking.'

'Oh, no?'

'No, I was making sand angels.'

A low chuckle. 'Sand angels,' he repeated.

'No snow in Hong Kong as far as I can see.'

'That would be a cold day in hell.' Quentin smiled and it was inviting. 'I thought V warned you off me.'

I nipped at my vodka. 'She's not your biggest fan.'

'There was a time she felt differently.' He held my gaze. 'Very differently.'

'Puppy love at Oxford?' I said lightly. 'Well, that was a long time ago. She and Jean-Pierre seem very devoted.'

'People seem to be a lot of things, don't they, Martina?' Quentin edged his bare foot closer to mine. He grazed my big toe with his accidentally on purpose. 'I think you're far more interesting than you appear. I'm intrigued.'

'Should I be flattered or offended?'

'Perhaps a bit of both.' His big toe slid gently up my left ankle, the nail creating a certain friction. 'Do you know, I was first inspired to host these parties because of swine flu?'

I whipped my head around to meet his eyes. 'Excuse me?'

Quentin laughed. 'Before your time. Back in 2009, there was a swine flu outbreak. The government was on high alert because of SARS and ended up quarantining an entire love hotel – the kind that charges by the hour – in Wan Chai. The couples were stuck for days together while their spouses discovered where they went on their long lunches.'

His toe moved up my calf. 'Wealthy Hongkongers have their mistresses in Second Wife Village, of course.' Seeing my confusion, he elaborated, 'Shenzhen.'

'Oh.'

'I thought, why don't we just keep things honest?'

'And how precisely are you doing that?'

'I think you know.' Quentin placed a hand on my knee and ran his fingers up the inside of my thigh before I realised what was happening.

I snapped my thighs shut. 'I think there's been a misunderstanding.'

He wrapped his other arm around me and pulled me closer. My breath grew shallow, panic tightening my throat.

'I don't think there has,' Quentin said. 'You wanted to be here. You wanted this. It takes two to tango.' He pressed his lips to mine and I jumped to my feet, fighting against his strength.

'No. I don't know what you think is happening here but I am not going to cheat on my husband with you.' Anger and confusion swirled inside me, making me nauseous.

'Then why did you come?'

'What are you talking about?'

Quentin shook his head with a chortle. 'Didn't Spencer tell you this was a swingers' party?'

Sucker punch.

Quentin's parties aren't everyone's thing, Eden had said. The barely clothed couples openly eye-fucking each other suddenly made sense. How could I have been so naive?

Without a backwards glance, I strode back into the party with determination. This was all a big mistake. Spencer couldn't possibly have known what we were walking into. He wouldn't just throw me into the lion's den.

But why did I feel so cold?

I bobbed and weaved through the partiers – through the swingers – scouring every face. Bile rose from my stomach. Pushing my way into the house, I saw that Andy was right. All of the doors were labelled: Oral, Anal, Petting, 69. My eyes burned. Knees weak, I leaned against the wall for support. Afraid I might puke, I continued down the hallway in search of a bathroom.

With some relief, I found a door without a label. I turned the knob. Immediately I knew I'd made a terrible error.

Masculine groaning filled the air, together with sucking sounds. The light in the bathroom was off but enough glow filtered in from the hallway for me to make out a woman on her knees. I was about to hastily close the door when I recognised the lobsters.

I knew those damn cartoon lobsters. I'd bought them for my husband as a joke before our trip to Nantucket last summer. I was surprised when he seemed honestly to like them.

There was no turning back once I flipped on the light switch. I hesitated for a moment. Rage turned my vision white.

Flick.

Sometimes things fall apart with alarming speed.

'Hey, what the hell—' All the colour leeched from Spencer's face when he saw me in the doorway.

Eden looked up from the floor, my husband's cock in her mouth making it difficult for her to speak.

Spencer looked between the girl on her knees and his wife. He wracked his brain for some kind of excuse. 'Mart—'

I held up my hand to stop him.

'I'm leaving and I don't want you to follow.'

Whatever dignity I had left went out the window. I ran through the house, out into the night. It was only when I got to the plaza in front of the ferry terminal that I realised I'd left my wallet in the canvas tote bag at the party. I'd walk over broken glass before I went back.

All I had was my phone.

'Veronica?' I said, my voice croaky. 'I'm in Discovery Bay. I don't have any way to get home.'

'Slow down, darling. What's going on?' Her concern soothed me.

'Spence took me to a party at Quentin Turner's. I turned tail and ran, but now I'm stuck.'

'Where are you exactly?'

Tears threatened again. 'DB Plaza.'

'I'll be there in half an hour.'

Veronica's chauffeur must have broken a bunch of traffic regu-
lations to get to me so fast. She threw open the door and I was
engulfed in the contrasting scent of fiery ginger and clean, rain-like
jasmine. She pulled me into a hug.

'This is all my fault,' Veronica proclaimed as the Bentley sped past
Hong Kong Disneyland towards Kowloon. 'I introduced Spencer to
Quentin at the ball just to make my own escape. I knew about his
parties but I never in a million years thought you'd be invited.'

'It's not your fault. It's *Spencer's* fault. He clearly knew what kind
of party it would be but failed to inform me.'

'Bastard,' Veronica hissed. 'Tell me everything that happened.'

Dabbing at my tears, I drew in a long breath and tried to keep my
voice from breaking. 'Right from the start, I had an uneasy feeling.
One of Spence's co-workers from Hutton Brothers and his wife were
there. It was like they were speaking in code. I decided to take a
break from the party on the beach – that's when Quentin found me.'

'What did he do, Marty?' She gripped my hand like a vice.

'He started coming on to me. He got overly friendly. I pushed
him away and he got pissed, saying I knew what kind of party I was
coming to. He said he was just trying to keep things honest.'

'Bloody typical.' Veronica cursed under her breath.

Had Spencer thought he could wife swap without telling me?
Quentin seemed so confident. Had they discussed it – *me*? More
silent tears streaked down my cheeks. A wife like Eden would be
much less work. Is that what Spence wanted?

I gazed out at the twinkling lights as the road snaked along the
water.

'Listen, Marty. Quentin is a law unto himself. Don't let him
make you doubt yourself.' Veronica inhaled and exhaled rapidly. 'I
need to tell you something I've never told anyone.'

The tenor of her voice gave me pause.

'Quentin and I ran in the same circles in Oxford,' she said. 'The public school set. He went to Eton. I didn't know much about him except that he was a heartbreaker. On the night Uncle Rupert telephoned me with the news that my whole family was dead, I went to the college bar and got absolutely shitfaced.'

'Who could blame you?' Tenderly, I pushed a loose auburn hair behind her ear.

'Quentin was there being Quentin, flirting up a storm, trying to jolly me along. The next thing I remember, I was waking up in his bed at New College on the other side of town. To this day, I'm not a hundred per cent sure if it was consensual, but I was left with this empty, wretched feeling.'

'Oh, Veronica, I'm so sorry. It doesn't sound like you were in any state to give consent.'

'Yes, well.' She chewed her lip. Something I'd never seen her do. 'Some years later, Quentin moved to Hong Kong. He'd finagled a position at a Hawkins Pacific subsidiary. A sexual harassment charge was brought against him but the internal HR investigation was inconclusive. Since it was my company, I had him fired.'

'Good for you.'

'He's nursed a grudge against me for years. He knows he can't publicly smear me because of who my family is, but he's always trying to corner me at parties. Not letting me forget. He likes to have power over people – especially women.' Veronica heaved an uncharacteristically big sigh. 'Marty, I'm so sorry. I think he targeted you because I introduced you to him. Because he could see how important you are to me.'

'Veronica,' I said sternly, 'you're the victim here. Not the perpetrator. None of this is down to you.'

A tear leaked from her eye. 'Thank you, Marty. Thank you for saying that.' Another deep breath. 'But what happened when you told Spencer what Quentin did?'

'I didn't. I didn't have the chance. Not while his dick was in another woman's mouth.'

'Oh *fuck*. I'm so sorry. I'll kill him.'

I released a sad laugh. 'I'd like to.'

'I've suspected Jean-Pierre of having another life. Sometimes I hope it's just his gambling.'

'Shit, Veronica. I'll kill him.'

Veronica laughed darkly. 'We could kill each other's husbands? Like something Hitchcockian?'

My eyes dried as I chortled. 'Sounds perfect.'

'But no, unfortunately I don't want to kill Jean-Pierre. People only have their own brand of love to give – Arthur taught me that. I'm not sure my husband and I give each other what we need any more.' She sighed. 'Or if we ever did.'

The Bentley sluiced through one tunnel after another as I leaned my head on Veronica's shoulder.

'Veronica, I don't want to go home tonight. I don't want to face Spencer.'

'Then you don't have to. I've got plenty of guestrooms.'

'Thank you. Really.' When I was at my nadir, I spent the night on the Peak.

Veronica had rescued me the way I'd always longed for but it had never happened. Not by my parents. Not by my husband. She gave me the brand of love I'd always craved. Recounting these memories of her is my futile attempt to hold on to them, to make them real for that much longer.

Veronica brushed my cheek. 'That's what friends are for,' she said.

I can still feel the warmth of her hand on my face.

Chapter 10

Hell's Bankers

*L*ate in the afternoon following Quentin's party, I finally gathered the nerve to return to Star Street. There was a note from Spencer saying he'd had to travel last minute to Shanxi province in the north of China to meet with the owner of a coal mine. He apologised for the short notice and signed off with *Love you babe, Spence.*

Iris watched me carefully. She was concerned when I didn't want her to cook for me. Her eyes were filled with sympathy but also the detachment of someone who has seen this particular play a thousand times before. Without comment she went to the overpriced supermarket in Pacific Place to buy me Cloudy Bay and the Japanese apples the size of a baby's head that cost five bucks apiece. I couldn't stomach anything more.

When Veronica wrote with an invitation to a much-needed girls' weekend at her beach house, I didn't hesitate.

By the time I packed my bags and headed for the ferry to Lamma Island, the dead were walking the streets. The Hungry Ghosts had arrived. My own ghosts were close, visceral.

Billions of Hong Kong dollars' worth of Hell banknotes were being burned on street corners throughout the city in red metal barrels, offerings to the souls of forgotten ancestors. I noticed at least three barrels on Star Street as well as styrofoam containers filled with dumplings and noodles, sustenance for the wandering dead.

Iris reiterated what I already knew: that my street was soaked with blood, filled with restless souls, and more than one resident had claimed to see a headless woman chasing her rolling skull down the street.

The flames from the Hell notes licked the near-twilight sky as I wheeled my Tumi bag towards the MTR.

Food offerings are left in great quantities around hospitals because it's believed that it's easier for the deceased to attach themselves to sick people, those between life and death. Distract them with candies and pork buns and they won't suck your life from you, or so the logic goes. Veronica believed that the ghosts of her family hovered around her. Perhaps they lured her off the side of the boat, perhaps they were too attached. Always feeding, always ravenous. Or maybe she just wanted to join them.

As I stood on the deck of the ferry to Lamma, Veronica texted me: *Running late at the office. Felipe will let you in. Champagne chilling.*

Watching the water, I wondered if perhaps relationships have ghosts too. Is nostalgia a hungry ghost latched to your heart, sapping you dry? What had happened to the Spencer who'd stood at the altar and promised to forsake all others?

When the ferry docked at Yung Shue Wan – Banyan Tree Bay – it was as if I had travelled to another world entirely, a much longer journey than the twenty-five-minute ride. Only about six thousand people, including a high proportion of expats, live on the island. At night, the houses on the verdant slopes surrounding the bay twinkle like lights on a Christmas tree.

No cars are allowed on Lamma Island. No skyscrapers. No chain stores. It's a collection of villages much closer to the subtropical islands the British first encountered. The present-day clans came from Shenzhen in the nineteenth century to make their home on Lamma fishing and farming, but a stone circle dating back to the Bronze Age has been discovered in the northern part of the island, more than three hundred feet above sea level.

The scent of sizzling salt-and-pepper squid and chilli clams filled my nostrils as I walked past the seafood restaurants near the pier. I sweltered as I made my way on foot to Veronica's country house, as she called it, wondering if the storm warnings would amount to anything.

The Hawkins family home was called Strawberry Hill, about a half-hour walk from Banyan Tree Bay and set back from a secluded strip of sandy beach, beneath a vibrant jungle canopy. I stopped and bought a slice of frozen pineapple from a hawker along the trail. Snakes slithered in the undergrowth; frogs began their nocturnal serenade.

At long last, the villa came within view.

It wasn't what I expected. In my mind's eye, I had pictured a haunted stone mansion akin to Daphne du Maurier's Manderley. Instead, a stunning masterpiece of art deco architecture emerged from the fig trees. Sunset tinted its curved white walls tamarind. This was a setting worthy of one of Gatsby's parties. Listening to the waves batter the rocks from its veranda, the stock-market crash wouldn't have seemed so bad.

I had yet to sight one of Hong Kong's rare pink dolphins but I imagined if I did, it would be here.

Lugging my rollaboard up the steps towards the mansion's gates, I noticed a particularly elaborate feast for the dead nestled among the strawberry bushes. Seven different dishes were offered to the great-greats, laid on an embroidered red silk place mat. Seven dishes are never served for the living, only for the dearly departed. White orchids were carefully sprinkled between the dishes. I inhaled the delicious aroma of stir-fried eggplant and lotus root glazed with golden syrup but this food was not for me. Not a single fly dared to land.

On either side of the gate, two shallow metal bowls were filled with burning joss.

Two centuries' worth of Hawkinses might come calling tonight when the doors to Hell were flung open. I shivered in the balmy breeze and the ashes of Hell notes landed on my tongue.

The entrance to Strawberry Hill stood beneath the portico of a smooth, curved tower that divided the mansion into two parts. Three terraced levels of balconies called to mind the ocean liners of yesteryear. Before I could lift the dragon's head knocker, I heard the groan of hinges.

'Felipe?'

The Filipino man nodded, eyes darting behind me, shoulders tense. His tawny skin contrasted with the white of his linen shirt and trousers.

'Come in, Ms Martina. It's almost dark.'

The living are meant to leave this night to the dead. Unless you're honouring them or entertaining them, it's best to let them run riot in the streets.

Felipe shut the door firmly and swiftly behind me. Sneaky spirits are known to slip through the thinnest spaces.

He took the Tumi bag from my grasp. 'I'll show you to your room. You can change from your journey.' I got the hint that my sweat-stained clothes did not pass muster.

'Thanks so much, Felipe. Veronica said she was caught up at the office.'

'Ms Veronica works too hard.' He huffed a laugh. 'I have prepared some small snacks for you before dinner.'

I followed him up the spiral staircase of the central tower to the top floor. He led me down a hall towards a room with a sea view. 'This is gorgeous.' I'd sleep well in the four-poster bed, I had no doubt. Bowers of wild indigo hung from the window boxes.

'Come downstairs when you're ready for your aperitif. Take your time.' Felipe padded from the room in soft-soled leather sandals.

This place is amazing. What's your ETA? I texted Veronica.

I availed myself of the clawfoot rolltop bathtub and rinsed the winding trails from my body. Ylang-ylang and lavender bath oil helped me unwind. With no reply from Veronica, I soaked a little longer. Full night cloaked the sea as I dragged myself from the tub and changed into a sailor-striped summer dress, blue and white.

Unable to squelch my curiosity, I studied the various abstract paintings in bold colours that lined the walls. 'JP' was scrawled in the corner of each canvas. On the dresser were several old-fashioned silver picture frames. I recognised Veronica, perhaps age eight, with a toddler in her arms. I'd put money on it being her sister. Another showed Veronica in the ridiculous robes Oxford students don to sit their exams.

Making my way in the direction of the sounds I heard coming from a reception room, I encountered Felipe expertly throttling a cocktail shaker, straining the contents into a flute and topping off the concoction with champagne. Felipe was a man of all work: bartender, butler, gardener. He lived in a small cottage on the grounds of the estate with his wife. Bringing over a married couple is rare, the sponsorship requiring more layers of red tape. His brother, Alejandro, was Veronica's chauffeur. Veronica was loyal to all those who were loyal to her.

'Cocktail?' said Felipe.

'Yes, thank you.'

I seated myself on a grand, cream leather Chesterfield sofa. The surf broke on the beach below, which I could no longer see through the large convex windows.

A single jagged lightning bolt pierced the sky. 'Will they stop the ferries if there's a storm?' I asked Felipe as he handed me a flute with a maraschino cherry at the bottom.

'Only if it's Signal 8. Tonight shouldn't be so bad.' He swept his hand across the coffee table where several plates of nibbles were waiting for me. 'Jamón ibérico, Nocellara olives and shrimp toast.'

'It looks delicious, Felipe.' He bowed his head and left me to my own devices.

Tart passion fruit juice complemented the sweetness of the cherry as the champagne swirled down my throat.

Felipe makes a mean cocktail. Are you almost here?

Ten minutes passed. I ate two of the prawn toasts. Still no reply from Veronica.

I decided to explore the rest of the house. The teak flooring creaked. I removed my shoes and set them by the entrance to the reception room.

The corridor was tiled, cool on the soles of my feet. Brightly coloured, their patterns reminded me of Spanish *azulejos*. In fact, Felipe informed me they were Peranakan tiles imported from Malaysia in the 1890s – British Malaya at the time. The tiles had been harvested from the first Hawkins family abode on this site when it was torn down and the current structure was built. It's hard for me to fathom having such a tangible link to the past, such a strong continuous family history. And it was all about to come to an end.

A small yelp escaped my lips as I entered the library.

Lightning shone off the marble eyes of a formerly cunning fox. Its red fur had faded in the years since one of Veronica's great-greats had shot it, but its snout remained open in a silent scream. My mind raced back to our dinner at Felix when she'd mentioned it and how my life had changed so dramatically in a few short months.

Quaffing my champagne, I exited the library as quickly as I'd entered.

As I carried on down the hallway, it opened into a larger, high-ceilinged room with a grand piano in the corner. Oil paintings of grumpy Victorian men and haughty women with daring décolletages watched their descendants, eyes full of reproach. Arcing windows met in a pair of double doors that rattled in the wind.

Thunder boomed like a kettle drum and I jumped.

I have no particular talent for music but my mother insisted I take piano lessons for twelve years. She wanted me to master Mozart and Bach. I preferred showtunes.

Setting my champagne flute down beside a frangipani plant on a side table, I pulled the piano bench out from beneath the Steinway.

A needlepoint cushion cover depicted the cascading hills of Hong Kong as they must have looked when the villa was built, at a time when hikers had to watch out for tigers.

Lifting the lid of the keyboard, I rolled my shoulders and lowered myself onto the bench. I stroked the keys, which were smooth and a tad opalescent – real ivory. My right thumb tested the middle C, then high C. The note was full-bodied, perfectly tuned. We only ever owned a Wurlitzer upright – it was all that would fit in our apartment – but my piano teacher insisted that I respected my instrument and that I understood how the sound quality was maintained.

Closing my eyes, I let muscle memory guide me as my fingers started to fly over the keys. The opening bars to 'So in Love' echoed around me. There's a Cole Porter song for every occasion. I laughed caustically to myself. What was my husband doing in the north of China tonight?

My lips curled inwards, my teeth pressing down painfully. I kept playing.

Perhaps Veronica was right and the kind of love I needed wasn't the kind that Spencer could give me. Maybe neither of us was to blame. We were just built differently. Maybe it was a mismatch from the start. Lord knew my in-laws would agree.

Hot tears beaded my lashes. I kept playing.

I'd tried to give Spencer what he needed but I could feel myself slipping further out to sea, whittling myself down to size. I would always have to make myself be less so that he could feel more – feel that he *was* more. My husband was supposed make me whole, to fill the emptiness that ached night and day.

I had made *myself* a dependent and that was how he'd started to treat me.

My fingers pounded the keys. At least we hadn't brought a child into our battlefield, for that I was grateful. We could each lick our wounds and walk away.

Was that what happened next? Could I really do it? Quitting wasn't in my DNA.

Suddenly, my head jerked up at the sound of footsteps.

'Veronica?'

'*Désolé.*' Jean-Pierre stood in the doorway. 'It seems we've both been stood up.'

'She's running late at work.' Blinking furiously, I tried to dry my tears.

'You play well,' he said.

'Not really.' Gently, I closed the lid back over the keys.

'Have you eaten dinner yet?' Jean-Pierre ran a hand over his head, his hair damp. He looked weary, shoulders slumped. What was this other life his wife thought he had?

'I'm waiting for Veronica.'

'You could be waiting all night. Come. Let's eat. *J'ai faim.*'

Not seeing any other option, I followed Jean-Pierre to a dining room I hadn't yet investigated. The back of his shirt was wet. 'Is it raining?' I asked.

'Only spitting, as the English say.'

Thank goodness. The ferries hadn't stopped. I bit back my annoyance that Jean-Pierre had crashed our girls' weekend.

Felipe was already lighting a silver candelabra at one end of a stately dining table that could easily seat twelve. Numerous dignitaries had no doubt supped here over the years. 'We're ready to be served,' Jean-Pierre declared.

'Of course.' Felipe dimmed the overhead light on his way out.

The Frenchman pulled out a brocade-backed chair for me before taking his own seat at the head of the table. 'Do you prefer red or white?'

'White, I think. It's so hot.'

Jean-Pierre smiled. Wavering candlelight made his wrinkles more distinct. 'So American. I assure you the Brouilly is chilled.'

Humiliation scalded me. 'All right, I'm game.'

'You know, in Hong Kong they say a man treats his wife "in the French way" when he's being romantic. I don't think Veronica would agree.' He chuckled to himself. 'You can have the Chablis if you want.'

'No, I'll have the Brouilly.'

'*Bon choix.*'

Jean-Pierre poured the red wine into my heavy crystal goblet, then served himself. Felipe returned with Drunken Chicken, a cold dish prepared with rice wine that I knew Veronica's *amah* had made for her as a girl. It was accompanied by *dan dan* noodles smothered in sesame paste, also cold, both suited to the muggy night.

Twirling a noodle with my chopsticks, I asked Jean-Pierre, 'Have you seen Veronica today?'

He shook his head. 'I left early this morning to see a client in Repulse Bay. I've spent all day painting her beagle, Duke, into her family portrait. *Mon dieu.*' Jean-Pierre drank deep of his Brouilly. 'Veronica prefers to be on Lamma for the Hungry Ghost festival. I assumed she'd be here.'

'She feels closer to her family here.'

'*Ouais.* To Lulu.'

Veronica's grief over her sister's death hadn't dulled with the passage of time. The visceral loss had been etched into her face when we visited Macau. She was a study in regret.

Jean-Pierre cut into his chicken. Felipe had set his place with a knife and fork rather than chopsticks. The knife scraped against the plate. Thunder shook the house; I gritted my teeth.

'The ghosts are knocking at the door,' he said, amused.

'Do you think so?'

'You look scared.'

'I'm not. I just don't like storms.'

'*Je ne te crois pas.*' Jean-Pierre spoke low, a taunting purr.

'Don't believe me all you want. I'm telling the truth.'

Candlelight glinted on his teeth. 'Your French is excellent. A woman of many talents.'

'My French is passable,' I replied, but I'd studied harder than any of the other girls in AP French to make sure I didn't just speak the doorman's language fluently.

'What about you,' I asked Jean-Pierre, 'not afraid to encounter any ghosts?'

His hand stilled on his knife. 'I was married before, in Paris. We got married too young. Because she was pregnant.' He rested the knife on the edge of his plate. 'We named the baby Adèle, for my mother.'

I felt a pinch in my stomach. Jean-Pierre's voice had taken on a different timbre. Something wistful that filled me with foreboding.

With a long exhale, he continued. 'I'd been a reluctant father but when Adèle smiled at me, I would have given her anything. Instead, I watched her die, slowly, for eight years. Leukaemia.'

'I'm so sorry, Jean-Pierre.' I reached out and placed my hand on his. 'I don't know what to say. That's terrible.'

'Nothing. *Il n'y a rien à dire.*' A shrug. 'I wouldn't mind if Adèle came to visit tonight.' He looked at my hand, still covering his. 'You have beautiful bones,' he said.

Instantly, I withdrew my hand as if I'd been burned. He resumed cutting his chicken. I couldn't imagine the pain of losing a child – a child that I had brought to term, nursed, watched take her first steps. The bond between Jean-Pierre and Veronica began to make sense. They had both suffered horrific losses. And yet, I was coming to understand that wasn't enough to sustain a marriage. A partnership couldn't survive without mutual respect.

Jean-Pierre refilled my wine glass, which I hadn't realised I'd emptied.

'Maybe we should text Veronica?' I suggested. 'Make sure she's OK?'

'Veronica is fine. Veronica is wherever she wants to be – which is usually the office.'

'If you say so.'

He shifted in his chair, squaring his shoulders in my direction. 'You're a little in love with her, *non*?'

'*No.*' The protestation came out a bark. 'I mean, not like that.'

The corner of Jean-Pierre's mouth lifted in a quarter-smile. 'No, not like that. But it's hard for anyone not to fall in love with my wife. After Adèle, I was a shadow. I didn't realise it until I met Veronica.'

'She is very charismatic,' I agreed.

He nodded. 'I understand you falling in love with my wife. I cannot understand why you fell in love with your husband.'

This time the protest didn't come. 'We also met when we were very young.'

'You're still young, *ma puce*. Take it from an old man, you should be enjoying yourself.' Jean-Pierre laughed at himself. 'You need someone who can keep you on your toes.'

'Oh, Spencer is just full of surprises.' I couldn't keep the vitriol from coating my words.

'Veronica told me.'

I coughed several times. The kaleidoscope of their relationship reconfigured itself in my mind. I didn't think she confided in Jean-Pierre much at all, but their relationship was knottier, thornier than I had grasped.

'Cheating isn't the worst thing you can do to your spouse,' he offered, his tone careless, and it was perhaps the most French thing I'd ever heard him say.

'What's worse?'

'You can no longer love someone but also not be willing to let them go.'

I had no response to that. Did Jean-Pierre feel trapped? Would my own husband be willing to let me go? Was that what I wanted deep down? We finished eating as the skies broke open and rain began to pound the veranda. Later I would think back on this conversation and it took on a more sinister tone in the wake of Veronica's death.

What would a man be capable of when the woman he loved no longer loved him back?

Felipe started clearing the dishes and I jumped up from my seat. Telling Jean-Pierre, 'I'm going to call Veronica,' I dashed back to the reception room.

I'd expected a flurry of texts to have accumulated on my phone's home screen. There was nothing. Anxiety tightened my scalp. She'd never flaked on me before.

I hit the call button. The phone rang once before a recorded message in Cantonese and English told me the number couldn't be reached and sent me to voicemail. I tried again. And again. I've never claimed to have a sixth sense but that night I did sense something amiss – another domino falling.

'No answer?'

Jean-Pierre looked at me in a pitying way as he walked towards me.

'It went straight to voicemail.' My eyes whizzed back to my phone, willing it to ring. 'You're not worried?' I asked.

'Veronica is her own master. I learned long ago that she doesn't like questions and she doesn't like worrying.'

That I could believe. 'Right. I'm sure she has a good excuse.'

He tugged at his collar.

'Well, don't feel like you have to entertain me,' I said. 'You've had a long day.'

A wry laugh. 'You are *mignonne*, Martina. I'd like to draw your hands – if you don't have other plans.'

'My hands?'

'They're the most telling part of the human body. The most expressive. For some artists it's lips or eyes. For me, it's hands.'

Hands seemed innocent enough. 'I suppose I'm free.'

Jean-Pierre retrieved his sketchbook and a set of Faber-Castell pencils while Felipe brought us Armagnac as a nightcap. The scratch of a record player drew my attention and Édith Piaf began to croon.

'Relax,' Jean-Pierre told me. 'Just rest your hands in your lap.'

He sat on the chair opposite, gaze intensely focused on my wrists, my knuckles, my fingertips. It felt like a touch. The sensation was warm.

I listened to the rain and closed my eyes. I didn't think about Spencer. I didn't think about anything.

When he was done, Jean-Pierre flipped the sketchbook around for me to see.

He had drawn my hands in shades of grey. The only colour on the page was my jade bangle.

'Veronica gave me this bracelet,' I told him.

'My wife loves giving gifts – and taking them away.' He tore out the page. 'From me to you.'

Upstairs, ensconced beneath the sheets of the guest bed, the wind howled. Jean-Pierre's tragic story about his daughter had left me with a profound disquiet. A pang of need squeezed my chest as I picked up my phone and dialled my father.

'*¿Mija?*' Papi answered in his perpetually brusque tone. It was the middle of a work day in Manhattan. I'd been taught from an early age that I was only to telephone Papi at the office if someone was dead or dying.

'Hi. How are you?' The line crackled and my voice cracked too.

'*Ocupado.*' A pause. '*¿Qué necesitás, vos?*'

What did I need? I couldn't help but laugh. I had no idea. So many things. Too many things. The words crammed together, fighting each other, none of them able to make their way out of my mouth.

'I . . . um. . . *No sé.*'

'Martina?' Papi infused my name with his habitual combination of tenderness and frustration, daring me to waste his time or ask him for a hug.

'I don't think I'm doing very well here,' I forced myself to admit. 'I need some support.'

'You have Spencer for support.'

'Not money, Papi.'

'*¿Entonces?*'

'Everything is just so different here in Hong Kong . . . for *me* here . . . I'm afraid of getting lost.' I struggled to hold back fresh tears. 'I don't know what I'm doing. At all.'

'This is girl talk, *mija*. Talk to your mother.'

A snort escaped me. 'I wanted *your* advice, Papi.' But what I wanted more than anything was to feel close to him. To imagine he would talk about me as mournfully as Jean-Pierre had his daughter if something terrible were to happen to me.

'*¿Mi consejo?* What's between you and your husband is none of my business – you'll work it out. *Ojo*: you can only ever be where you are. You're in Hong Kong, be there. Then you can never get lost.' Before I could reply, he added, 'I've got a call on the other line I have to take.'

Click.

I stared at the screen as Papi vanished, a phantom glimpsed from the corner of my eye. Wishes were another category of spectre, I realised. Wishing for someone to be other than they are can only ever haunt you, torment you.

Papi never met a platitude he didn't like and I don't know why I'd expected anything else. Desperation, I suppose. But, for once, he'd given me good advice.

I could only be who I was, where I was.

I was no longer New York Martina.

Who would Hong Kong Martina turn out to be?

Chapter 11

A Visitation

*W*aves slapped rock. I woke up with a start several times throughout the night. Around daybreak, I heard a soft shushing in my ear. Light tickled my eyelids.

You're safe, Martina. Go back to sleep.

Rolling over, I pulled the covers tighter around me. A floaty feeling made my limbs weightless and I slept peacefully at last.

I woke up circling the jade around my wrist. There was a body next to me on the bed.

Fully dressed, Veronica dozed on the outside of the coverlet. She snored softly. Her auburn hair was mussed, slightly frizzy from the humidity.

The storm had passed. Strong yolky sun streamed in through the windows. Veronica looked younger in her sleep. Vulnerable. The eyes that watched everyone and everything like a sentinel taking a moment's respite. Plum-coloured circles ringed them. She must have arrived with the dawn.

What had kept her out all night?

I sat up gingerly, not wanting to wake her. The scent of peat smoke tickled my nose. Sunlight winked off a whisky glass on the nightstand on Veronica's side of the bed. Goosebumps erupted on my chest. Scanning her more closely, my gaze became focused on her wrists. I blinked, confused.

Deep lacerations cut into the skin, red and angry. Scratches, razor-thin, marred the backs of her hands. Darker bruises shadowed the cuts. I inhaled sharply.

It looked like she'd been restrained. Panic hit me.

What the hell had happened?

The tide lapped against the beach below, echoing my heartbeat as I sat paralysed with indecision. *Do I wake her? Do I call the cops?* A seagull screeched as it dove past the window. Each and every muscle in my body grew taut.

Where was Jean-Pierre? Had *he* done this?

Poor Veronica. My poor friend. An icy calm descended over me. The wounds needed to be treated. First things first.

Slipping silently from the bed, I grabbed my striped dress from the armchair where I'd thrown it and went into the bathroom to change. I splashed some cold water on my face and checked the cabinets but couldn't find any first-aid supplies.

Reluctantly, I left Veronica alone and went in search of Felipe.

'Good afternoon,' he greeted me when I found the kitchen. Was it afternoon already? 'I hope you slept well.'

I showed him an anxious smile. 'I did, thank you, Felipe.' Taking a breath, I said, 'Do you have any first-aid cream? Gauze?'

'Are you hurt, Ms Martina?' He stared at me curiously. He must not have seen Veronica come in.

Not wanting to betray her confidence, I nodded. 'Nothing serious.'

Felipe's face brightened with relief. 'I can bring it to your room.'

'No, no. I'll wait here.'

His eyes grew uncertain again but, 'Of course,' he said. 'Wait just a moment.'

The kitchen backed on to the garden. Through the open doorway I could see the fig trees swaying in the breeze. It was a gorgeous day in a tropical idyll but dread pooled in my belly. My eyes skittered around me, my senses on high alert.

Where was Jean-Pierre *right now*? My bare foot tapped against the tile.

Felipe reappeared a few minutes later with cotton balls and a brown bottle of rubbing alcohol but it felt like it had taken hours. Impatiently, I grabbed them from his hands and sprinted back upstairs.

Turning the handle of the bedroom door, I tried to enter as stealthily as I could.

'Morning.' I startled at Veronica's sleepy voice. She was sitting up, lounging against the headboard and saluting me with her tumbler of whisky.

Her hand was shaking as she took a swig.

'Where were you last night?' The words rushed out of me. 'What happened?'

'You sound like my mother,' she snapped.

I closed the door. Bracing myself, I dropped beside her on to the edge of the bed and let the cotton balls fall into my lap.

'Let me take a look at your wrists,' I said.

'Now you sound like *amah*. Are you always this bossy in the morning?'

'It's afternoon.'

Veronica threw back the rest of the whisky and extended her arms. 'Looks like I'll be wearing long sleeves for a while.' She laughed darkly.

I uncapped the rubbing alcohol, pressed a cotton ball to the lip and swished until it was half soaked. 'Did Jean-Pierre do this to you?'

'Not as such. Is he here?'

'I don't know. He was last night.' Holding out the cotton ball, I warned, 'This will sting.'

'I'm a big girl.'

Veronica hissed as I daubed the alcohol against her broken skin. She jammed her lips together. Examining the marks, I said, 'I don't see any dirt, but I need to make sure they're clean. You don't want the cuts to get infected.'

'You're a regular Florence Nightingale.'

Pausing for a moment, I met her gaze. 'Veronica,' I said, 'what causes these kinds of wounds?'

'Zip ties.'

'Zip ties?' There was a part of me that had been hoping she would say silk ropes or the equivalent, that she had a lover with whom she engaged in kinky fantasies. The fear in her eyes told me it was nothing of the sort. Nothing fun had happened last night.

'We need to phone the police.'

'No!' Her tone was vehement. She leaned closer. 'There is no need to go to the police because the situation has been resolved.'

'How is that possible?' I heard a hysterical note in my voice. '*Please*, Veronica. Talk to me. You can trust me.'

'Can you ever really trust anyone?'

She let the question hang in the air. The silence swelled until it was oppressive.

Then all at once she deflated.

'Jean-Pierre's trips to Macau have caught up with him – or, more accurately, with *me*,' Veronica began. 'He owes money to men you should not owe money to.'

Headlines of gang killings and disappearances of prominent businessmen flashed through my mind.

'They approached me outside my office last night,' she said.

'They *who*? The Triads?'

'They didn't offer me a calling card.' A hollow chuckle. 'I was taken somewhere in the New Territories where they requested I make immediate payment.' Veronica glanced down at her wrists. 'I shouldn't have struggled so much.'

'Did the men . . .' I swallowed. 'Did they assault you, Veronica?'

She shook her head. 'Nothing like that. They just didn't want me leaving before my banker was able to assemble and transfer the funds.'

'That should have been easy.'

Her mouth pinched. 'Jean-Pierre's debts were more than I'd realised. My liquid assets do have their limits.'

'But isn't he an aristocrat?' I said, repeating the gossip I'd gleaned at parties. 'Doesn't he have a trust fund?'

'French aristocrats are mostly cash poor, darling. The sans-culottes saw to that.'

I took Veronica's hand and resumed disinfecting the cuts. She grimaced.

'Even so,' I started. 'I thought Ao Wing was your friend. Why would he send his goons after you?'

'Vasco? No, it wasn't him. Of course not.'

'Then who?'

'It doesn't matter, Marty. We've come up with a payment plan.' Her smile was bitter.

'I still think you should tell the police.'

Veronica flopped back against the headboard, pulling her hands from my grasp. 'That's not how things work.' She circled her wrists in front of her, the pain evident from her clenched jaw. 'I will have a word with Vasco – much more effective.'

Menace laced her voice. Maybe she was right. Perhaps Vasco was better equipped to help her than the police. This was Veronica's world, not mine.

Still, I often lie awake at night berating myself. I should have pressed her to go to the authorities. *I* should have gone. Would it have changed anything?

Would she be alive?

Guilt tastes like the sickly sweet candy that I was given at Veronica's wake. Every mourner receives a candy to ease their sorrow and a coin to spend on their way home. I threw mine in the harbour.

Veronica's eyelids fluttered. 'If you don't mind,' she said with a yawn, 'I'd like to sleep a little more.'

'Whatever you need.'

'You'll stay though, won't you? I'd rather not be alone.' She spoke with the barest hint of a tremble.

'I won't leave you,' I promised. Veronica had provided me refuge and I wanted to be hers in return.

I kissed the crown of her head.

'If you see my husband, Marty, tell him to go. He's not welcome.'

While Veronica rested, I needed to stretch my legs. I was absolutely enraged for her and totally powerless to help. The metal gate banged behind me as I followed the trail towards the cove. Offerings for the ghosts were strewn just off the path. Incense smouldered.

A dark silhouette had its back to me, wading in the surf up to his knees.

'Jean-Pierre!' I called out.

He looked over his shoulder and waved. I jogged toward him, bursting to give him a piece of my mind. I kicked off my espadrilles and ran into the water.

'How could you?' I demanded at the same time he nonchalantly bid me a '*Bon après-midi.*' I shoved him and he stumbled back.

Shock widened his eyes. 'What's wrong, Martina?' Deep ridges formed on his brow as he regarded me like a crazy person.

'What's *wrong*?' I repeated. 'Nothing's wrong with me! Something is wrong with you! Have you seen what you've done to your wife?'

'*Comprends pas.* You're not making any sense.' He wrapped his hands around my shoulders. 'What's happened to Veronica?' I heard terror in the question.

'You were so convinced she was fine! That she was just working late!'

Jean-Pierre gripped me tighter. 'Where is Veronica?'

'She's at the house. Sleeping. She doesn't want to see you,' I spat, as *Putain, dieu merci*, he whispered under his breath. His chest rose and fell.

I couldn't keep frustrated tears from blurring my eyes.

He caught one of my tears. 'Don't touch me. This is all *your* fault,' I accused him.

He dropped his hands to his sides and took a deliberate step back. 'Where was my wife last night?' His composure began to fracture.

'What do you care? You didn't last night.'

'Give me a straight answer,' Jean-Pierre growled, low and harsh at the back of his throat. For a moment, he frightened me.

'Your friends from Macau kidnapped her, you prick!' I rushed toward him in the surf, wet sand slowing my charge, shells splintering beneath my feet, and hammered a closed fist against his solar plexus.

He let out a string of curses. '*Ce n'est pas possible.* Vasco and I have an understanding.' He struggled for his next breath. 'He's known Veronica since she was a girl. He wouldn't touch a hair on her head.'

'But he's not the only casino owner in Macau, is he?' I shot back.

'Listen to me, Martina. There has been a mistake.'

'Do you or do you not lose more money than you have at the tables?'

Another blush-inducing litany of *verlan*. I only understood about a quarter of the profanity. 'There was one night – *une seule nuit . . .*'

'Only one night when you did what?' My blood pressure was steadily climbing.

'Vasco cut off my credit. I was down, way down. I needed to pull myself out of a hole. I went to a less salubrious establishment, near St Paul's. The Conquistador.'

'And let me guess,' I said with derision. 'You dug yourself deeper into that hole?'

Jean-Pierre hung his head. 'I let someone stake me. Someone connected.'

'Jesus Christ! Why the fuck would you do that? Don't you have enough money?'

He scoffed. 'The real money belongs to Veronica. My shitty society portraits don't even cover the fuel for her private jet. We may be husband and wife – but we're not equal. I just wanted to earn enough to pay for a few things in our lives.'

His contempt was palpable, corroding his remorse. What could that kind of shame drive a man to do?

Tugging at his hair, Jean-Pierre said, 'It doesn't matter, I paid back the loan shark. My ledger is supposed to be clean.'

Unconvinced, 'How?' I demanded.

'Antiques – family heirlooms from the Napoleonic era. Nouveau riche Chinese like to collect royal trinkets.'

'Veronica doesn't want the police involved so I'll keep my mouth shut. She *does* want you gone for a while.'

Jean-Pierre's lips pursed, his nose scrunched. 'This isn't what the loan sharks do. They don't kidnap Western women. *Certainement pas Veronica.*'

'Tell that to the lacerations around her wrists from the zip ties.'

His head fell in his hands. He made a low keening sound.

'They should have come for me,' he murmured.

'Well, they didn't. Your wife is the one they made *bleed*.'

When Jean-Pierre met my eyes, his were glassy. 'I'll make this right. I have other antiques.'

'Veronica doesn't want you to do anything but leave.' My voice turned hard. '*Go*.'

'I love her.' The anguish in his eyes was real. 'I would never hurt her.'

'You did.'

'Looks like the ghosts came knocking last night, after all.' He ran his hand through his hair in a slow, arthritic movement. For the first time I saw each of his fifty-four years.

When Veronica's body finally washed ashore, speculation swirled that she'd taken her own life. I didn't want to believe that the stress of her husband's gambling debts had led my friend to kill herself, and I still don't.

Could she have been murdered for not paying quickly enough? I don't want to believe that, either, but the doubts crowding my mind at 3 a.m. have everything to do with the night the dead roamed the earth.

'I'll protect Veronica,' I told her husband that afternoon on Lamma. 'She doesn't need you.'

'*Bonne chance.*' Jean-Pierre afforded me a listless smile, then strode along the beach in the opposite direction from the villa.

He stamped his footprints into the wet sand.

Later, I tore the sketch he'd done of me into teeny-tiny pieces and flung them into the sea. The whitecaps devoured them.

Bonne chance, he'd said. Good luck.

Did he know I would fail?

Statue honouring Hawkins hong unveiled

T his afternoon a statue of the founder of Hawkins Pacific Ltd, Alistair Hawkins, shaking hands with his descendant, Arthur Hawkins, was unveiled outside the Barron Industries headquarters in Central. The dynamic bronze sculpture by lauded local artist Sze Ma captures a sense of motion and dynamism appropriate for the two taipans. The Futurist style of the artwork recalls Marcel Duchamp and is also a clever nod to Hawkins Pacific's recent investment in Tsinghua University's quantum computing program.

Iain Barron, CEO of Barron Industries, and his sister, Elsie Barron-Jones, were on hand for the ribbon-cutting ceremony. 'Hawkins Pacific was the first *hong*, with a noble and rich history,' Ms Barron-Jones told those assembled. 'Alistair Hawkins helped make Hong Kong what it is today. My father, Rupert Barron, considered Arthur Hawkins to be his brother – his best friend in the world. If he were still alive, he would have wanted to honour Arthur and Veronica, his goddaughter. It's a tragedy that she's not here to see it. This statue will ensure that the Hawkins *hong* is never forgotten.'

The Criminal Investigation Team of North Lantau Police District has used DNA from a hairbrush belonging to Ms Hawkins to identify the body that washed ashore on Discovery Bay beach last month. Police Commissioner Raymond Kwan confirmed that 'sadly' the DNA analysis concluded the body did indeed belong to the drowned heiress.

A funeral is being planned for next week.

In the wake of Veronica Hawkins's death, it has come to light that Hawkins Pacific was in the process of selling itself to a sovereign wealth fund based in the United Arab Emirates but that the deal fell through. Asked by the *South China Daily* whether there was any truth to the rumours that Barron Industries had made a bid to acquire Hawkins Pacific, Iain Barron said he had no comment.

Chapter 12

Say My Name

*S*tanding on the slow-moving travelator that ran through the tunnel connecting Star Street with the MTR station, I was jostled by a deluge of office workers calling it a day. The hustle and bustle seemed alien after the tranquillity of Lamma.

I'd been at Strawberry Hill for five days, my cell phone off. The outside world had ceased to exist. Veronica had refused to discuss her captivity further, yet she didn't want to be alone, either. We ate fresh grilled fish, drank Felipe's cocktails and swam in the sea – Veronica was fearless against the pull of the tide.

Ping!

I was inundated with texts and WhatsApps as soon as I switched my phone on. Spencer had returned from Mainland the day before. His messages made his displeasure at his inability to reach me clear.

I didn't care. I'd been taking care of my friend – my only real friend. We stayed in our bubble until the siren call of the office proved too much for Veronica and she declared she'd licked her wounds long enough. She promised me she'd hire a bodyguard.

She never did.

It took two more escalators to climb the hill to the entrance of my apartment building. I didn't want to go home but I couldn't live with Veronica forever. Instead, I dragged my rollaboard reluctantly towards Starscape.

The doorman greeted me with a cursory smile and I proceeded towards the elevators as if I were walking towards my own execution.

Opening the door, I wasn't sure what would greet me.

The first thing I saw were gorgeous raw-silk draperies in pearl, ivy and sunset rose; the valance fitted like a glove across the enormous windows of the living room. Window treatments, my mother would say, are what pull together a room.

Iris must have let the workmen in to fit them while I was away.

They were exactly what I had wanted. The colours of my wedding bouquet writ large. Their private meanings now a billboard to my failure: desire, love, fidelity.

I hated them.

An irrational urge to tear them down surged through me. To shred them. To burn them. My skin was hot and it wasn't from too much sun. I gasped.

'Ms Martina?'

I whipped around. Iris had stepped out from the kitchen. She wore a patient smile. Tears threatened and I forced them back.

'I'm making Hainanese chicken rice,' she said. Her glasses were slightly fogged with steam. Chicken and rice are comfort foods the world over.

'Thank you, Iris. It smells delicious.' The scent of frying ginger and garlic wafted my way but my appetite had evaporated again. 'Is my husband home?'

I held my breath waiting for her answer.

'Mr Spencer just left. He said he was meeting a client for a drink but would be back to eat.'

Iris relayed the information cheerfully, without hinting that she knew neither of us had been home for nearly a week; nor had we been together. I hoped at least she was enjoying the penthouse.

'Great,' I said, nodding. A tear slid from my eye.

She studied my face and mortification seared me. This stranger saw the truth I'd been hiding from myself. My marriage was really and truly over.

Smoothing my hands over my face, I feigned a yawn, heading for the hallway.

'My husband is a weak man,' Iris said. I stopped in my tracks. She twisted a gold band on her ring finger I hadn't noticed before. She'd never shared any personal details, and I hadn't wanted to pry. 'I came to Hong Kong to work when my daughter was two. I sent money home every month and my husband would drink it away. Not buy our daughter clothes or toys, books for school.'

'That's awful,' I said, unsure where this story was going.

'Years went by. Past hope, I confided in Ms Elsie's mother. Ms Philippa told me I could let my husband's weakness be my weakness, or I could be strong.' Iris tugged on her ring. 'I sent my daughter to live with my mother and I never sent my husband another peso. She's the first person in my family to go to university.' The corner of her mouth hitched up in a smile. 'Nothing is without a remedy.'

I laughed with gusto. Iris was tough as nails. 'I suppose you're right. Thank you. I'm going to take a shower – it always makes me feel better.'

As I started down the hallway again, something occurred to me. Pausing mid-step, I asked over my shoulder, 'How long did you work for Elsie? She didn't mention it.'

'No, I worked for her parents.' Her demeanour changed. 'At their country home in Shek O. When Mr Rupert died, they shut up the house.'

'Elsie said he died a few years ago.' I shook my head. 'I'm lucky to still have both my parents.'

Iris crossed herself. 'So sad what happened. He was a good man.'

'Heart attack?'

'Stabbed. A robbery in Mainland. Terrible.'

'Terrible,' I agreed. Poor Elsie. I needed to invite her to lunch.

Veronica's friendship made me want to share that sisterhood with others.

Sizzling from the kitchen grew louder, like firecrackers. 'I'll finish the chicken rice,' said Iris.

I thanked her and wheeled my bag into the bedroom. Looking at the super king Spencer and I shared, my stomach gurgled.

Where are you? I texted him.

Stripping out of one of the dresses Veronica had loaned me since I'd only packed one change of clothes, I jumped in the shower. Lukewarm jets streamed over me. I washed the saltwater from my hair, remembering the first time I'd been asked for my hand in marriage, the feel of linoleum beneath me, blood gushing from my nose.

I was four years old again, lying on the floor of the prestigious Diller-Quaile music school for tots whose parents wanted little prodigies to brag about. I'd turned down a marriage proposal and the suitor counteroffered with his fist.

Later that afternoon, the pre-school heir to a real estate dynasty arrived with his mother at my apartment. He held out an aqua box tied with a white ribbon.

I'd stuck my tongue out at him but my mother pushed me forward, forced me to thank the tyrannical tyke. 'A tennis bracelet,' said my mother, examining the silver heart that dangled from the chunky, shining links. 'Elsa Peretti. How lovely.'

The boy's mother smiled tightly, pancake-thick foundation slathered on her cheeks.

'It's a tad big, but she'll grow into it.'

'Indeed she will,' my mother agreed. When they were gone, she told me, 'Diamonds would have been better.'

Wrapped in a towel, I snatched my phone, checking for Spencer's reply.

The Pawn.

I glanced at the diamond on my finger. *Be there in 15.*

Neon illuminated my stroll towards the seedier side of nightlife in Hongkers.

If the Peak is the Upper East Side and Central is basically Midtown, then Wan Chai is Times Square before it got the Mickey Mouse treatment. Sugar refineries, the raw material imported from Java, were once located here. Tobacco factories belonging to British-American Tobacco Co. Ltd. Some of the best cheap dumpling shops catering to both labourers and office stiffs are yet to up sticks. *Shui gao* filled with water chestnuts and a glass of soy bean milk will only set you back HKD 30.

The bamboo scaffolding-covered tenements with their laundry drying out the windows, soaking in the pollution, and the ramshackle shophouses, accented by rattan birdcages, that give Wan Chai its grit and history were facing a barrage of redevelopment plans, however. Hongkongers prefer to live in buildings that are new. Tower blocks only twenty or thirty years old are regularly demolished.

Anxiety was a rabbit thumping in my chest and I was in no rush to meet Spencer at his favourite watering hole. I meandered toward Wedding Card Street, a lane near the 1930s wet market, which sells precisely what it says on the tin. Ornate traditional Chinese wedding invitations, mostly in red and gold. There are other printers for business cards, red packets and *fai chun* – square or rectangular doorway decorations for Chinese New Year. But I liked the elaborately embossed wedding cards best.

The sparkling storefronts mocked me.

As the dusk thickened through the many passageways that comprise this part of the city, I cut down Li Chit Street lined with rundown shophouses. Narrow alleyways darted off the sides at random intervals. In one I found the best seamstress I've ever encountered who fixed a slight tear in my Vivienne Tam as if by magic; down another lay a barber who would trim your beard al fresco beneath a blue-and-white-striped plastic canopy. I stopped to admire the birds outside the exotic pet shop.

Around Wan Chai, I felt anonymous and safe to get lost.

Wan Chai means 'small bay' in Cantonese but its big international reputation for prostitution is courtesy of the American seamen who took R&R – otherwise known as I&I (intoxication and intercourse) – from the Korean and Vietnam wars here. American officers called the brothel keepers mama-sans like they did in Tokyo because to them the liberty ports were all one Shangri-La for twenty-four-hour party people. An Orientalist fantasy.

A fantasy in which my husband was partaking with relish.

When I'd dawdled long enough, I followed a spindle-thin staircase up from the street to the lounge area of the renovated nineteenth-century pawn shop. In the back were the pool tables. I knew I'd find Spencer there.

The bar was hopping with the after-work crowd. It was now around seven and buffalo wings and chips were being greedily gorged on by patrons on their second or third cocktail. Needing some fortification, I ordered myself a Hendrick's.

Spencer was leaning over the billiards table, his cue lined up with the eight ball when he spotted me. He was about to break.

'Marty,' he said, a swagger to his stance. I gritted my teeth at the way my husband used my nickname, like it was a trifle, an amusement – something he owned.

'Hi. Where's your client?'

'Gone home.' He straightened, grabbed the chalk and polished the end of his cue. 'So, you decided to stop running away from me?'

I lowered an eyebrow. 'You ran away to China first.'

'You fled the party.'

'What did you expect me to do, Spence?'

'Play with me.' He bent from the waist and hit the eight ball. The rest went spinning. 'Grab a cue.'

Crossing my arms, 'I'm sick of games,' I told him.

'Come on. You were always better than you let on.' There was something plaintive in his tone. Examining him closely, his eyes were bloodshot. He looked like he hadn't been sleeping well.

Good.

'What do you mean I was always better than I let on?' I asked.

Spencer grinned. 'I remember you skulking around Eastside Billiards on Eighty-Sixth. Never quite daring to come over to the seniors' table.'

'I didn't think you knew I was alive. You were so wrapped up in Sloane de Graaf.'

I'd watched him and the blonde heiress from afar, my nose pressed against the proverbial glass.

'Oh, Marty.' He rounded the billiards table and snaked an arm around my waist, drawing me close. 'Sloane's mom is my mom's best friend – as much as she has friends, anyway. It was my mother's idea. She wanted to micromanage the rest of my life.'

Spencer turned me in his arms to face the table. He slipped the pool cue into my hands. I assessed the balls and the pockets. His chest connected with my back as I leaned forward and he helped me guide the cue.

My body reacted to him instinctually. Desire began to rise, but so did loathing – self-loathing.

With a crack, I sent the yellow ball careening into a side pocket.

He hovered over me, inching closer so I could feel the tell-tale evidence of his erection. I breathed him in. The same Dior cologne he'd been wearing since high school. I'd seen Spencer teaching Sloane de Graaf to play just like this and I'd wanted to be her – I thought if only I could be like her, then my life would make sense. But I never could be, and that was what Spencer liked about me most of all.

The truth stabbed me. It was a mortal wound.

I spun in my husband's arms to face him. 'I was your rebellion,' I said. It was so obvious, a sudden realisation I should have seen years ago.

'Maybe.' A smirk. 'Take it as a compliment.'

'Maybe I would if I hadn't found you with your dick in someone else's mouth.'

Spencer's eyes bulged. 'Keep your voice down,' he said in a harsh voice. There was nothing a WASP hated more than displaying emotion in public. He was the one caught *in flagrante* but I was the one making a scene.

'Why should I?' I charged.

He blew out a frustrated breath. Little Boy Blue. 'You didn't give me a chance to explain – it was all a big mistake.'

'Eden tripped and fell on your cock with her mouth?'

'*Shh*, Marty. Come on.' My husband got right up in my face. He curled one hand around my elbow.

'I don't feel like being quiet. That's what you like in your women, huh?' I leaned closer. Our foreheads touched. 'Silenced with your cock?'

Disgust riddled his face. '*No.* How can you say that?'

I just stared at him.

'Look, I thought it was a joke. I knew Quentin's parties were laissez-faire but when Eden said she wanted to blow me, I didn't believe her.' Another frustrated breath, hot and scented with hops. 'You walked in at the wrong moment, Marty – I was about to tell her to stop. The joke had gone too far.'

I took a giant step back from my husband.

'The thing is, Spencer: I don't believe you.'

Not giving him a chance to spew any more lies, I marched out of the pool room and scurried back down the stairs to the street like Cinderella who's seen through her own delusions.

I shouldn't have left my Xanax at home. I pushed my way through carousing foreigners and locals, my chest tightening by the second. Striding up Tai Wong Street, I wished I could breathe fire while feeling myself disintegrate.

Who was I if I wasn't Spencer's wife?

I found myself outside the Hung Shing Temple on Queen's Road

East. Built into the hillside, it's a simple temple overshadowed by greenery, trees that will not be moved. Hung Shing is the god of the Southern Sea, touted to save people amidst tempests. I was weathering a tempest that evening.

'Torres! Marty!'

My husband had caught up with me. 'What do you want?' I snarled.

'Let me walk you home,' Spencer said, halfway between a whine and an edict.

'I'm perfectly safe.'

He laughed, chagrined. 'Stop it, Marty. Just stop. I've apologised.'

'Have you?' I balled my hands into fists.

'Jesus. I *am* sorry. This all got blown out of proportion. But I'm sorry.'

'Fine.'

'Fine? Does that mean you forgive me?' Spencer looked at me like a man who's just slipped the noose.

'Does it even matter to you?'

He jerked back as if I'd struck him. 'Hong Kong has changed you. I don't know who you are any more.'

Boom. Boom. My pulse raced. I was nearing the point of no return.

'All you care about is Veronica. She snaps her fingers and you run to her side like a dog.' Spence raised his voice, dragging a hand through his hair. 'You can't even see it – she's collected you like some kind of doll. That's it – a marionette. She's pulling your strings.'

'That's *enough*, Spencer.' If we were still in New York, I'm ashamed to admit I would have forgiven him. Clung to him like barnacle. But not here. Not when I had the chance at something different.

Spencer's eyes darted to the jade bangle. 'I didn't think your affection was so easy to buy.'

I slapped him. 'Hong Kong may have changed me, but it's made you more who you are.'

'What the fuck is that supposed to mean?'

'Poor little princeling. Can't take the competition. Go back to Johnston Road and find yourself a girl for the night. If you come home, you're sleeping in the spare room.'

Spencer stared at me, stunned.

'It's *my* apartment. You're *my* dependent. You're only here because of *me*.'

He wasn't wrong, and the knowledge gutted me. Without Spencer, I wouldn't be able to stay in Hong Kong. I'd have to leave the city. I'd have to leave Veronica.

'OK, you win,' I said. 'I'll sleep in the spare room.'

'Cut me a break, Marty. Don't be like this. I'm sorry – genuinely sorry.' There was a quaver in his voice now. I saw apprehension in his blue eyes. He didn't want to lose me. He didn't want to *lose*. He was invested in the idea of us too. He wanted me as his wife.

And I realised it didn't move me. I felt nothing.

'I'm going home. I'm tired. Do whatever you want, Spence.'

He stepped closer, cradling my jaw with this hand.

'You, of all people, I didn't think would stop loving me, Marty.'

Me, of all people.

Me, who wasn't good enough.

Me who should be grateful.

I looked at my husband one last time. 'My name is fucking Martina.'

Chapter 13

Lady in the Moon

'Have you made a decision about Thanksgiving yet?' my mother asked me from the other side of the planet. Somehow it was still too close. 'Surely Spencer wants to come home for the holidays,' she said. 'Your father and I would be happy to join the Merton clan gathering in Newport again this year.'

Internally, I groaned. Spencer had slept in the spare room the night of our big fight and decamped the next day to the Four Seasons in the IFC complex – the preferred hotel of philandering husbands. Room service and an elevator ride to the office.

'I don't know, Mom. We're still thinking about it,' I lied. 'Spence needs to be in China a lot at the moment.'

A couple weeks had passed and Spence was giving me time to 'cool off' in his words, but I didn't need the time; my feelings for him had cooled like lava. The trouble was I couldn't afford to leave him – not if I didn't want to move back in with my parents.

How could I return to Manhattan a failure? A failed wife. A failed career woman.

Nobody on the Upper East Side would believe that *I* had left Spencer Merton. Least of all my mother. Marrying someone like him was her main goal in sending me to The Buxton School in the first place. She might not forgive me if I ruined that for her.

Trying to redirect the conversation, I said, 'Aunt Dagne has been inviting you to Thanksgiving every year for the last decade. Why don't you take her up on it?'

'Minneapolis isn't Newport.'

Growing up, I'd envied Aunt Dagne flying the friendly skies, seeing the world from thirty thousand feet. To me she wasn't a stewardess; she was Amelia Earhart. She brought me a doll in national costume from every country she visited. My mother thought the only redeeming feature of being an air hostess was to marry an airline captain – and Dagne had settled for a fellow steward. I barely knew my younger cousins but their towheaded Christmas photo collages were very *Village of the Damned*.

'Don't be such a snob,' I told her.

'I'm not a snob because I don't want to spend hours wandering around the Mall of America.'

My fingers tensed around my cell phone. 'No, you prefer Tiffany's.' When she was still Anette Olson from backwoods Minnesota she'd had delusions of becoming Audrey Hepburn. She jilted her high-school sweetheart at the altar because she thought she could do better – marry better. A career had never been her priority.

Mom laughed. 'The best things in life come in little aqua boxes.'

'Fine, Mom,' I huffed. 'I'll talk to Spence about Thanksgiving.' Wherever he decided to spend Turkey Day, I already knew I wouldn't be with him. But I wasn't ready to tell my mother yet, not until I knew what my next move was.

'How are your little stories going?' my mother asked, and I felt my shoulders grow taut.

'Quite busy at the moment. Lots of commissions.'

She yawned. 'Oh, it *is* getting late here, but I'm glad to hear it.' Another yawn. 'It's nice you have something to keep you occupied while you work on giving me grandchildren.'

'Right, Mom.' She had a point. The puff pieces for *HK City Chic* weren't going to pay the bills. It certainly wouldn't pay for HKD 80 lychee iced teas at Cova where I liked to write my stories longhand.

They were something to keep a *tai tai* occupied between kickboxing and macramé.

It was all so unfair; I didn't want to leave Hong Kong. Spencer didn't deserve to stay. He didn't deserve to have this city all to himself.

'Anyway, I'll tell your father hi from you. Get back to me about Thanksgiving.'

'Will do. Night, Mom.'

I followed up the frustrating conversation with my mother with an even more infuriating encounter at the HSBC branch in Pacific Place where I was told I wasn't eligible for a credit card of my own because I didn't have a contract job or a work visa.

When I said I'd settle for a checking account with a debit card, the man behind the counter said, 'But you already have a joint account with your husband. Why would you need your own?'

I turned on my heel and walked out of the branch before I did violence to the flawlessly groomed clientele.

My blood boiled as I headed through the shopping mall to meet Veronica for high tea. Red paper lanterns peppered the ceiling in honour of Mid-Autumn Festival. Riding up the elevator to the Café Grey, I tapped my gel nails against my jade bracelet.

The restaurant was located in a swish boutique hotel called the Upper House that occupied several floors in the same building as Veronica's headquarters. She'd been in Beijing for business since we got back from Lamma so I hadn't been able to properly debrief her about Spencer yet. I suspected she was avoiding Jean-Pierre, and I couldn't blame her.

I also couldn't wait to see her.

The hostess welcomed me with a big false smile. She showed me to Veronica's regular table at the corner of two enormous windows with panoramic views of the harbour and Kowloon bathed in afternoon sun. I'd arrived first. Doing a lap of the restaurant with my gaze, I wondered how many of the other ladies who do high tea secretly longed to flip the table and throw it from the forty-ninth storey.

The Chinese don't believe in a man in the moon, but in a woman named Chang'e. Her husband was a tyrannical ruler who had come into possession of an elixir for immortality. Not wanting the cruel king to live forever, Chang'e took the elixir and floated up to the moon. She became the goddess of the moon and people celebrate her protection by eating mooncakes and floating lanterns in the sky.

Veronica walked into the café chatting with the hostess as if they were old friends, utterly poised in her Armani pantsuit. The vulnerable woman on Lamma had been replaced by the wheeler-dealer most of Hong Kong saw. Her sleeves were still long, hiding the marks from the zip ties that no doubt still grazed her wrists.

'Don't get up,' she said, bending down to kiss me. I wiped off a smudge of her signature lipstick from my cheek. She sat down on the grey velour banquette.

The hostess's smile pinched her pretty face as she waited to do Veronica's bidding.

'Minnie,' Veronica said, 'we'll both have the Mid-Autumn High Tea. With two gin and Earl Grey tea cocktails – emphasis on the gin.' She winked and Minnie laughed demurely. 'Mooncakes have been arriving at the office all week both here and in Beijing and I don't think I can eat any more red bean paste. Do you have any other flavours?'

Presentation boxes of mooncakes are given to most friends, family and business associates. Several had arrived for Spencer on Star Street. And they weren't cheap. A basic box of four will run you at least fifty US dollars.

Minnie smiled. 'Of course. We have Earl Grey ice cream, snow skin cakes, and chocolate with sea salt.'

Veronica clapped her hands. 'Wonderful. I can always count on the chef here to be creative. Oh, and two glasses of osmanthus wine. It's my friend's first Mid-Autumn festival.'

'How wonderful,' Minnie told me and ambled away.

Arching an eyebrow at Veronica, I asked, 'Osmanthus wine?'

'It's part of the legend of Chang'e. The sweet-scented osmanthus tree on the moon can grow back after it's been chopped.'

'That's a handy trick,' I said but my tone was muted.

She regarded me evenly. 'What's wrong, Marty?'

I lowered my eyes and swept them towards the harbour, sighing. 'I'm going to miss Hong Kong.'

'Where are you going?'

I flattered myself that I heard a note of panic in Veronica's voice. 'Spencer is unrepentant,' I said. 'All he could muster was a hollow apology.'

She set her elbows on the table, leaned toward me. 'You want to leave him.'

'I don't see how I can stay. I'm just not sure where I can go.'

Living with my mother was out of the question. Bitsy would give me a place to stay, I supposed, but doors that had been open to me as Spencer's wife would be shut in my face. The last couple of years in New York had revolved around his college buddies, his family, his work colleagues. Would I even be able to get a job with such a big gap in my CV? Thinking about my student loan payments made me nauseous.

'You're done, then?' Veronica watched my reaction. 'No second chances?'

Blowing out a long breath, I said, 'You think I should give him a second chance?' I was more than a bit surprised. 'We haven't been married long, it's true.'

'God, no, darling. Spencer is a jackass.'

I snorted, and then I guffawed.

'He really is,' I agreed. While my life was falling apart Veronica could still make me laugh. The cloud over my head lifted in her presence.

A waiter returned with two fine white porcelain cups filled with amber liquid. Veronica and I clinked cups. The floral wine was sweet and mellow.

'How was Beijing?' I asked. I didn't want to bore Veronica rehashing my problem over and over when it had no solution.

'So much turmoil in the government at the moment. The old guard is getting swept away – charged with corruption, which is probably true, but it's more about disposing of political rivals.' Veronica drank most of the osmanthus wine. 'Ah, well. Hawkins Pacific has been around longer than the Communist Party.'

I laughed. 'What are you working on?'

'Telecoms.' She didn't elaborate.

'Have you seen Jean-Pierre?' I lifted my cup to my lips.

'Yes. He's trying to make amends.'

I finished my wine, contemplating the softness in her voice. Spencer had done far less than get me kidnapped by gangsters. I nearly suggested we both leave our husbands but Veronica was obviously in the process of forgiving Jean-Pierre.

'He sold a comb that belonged to Marie-Antoinette to a private collector in Shanghai,' Veronica explained.

'So you're out of danger, then?' I stared pointedly at her hands. I had sworn to Jean-Pierre I would protect her and already I was worried about keeping that promise.

She rubbed two fingers on top of the silk cuff hiding the other wrist. 'Who knows? Artistic temperaments being what they are. His mood swings get tedious but he's certainly never boring in the bedroom.' A throaty chuckle escaped her lips.

'You must love him,' I said. I didn't understand it, to be frank. Jean-Pierre was a volatile man, charming as the devil but deeply flawed. He was passionate, especially about his wife, and yet his self-destructive urges seemed even stronger. I was afraid he couldn't help himself – that his need to assert his independence, financial and otherwise, would continue to put Veronica in danger. Now I'm afraid I was right.

Veronica's mouth puckered. 'I'm not indifferent. I wish I were.'

'I think I am.'

'Indifferent to my husband?' she teased, eyes flashing with delight.

'Ha. No. Indifferent to my own. I've known him since I was fourteen . . .' I broke off. 'I thought I knew him . . .' Shaking my head, I took another drink. 'Maybe we never know anyone.'

Veronica placed her hand atop mine. 'I don't envy you. That's a hard place to be.'

'The thing is, I don't have many savings. If I separate from Spencer, I'll need to go back to New York. I have about a year left on my Dependent visa, but it's not like I can cover rent anyway.'

'You're not going anywhere.' Veronica's voice was stern, as commanding as someone telling you to run into no man's land under artillery fire. Some of her great-greats undoubtedly did do just that.

Minnie returned carrying a three-tier cake stand toward us, while a waiter followed behind her with a tray containing two crystal balloon glasses of gin.

The lowest tier of the cake stand was piled high with tea sandwiches (smoked salmon, egg salad, roast beef with horseradish) as well as savoury mooncakes containing roast pork or abalone and seaweed. The pastries were, unsurprisingly, full-moon round and their crusts stamped with traditional Chinese characters for harmony and longevity. On the second tier were to be found jasmine-tea-scented panna cotta and mini-shrimp cocktails.

The sweet mooncakes Veronica had requested were arranged on the top tier in between candied ginger and pineapple *pâte de fruits*.

'Enjoy it,' Minnie told us.

I curved my hand around the gin balloon as soon as it was set in front of me. The condensation was cool on my fingers.

Veronica plucked one of the delicate snow skin cakes from the stand. Served cold, a bit like Japanese mochi, the white skin was almost translucent.

'Go on,' she urged me. I decided to try the chocolate. The pinch of sea salt balanced the rich, dark chocolate on my tongue. A small smile wavered on my lips.

'See, you're smiling.' Satisfaction imbued her words. 'There's nothing that tea and scones can't fix. It's hard to be sad while eating jam and clotted cream. That's what the headmistress at St Edith's would say. Mooncakes are even better.'

'This is delicious.' Discreetly, I licked a daub of chocolate from my forefinger. I took another bite.

Veronica chewed deliberately. 'Mmm. Lulu loved mooncakes. She had a sweet tooth. Like any twelve-year-old.' She paused, savouring the memory. 'Marty,' she began. 'I think you're the answer to my prayers – and I'm the answer to yours.'

Anticipation tasted like sea salt. 'What do you mean?'

'Lulu. She had a trust, of course. But when she died it triggered a clause that the assets could only be used for charitable causes.' Veronica chased the snow skin with some gin. 'I've been wanting to set up a charitable foundation in her name for years but something's always come up and I didn't know who would run it. Etcetera, etcetera. I've been full of excuses. But I had an idea while I was visiting the 798 artists' commune in Beijing last week.'

I tilted forward eagerly.

'Lulu was an aspiring artist. She had real talent, like our mother. I want to establish the Lourdes Hawkins Foundation to support emerging artists from Hong Kong, China – all over Asia.'

'That's a brilliant idea, Veronica.'

She raised her glass. 'And I want you to head it up. You have the academic credentials. You understand art. You're perfect.'

I was so stunned I couldn't speak. *Yes, yes!* said my heart, but my impostor syndrome kicked in full throttle. What if I wasn't up to the job? What if I took the leap and fell right off a cliff?

'I'm flattered, Veronica, truly I am. But I don't have any experience running a non-profit.'

'You won't be doing it alone.' She laughed. 'You'll have men in suits to crunch the numbers. I'm too busy to oversee it properly and I need someone I can trust with my sister's legacy.'

My mouth opened and closed and opened again. 'I'm honoured. So honoured. I just wouldn't want to screw it up.'

'I believe in you, Martina.'

I dug my fingernails into the pads of my palms to avoid water-works in the middle of the restaurant. No one had ever told me that before. 'If you're sure?' I said in a hush.

'I haven't been so sure of anything for a long time. You'll have a salary and a work visa of your own. *Et voilà*, Spencer has no hold over you.'

It was one of those lightbulb moments. Veronica made me real-ise I would always be Spencer's trailing spouse no matter where we lived. She gave me the courage to blaze right past him. 'That sounds pretty fabulous,' I told her. With a self-deprecating laugh, I added, 'And maybe HSBC will actually give me a credit card.'

'What are you talking about, darling?'

'*Ugh*. It's so embarrassing.' My chest tightened, getting angry again. 'This pencil-pushing bureaucrat downstairs refused to let me file a credit card application and even suggested I shouldn't have my own bank account separate from my husband.'

Veronica frowned. 'Well, that won't do at all. Once we've fin-ished tea, we'll go have a chat with my Premier relations manager.'

'Oh no – you don't need to get involved,' I protested.

'Nonsense. You're my friend, I *am* involved. Besides, I wish I could solve my own problems so easily.'

We gobbled up the tea sandwiches and split the Earl Grey ice-cream-filled mooncake. The notes of bitter orange and bergamot were subtle.

When we'd finished, I asked Minnie for the bill. Veronica started to withdraw her wallet from her Kelly bag and I wagged my finger at her.

'Absolutely not,' I said. I laid down the Black Amex – I was only a signatory on Spencer's account but I might as well put it to good use while I could. 'This is on my soon-to-be-ex-husband.'

With a devilish smile and a wink, Veronica told me, 'Too right. Your new life in Hong Kong begins today.'

Chapter 14

Girls in Pearls

I blinked and my life had changed.

'A good challenge is what you need,' Veronica told me as I signed my contract with the Lourdes Hawkins Foundation, and she was right. When I'd married Spencer, I'd stopped challenging myself. All my years of higher education counted for nothing. All that was required of me was hosting the perfect dinner party. A lifetime of being a lady who lunches would have hollowed me out until there was nothing left.

But a New York minute is nothing compared with a Hong Kong minute. Masses of Mainland tourists and Hongkongers buffeted me in the Hung Hom station as I ran for my train to Guangzhou. Golden Week was in full swing. Like during the spring festival, millions of people travel across the country to see relatives and celebrate the official establishment of the People's Republic of China on 1 October 1949.

Veronica was taking me to watch a special National Day performance of *Madame Butterfly* at the recently completed, Zaha Hadid-designed opera house. The guest list would be a who's who of creative types from around the PRD, the Pearl River Delta, and potential donors to the foundation. The Hawkins Pacific lawyers had incorporated it with alacrity and I had a shiny new business card with EXECUTIVE DIRECTOR printed on it. There was a lot to learn, but I was determined to surpass Veronica's great expectations.

I also now boasted my own Premier bank account and a credit card to go with it.

By the time Spencer had decided he was finished with his self-imposed exile at the Four Seasons, I had found a new apartment. I couldn't afford anything comparable to the Starscape penthouse, of course, but my salary was higher than anything I'd ever made in publishing and I was thrilled with my one-bedroom in the heart of Wan Chai, closer to the water. The building was called Incens8 and populated with mostly single expats in their late twenties. When I signed the lease, I popped the cork on a bottle of Veuve I'd purchased from the 7/11 downstairs and drank it on my Barbie-sized balcony.

I had the dragons of Kowloon and the shimmering sea – what more did I need?

'Do you want to come with me?' I'd asked Iris, breaking the news to her first. 'The apartment's smaller but you'll have your own room.' It was still a broom closet, but fortunately Iris didn't mind.

She negotiated herself two plane tickets a year to Manila and an additional day off every other week before agreeing. She knew her value to me and I was happy to pay. I asked her to pack our bags that same afternoon.

We left the drapes behind.

Spencer didn't believe me, not straight off. He couldn't comprehend that I was leaving him. He decided to take a vacation back to New York and said we'd talk when he returned.

I didn't see him again until the night Veronica died.

But when I boarded the train to Guangzhou, I didn't know what was coming. All I knew was that I couldn't stop smiling.

Veronica was already ensconced in the first-class compartment, tapping at her laptop. I gazed at the countryside as the train passed through greenery I wasn't expecting. The Pearl River Delta is known as the world's factory and the rural villages that used to dot this region are mostly gone, yet a few pastoral patches remain.

Guangzhou, like Macau, was a city whose fate was interlaced with Hong Kong's. During the eighteenth century it earned a reputation as the Silk Road of the Sea. Its location in the middle of the Pearl River Delta with access to the internal waterways of China through the West, North and East Rivers attracted ambitious and unscrupulous foreign merchants, such as the British East India Company, who came for tea, silk and porcelain. (Think Amazon but with firepower.)

As soon as Deng Xiaoping decided to begin opening China to foreign investment in the 1980s, Guangzhou once again became a special economic zone and the 'business, business, business' attitude radiated from strangers in the street confirming *dui, dui, dui* – yeah, yeah, yeah – into their cells as they hustled past. Everyone here wants to know, 'What have you done for me today?'

We were picked up at the Guangzhou East station by a chauffeur employed by the Hawkins Pacific satellite office. Veronica informed me we were on a tight schedule. There was something unsettled about her demeanour, an edginess I couldn't quite put my finger on.

Maybe she felt the grains slipping through the hourglass? I had no inkling that our friendship would end with her death, but in the final days and weeks of Veronica's life she showed me how to truly live mine.

The morning zoomed by at hyper-speed, straining all the senses, and I was more than ready for lunch. The frenetic energy of the many construction sites across the city was positively infectious. Our chauffeur navigated us through heavy traffic to the old town of Xiguan, which abounded with narrow *tong lau* shophouses, three or four storeys tall. The terraced structures provide an arcade for the pedestrians below to shelter from the sub-tropical rains and browse their wares.

Veronica turned to me before we entered the restaurant and said, 'We're meeting Peony Huang. She can make or break the founda-tion.' I'd never heard such reverence in Veronica's voice. The fact that I didn't know who Peony Huang was merely betrayed my igno-rance. My skin suddenly felt too tight.

The Guangzhou Restaurant is the oldest in the city, first estab-lished in 1935. Forced to close during both the Japanese Occupation and the Chinese Civil War, it reopened in the 1950s and has been renowned as the home of true Cantonese cuisine ever since. I noticed a banyan tree sprawling out from the middle of the main dining room as we were led through a corridor and a courtyard to a private room.

Sunlight filtered through Qing dynasty stained glass. Veronica ordered tea while we waited for Peony and I followed suit. She reap-plied her cerise lipstick.

'Did I get any on my teeth?' she asked me.

Laughing, I shook my head. 'I've never seen you nervous before.'

'Peony Huang is the smartest person I've ever met.'

My gulp was audible.

A quarter-hour later, a petite woman in her late fifties or early sixties arrived. Her skin was flawless but her hair was streaked with white.

'Auntie Peony,' Veronica exclaimed, standing immediately.

Peony's presence was imperious yet relaxed. She walked towards us at an unhurried pace. 'So good to see you, Veronica. Traffic is terrible.'

The two women embraced.

Discreetly, I surveyed what was certainly a bespoke pastel dress suit. The lapel was accented with an antique pearl and enamel brooch that wouldn't look out of place in a Christie's catalogue. Yet I wouldn't have guessed from her understated style that she was the wealthiest woman in Guangzhou. A self-made billionaire property developer.

Veronica stepped back and said, 'Auntie Peony, let me introduce you to my good friend, Martina Torres.'

'Delighted to meet you,' I told her, extending my hand. She

shook it with an 'And you,' and an assessing eye. I had put together what I deemed to be a business chic ensemble: a silk blouse from Shanghai Tang, a pencil skirt and Marni flats I'd picked up on sale at On Pedder in Central.

'Please, sit,' said Peony, gesturing at our seats. 'I only have an hour so I took the liberty of ordering the best dishes in advance.'

'Thanks so much for making time for us,' Veronica replied. 'I know how busy you are, Auntie.' The chairs scraped against the tile, echoing in the empty room. Beneath the table, I fidgeted my jade bracelet, a new compulsion of mine.

Peony motioned at the waiter hovering in the doorway and he entered briskly, carrying a tray laden with platters. Veronica poured the jasmine tea into Peony's cup while we were served. To calm my nerves, I studied the butterflies on the amaranth-pink teapot.

Sipping her tea, Peony asked, 'When was the last time I saw you, Veronica dear?' She paused. 'Something for the M+ museum in West Kowloon, wasn't it? I don't think it will ever be finished.' She released something halfway between a tut-tut and a laugh.

'Me neither. They should have asked you to build it.'

One corner of Peony's mouth curved upward. 'What brings you both to Guangzhou for Golden Week?' she said and looked directly at me.

'We're going to see *Madame Butterfly* tonight,' I answered. 'And Veronica is showing me the town.'

'Ah, yes. I received an invitation. Your first trip?' Peony said, and I nodded. 'You have a good guide. Veronica's been coming since she was a girl. And this is the right place to try authentic Cantonese cuisine – we invented it here in Guangzhou.' She pointed out the dishes for my benefit, a gracious hostess, explaining that real Cantonese food is lighter and more fragrant than what I would find in an American Chinatown.

I helped myself to tea-smoked duck, steamed white fish dressed with strips of scallion and ginger, and *shahe fen* – wide, flat rice noodles.

'If I know you, Veronica,' Peony started, 'you are not just here for fun.' She watched me as I took a bite of the fish, waiting for Veronica to answer, and said, 'Tasty, isn't it?' Her tone was matter-of-fact, yet I detected a note of pride. I made a murmur of agreement.

Veronica blushed – not something I'd seen before. 'You know me well, Auntie.'

'Arthur was the same.'

'He was.' She cleared her throat. 'As you know, I've kept Maman's gallery going all these years but I've decided I want to do more to promote young artists around the region. Lulu had dreams of art school too. Which is why I've created the Lourdes Hawkins Foundation.'

Peony plucked a rice noodle with her chopsticks as she listened. Her expression was inscrutable.

'I should have thought of it years ago,' Veronica added. A muscle in her jaw twitched.

There was silence as Peony finished chewing.

'So, you want my money.'

Veronica laughed a little too loudly. 'I was hoping you might consider funding the endowment, yes. I've appointed Martina as the executive director.'

The searchlight of Peony's gaze landed on me. 'Ah, so *you* want my money.'

Forcing myself to meet her eyes, I said, 'Yes.'

'Martina studied art history at Columbia and did a masters at Cambridge. She's very well qualified,' Veronica told Peony. 'Plus, I trust her, Auntie.'

The older woman's eyebrows lifted slightly. 'Well, your father had an eye for talent.' They exchanged a look and then they both smiled.

'That he did,' she agreed.

Peony returned her attention to me. 'I am what you a call a rags-to-riches story. I started work in a factory near Shenzhen when

I was fifteen years old. We made small electronic products for different companies – including Hawkins Pacific. I worked my way up to assistant manager. I had ideas for how we could organise the workflow more efficiently. The factory manager was lazy and sexist, he wouldn't listen.' Her lip curled. 'One day Arthur Hawkins came to review the operations and I took my chance. Despite being a *gweilo*, he listened to me, gave me his full attention.' A new fondness crept into her voice. 'He offered me a job in Hong Kong, in his import–export department. I learned English and I started to save my money. What I had learned working in a factory is that the products come and go, but the buildings remain. I didn't want to make things. I wanted to *own* things.'

Peony Huang's spine was made of steel and it was terrifying.

'And now Auntie Peony owns many things,' Veronica chimed in. 'She's passionate about architecture. And she's responsible for many of the landmarks you saw in the new CBD this morning, Martina.'

'Indeed. Beijing and Shanghai like to view us as the third city of China.' She clucked her tongue. 'They forget that we *guangdongren* are revolutionaries. Without us they'd still have an emperor!' She tut-laughed again. 'Here you'll be trampled if you rest on your laurels.'

'I'll make sure to remember that,' I told Peony.

She smiled broadly.

Veronica and Peony made chitchat about mutual friends, Peony occasionally glancing at her golden watch, until the main courses had been cleared.

'Veronica dear,' she said. 'I've ordered black sesame soup for dessert – you've always loved it, but I'm afraid I'm running late for another engagement.' Her attention to detail and her long memory undoubtedly contributed to her success. 'Always so many people to see during Golden Week.'

'Of course, Auntie.'

Peony stood. No one else would have dared dismiss Veronica Hawkins so easily. We both hopped to our feet.

'Martina, send your prospectus to my office. Let's see what I can do for Lulu's foundation.'

'Thank you so much, Mrs Huang.'

'It's *Ms* Huang. But call me Auntie. I am everyone's auntie in the PRD.'

Before heading to the opera, we quaffed several glasses of champagne in the hotel lobby bar, the waterfall at its centre a cinematic backdrop. The White Swan had for a long time been the only hotel open to foreigners, hosting everyone from Queen Elizabeth II to Dear Leader Kim Jong-il.

Veronica looked to die for in a one-off creation by an up-and-coming Hong Kong designer: a mandarin collar sprouted from a strapless bodice attached to an asymmetrical skirt with a ruched train. The two-tone chartreuse satin enlivened Veronica's complexion, although it couldn't entirely hide her fatigue. Stitched into the bodice using the same lime-coloured thread, demanding the viewer's eye, read 'Fashion is my Revolution'.

I wore another Horizon Plaza discount find, an Armani A-line evening gown that I'd embellished with a satin scarf doing double duty as a belt. My foundation salary wouldn't stretch to a new gown every month. Veronica had been so kind as to loan me a necklace comprised of gumball-sized pearls.

'Did lunch go well?' I asked. I was desperately afraid I'd blown it already.

'I think so.' Veronica shrugged. 'Peony patronises lots of artistic causes but she's always held my family in high regard. Loyalty is important to her. If she makes a donation, her friends will too.'

'What did Peony mean about Guangdong being full of revolutionaries?' I asked and tilted my champagne flute at the bodice of her gown.

'Sun Yat-sen came from Guangdong.'

Veronica pinched her lips at my blank face. 'He was a doctor who led the revolution against the Qing dynasty. The first uprising took place in Guangzhou. He's revered in both Mainland and Taiwan. Without him, the People's Liberation Army and the Kuomintang wouldn't have had anything to fight about.' She took a sip of champagne. 'It's why Beijing will never fully trust the south – Hong Kong or the PRD. Far from the watchful eyes of the central government, filthy rich, and with revolution in their blood.'

'Revolution in the blood, huh. Sounds like us.' I clinked my glass against hers. In that moment, on that night, I did feel like I was toppling the old order – my old beliefs. I was declaring independence from my past.

On the drive to the opera, we passed the nearly two-thousand-foot-high Canton Tower whose sleek knotted design is nicknamed 'twisted firewood', but it reminded me of the friendship bracelets so many pre-pubescent girls disingenuously weave for one another. I cast a fond glance at Veronica. Before we'd met I hadn't understood just how starved I'd been for true connection. She didn't look up from the screen of her phone, a deep crease in the middle of her brow, worrying her lip between her teeth.

The new opera house was radiant against the night sky, basking in the glow of the Pearl River. Its organic form undulated like a celestial body. Rising from a vast pond, the mostly glass structure was reflected in the water below, an elegant boulder contrasting with dark skyscrapers behind. It was an iconic building. A statement of wealth and power.

New Yorkers must have felt the same when the robber barons erected the Metropolitan Opera. Our Gilded Age had long since passed. This was a city in its ascendancy.

I inhaled shortly and Veronica gave me a curious sideways glance.

'This is the future, isn't it?' I said. Why would I want to go back west?

'You get it. I knew you would.' Sweeping her arm from the opera house to the river, 'This is *our* future,' she pronounced. Veronica was looking forward to the future that night.

Yes, she had troubles but she *loved* life. She was more alive than anyone I've known before or since. Either her death was a tragic accident – or she was murdered.

Arm in arm, Veronica and I processed up the space-age ramps to the main entrance. We stopped every few feet from the veranda to the lobby until we took our seats in the central mezzanine so that Veronica could introduce me to her myriad acquaintances and discreetly announce the creation of her foundation. By the end of the evening, half of southern China would be aware of Veronica's new venture.

The inside of the theatre pulsed with energy. All of the opera-goers admired the rhythmic lines of the internal space, not a right angle in sight. The walls and terraced balconies were a haze of earthy gold expanses. This was where Jason had hidden his fleece. As the orchestra's tuning grew louder, then softer, the ethereal lights winked off one by one.

Veronica removed a pair of opera glasses from her clutch. 'Now the real show begins,' she said. She wasn't looking at the stage.

At the second intermission, we went in search of more libation. The cavernous atrium of the lobby was what a hollow mountain would look like. Men in white tie gallantly offered champagne to decadently dressed women.

'Oh, look,' I said, spying a familiar sylph making her way towards the bar. Elsie Barron was ephemeral in silver, a shooting star. I waved her over.

Veronica embraced her surrogate sister. 'The whole world is here,' she said and offered Elsie her champagne flute before commandeering another from the barman.

'Thank you,' Elsie said. She touched the lip of the flute to her mouth but didn't drink. 'You know how much Philippa loves Puccini.' Elsie leaned over to greet me with a kiss on the cheek. 'You look divine,' she told me.

We clinked our glasses as an enthusiastic voice called, 'Martina! Veronica! Elsie!'

Cressida took coltish steps towards us in a red Valentino gown. 'I didn't know you'd be here, Martina.' She seemed glad to see me.

Veronica replied, 'I wouldn't let her miss it.'

Although I'd turned down her job offer, Cressida still wanted me on her charity committee and I didn't feel like I could say no to that as well. We'd seen each other at meetings over the previous couple months and she remained cordial, friendly even.

'Are your husbands here?' Cressida asked, her gaze roving between the three of us.

'Is yours?' Veronica said.

'No. He's in Chongqing visiting his mother.'

'What a dutiful son.' Veronica smiled and I could see her teeth.

'Girls-only evenings are the most fun anyway,' I interjected, trying to broker a peace.

Elsie agreed with an enthusiastic, 'Hear, hear.'

Cressida trilled a laugh. 'Perhaps we should have made the fundraiser ladies only.' She paused to consider it. 'Maybe next year.' Looking at Veronica she said, 'Did you get my text?'

They stared at each other like steers about to lock horns. A vein pulsed above Veronica's eyebrow. Several heartbeats passed.

'We haven't received your RSVP,' Cressida elaborated. 'For the fundraiser?'

'Which fundraiser is this?'

'Lifting Hope,' Cressida replied. I watched her chin tremble as she tried not to let her face fall.

'Oh yes, the boat party.' Veronica's tone dripped with disdain. 'Hottest ticket in town. I'm not a fan of boats, as you can imagine.' She necked her champers.

'Of course.' Cressida allowed a shadow to fall on her face. Then she cocked her head at me. 'But the junk was Martina's idea. Wasn't it, Elsie?'

Elsie winged her eyebrows and took a small sip of champagne.

'Your idea?' Veronica crinkled her brow, confused. She stared at me.

Shit. 'Didn't I tell you? Cressida invited me to join her committee. Elsie's on it too. We're helping orphans in Cambodia.' My stomach roiled. I hadn't mentioned it to Veronica but it seemed like a relatively small fib.

'Who can resist a cute orphan? Please, sir, may I have some more?' Veronica let out a laugh that was nearly a cackle.

'Be nice,' Elsie said, but she laughed along. 'It *is* a good cause.'

'Perhaps the junk party is a little cliché,' I began dissembling. 'I thought it would be romantic.' My cheeks heated. 'A vintage throwback. I guess I'm still seeing Hong Kong through tourist-tinted glasses.'

'Rubbish, darling. I'm being an old grump. If you're organising the party, Marty, it will be a smashing success.'

Cressida made an *ahem* noise. 'I'm the chair.'

'Of course, of course. Well, the Gallery de Ladrones will be happy to donate a painting for the silent auction.'

If it hadn't been for me, if Veronica hadn't been supporting me, she never would have been on the boat that night.

Could her kindness have been her undoing?

'That's very generous, Veronica. The orphans will appreciate it.' Turning to me, Cressida said, 'Do you think you'd be able to get us a cover story at *HK City Chic*?'

'Martina will be far too busy with her new job.'

Cressida's mouth puckered like she'd sucked a lemon. 'What new job is that?'

'Martina is the new executive director of the Lourdes Hawkins Foundation to promote emerging artists in the region. It's a much better career move than an in-flight magazine, don't you agree?' Veronica's eyes flashed. 'We had lunch with Peony Huang today – she thinks it's a splendid idea.'

'Does she? Peony Huang?' Cressida's voice betrayed her awe.

Elsie lifted her glass to me. 'Hearty congratulations, Martina. I hadn't heard the news,' she said. 'Veronica, I know Rupert would be so proud of you for honouring Lulu's memory like this. We all are.'

Veronica choked up. 'I hope so, Elsie.'

Elsie gave her a swift embrace as the lights flickered. Intermission was nearly over.

'It's important not to forget.' Drawing back, she said, 'I'd better go find Mum.'

The lights flickered again.

'We should head back in too,' Veronica said to me.

'Oh, I wouldn't be in too much of a rush,' Cressida countered. 'She dies at the end.'

When we reached our seats, the house lights were dimming.

'You don't have to come to the fundraiser,' I said, heart hiccupping, as I lowered myself into the seat beside Veronica. She didn't acknowledge me. 'I'm terribly sorry if it caught you off guard. I know how much Cressida bothers you, but . . .'

My eyes dropped to the phone that had Veronica rapt. A text message glowed on the lock screen.

> **Unknown Sender**
> You think you can get away with it?
> I'll make you pay.

I froze. A backwash of Veuve filled my mouth. I reread the message.

'Who's threatening you?' I asked in a low voice.

The curtain began to rise.

'Threatening me?' Veronica repeated. She let out a full-throated laugh that attracted disapproving looks from fellow patrons. 'Oh, darling. This is nothing. Probably someone with an axe to grind against Hawkins Pacific.'

'It doesn't seem like nothing,' I insisted.

'Trust me, it is. You can't run a global company without making enemies.'

'I can't say I find that very reassuring.'

'You're too sweet.'

'I'm *worried* about you, Veronica. What if Jean-Pierre has more debts you don't know about?'

A rueful expression passed over her face as the stage lights came up. 'I love you for worrying, I do. But trust me, the Triads don't text.'

Imagining the Chinese mafia text-feuding like schoolgirls, I couldn't restrain a small laugh. This time I received the disapproving stares.

'Even so,' I whispered, relenting. 'How did whoever it is get your number?'

'That's simple.' Veronica opened up her clutch and withdrew another iPhone. '*This* is my personal number. The one that got the text is my business number. It wouldn't be too Herculean to obtain. Maybe I'll fire my PA.' She said it with mirth and she was only half joking.

Neither of Veronica's cell phones were recovered from the boat after she went missing. If the police were able to retrieve the messages from the phone company servers, they didn't lead to any arrests.

'Or perhaps Cressida has something worse in store for me,' Veronica suggested.

'Worse like what?'

'Worse like getting me to join one of her damned committees.'

We both laughed as Madame Butterfly entered from stage right.

Cressida's words meant nothing to me at the time but now they seemed eerily prescient. *She dies at the end.*

Heiress laid to rest at St John's Cathedral

The grandees of Hong Kong dressed to the nines to honour the city's favoured daughter, Veronica Hawkins. The chimes at St John's rang out, a forlorn peal, having been donated by the Hong Kong Club to the cathedral in 1953 on the occasion of Queen Elizabeth II's coronation. During the funeral, a ferocious thunderstorm shook the church, which Veronica's many friends said was in keeping with her character and how she would want to be remembered.

In addition to Ms Hawkins's widower, Jean-Pierre Renard, who gave a short speech about his wife, a longer eulogy was given by Mrs Philippa Barron. After the deaths of Arthur Hawkins, Geneviève Varenne and Lourdes Hawkins in 1997, the Barrons became Veronica's surrogate family. Rupert Barron was Veronica's godfather and they had a close relationship until his murder in 2009 during a robbery gone wrong in Guangzhou. Iain Barron and Elsie Barron-Jones also spoke about their childhood together.

Other notable guests at the funeral included Ao Wing, the Macau casino impresario, and Peony Huang, founder and CEO of Park Lane China.

Cressida Wong, the hostess of the infamous pleasure cruise, told *South China Lifestyle*, 'Veronica and I have known each other all our lives. We went to boarding school in England together and knew things about each other that no one else did. Hong Kong won't be the same place with her gone.' The fateful boat party took place on the Double Ninth Festival, which some Hongkongers see as inauspicious, suggesting that the event courted danger.

New on the social scene is Martina Torres, the executive director of the Lourdes Hawkins Foundation, who pledged to continue the work that Veronica had begun in using her family legacy to promote young Asian artists.

Ms Torres brought the ceremony to a close with a reading of a John Donne poem that was said to be beloved by Veronica: 'One short sleep past, we wake eternally, / And death shall be no more; Death, thou shalt die.'

Chapter 15

Little Mermaid

*A*utumn is the best season in New York, when Central Park transforms into a sea of flame and gold. Leaves turn, curl up around the edges, and fall to the earth. I missed the changing of the seasons – or I would have if I hadn't been so busy with my new job, my new friends, my new life. Amidst the ever present hum of my adopted city, I felt myself moulting, becoming the me I'd always wanted to be.

The seasons in Hong Kong hardly change. It was still in the high seventies as I got ready for the Lifting Hope charity gala. I didn't want to be seen in the same gown twice so I put some mileage on my new credit card, purchasing a flowy chiffon tea-length dress from Shiatzy Chen, the Chanel of Taiwan.

I prayed my deodorant would last the night as I hailed a taxi on Queen's Road East. Cressida had arranged a cocktail reception at the Royal Hong Kong Yacht Club before the gala guests boarded a luxury junk for an evening of dinner and dancing. Cressida wanted all of the committee members at the yacht club by 5.45 p.m. sharp to greet the guests as they arrived. She had the entire event planned down to the nanosecond. She would have been an excellent drill sergeant. Thinking about it, I suppose Cressida's strict schedule must have helped with the police investigation.

The Royal Hong Kong Yacht Club is located on Kellett Island, which is no longer an island – land was reclaimed in the 1960s joining it to Causeway Bay but, like so much else in Hong Kong, the colonial legacy remains. Sir Henry Kellett was a vice admiral in the Royal Navy and a small fort was built on the island when Hong Kong was ceded to the British. The navy stored their ammunitions on the island before the yacht club was bequeathed it for their new headquarters in the 1930s. (I'd love to know the backstory there.)

The taxi dropped me off out front at precisely 5.44 p.m. I remember noticing the time while ignoring another text message from Spencer. He was back from visiting his family in Manhattan and had been asking or, rather, demanding to see me.

If it hadn't been for Spencer, I might have been more alert, less preoccupied, more aware of Veronica's movements that night.

The clubhouse reminded me of Strawberry Hill in style and I wondered if they'd had the same architect. Reminiscent of Le Corbusier, the clubhouse sits atop a rocky shoreline as a monument to modernism: a circular structure of smooth white concrete punctuated by undulating glass windows. It's deceptively large and Cressida had hired the entire poolside area for our cocktail hour. The bottom of the pool is tiled in shades of blue, resembling rolling waves, and my gaze was immediately drawn to them.

'Oh good, you're finally here,' Cressida said, nerves vibrating in her voice. It had taken me all of two minutes to traverse the club and arrive at the pool.

Elsie rolled her eyes from where she stood beside Cressida. They both looked drop-dead gorgeous and I was glad I'd splurged on my new dress. Elsie's hair was swept up in a strawberry-blonde chignon, her dusting of freckles set off by her sleek violet gown. I recognised Cressida's quartz-pink, sleeveless Alexander McQueen gown with the romantic cape down one side from my window shopping. What surprised me was that she had a glass of champagne in her hand – and that she took more than a sip.

With a small giggle, I said to Cressida, 'What are my marching orders?' Things had been a tad chilly between us since our run-in at the Guangzhou Opera House, although I had ensured that a photographer and columnist from *HK City Chic* would cover the fundraiser. I wasn't exactly Switzerland, but I did my best.

'Martina, I'd like you with me at the entrance to hand out the raffle tickets as people arrive,' she said, just a hair's breadth from being curt.

I gave her a mock salute and Elsie winked at me. She was fairly easy-going for an heiress, but an aura of sadness clung to her. Given that her father had been murdered and her husband was MIA, spending most of his time in Singapore, how could it not? She and Veronica had led such tragic lives, almost mirror images of each other.

Cressida gave the rest of the committee their assignments and pinned us with the orange ribbons that indicated our status. The women represented the diversity of Hong Kong's upper crust: Wanda Shen came from a prominent Shanghainese family, Elizabeth Foo was Malaysian Chinese whose husband made a killing in palm oil, Lilya Shroff was an elderly Parsee woman whose grandfather had established a wildly successful trading house in the early twentieth century, and Esther Samuel was distantly related to both the only Jewish governor of Hong Kong and the Sassoon banking dynasty.

And then there was me. I hoped they'd all make generous contributions to the foundation.

Grabbing my own glass of fizz, I headed towards the entrance with the book of raffle tickets in the other hand. Prizes ranged from an all-inclusive stay at the Aman Summer Palace in Beijing to a private concert by a Cantopop star. Waiters doing their best not to sweat beneath their bowties zipped past me carrying silver platters arranged with Wagyu beef puffs, black truffle and shrimp spring rolls, and steamed hairy crab dumplings (in season and imported directly from Yangcheng Lake).

Elsie was positioned further down the reception line to pass out the programmes with the evening's well-timed running order:

6 p.m. to 7.15 p.m. was the cocktail reception at the RHKYC, followed by boarding and setting sail to catch the Symphony of Lights in the middle of the harbour at 8 p.m. The front cover was adorned with the mostly toothless grins of grateful and photogenic Cambodian orphans while the lists of donors inside ran several pages from the Platinum Circle to the lowly epithet 'Patron'. The corners of my mouth tilted upwards when I saw my name on the inside cover under the 'Committee' heading.

It would all be logged into police evidence the next day.

The guests began to arrive, sporting hundreds of thousands of dollars' worth of jewels. Cressida introduced me to her parents, who were accompanied by her husband, Jack, and there was a discernible tension between her father and her husband. I handed out the raffle tickets, feeling like a coat-check girl, which I think was the point.

Cressida took another gulp of her champagne. 'I thought you didn't drink?' I whispered, still smiling. Holding an entire conversation with teeth clenched is a cardinal skill for surviving the Upper East Side that my mother had taught me before I started ovulating.

'Everything tonight has to be perfect,' Cressida said, eyes too bright. 'I want the gala to be the talk of the town.'

Well, it certainly was that. Just not for the reasons Cressida had been hoping.

Venus Lam had been comped a ticket for publicity and she arrived with more of an entourage than we had room for safely on the boat. A quiet negotiation took place that resulted in several of the hangers-on agreeing to stay on dry land. I have to admit that I hadn't seen any of her movies but she exuded glamour. Word on the street was she was starring in an as yet unreleased but sure to be classic film by Jia Zhangke.

Editor Evelyn came decked out in a bold-print vintage Christian Lacroix frock with a beaded tassel trim. 'You look radiant,' she told me. 'I think you and Veronica will both be pleased by the feature we're doing on the foundation.'

I was coming up in the world, thanks to my best friend.

Iain Barron was attending the gala stag, which I wouldn't have predicted given that he was one of the most eligible bachelors in Hong Kong – hell, in Asia. Elsie divulged that Iain had had a huge crush on Veronica in his teens and I couldn't help but wonder whether he still carried a torch. He gave me a friendly grin as I handed him his raffle ticket and he went in search of his sister.

Veronica and Jean-Pierre didn't show their faces until 7.05 p.m. I remember the exact time because Cressida was adamant we keep an eye on the clock to ensure all of the guests were aboard the *Tin Hau 8* by 7.25 p.m. We would cast off at 7.30 p.m. *on the dot!* The name of the junk ship had struck me as a funny coincidence but it was only in retrospect that it seemed foreboding. It seemed like fate.

The strain between Veronica and Jean-Pierre as they entered was palpable, as was the frisson. Whatever was going on between them, it wasn't over. More like a powder keg – and the fuse was about to be lit.

Maybe if it hadn't been the last dress Veronica would ever wear, I wouldn't have remembered every detail. Or maybe I would. A sequined scarlet mini-dress was moulded to her body, matching the cerise lipstick she had custom made. Even beneath the floodlights that illuminated the poolside, Veronica was ablaze. The looming hills and skyscrapers couldn't extinguish her fire.

She was impossible to miss. And yet no one saw her go over the side of the boat. I still can't wrap my head around how that happened.

When Veronica washed ashore, I'm told, the sequins still burned blood red.

Jean-Pierre looked uncomfortable in his tux. '*Bonsoir*, Martina,' he said, giving me one impersonal kiss on the cheek. We hadn't spoken since I'd yelled at him on the beach in Lamma.

'*Bonsoir*,' I said all sweetness and light. 'Maybe you'll be a winner tonight.' I presented him with the raffle ticket and his lips flattened.

'You know my husband,' said Veronica. 'Loves to chance his arm.' She drew me in for a quick embrace and the patchouli base notes to her perfume made me sneeze. Stepping back, 'You look good enough to eat, Martina,' she told me. 'Lots of potential backers for the foundation here. Well done.'

I beamed at her praise. Veronica had been distant, frantic since our trip to Guangzhou, city-hopping for business, and I hadn't looked for a deeper explanation. Now I wish I had. I'd been incredibly self-absorbed in the weeks leading up to the fundraiser. I should have been paying more attention. I should have been a better friend.

Cressida coughed, waiting to be acknowledged. 'Hello, Veronica. Jean-Pierre,' she said after a beat.

'Cress,' said Veronica. 'Fab party. I trust Apple got the painting for the silent auction onto the boat without any hiccups.'

'Yes, thank you, Veronica. The Yue Minjun is sure to fetch the highest price.'

'You're welcome. Is your husband Jack here?' Veronica asked. 'I'm up in Beijing every other week lately and I may have some business for him.'

I knew Veronica was lying but Cressida's eyes widened and her features softened. 'Oh yes, he's around here somewhere. He recently received the Order of the Bauhinia Star.' She sounded sincerely proud of her husband and I envied her that feeling.

'Oh, that's nice.' Veronica's tone was unenthusiastic. Cressida's face fell. Even if she'd warned me away from Veronica she still wanted her approval.

'Of course those honours don't mean what they used to,' Veronica continued. 'It's not like it's the Queen giving them out. Still, who would turn down a shiny medal?'

She laughed and Cressida stuttered out a croak.

'We Americans don't have any kinds of honours at all. Not proper ones. I can only dream of receiving the Order of the Bauhinia Star,' I said.

Veronica pinched my cheek. 'Marty, darling, you're one in a million.'

Cressida's complexion grew blotchy as she downed the rest of her champagne. Glancing from the flute to meet Cressida's stare, Veronica noted, 'That's not a great idea, is it? You've never had a hollow leg.'

The flute wavered in Cressida's hand. Her eyes began to gleam. I swallowed.

'Have you met Ao Wing?' Veronica said, motioning to the un-assuming Chinese man behind her. 'I forgot to get him a ticket but I'm certain that's not a problem.'

To her credit, Cressida recovered in a heartbeat. She blinked back any nascent tears. 'Of course not. It's a pleasure to meet you.'

She extended her hand. Ao Wing was not what I expected of the man who controlled much of Macau's gambling and other motley activities. He was shorter than me with a full, jolly face, although built like a Graeco-Roman wrestler. He wore an expertly crafted tuxedo and a red bowtie.

When he smiled, deep wrinkles accentuated his round eyes, yet they reminded me of the stuffed fox at Strawberry Hill. Vulpine and calculating. How exactly had he taken care of Veronica's kidnap-pers? Did they return to the *Tin Hau 8* that night? The police didn't think so. But we'll never know.

After Cressida and Ao Wing had exchanged formalities, Veronica presented me.

'This is Martina whom I've told you so much about. She's the one helping me with Lulu's foundation.' Veronica tucked a loose hair behind my ear. 'When she walked into my gallery it was like meeting a long-lost sister.'

'Veronica is too kind,' I said.

Ao Wing shook my hand. 'I'm not sure if she's that, but she knows people.' He darted her a glance and I saw something almost paternal surface within his eyes.

'Thank you,' I told him. 'I think.'

He laughed.

When all was said and done, it was Ao Wing who arranged Veronica's funeral. Jean-Pierre was too paralysed by grief. Whatever the alleged gangster's sins, that's what I'll always remember.

'Champagne is that way,' I told them, a prickly feeling beneath my skin.

Cressida daubed at her eyelashes. Mascara was flecked beneath her eyes.

'Why don't you visit the ladies?' I suggested. 'I'll make sure everyone knows where to go and when.'

She nodded. My chest twisted. How many times had I sought refuge in the bathroom at Buxton? If I'd stayed married to Spencer, I would have remained trapped in the same paradigm forever, frozen in time. Veronica offered me a way out. She was acting unnecessarily viciously that evening but circumstances we'll never fully grasp were bearing down on her, turning the screws bit by bit.

Before Cressida hurried towards the corridor, she grabbed my arm. 'Don't say I didn't warn you about getting into bed with her,' she told me, voice raw. 'One day Veronica will get what she deserves.'

Did Cressida make sure Veronica got her just desserts a couple hours later?

The next guest to arrive blindsided me.

'Spencer?'

'Marty.'

'What are you doing here?' I asked in a low voice.

'You're not the only one in the know.'

'Congratulations.'

Spencer heaved a sigh, tugged at his floppy blond bangs.

'Wait, that came out wrong,' he said. 'I bought a ticket. I wanted to see you.'

I wish I could say he didn't pull at my heartstrings but he did. He had been my girlhood crush. He was technically still my husband.

His shoulders filled out his evening suit, his eyes a tad shy and shimmering.

Spence took a step closer. 'The bed's too big without you.'

'The bedroom was never our problem.'

'No.' A naughty yet cherubic grin curved his lips. 'But it's more than the bed. It's the apartment. You even stole Iris.'

'She likes me better,' I said.

'No doubt.' Taking my hand, Spence said, 'It's not just the apartment. It's the whole city. Hong Kong is too big for me without you – I *need* you, Marty.'

But Hong Kong wasn't too big for me. It was just right. And Spencer was still thinking about Spencer.

'I'm sorry, Spence. I don't need you any more.'

He stumbled back a pace, jaw agape. 'You can't mean that.'

'But I do,' I said in the gentlest tone I could manage.

His chest inflated as he took in a large breath. 'OK. OK. Sidekick said I would need to win you back.'

'Jesus H. Christ. You told Merritt about your catting around?' Icy tingles erupted across my skin. Merritt would no doubt have spread that around the Carnegie Hill whisper network by now.

'She's my best friend, Marty – and she's on your side, believe it or not. She told me I needed to grovel.'

My jaw slackened. I hadn't anticipated Merritt Merton siding with me against her Golden Boy older brother, not after all her years of taunts at Buxton. But it didn't matter. It was too late.

'You don't need to grovel,' I told him.

He looked up at me with his big blue eyes. 'I don't?'

'No. I called the US Consulate. Since we're both residents in Hong Kong, a divorce should be pretty straightforward.'

Spencer slipped an arm around my waist and pressed me flush against him. Totally inappropriate in the midst of a gala, he launched his mouth at mine. He tasted of whisky and desperation.

Pushing him away, I said, 'Isn't it a bit early for the single malt?'

'You're one to talk. You uncork the Sauv Blanc at noon.' He nodded at my empty champagne flute. 'We each pick our poison.'

Spencer wasn't wrong and that was the problem.

'You're right. We're not happy. We're not happy together.' My bottom lip quivered. 'Don't you want to be happy, Spence?'

'My parents have been together thirty-five years.'

'That's not the same.'

'What does "happy" even mean? We're *married*, Marty. Not even two years. We can't get divorced.'

In that moment I felt sorry for him.

Then he added, 'Mertons *don't get divorced.*'

And suddenly my pity turned to smoke.

'But I've never been a Merton, Spencer. I'm a Torres – through and through.'

Spencer grabbed for my wrist and I dodged his grip. I walked away as quickly as I possibly could in my high heels without knowing where I was going. I abandoned my post. Cressida could read me the riot act later.

I found myself on a veranda overlooking Victoria Harbour, leaning against the Little Mermaid. A replica of Copenhagen's mascot stared out at the black water. I don't know how she got there, either.

If only Veronica had been a mermaid perhaps she would have survived whatever happened to her. To me, she was magical. But, in the end, she was only mortal.

'I'm not spying on you,' said Elsie as she stepped out from the other side of the statue. 'I'd just had enough of the glad-handing.'

With a watery smile, I said, 'She's a long way from Denmark.'

'It's your party and you can cry if you want to.'

'Actually, it's Cressida's. Speaking of which . . .' I opened my clutch to check the time on my iPhone: 7.17 p.m. 'We need to herd the guests toward the junk.'

Elsie placed a hand on her belly. 'I'm feeling pretty peaky.' She swallowed. 'Don't tell anyone, it's not quite twelve weeks yet.'

'Oh!' I exclaimed. 'Oh, congratulations!'

'Thanks. The morning sickness tends to hit me pretty hard. And I don't want to jinx it.'

'Jinx it?'

'It's Chung Yeung. Ninth day of the ninth month in the Chinese calendar. Some people think it's an unlucky day. That tragedy is more likely to strike.' Elsie circled her hand around her invisible baby bump. 'I don't know why Cressida picked today of all days for her gala.'

It's a question I still ask myself.

'Will you cover for me?' Elsie said. 'I think I need to go home.'

'Of course. Do you want me to find Iain for you?'

'No, no. Let him enjoy himself.'

'If you're sure?'

Elsie traced a finger along the Little Mermaid's silhouette. 'She wasn't meant to live in our world. She gives up her voice to be human and then she can't go through with killing the prince because she's fallen in love with him. She fades away to nothing, becomes seafoam.'

'That's not how Disney told it.'

A faint chuckle. 'Kill the prince or become seafoam; which would you choose, Marty?'

'I don't know.'

'I think you do. Now it's back to the sea for me.'

Elsie wandered off.

I reached my hand atop the Little Mermaid's, breathing in and breathing out. A few tears fell on the oxidised bronze tail.

Kill the prince or become seafoam: which would you choose?

Chapter 16

Seafoam

*I*n this digital age, I used my text messages to help me reconstruct the final hours of Veronica's life. Eyewitnesses are notoriously unreliable but I've done my utmost to sketch an accurate timeline. I wracked my brain for every shred of memory, for anything that could be useful during the investigation. In the darkest hours of my grief, I filled notebooks with graffiti-esque scrawl, circling words and ideas in red pen, only just restraining myself from creating a Big Board littered with twine and thumbtacks.

Here's what I've cobbled together:

I rushed up the gangway with about thirty seconds to spare and the captain cast off at 7.35 p.m., give or take. Red sails unfurled, the engines rumbled below – cheating, really – but I pictured setting out to cross the ocean the way Chinese sailors had during the Song dynasty a thousand years ago. At the far end of the wooden deck, a Filipino band was in full swing with a cover of 'Fly Me to the

Moon'. A not-quite full moon hung above the Peak, somewhere between a sigh and a whisper.

> **Spence**
> You can't keep running
> away from me, Marty!
> Sent 7:38pm

Yes, I could.

Glowering at my phone, I stashed it back in my purse and decided to go in search of Veronica. I smacked immediately into a firm chest, then raised my eyes to a distinctive chin.

'We meet again.' Quentin's blue eyes glinted.

'Just my luck,' I muttered. 'I don't remember sending you an invitation.'

He blocked my path, keeping me trapped against the railing of the ship.

'I'm invited everywhere, Martina.' His smile was feral. 'Who do you think got your husband his ticket?'

'And why would you do that?'

'Because I believe in true love?'

I answered with a snort, and he laughed.

'I did once,' Quentin said. 'Ended with a shotgun wedding in Tashkent the year I left uni . . . but hey ho, Uzbekistan in the nineties. Heady times.' He chuckled to himself, saying, 'No, I didn't think your husband would get what he wanted out of this evening. But friends do each other favours. I like to collect favours.'

Quentin lifted a tumbler almost to his lips. Pausing, he said, 'I'd be lying if I said I wasn't glad when I heard you'd left Spencer.'

'You're a real pal.'

'I do love a smart mouth on a woman.' He leaned closer. 'And now there's nothing to stop us from continuing the tryst we started on the beach.'

'We didn't have a *tryst*!' I told him, exasperated, straining to keep my voice down. Cressida would have killed me if I'd caused a scandal. Ironic, isn't it?

'I think we did,' he countered. 'And I think a revenge fuck is just what the doctor ordered.'

'Of course you do.'

'Here.' He offered me the tumbler. 'You need this more than I do. It will take the edge off. Just relax, Martina.'

'I don't need to *relax*. I need to go find my friends.'

'V has that effect on people.' Quentin swirled the drink in his hand.

The muscles in my jaw tightened and I stabbed his chest with my index finger. 'Veronica told me what you did to her in Oxford,' I practically spat. 'Stay away from her and stay away from me.'

His eyebrows shot up but otherwise his face remained blank.

'You shouldn't believe everything that V tells you, Martina. I remember things quite differently.'

He was full of shit, and we both knew it. I grabbed the tumbler from his hand, wanting to dump the drink over his head in the worst way, but I couldn't risk ruining my reputation among the city's elite. Instead, I tossed the contents into the harbour and shoved the tumbler back against his chest.

'Looks like you'd better freshen your drink,' I said.

'Oh, I do like you. We'd have so much fun together.' He wielded another smile like a knife. 'You play rough – and so do I.'

'Fuck off, Quentin.'

Hands up, he stepped back. I strode away from him, forcing myself not to run, as the Symphony of Lights began to dance along the skyline. That made it 8 p.m.

Just relax, Martina.

The words skitter through me, taunt me. When the police investigation revealed Veronica's lipstick and fingerprints were found on a glass containing traces of GHB, my stomach churned wondering precisely *how* Quentin had wanted to help me relax. I reported the suspicious encounter to the inspectors and they said they'd made a note. The sad truth is that any of the men at the fundraiser had the means to procure the incapacitating drug. Or the women.

As the investigation dragged on, I also got the distinct impression that the police were loath – or perhaps didn't have the authority – to root around for skeletons in the closets of the city's most influential inhabitants.

Did someone drug Veronica on purpose? Was it Cressida finally getting revenge for what happened at boarding school? Or did Veronica sip a drink intended for someone else? If someone did mean to drug her, did they mean to murder her?

But, more importantly, why?

Elsie Barron

Thanks for the out.

In bed with a cup of tea.

Let's get lunch next week.

Sent 8:07pm

While the majority of the guests flocked to the starboard side of the ship, I turned my back on the effervescent skyscrapers of Hong Kong Island. I pressed my hands flat against my sides to hide how much the conversation with Quentin had rattled me.

Where the hell could a girl get a drink?

The Symphony was reaching its crescendo as I climbed the stairs to the upper deck. Swanky lounge chairs were arranged around the bar. Waitresses circulated with heavy hors d'oeuvres and a multitude of sweet and savoury canapés. The committee had decided to forego a sit-down dinner for logistical and cost reasons.

Fireworks glittered against the never truly dark panorama. We were illuminated by thousands of LEDs. Very *Blade Runner.* Like the first day in Veronica's gallery, I had the sense of watching myself from somewhere else entirely.

Sometimes I think I dreamed it all. Then I touch the jade on my wrist, and I remember.

The pyrotechnics fizzled, signalling the end of the show, which put the time around 8.15 p.m. That's when Spencer ambushed me.

He was sloppy drunk now.

'Go home, Spence. I'm not doing this again tonight.' The words were a growl. I'd had enough of entitled men for one evening.

'We're on a boat, Marty. I'm not going anywhere.'

'You could always swim to shore.'

I regret the words now, I do. But not because of Spencer.

He stumbled closer, bowtie askew. I'd always tied it for him. He reached for my left hand. Lifting it to eye level, the diamond on my ring finger winked.

'You're still wearing it,' Spencer said, and I detected a quaver to his voice. He stroked his thumb over the stone. 'Wearing your engagement ring means something.'

It was the most valuable piece of jewellery I owned. I'd slipped it off with the platinum wedding band a few weeks ago, but I replaced it again tonight. Just for show. A paltry attempt to compete with my fellow committee members.

Our entire marriage had been for show. The depths of my self-deception still astonish me. Rebuke me.

Blowing out a breath, I told him, 'The ring doesn't mean what you want it to mean, Spencer.'

His brow furrowed, a toddler about to throw a tantrum, and he gripped the ring harder. The rose gold dug into my skin.

'Then I want it back.'

'What?' I gasped, speechless.

'The ring belonged to my great-grandmother. It belongs in the

Merton family. If you're leaving me, I want it *back*.'

'No.'

He squeezed tighter. 'You don't deserve it.'

White heat scorched me. 'You never thought I deserved it, did you, Spence? You never thought I deserved *you*. But now I know it's *you* who never deserved *me*!' My shoulders heaved as my pulse accelerated. 'Ask your mother or goddamn Emily Post, you gave me the ring and now it's *mine*!'

Spencer yanked harder, trying to pull the ring from my finger. I yelped and pulled back. 'Get *off* of me!'

'What the devil is going on here?' Veronica appeared in her flame-red dress like the sword of an archangel. (Blame *Abuela* for dragging me to all those Catholic masses.)

'This is none of your fucking business,' Spencer slurred.

Veronica smiled, unfazed. 'Testy, testy.'

'You ruined our marriage!' He thrust out an accusing finger, eliciting a few stares from the other guests. 'You ruined my wife! You *changed* her. Turned her against me!'

She drew in a patient breath. 'It's not my fault you took Martina for granted. All I did was believe in how smart and capable she is. You're the one who didn't realise what you had until she was gone.'

Despite my mortification, I basked in Veronica's praise. She saw me like no one else ever has. She believed in me more.

I want to live up to her expectations. I want to be the version of me she glimpsed beneath the surface. Every day since she died, it's the reason I pull myself out of bed. I honour my best friend by trying to fulfil my potential.

Veronica pried Spencer's hand from mine. 'You don't want me to call security,' she warned him. The colour leached from his face. He was all bluster, as usual.

Shoving his hands in his pockets, Spencer said, 'You keep destroying people's lives and you'll get what's coming to you.'

'Sticks and stones.'

Spencer opened his mouth, distorted with anger, but Veronica placed a finger to his lips to shush him.

'Walk away now,' she said, 'and I won't ask Edwin Leung to fire you.'

He looked from Veronica to me. 'She owns you, Marty. It's pathetic. You should be embarrassed.'

I plucked the ring from my finger, held it up so it twinkled like a star. Spencer stretched his hand toward me. I took two quick steps towards the side of the upper deck.

'What I am is free,' I declared.

Dizzy with elation, I tossed the diamond into the sea.

'Are you fucking crazy?' Spencer screamed at me. He rushed to the railing and watched his family heirloom disappear.

A few hours later Veronica would disappear in the same way.

'You're gonna pay for that,' he threatened.

'I'm sure the Mertons have insurance. From now on, we'll talk through lawyers. Goodbye, Spencer.'

Veronica hooked her arm through mine. 'You're simply inspiring, darling.'

Giggling, still in shock, we processed to the lower deck arm in arm. Veronica whispered a request to the band leader. The opening notes of 'I Will Survive' rang out across Victoria Harbour.

Veronica twirled me as we shouted the lyrics from the tops of our lungs.

Veronica was vitality incarnate. She danced her heart out. She had so much left to give. We both danced like there was no tomorrow.

And there wasn't.

> **Cressida Wong**
> Can you come chat
> with a donor?
> Lower deck
> Sent 10:16pm

I ate far too many of the caviar-topped blinis and grilled oysters with parmesan but they were no match for the quantity of alcohol I'd consumed after throwing my engagement ring into the fathoms below. The dramatic gesture was a *pièce de résistance* but later, much later, I regretted not pawning it or selling it to a jeweller on the Golden Mile of Nathan Road in Kowloon.

As I said before, if it hadn't been for Spencer, how discombobulated he made me, I would have been better able to keep track of Veronica's whereabouts on the *Tin Hau 8*. I blame myself. In every nightmare. With every unanswered prayer.

Did Spencer push Veronica off the side of the junk? He was drunk and angry. He'd threatened her. He had motive. He had means.

Did he have the opportunity?

Still, I can't make myself believe it. He's too much of a coward.

The police questioned him. Other guests had overheard his altercation with me and Veronica. But no charges were brought. Spencer resigned from Hutton Brothers and returned to the States by Christmas. Oddly enough, my parents weren't invited to Newport for the holidays.

The band played on while I plied myself with the free Martinis – we would never have been so gauche as to stem the free flow of alcohol for our guests in order to send more of the proceeds to the Cambodian orphans.

Cressida wanted to introduce me to one of the gallerists who had donated a sculpture of Elvis made from ashes collected in Burmese temples. He was an enthusiastic young man from a frightfully wealthy Thai family (they even own an English football club) who thought a twenty-two-year-old who'd never made his own bed capable of running his own business. Just a starter business. The way Baby Boomers have starter houses and the rest of us have starter furniture from Target.

The Hong Kong skyline bounced on the horizon. I made polite conversation for an appropriate amount of time before making my excuses to be elsewhere. I'd last seen Veronica rocking out to 'Stayin' Alive' on the dancefloor and I was eager to re-join her. As I made my way back towards the bow of the ship, I spied Veronica and Quentin standing together on the upper deck.

Between the din of the crowd and the overzealous drummer of the band, I was too far away to hear anything they were saying. But, from their violent hand gestures, they weren't talking about the weather.

Quentin grabbed her shoulder. Veronica clutched a Martini glass in one hand and shoved him with the other. Hard. He stumbled back a few paces.

Quentin seemed to be shaking his head. Then he stormed off. I held my breath as I watched him race down the stairs from the deck above.

Unfreezing, I headed towards the stairway but did a U-turn when Spencer came into my field of vision. The boat was too goddamned small. There were too many people altogether and too many people I wanted to avoid.

Of course, I walked straight into another one of them.

Jean-Pierre's silver locks were lifted by the breeze, expertly mussed. He needed a haircut but the haphazard length gave him a bohemian air. His suit was tinged with the scent of clove cigarettes.

'Martina.' He made my name a purr. Touching a finger to the saffron-coloured ribbon pinned above my clavicle, 'Gamboge,' he said.

'Excuse me?'

'It's the name of the pigment. From *Gambogia*, the Latin word for Cambodia.'

'Oh. Fascinating.'

'I love her,' he said. '*À la folie.*'

Talk about a non sequitur. I didn't respond. We stared at each other as the bass guitar reached fever pitch.

'I'm doing everything I can to set things to rights,' he insisted.

'It's not me you need to convince.'

Jean-Pierre ran his fingers through his silver strands. 'Have you seen her?'

'No,' I lied. If Veronica was avoiding him, I wouldn't give her away. Why had she brought him to the gala at all?

Nodding, agitation stencilled itself on to Jean-Pierre's brow. How had he lost track of his wife? Why? Resignation striated his next breath.

'Veronica will be found when she wants to be,' he said. Another huff. 'I'll keep looking.'

'You do that.'

Jean-Pierre opened and closed his mouth, thinking better of something he wanted to say. Then he walked into the throng of partygoers huddled around the bar of the lower deck. It was the last time I saw him before Veronica went missing.

What did he get up to over the next hour?

> **Cressida Wong**
> Raffle draw starts at 11 p.m.
> I need you now!!!
>
> Sent 10:50pm

Here's the thing: you usually don't know the last time you see someone that it's going to be the last time. If I'd known these were my last few hours with Veronica, I wouldn't have wasted a single precious minute doling out raffle prizes.

I'm embarrassed to admit I downed another glass or two of bubbles during the prize draw so I'm not entirely sure what time it finished. It took about half an hour. I felt pleasantly warm, even if my head was already a bit sore.

Veronica was on the upper deck, ensconced on the last sofa

towards the stern of the ship, when I finally caught up with her. Her long legs were crossed, her mini-dress showing off her sleek limbs. She gazed out toward the rippling wake of the junk, Martini glass in hand.

If I'd had my wits about me, I might have noticed that her head swung towards me with a jerk. That her movements were too lethargic. Her pupils were too dilated – but, then, so were mine.

Veronica greeted me with an enormous smile. She tried to get up but fell back against the sofa cushions.

'Are you having fun?' she asked me.

What a question. What a night it had already been. 'I think the fundraiser is a success,' is what I replied as I sat down beside her.

She released a throaty laugh. 'You're good at this. Very good. I know Lulu's foundation is in good hands.'

There was something amiss. That much I recognised. Veronica was not acting herself. I hate myself for not realising sooner that she was drugged.

'Are you all right?' I asked her. Lowering my voice, I said, 'I saw you arguing with Quentin earlier.'

Veronica drank deeply from her gimlet. 'Quentin?' she said dreamily. 'Oh, right. *That.* He's such a bore.'

'Did he hurt you?' I said, urgency rising within me.

Not answering, she picked up a discarded dessert plate from the side table next to the sofa. 'Look. A *pastel de nata.*' Plucking the half-eaten egg tart from the plate, Veronica said, 'Lulu loved these. "*Natas, natas!*" she would say.'

'I know. You told me,' I said quietly. Veronica never repeated herself. She didn't forget what she'd told to whom.

She plopped the egg tart in her mouth and chewed slowly.

'I'm the bore now,' she said. 'Oh, well.'

'You could never be boring.'

Veronica set down the plate and took my hand. 'If only my husband felt the same way.'

'What are you talking about?' I crinkled my brow. 'He adores you.' Of that much I had no doubt.

'Maybe so,' she said. 'But I've left him.'

Words lodged in the back of my throat as my mouth fell open.

She slurped her gimlet. 'He lost more money in Macau,' Veronica said, her voice becoming a hiss. 'He can't help himself – and I can't keep helping him. Enabling him only hurts us both.'

'I'm so sorry,' I told her and I meant it. Our hands were still intertwined so I gave hers a squeeze. 'Is there anything I can do?'

She drained her glass. 'I'm foxed . . . I want to get more foxed.'

'Foxed?'

'Drunk, Marty. Arthur liked old-fashioned words – and I adored my father, well . . . most of the time . . .'

'Maybe I should get you some water.'

Veronica laughed. 'You're the best friend I've made in years, Martina. The best I've ever had.'

'You too.'

'Let's go on a Grand Tour like my great-greats did. Just the two of us,' she said, her syllables fuzzy around the edges, her smile hazy. 'I've been taking care of people my whole life. Now I'm light. So light. Jean-Pierre is on his own. I only have to take care of me – what an amazing feeling. St-tupendous . . .'

Veronica raised her empty glass to the Hong Kong skyline.

It's always the husband. Isn't that what detectives say in police procedurals on TV?

Did the Frenchman shove his wife off the side of a ship to get her fortune? Insurance money? If that was Jean-Pierre's endgame, Veronica outsmarted him. When the last will and testament of Veronica Hawkins was read, she'd bequeathed only a middling estate near Paris to her husband.

Veronica clutched my hand tighter, drew me closer. I remember the scent of her perfume, tinged by night and sea salt.

'Promise me we'll escape together,' she said.

'A big trip sounds like fun.'

'*Promise me.*' Veronica was adamant.

'I promise.'

She made a liar of me. There was no escape. Not for her. Not for me.

'But first, I'm going to find us some water,' I told her.

Veronica flopped back against the cushions. 'If you insist.'

'You'll thank me later.'

'Thank you, Martina.' Her sly smile turned genuine. 'I'm so glad you moved to Hong Kong.'

Veronica's eyes drifted closed and I went in search of the stuff of life.

It was the last time I saw her alive. She was beautiful in repose, framed by the city she loved so much.

When I finally managed to elbow my way through the other partygoers for a highball glass full of H_2O and returned to the upper deck, Veronica was gone.

Her purse remained on the sofa. The glass that tested positive for GHB was set beside the demolished egg tart.

There were signs of life. Signs of a vivid life. But Veronica herself was gone.

Evaporated.

Dust to dust.

Epilogue:

Orpheus

Me to Veronica

Veronica, where did you go?

Sent 12:34am

Veronica

Nowhere. The lhigts. Prettyy

Read 12:40am

This is when my five stages of grief began. I just didn't know it yet. I couldn't know it. My conscious mind built a moat around my heart, poured hot oil over my intuition.

Me to Veronica

You aren't where I left you

I'm getting worried now

Sent 12:45am

Stage One: Denial. I was worried, but I was a teensy bit pissed. My strappy open-toed Louboutins were cutting into my big toes, a border of blood forming around the Swarovski crystal appliqués set in a daisy pattern on the nails.

I found Jean-Pierre near the band. The singer belted out 'Dancing Queen' at the top of her lungs. He'd undone his bowtie and his tuxedo shirt looked damp. I could smell gin emanating from him.

'She hates boats,' he said. 'I don't know why she wanted to come.'

'She told me she left you.' And I knew why Veronica had come. She had come for me. To stand by my side. I don't think my fog of guilt will ever lift. Perhaps it shouldn't.

'We had a fight.' Jean-Pierre gave an exaggerated shrug. 'This isn't the first time she's left me. She never means it.'

'I think this time she does.'

Raking a hand through his silver hair, he said, '*Peut-être*. Either way, I need to find her. She didn't seem . . . she's not Veronica. Something – *ce n'est pas normal*.'

On that we were agreed. 'She has to be here somewhere,' I said. 'It's not like she can go anywhere.'

A haunted look passed over his face. 'She hears Lulu sometimes. She hears her crying.' Jean-Pierre exhaled harshly. '*J'ai peur*.'

Stage Two: Anger. I grabbed his lapel. 'Stop it,' I said coldly. 'Being afraid won't help anything. I'm going to find her. You go find the captain. Just in case . . .'

As I spoke a chill stole through me. I was lying. Somehow I knew I was lying.

'We'll find her,' I repeated. Jean-Pierre and I went our separate ways to scour the junk for her.

Why was his shirt damp?

Was it the remnants of Veronica's gimlet or a splash from the sea?

I shivered in the subtropical night.

> **Me to Veronica**
> If you don't turn up in 10 minutes
> I'm telling the captain
>   Sent 1:05am

Stage Three: Bargaining. I thought by threatening Veronica like a naughty child that I could coax her out of wherever she'd absconded to.

Ha. I should have known better but I wanted to believe I had some control. That I could *fix* something.

Jean-Pierre had reached Stage Four: Depression. I could see it in his glazed eyes. I wasn't there yet. I bounced between anger and bargaining. Mostly fury.

> **Me to Veronica**
> I'm with the captain. Jean-Pierre too.
> They're radioing for help.
> No joke.
>   Sent 1:15am

> **Me to Veronica**
> Veronica?
>   Sent 1:20am

Jean-Pierre let out a string of curses in French. The captain was unmoved. I texted furiously. Jean-Pierre texted furiously. The revellers continued their bacchanale, gyrating bodies above the pitch-black waves.

Acid gurgled in my gut. My world was coming apart at the seams.

> **Me to Veronica**
> VERONICA????
> Sent 1:30am

I crumpled to the deck of the ship. I supplicated the goddess of the sea. Please. *Please.* But I couldn't sense her.

Was this Stage Five? Screaming into the digital abyss didn't feel like acceptance.

I still don't accept that she's gone.

Nobody can give me one good reason why she is.

You know what happened next. The search, the dead ends, the resignation. Rumour and innuendo swirling through headlines and blogs across the world, launching a thousand think pieces.

What really happened to Veronica Hawkins?

Motives abound. Veronica wouldn't have been Veronica without a bevy of enemies, but each of the suspects is slipperier than a shadow.

Could it have been the socialite with a grudge, finally giving Veronica a taste of her own medicine? Perhaps Cressida only meant to humiliate Veronica but she lost her footing and fell overboard . . .

The spiked drink also implicates Quentin Turner, who had a sordid history with women and had taken advantage of Veronica in the past. Did he spot an opportunity to put Veronica in her place?

Or was it her husband, in over his head with fresh gambling debts who had just learned Veronica was finally leaving him? Did love turn to hate for a single moment that changed everything?

I can't exclude my own husband from the list of suspects, either. For the exact same reason. Did his love of me and hatred of Veronica, fuelled by too much drink, cloud his judgement and result in one violent act that could never be taken back?

Or maybe it was someone else entirely? Someone at the periphery of Veronica's life I never met?

It doesn't matter. It won't change anything. She'll still be gone.

You were hoping for more answers? I don't have any.

Like I said from the beginning, this is a love story. I want you to remember Veronica as I do. As she was in life. She was radiant, generous, loved her friends fiercely, and yes, sometimes, she was casually cruel. She was human, so incredibly human.

This is my only truth: I look for Veronica in the seafoam now.

I walk along the beach where she washed ashore, letting the tide surge over my bare toes. She has returned to the sea like the Little Mermaid. Tin Hau reborn. She is with Lulu, I believe that. Veronica saved me – gave me a new life, the courage to be myself – even if she couldn't save herself.

At the end of a Chinese funeral, mourners aren't supposed to look back at the casket. It will bring bad luck. I can't help myself.

Was she murdered? Was it a horrible accident?

I'm learning to live with never knowing.

Yet I can't stop looking back.

Camden Press wins Veronica Hawkins tell-all at auction

Camden Press won world rights to *Hungry Ghosts: Life and Death on the Peak* by Martina Torres in a fierce ten-way auction for a rumoured high six figures. 'A compelling and unflinching account' of the final days of Veronica Hawkins as told by her closest friend – who was also the last person to see her alive. Pitched as *Eat, Pray, Love* with murder, the memoir examines the Hong Kong expat scene and gives context to the heiress's mysterious death that has captivated the world. Translation rights have been sold in twenty territories with planned simultaneous publication for next summer. Film rights have been optioned by Warner Brothers.

Part II

ENCORE

La Vie en Rose

Pull yourself together, Piggy. Men are coming to slaughter you.
Martina repeated this mantra to herself before any big interview, exam, social function. Just as her mother had repeated it to her as a child, as her grandmother had repeated it to her mother and so on and so forth back to the misty fjords.

To be fair, it sounded better in Swedish.

From where she waited in the courtyard, shielded by the massive French doors of the *hôtel particulier*, Martina listened for her cue. Her publisher had flown her to Paris to promote the French edition of her memoir at the Salon des Livres and her canny publicist had suggested an event at Martina's alma mater. Columbia owned a small house in Paris, all covered with vines. Well, not quite – but close. The mansion had once belonged to the wife of the United States ambassador to France in the 1890s, who had transformed it into a club and boarding house for American women.

'*Bienvenue à tout le monde.* Good afternoon and thank you for joining us. I am Professor Camille Lefebvre, the *directrice* of Reid Hall, and we are delighted to be hosting this special author event in conjunction with the American Library of Paris.'

The scent of early spring roses tickled Martina's nose although the first day of April was miserably overcast. She chewed her Nicorette gum with renewed vigour – that was a titbit she'd left out of the memoir. While Martina and Spencer were still married, he'd nagged her to quit and she'd decided not to give him the satisfaction. Early on in their courtship he'd bummed smokes from her, said the sight of her pink lip-print on the filter turned him on.

His attitude changed once they'd said, 'I do.' What he'd wanted from Martina the girlfriend and Martina the wife were two very different things.

Now she didn't want yellow teeth on Instagram, either. She'd been plenty neurotic about her appearance before the memoir was published eighteen months ago, but since then, being in the public eye had pushed Martina back towards some of the darker impulses she'd harboured in middle school. The two madeleines she'd allowed herself for breakfast weighed in her stomach like stones. But when in Paris, why not be Proustian?

'It is my great pleasure to introduce our speaker, Martina Torres,' Professor Lefebvre continued, 'who is not only the author of the internationally bestselling memoir, *Hungry Ghosts: Life and Death on the Peak*, but also a graduate of Columbia University. She majored in art history at Columbia before winning a Gates Scholarship to the University of Cambridge for her master's degree.'

Remaining out of sight, Martina discreetly surveyed the audience. In addition to the college students enjoying their Junior Years Abroad, the Anglophone expatriate community had turned out in force – bored American housewives trying to reclaim Lost Generation glamour and chattering classes Brits bemused by the upcoming Brexit vote. She very much hoped each of the hundred-strong crowd had purchased a copy or two of her book – she was within inches of earning out her foreign rights deals in addition to both the US and UK editions.

Martina would gladly suffer a few more hand cramps as she scrawled, *Live your own truth, M xx* on the title page for the zillionth time.

'Ms Torres currently resides in Hong Kong, where in addition to writing she is also the executive director of the Lourdes

Hawkins Foundation, promoting emerging artists from around Asia.' Professor Lefebvre paused to draw breath. 'Please join me in welcoming Martina Torres to the stage.'

Wetting her lips, she circled the ice-cold jade around her wrist. A niggling sense of dread had pursued her for the past few years. She squashed it with a smile, polite applause accompanying her entrance.

Martina had spruced up her wardrobe with some of the money from the film option on her book and today she had donned a black silk-crêpe Paule Ka suit, sky-high Louboutin boots adorning her feet. Her arches were already killing her. She understood Veronica better now than she had when she was alive. Martina could only claim a sliver of her friend's celebrity and yet she felt the pressure acutely. The pressure to be the best, most perfect version of herself at all times.

She didn't dare slip up or let down her guard. Someone might be watching.

Pull yourself together, Piggy.

Martina strode towards the front of the dark wood-panelled Grand Salle and shook Professor Lefebvre's hand. The other woman exuded confident elegance: silver hair in a severely cut bob, the few wrinkles that dared crease her porcelain complexion betrayed her age – perhaps sixty, an Hermès scarf looped around her shoulders. No dowdy academics in this ancient capital.

Hazy light filtered through the glass doors as Martina took one of the two seats positioned at the centre of the dais. Parisian grey wasn't the same as Hong Kong grey. The light was thinner. The humidity didn't cling to the skin in the same way. Martina missed the heavy sensation, its own form of armour.

Professor Lefebvre lowered herself gracefully onto the other chair and handed Martina a wireless microphone.

'Welcome,' said the older woman. 'I am delighted to have you here to discuss the art of memoir and the boundaries of memory.'

Martina curved her lips in a feline smile. 'The pleasure is mine.'

On the promotion circuit, she'd become more adept at taking control of interviews, of twisting questions to be answered with one of her canned responses. Even so, she held her body taut, waiting for the first sally. She preferred to be the one *asking* the questions.

Professor Lefebvre canted her head. 'Let us start with your writing process. How did you decide where to begin your story, which memories to include . . . how does one craft the truth?'

'Ah, wasn't it Baudelaire who said a painter must be an observer of modern life? A *flâneur* – a wanderer, a connoisseur of the street,' Martina replied, knowing a reference to the French art critic would score her points. 'I consider myself a *flâneuse*, a fly on the wall.'

'But you aren't just a fly on the wall – you're a central character.'

The professor's gaze was astute, piercing. Martina stroked the microphone.

'Memoir is a curated version of the past,' she replied. 'And memory is always faulty. When I was working as a journalist, I adhered to the three-source rule – that you need three independent confirmations of a story before you go to print. When you're writing your own story you discover that what you believe to be true may, in fact, be a fiction. It's very tempting to become your own hagiographer.'

'In that case, where is the line between memoir and fiction?'

'For me, it's all about intention,' she said, earnest as she could manage. 'I set out to celebrate Veronica's life and to work through my own grief . . . to try and make sense of my loss by recounting her final days.' Martina inhaled and held the breath for several beats. 'Veronica Hawkins is the stuff of legends but I wanted to share Veronica the *woman* – the friend I knew – with the reader. She was entirely unique but loss is universal, something everyone has experienced.'

The truth was Martina did mourn Veronica in a raw, bone-deep way that not even she completely understood. How could she crave her like marrow? Like sustenance? She'd known Veronica less than a year when she went overboard. She'd been talking and writing about her friend longer than she'd spent in her company.

And yet the connection between them, the spark she'd felt in Veronica's presence was something Martina hadn't experienced before or since.

Not with a lover. Certainly not with a friend. The exhilaration of walking a high wire.

Professor Lefebvre nodded sagely and shifted in her seat. 'How do you approach writing yourself as the narrator? As the heroine?' A hesitation. 'Especially in someone else's story?'

'I'm no heroine.' Martina released a practised laugh, fluttery and somewhat disparaging. 'Creating yourself as a character is a complicated business.' She heard herself speak the same words she had on multiple other occasions, as if from a long distance. 'Almost akin to shapeshifting.'

She'd made herself both less and more on the page. More likeable but less relatable. The reader needed to want to be Martina's friend – needed to think of her as simultaneously approachable and intimidating. A Mean Girl with a soft, chewy middle.

Martina revealed just enough of her private pain to be sympathetic yet not pathetic. As much as she could stand. She didn't owe the world all of her scars.

'Shapeshifting – *mmm*.' The professor peered at Martina sideways. 'You touch on questions of identity throughout your book, of existing in liminal spaces, of never feeling like you belonged on the Upper East Side. Do you feel a sense of belonging in Hong Kong?'

'What an interesting question.' Martina crossed her legs. 'As a very pale-skinned Argentine, I am able to pass and blend in mainstream white America, which was a matter of social survival growing up. Having said that, there is always a space between us . . . a caveat to my identity.'

The summer Martina was sent to Swedish language camp in the Midwest was seared into her memory. In a sea of Swensons and Johanssons, she was the only Torres. *What are* you *doing here?* she was asked on a daily basis and she'd had no good answer.

Martina surveyed the audience wistfully. 'Hong Kong is a city built by immigrants – it's what defines the Hongkonger identity. As a Westerner, I am in the minority, of course, but I am also an immigrant to the city seeking something better than what I had in my home country. And I believe I've found it.'

Spine erect, Professor Lefebvre's lips pinched ever so slightly to the left.

'Yes, the proximity to whiteness is a theme of utmost importance in your work. Yet there are some critics who have voiced concerns regarding the centring of two Western women in an Asian context. Some going as far as to accuse you of Orientalism.'

Martina's shoulders stiffened. The French publicist was supposed to have screened the questions so she wouldn't be thrown any curve balls.

'What is your question, Camille?' Martina tapped her fingers against her knee.

The professor held her ground. 'How would you respond to those concerns?'

'To them, I would say that I portrayed the world I know – the world I lived in. As each person has many facets, so does a city. There are many Hong Kongs and the expat world is its own particular beast. As I'm sure it is here in Paris.' Martina paused for a chuckle from the audience before continuing. 'I am no apologist for imperialism, yet you cannot tell the story of Hong Kong – or of Veronica Hawkins – without exploring its legacy, its role in shaping my adopted city. The glitz and glamour of the Peak are a direct result, among so many other things.'

She lounged back against the Louis XV chair, waiting. Anticipating.

Changing tack, Professor Lefebvre asked, 'You are very open about the dissolution of your marriage. Was that difficult for you?'

Like a root canal without novocaine, she wanted to say.

Martina touched the jade bangle, winter at her fingertips, cool and calm.

'I lost myself in my husband the way that far too many women do – even in the twenty-first century,' Martina said with chagrin. 'I'm not proud of it. Having Dependent Spouse stamped in my passport forced me to re-evaluate my life choices.'

Out in the audience, she noticed microscopic nods of agreement and tense jaws among the female members, as she expected she would.

'I knew that I would burn some bridges in talking about my ex-husband, in disclosing details about the reasons for the way our marriage unravelled.'

Divulging those gory details had also allowed Martina to control the story, more or less. Spencer would tell the grey-flannel-wearing dude bros at the Union Club his version of events, she'd been sure; his mother would spew her venom up and down Park Avenue. Everyone would pretend to believe them, cringe or smile at the right moment, all while reading Martina's truth in black and white. She'd received some private messages of support from New York friends upon publication, but mostly the consoling emails had come from strangers. The Mertons still held too much sway in Yorkville.

One arch-rival of Spencer's mother did invite Martina to speak at the prestigious Cosmopolitan Club book club, however. That had been a hoot.

Leaning towards the sea of rapt faces, Martina said firmly, 'I had to tell my truth. Fire can be cleansing.'

But also lonely. Martina's oldest friend Bitsy was terribly hurt by her depiction. Martina's mother had always warned her that no one looks good under a magnifying glass and Martina reminded her mother of this sentiment after she'd read the first complete draft. They hadn't talked since a perfunctory call at Christmas. Her father didn't seem to notice.

Veronica remained her most loyal friend, and she was dead.

'Speaking of complicated dynamics, you briefly mention those between women in Hong Kong and their helpers.' Professor

Lefebvre's nostrils flared. 'Your view on that relationship seems to change throughout your memoir.'

Martina did the fluttery laugh again. 'I never had staff growing up – we definitely couldn't afford it – and I found the idea all very *Upstairs, Downstairs*.' She pursed her lips. 'But Iris is an extremely capable woman and she's also now my PA. She's basically my Girl Friday and, for that matter,' she said with another laugh, 'I've lived with Iris longer than I did with my ex.'

Titters rose to the ceiling. That line always got a laugh.

She liked to think of Iris as friend, not as an employee, more like a roommate. Iris had taken care of her in the days after Veronica went missing, bringing Martina endless mugs of hot milk with turmeric when she couldn't sleep, even painted her fingernails to cheer her up, mothered her. They'd found a companionable domestic rhythm and Martina never had to worry about coming home to a cavernous, echoing apartment. She was a lonely only. She hated to be alone. Iris seemed to feel the same.

Professor Lefebvre redirected the conversation again. 'You present several potential suspects in Veronica's demise, several men – including your ex-husband – who might have had motive to kill her. Do you have a particular theory?'

'Ah, the sixty-four-thousand-dollar question. I might,' Martina teased. 'But I'd need to call my lawyer before I told you.' She was going to see one of those men straight after this event but that wasn't for public consumption.

The audience murmured and giggled. Approval was Martina's drug of choice and when the audience was with her, the electric feel was better than sex. Veronica's approval had been Class A, of course, but she'd take the garden variety.

Professor Lefebvre pushed a stray hair back into her bob.

'Has the success of the book surprised you? Do you think you've shown the true Veronica to the world?'

Martina's expression sobered. 'If you make someone feel, if a reader connects with your story and perhaps, even, it sheds light on something in their own lives – that's the whole reason behind writers doing what we do. *That's* success.'

'Indeed,' agreed the professor. 'Let's open up questions to the audience.'

The next thirty minutes raced by, Martina still feeling mostly detached, answering on autopilot, the stream of questions benign. Finally, Professor Lefebvre took back the microphone.

'The last question I must ask is: what's next for Martina Torres? Can we expect a follow-up?'

What's next? The question all writers dread.

Martina did have another book under contract but no clue what to write about. What else could she possibly write about that would be as captivating as Veronica Hawkins?

Herself? Ha.

Smile turning brittle, 'Now I do have to play coy,' Martina replied.

'We'll be waiting with bated breath for the announcement.'

'And don't forget to pre-order from your favourite independent bookstore.' She winked at the audience.

'Which today is the illustrious Shakespeare & Co.,' Professor Lefebvre jumped in. 'The signing table is prepared at the back of the *salle. Merci à tous d'être venus.* Thank you again to the audience for coming and a huge round of applause for this illuminating discussion with Martina Torres.'

Blood roared in Martina's ears as she prepared herself for the inevitable onslaught of small talk during the signing. She was grateful for the reader support, she was, but she was already preoccupied with her next engagement.

With her destination near the Fontainebleau Forest and the confrontation lying in wait. She couldn't help but feel like she was setting out for grandmother's house.

Men are coming to slaughter you.

Into the Woods

$\mathcal{M}$artina watched the city streak by as her chauffeured Mercedes carried her towards the outskirts of Paris. It was easy to lose yourself here. Paris was the antithesis of Hong Kong. Here, everyone strolled. No one was in too much of a rush to forego another kir or pastis. The city was backward-looking, a living museum.

Martina had been surprised and mildly alarmed when Jean-Pierre left a message at her hotel asking to see her. They'd hardly exchanged a word since Veronica's funeral.

What could he want? After all this time?

She fidgeted with her bracelet, then pressed the button to lower the window. A Vespa zoomed past.

Jean-Pierre had fled Hong Kong once news of his gambling debts hit the tabloids. Once the whispers of his potential involvement — or, at the very least, his potential culpability — in Veronica's death had reached a fever pitch. Martina hadn't revealed anything in her memoir that wasn't already in the public record, that wasn't already on everyone's lips.

Not really.

Still, Martina suspected Jean-Pierre hadn't been best pleased with her disclosure of what had transpired the night of the Hungry Ghost festival. When Martina's literary agent had signed her, she insisted that the book needed a better structure. There had to be clear heroes and villains, red herrings and suspects.

Don't lie, of course, she'd said. *Let's not do a James Frey. It's simply a matter of guiding the reader through the story, letting them draw their own conclusions.*

Jamie Jackson hailed from a working-class family in the north of England and had risen through the ranks of London's elitist publishing industry before founding her own agency in Manchester. She'd reached out after Martina's essay about losing Veronica had gone viral. Martina hadn't known how to take it when Jamie described her prose style as 'Jan Morris for American Soccer Moms' but she'd gotten her a six-figure advance and that's what counted.

Jamie knew what would sell, the story harried women in supermarket checkout lines were most likely to add to their carts full of baby wipes and Chardonnay. *Give them glamour, intrigue – everyone needs glamour in their lives.* Martina wanted to do Veronica justice in her writing, that much was heartfelt, she simply selected the details that would create the most tantalising story, doled out the breadcrumbs and let the reader gobble them up.

They'd had a wild ride together, her and Veronica, and when it abruptly came to an end, Martina was left devastated. If she massaged the truth a little bit, well . . . Veronica would understand. She'd lived her life unapologetically. Martina liked to think she'd approve of the memoir, be proud of how much their time together had transformed her.

What would Veronica do?

Her friend's advice was inevitably pragmatic rather than dogmatic. Yet an acid backwash coated Martina's tongue as the car traversed the Boulevard Montparnasse past the famous cemetery and catacombs housing centuries' worth of dead. Her journey continued south through the Quartier Asiatique, its signage in Chinese characters reassuring, making Martina even more eager to board her Cathay Pacific flight home.

Crossing the *périphérique* – the city limits of Paris – the car pulled onto the autoroute and picked up speed. She closed her eyes, letting the hum of the tyres on the road soothe her. Jean-Pierre had taken up residence in a chateau outside Barbizon that Veronica had left him in her will. The village of Barbizon had been popular with artists for a couple centuries now. Perhaps the chateau was all Jean-Pierre had wanted. He must not be running too low on funds these days since he'd sent his chauffeur for Martina.

The driver informed her that the journey would be just over an hour and soon enough they were turning on to a smaller maze of roads. Acorn-laden oaks and evergreens towered above them, thick with verdant leaves and sharp needles, the woods growing denser as the car plunged further into the countryside. Downy hairs on Martina's neck lifted as cold sunlight caressed the side of her face.

There was one significant detail Martina had omitted from her memoir. It had been so easy to take a red pen to history, erase an unforgivable mistake, correct her tragic flaw – dissolve it with lye. A secret she'd been waiting to be punished for.

Ten minutes later, the driver made an abrupt right at a blink-and-you-miss-it exit on to a long, narrow lane. The forest encroached, dark and alluring. Martina could have sworn she spied a stag from the corner of her eye.

'Château Vert,' the taciturn chauffeur announced as the seventeenth-century structure came into view. It was more ostentatious than any of Veronica's homes in Hong Kong. Four rounded towers of pale stone were perforated by arched Gothic windows outlined in red brick and topped with conical roofs like witches' hats. Ivy dripped from the balustrades. Martina could easily picture the Sun King frolicking here with his Musketeers while waiting for Versailles to be finished.

The Mercedes slithered its way down the serpentine drive, gravel crunching, making Martina think of bones being ground to dust.

She swallowed her Nicorette gum and reapplied her lipstick.

With a slight jolt, the car stopped in front of a stone fountain. Martina stepped out before the driver could open the door for her.

The Three Graces were bathing together, naked and smirking. Charm was splashing Beauty and Creativity – or she would have been if the water had been bubbling. Instead, a fetid smell rose from the filmy green substance that had formed along its surface.

The portly driver motioned towards the chateau. 'Monsieur Renard has left the door open for you.'

Martina would always be too much of a New Yorker to leave her door unlocked. She contrived a smile for the chauffeur and gathered her courage.

Marching up the steps, the wind whistled by her. The door was indeed ajar: heavy wood studded with iron bolts, resembling a drawbridge.

'Hello?' Martina called out.

Her chest tightened as she crossed the threshold, suddenly aware of how very alone she was. She hadn't told anyone where she was going. No one would notice she had vanished until it was too late. She grabbed her iPhone from her Birkin bag and checked the reception – a meagre two bars.

Don't be stupid, Piggy.

Jean-Pierre wasn't some madman who'd lured her to a remote estate to take his revenge. If he'd wanted payback for his portrayal in Martina's memoir, he had a much more effective weapon in his arsenal. She inhaled a deliberate breath, eyes circling the entrance hall.

Her gaze landed on a bas-relief coat of arms. A hawk unfurled its wings, ready to capture its prey. But theirs would be a mutually assured destruction.

'*Allo? C'est moi*, Martina!'

The floorboards creaked as a dark figure began to emerge from the shadows.

'I didn't think you'd come,' rasped a distinctively French voice.

'You invited me.'

Jean-Pierre's lips lifted in a wry expression as he stepped into the light.

He ran a hand through his hair, now entirely grey — nearly white — tied back in a ponytail at the nape of his neck. It looked greasy. In her memory, Jean-Pierre was always insouciant and immaculate. His tanned complexion had faded under European skies, grown sallow, his cheeks gaunt, his lips papery. His linen shirt was rumpled, stained.

As he leaned forward to give Martina a welcome kiss, something caught her eye at the edge of his widow's peak. Without thinking, she touched the spot and her forefinger came away dark red.

'Are you hurt?'

The Frenchman's laughter held the rumble of thunder, the rattling of windows in a storm, the metallic whir of a zipper, the rustle of sheets. Martina shivered.

'Paint, *ma puce*,' he reassured her.

Martina rubbed her forefinger and her thumb together, the substance smooth and sticky. Oil paint. She sucked in a breath.

'Your concern is touching,' Jean-Pierre said and Martina didn't know if he was still laughing at her or being sincere. Gently, he took her hand and cleaned off the paint with his shirt tail. A slight paunch poked at his waistband. His eyes dropped to the jade bangle but he said nothing.

'Thank you. You didn't have to ruin your shirt.'

'*Bof.* All my shirts are ruined. Come, I'll show you my studio before we eat.'

He gave Martina a long look, assessing. His black eyes no longer glinted. The past echoed in the dark voids.

Whatever happened to the portrait you did of Veronica when you first met?

It's upstairs. In my bedroom.

You sleep in separate bedrooms?

Veronica has nightmares. She doesn't like anyone to see her lose control.

Martina followed Jean-Pierre through the dimly lit rooms, most of the furniture draped beneath white sheets as if the house were vacant. There was no noise but the squeak of the occasional hinge.

'How long have you lived here?' Martina asked, her voice too loud.

'Since my return.'

Which had been nearly four years ago. 'It doesn't look like you've even moved in.'

Jean-Pierre grunted. 'It's too much house for one man.'

A gale howled in her memory, bayed. Martina was walking down a different corridor in a different life.

You have beautiful bones. If only she had slipped her hand from his grasp. *Your husband doesn't know how to appreciate you. He's not an artist, like us.*

Switching subjects, Martina said, 'I read about your exhibition at the Louis Vuitton Foundation. Congratulations.' The violent seascapes that she'd seen online were in a different league from the poodle portraits Jean-Pierre had churned out in Hong Kong, although the reviews were more concerned with his personal tragedy.

'You are *sympa*. The curator is a friend. He keeps pestering me to spend more time in Paris, show in more galleries.'

'Why not move into Paris, then? You must get lonely out here by yourself.'

Looking over his shoulder at Martina, Jean-Pierre replied, 'This is where she wanted me to be.'

He reached back, taking Martina's hand and tugged her forward, forcing her to quicken her pace.

'Besides, in Paris, I couldn't have this,' he said.

Diffuse light drenched a conservatory that must have been added to the chateau in the last century.

And everywhere Martina looked, she saw Veronica.

Veronica dancing. Veronica swimming. Veronica reclining on a chaise longue, a come-hither look in her eye.

Martina walked to the middle of the studio and spun slowly on the spot.

Happy Veronica, hazel irises bright. Angry Veronica, red lips a gash on her face, auburn hair a tempest. Dreaming Veronica, eyes closed and serene.

Canvas, after canvas, after canvas.

Martina's mouth grew parched. Large and small, there must have been a hundred canvases in all. Veronica watched Martina from every corner in the room.

Her friend could see everything from where she was now. Sailor stripes in a puddle on the floor – a dress Martina never wore again – her husband slipping it over Martina's head, kissing each vertebrae of her spine, whispering *You deserve to be worshipped*, her pain a beast that demanded to be fed.

'Veronica never wanted me to paint her after that first time,' Jean-Pierre murmured. He had moved behind Martina, his chest close enough to her back for her to feel his breath, his heat. 'We've both created portraits of my wife that come from our imaginations.'

With a sigh, he mused, 'I wonder if any of these portraits would make her fall in love with me again?'

'I wonder if she'd still want to be my friend.' The words came out more broken than Martina had intended.

'I'm not sure Veronica was ever your friend.'

Martina whipped around, right hand curling into a loose fist. 'Maybe I didn't deserve her but she *was* my friend.'

She had to believe it. If only she'd known what Veronica had in store for her, how she would change her life, Martina wouldn't have let her weakness overwhelm her. She wouldn't have stolen a few hours of solace, a temporary refuge.

She *wouldn't*. It wasn't worth the trade.

'Veronica trusted me with Lulu's foundation,' Martina insisted to Jean-Pierre. 'She put me in charge because she was my friend.'

'As you say.'

Let him think what he wanted. Veronica saw something in Martina nobody else had, pushed Martina towards her potential. She wished she'd had the chance to ask Veronica for forgiveness. Making the foundation a success was her attempt to earn it. Her penance.

Jean-Pierre pulled a pack of cigarettes from his trouser pocket and the aroma of cloves permeated the air. He patted the end against his other palm, then offered her one.

'I quit,' Martina told him.

'I tried giving up my vices for Veronica.' Fishing out a match-book, chocolate-brown cigarette dangling from his mouth, he said. *'Quoi faire?'*

The crow's feet that Martina had once found attractive on Jean-Pierre had deepened into grooves, a rockface worn down by trickling water.

Martina strolled towards a half-finished canvas, different from the others. This one sketched a villa surrounded by jungle, its design similar to those in the south of France except for the high-peaked wooden roof, the gold-leafed shingles resembling wings. Resting on the easel was a weathered snapshot showing Veronica aged eleven or twelve on the villa's liana-strewn veranda.

She pursed her lips. 'Is this in Hong Kong?'

'No, Laos. Her mother's childhood summer home.'

Glancing from the outline of the little girl, wraith-like, to Jean-Pierre, she said, 'Veronica never mentioned it to me.'

'You didn't know her very long.' He took a drag, exhaling the sweet-smelling smoke in Martina's direction. Lifting a shoulder, he said, 'I think the place was sold right after Veronica's parents died.'

Martina flushed, hating that he was right. What she didn't know about Veronica could fill a book. She had wanted to know more. She had wanted to know everything.

Now Veronica would remain forever out of reach.

'Why did you ask me here?' Martina snapped at Jean-Pierre.

'Why did you come?'

Their gazes locked. The quiet grew painful. Martina plucked the cigarette from his lips, her eyes never leaving his, and put it to her own. She inhaled deliberately, the rush going straight to her head.

Giving into temptation was inevitably far sweeter than the temptation itself. Martina felt sixteen again, drinking blackberry brandy in
the girls locker room at Buxton, half hoping to get expelled.

'I needed that,' she admitted and Jean-Pierre snorted, shaking
his head.

'This is how I'd paint you,' he said. 'The real Martina. Not the
girl from your book.'

Her stomach dropped. Everyone liked Memoir Martina so much
better. She was nicer, funnier, cleverer. She was the woman Martina
had aspired to be her whole life.

She'd almost forgotten she wasn't her. But Jean-Pierre was a
skilled portrait artist.

'I didn't destroy the sketch you made of my hands.'

'*Non?*'

'No.' Martina sucked and the embers flared.

She'd wanted to blow up her life that night – before Spencer had
the chance. *She* wanted to be the one to pull the pin on the grenade.
It was selfish and cruel but, in the moment, it had felt like her only
ounce of power.

Martina kept the sketch to remind herself how close she'd come
to ruining everything. Her own private scarlet letter.

With an exhale, 'I'm sorry if the memoir made things more
. . . difficult for you,' she told Jean-Pierre. 'You never talked to the
press. You never told anyone about . . .' Martina nodded at the space
between them.

He trailed one finger along her jaw and stole the cigarette back.

'Life is difficult, *ma puce*. The ghosts have it easy.' He flicked the
ash on to the floor. 'I was losing my wife *petit à petit* before she died.
The more she pushed me away, the more reckless I became.'

Desperation sent him running to Macau. Desperation sent him
running to Martina. There was honesty in desperation, at least, but
no relief. She knew it all too well. She'd needed to be worshipped
into oblivion more than she'd cared about vows or friendship.

Jean-Pierre twiddled the cigarette. 'What I will never under-stand is what happened to Veronica during the festival. Vasco swore to me that he could find out nothing and he is a man who knows everything.' He stared at Martina hard. '*Dites-moi la vérité*. You know nothing more than what's in the book?'

'I'm sorry, Jean-Pierre. Veronica wouldn't tell me any of the details. I told the police everything I know. I promise you I did.'

He threw the cigarette to the ground, stamping it out.

'*Alors, c'est fini*. We are both alone now . . . with our regrets.'

'We are.'

Martina jumped as a shrill sound sliced through the conserva-tory. It took her a moment to recognise her ringtone.

'Sorry,' she said. Jean-Pierre waved vaguely and reached for his cigarettes.

Fumbling for the phone, Martina flipped it over to see the Caller ID. The call was coming from the Lourdes Hawkins Foundation – but it was nearly 9 p.m. in Hong Kong. Nobody at the foundation ever worked this late.

'Martina Torres,' she answered. Apprehension tightened her throat.

The line crackled.

'Oh, thank goodness. I'm so sorry to bother you in France but this is . . . this is an emergency. Peony Huang was here earlier and she needs to speak with you right away . . . and I told her you were in France but she said that she doesn't care where you are and I . . . I couldn't reach my boss and . . .'

Martina didn't recognise the young-sounding female voice on the other end of the line but she was clearly panicked, talking a million miles an hour. The mention of Peony Huang was enough to make Martina hyperventilate.

'Slow down,' Martina commanded. 'Who is this?'

'Oh, I'm so sorry. Oh goodness. I'm Priscilla Yip – I just started in the fundraising department.'

'Priscilla. Right. Tell me what's going on.'

'I . . . I don't know exactly . . . I'm sure it's not true . . . I mean, it can't be true . . .'

'Priscilla, what did Peony Huang say?' Martina spat.

'She said that the foundation accounts don't add up. Something about the annual gala. That someone is embezzling. And . . . she thinks it's you.'

Beneath her silk-crêpe suit, Martina's skin began to itch. It had been years since her anxiety had provoked hives. She was going to be sick.

'Listen to me very carefully,' she told Priscilla in the icy WASP tone her ex-mother-in-law had used on her. 'There has been a misunderstanding. Does anyone else know about Peony Huang's concerns?'

'No, I don't think so.'

'Let's keep it that way. Don't breathe a word of this to anyone – not your boss, not anyone. Do you understand?'

'Ye . . . yes.'

'Good. I'm getting on the next flight to Hong Kong and everything will be sorted out. I want you to go home. Take the rest of the week off.'

Martina hung up. Her hands shook. She stared into the middle distance.

Peony Huang could destroy the foundation. She could destroy Martina before breakfast. There had been some huge mistake. There *had* to be. No one was going to take away everything she'd worked so hard for.

Martina had spent the last few years waiting for her *abuela*'s wrathful god to smite her for her sins, and it seemed the wait was over.

Who would want to destroy her? Who had the means and motive?

Not Spencer. He'd already chucked in banking for law school and got remarried to his high-school sweetheart Sloane de Graaf, to the absolute delight of the *New York Times*'s 'Sunday Styles' section.

If Quentin had taken issue with Martina's depiction of his predatory practices she didn't think he'd have waited more than a year to take action. Impulse control wasn't exactly his strong suit.

Cressida Wong gave her a distinctly cold shoulder when their paths crossed at social functions, but she hadn't asked Martina to step down from the Lifting Hope charity committee. How could she without seeming churlish? Besides, Martina hadn't painted Cressida in *such* a negative light.

Who, then? Some disgruntled foundation employee?

'Ça va?'

It took several moments before Jean-Pierre's voice filtered into her consciousness.

Things were pretty fucking far from OK.

'Just someone playing an April's Fool,' Martina lied, turning back to him. He didn't believe her, she could tell.

'Another smoke before you go?' he asked. Jean-Pierre held her gaze, need tangled with melancholy, and she knew what he was really asking.

What could it hurt? She felt the pull like a lariat, wrapping itself around her, tethering her to old habits.

'I'm desperate for one.'

Red Eye

*T*welve hours alone with her thoughts in a tin can in the sky did not a happy Martina make. Even if it was a first-class tin can and she was snuggled in a cashmere throw. She quaffed a couple too many French 75s with her Xanax, still only managing the occasional catnap. Withdrawing a sketch from her purse, she admired the cigarette drooped carelessly from disembodied lips.

One for the road was scrawled on the creamy, textured paper.

Martina's shrink would have had a field day with the fact she'd fabricated a phone call with her Papi in the memoir instead of what had actually happened that night. If she ever brought it up, that was. She could only trust her therapist with so much.

Availing herself of the freebies in her amenity kit, Martina rubbed the Jurlique hand cream over her knuckles like she was Lady Macbeth.

The scent of lemons filled her private cabin.

She loved nothing more than freebies. Her mother had taught her to help herself to the toiletries on the housekeeping trollies in fancy hotels. It wasn't like anyone would miss them. Martina filched free toothpaste samples at the dentist too — no doubt something else she should mention to her HKD 2500-an-hour shrink at the expat clinic on Queen's Road that looked more like a day spa. But, then, she'd once heard an irate white woman yell bloody murder at the receptionist for giving her helper the wrong prenatal vitamins for her surrogate, which made Martina feel like she had her head screwed on pretty straight.

Except that as she disembarked the 777 and began wheeling her Bottega Veneta trolley through Chek Lap Kok Airport, Martina's nausea sent her racing to the ladies room where she dry heaved in the disabled stall (which she preferred because they were roomier). She flinched as the hard square tiles impressed themselves into her knees, biting like baby teeth. Heart pounding, she scratched at the hives that had erupted beneath her travel Lululemons, a dark spot welling on the beige leggings.

The iPhone burned a hole in her pocket. As soon as she'd left Jean-Pierre at Château Vert, Martina had called Iris and told her to retrieve all of the files related to the annual gala from the foundation offices in Kennedy Town. She was afraid to switch off airplane mode.

What fresh hell would her inbox reveal?

The remnants of champagne, smoked duck and nicotine made their way up Martina's throat and she gagged. She'd caved and bought a pack of Gitanes at Charles de Gaulle.

In. Out. In. Out.

Through sheer force of will Martina peeled herself off the tile, straightened her spine and threw her shoulders back. She swiped at the moisture beneath her eyes. That's right, she was mindful as fuck. She would *not* fall apart. She had come too far.

'Let's go, Piggy,' she breathed.

Zipping through the automatic immigration gates with her HKID card, Martina felt a small surge of triumph as she watched the poor schlubs with raccoon eyes and screaming toddlers waiting in the non-resident queue. In no time, she was being shown to her town car and hurtling across the death-defying suspension bridge that connected Lantau Island to the Mainland, skyscraper-dense slopes rising on either side.

Hong Kong Island grew steadily closer and closer. There was no skyline like it. Despite her altered state, the expanse provoked an inward smile.

Veronica had propelled Martina into a new life, but Martina had made it a success on her own. When she walked into a room, she expected a warm welcome. Her parents defined friendships as useful relationships and here, in Hong Kong, Martina was very useful.

She couldn't give it up. Everyone deserved a home.

Clutching the armrest, Martina connected her phone to the Pacific Star mobile network. The telecoms company had until recently been the jewel in the Hawkins Pacific crown. Following Veronica's death a majority stake of her company had been sold to Barron Industries, which made it the jewel in Iain Barron's crown now, Martina supposed.

Veronica had never even hinted that the Hawkins empire had been in dire straits. Her house on the Peak, the private jet, the apartments around the globe had all belonged to the company and all of her assets had been liquidated shortly before her death. Barron Industries kept the branding for posterity, Elsie confessed to Martina, but the Hawkins Pacific *hong* now existed in name only.

Martina was glad, in a way, that Veronica hadn't lived to see the end of her dynasty.

And *swipe*. Let the email deluge begin.

Thirty minutes later, Martina cruised into the lobby of Starscape just before 9 a.m., even with the cross-harbour traffic, and asked the doorman sweetly if he wouldn't mind bringing her luggage upstairs while she got herself a triple espresso from the Italian café on Moon Street. She'd made sure her red packets were extra fat this Chinese New Year since moving back into the building. Martina still couldn't afford the penthouse she'd shared with Spencer, of course, but she could handle the rent on a one-bedroom with a hill view.

She'd wanted to be congratulated on her address again. So sue her.

Guzzling her espresso, bleary-eyed, Martina waited for the

elevator, already deciding to send Iris out for more caffeine. The brass doors slid open to reveal a bleach blonde in a short, skin-tight leopard-print dress, mascara flaking, toting her own wheelie. Well, it *was* Sunday morning. The woman stared through Martina and brushed past her close enough for Martina to get a whiff of a man's aftershave.

Martina hit the button for the eleventh floor and downed the bitter dregs of her espresso. No doubt Spencer had entertained similar guests here after she'd moved out.

Had Martina looked similarly bedraggled when she left Château Vert?

'Welcome home!' Iris shouted from the living room as Martina turned the key in the lock.

Ducking into the kitchen, she saw freshly prepared *torta* on the countertop. Martina usually allowed herself to eat the Filipino omelette with one teaspoon of banana ketchup but her stomach still gurgled from her ill-advised indulgences at thirty-five thousand feet. Instead, she grabbed one of the fluffy *pandesal* rolls that Iris picked up at World-Wide House every Sunday when she met up with her other helper friends.

Tearing off a chunk of white bread, Martina shoved it indelicately into her mouth.

Iris's brow furrowed, tiny creases appearing on her golden brown skin. The sight of Martina eating carbs was a worse indication of her mental state than snorting lines of coke from the Pilates-flat stomach of the bleach-blonde hooker in the elevator would have been. Iris stopped tapping at the laptop on the dining table.

'What did you find?' Martina said. God, she wanted another cigarette.

Iris pushed her glasses up the bridge of her nose. The Fendi cat's-eye frames suited her round face, making her look younger than her forty-eight years. They'd been a gift from Martina when Iris completed her diploma in secretarial studies at Hong Kong University.

Gesturing with the bread roll, '*Well?*' Martina demanded. She winced at the whine in her own voice.

'There is a problem,' Iris said with a swallow. 'I've looked at the itemised invoices for foundation galas the last three years running and there is a discrepancy between the listed hotel prices per item and what the events company charged the foundation.'

Iris coughed as Martina continued to glare, waiting for her to get to the point. 'For example,' she continued, 'the per-hour hire charge of the Dom Pedro V ballroom is double what it should be for the first annual gala. It's triple for the second annual gala. And it's quadruple for this year's gala in January.'

Martina let the carbs sink down her gullet. 'Almost as if someone was seeing what they could get away with. Increasing the prices each year, wondering if we'd notice.'

'That's what I thought too,' agreed Iris. 'Sneaky.'

'And clever.'

Because Martina hadn't noticed. She'd signed off on all of the expenses without scrutinising the invoices. She'd been so busy getting the foundation off the ground and trying to make the deadlines for her memoir – there'd been yet another email from her agent in her inbox this morning saying her publisher was getting restless about the proposal for her next book – that it hadn't occurred to Martina someone might be stealing from her. Ao Wing had offered to host the foundation gala at the Lusitano Palace in Veronica's honour, after making a seven-figure donation, and Martina had delegated all of the party details to a coterie of society ladies. What did she care about napkin rings or floral colour schemes?

Fuck.

'I presume they ran this racket with most of the expenses?' Martina said to Iris.

The other woman nodded. 'Especially the food and wine.'

Which made sense. All the gala guests were booze hounds. 'Print out the files, would you? I'm going to see Elsie.'

'Ms Elsie?'

'I want to see what she knows about the events company,' Martina replied. It amused her the way Iris always said Ms Elsie with a mix of respect and pity when she'd long stopped calling Martina 'Miss' anything.

She strolled towards her carry-on, opened the side pocket, and retrieved an itsy-bitsy Chanel shopping bag. 'Here.' Martina held it out to Iris. 'A souvenir from Paris. And now you've definitely earned it.'

Subsidising Iris's tuition for her diploma had been one of the best investments Martina ever made. Once she'd learned that Iris had painstakingly studied for the exams required to obtain a Hong Kong secondary school certificate on her own time over many years while working as a helper, it was a no-brainer. Iris was a go-getter with ambition for miles, and Martina admired that about her. She was ambitious yet kind.

The first Christmas after Veronica died, Martina was too busy to fly home to New York. She also hadn't wanted to take the risk of running into Spencer. Iris would normally go back to Manila for the holidays but, instead, she had her daughter come to Hong Kong. The three of them drank eggnog and sat around a virtual fire screensaver on the smart TV, singing about a White Christmas along with Bing Crosby.

Light caught on the gold-tone keychain as Iris dangled it from her finger.

'It's a Parisian street sign,' Martina informed her. 'Thirty-one rue Cambon is Coco Chanel's original boutique. I picked it up for you there especially.' In actual fact, Martina had picked it up at Duty Free, but white lies were like snowflakes – they made everything fresh and new.

'Thank you,' said Iris. 'It's very pretty.'

'Don't give it to Angelica,' Martina said with a knowing smile. She had a feeling most of the presents she'd given Iris had ended up in a box on their way to her daughter in Boracay.

Iris puckered her lips. 'I won't.'

'You deserve nice things too.'

'Yes.' She closed her hand loosely around the keychain. 'What are you going to do about the accounting irregularities?'

Martina let out a long sigh. 'I'm relieved that's all it is, truth be told. I'm going to talk to Elsie and then I'm going to have a nice long chat with the events company.' She rubbed her temples, which had started to throb during the car ride from the airport.

'Would you be a saint and run out to San Marco's and get me another triple espresso while I take a quick shower?' Its logo was a winged lion and everything.

Iris gave her what could only be interpreted as a maternal look of disapproval.

'You should eat some *torta*.'

'*Pleeease.*'

The other woman huff-laughed. 'Fine, fine.'

'I wouldn't survive without you, Iris.'

Her right-hand woman placated Martina with a smile.

'No, you wouldn't.'

Halcyon Days

*A*scending the Peak felt like travelling to another world, a rarefied environment where Martina merely clung on to the cliffs' edges. She leaned back in the red-and-white as it zig-zagged its way past the High Court and the US Consulate, climbing the Mid-Levels. If you looked closely, you could spot graffiti in the shape of umbrellas on government buildings, which were regularly scrubbed clean only to reappear soon thereafter. Most of the Hong Kong elite with whom Martina socialised were more annoyed by the disruption to their daily lives caused by the occupation of Central than the lack of genuine democracy.

Nobody believed 'one country, two systems' was going any-where. The students were getting worked up over nothing, they'd gripe. Nor did the Western bankers believe their playground would be taken away, either. Martina kept her mouth shut when the topic came up at cocktail parties. No point in alienating the foundation's donors. Besides, the foundation had organised an exhibition of pro-test art by members of the Umbrella Movement. She'd done her bit for freedom of speech.

Wintry-grey clouds descended as the taxi drew closer to the Barron family mansion. Whenever Martina couldn't sleep, she'd end up down an internet rabbit hole obsessively researching something – a habit formed in the days of *Encyclopædia Britannica* and a flashlight. One night recently it was cloud classifications. These were cumulus mediocris, if she wasn't mistaken, but she wouldn't let on to any of the Peak dwellers.

Elsie's 'bungalow' was at the top of Mount Kellett and she, like Veronica, had been born at the chichi Matilda Hospital at its foot. Rockyda Manor was among the first mansions built as summer homes to beat the heat of Central in the mid-nineteenth century and it retained its original name. If the price tags of other houses on their road were any indication, today it was worth around 100 million greenbacks.

There was a reason Hongkongers called the neighbourhood 'wealth mountain'. Hard to imagine colonists had once considered farming it. Maybe for money trees.

Martina's iPhone started vibrating in her pocket. *No Caller ID.*

'This is Martina,' she said with more than a little trepidation.

'Good morning, Martina. My office says you've been trying to reach me.'

She nearly dropped the phone.

'Yes, yes – Peony, hi. Th-thanks so much for returning my call.'

'I assume you called to tell me you've located the missing funds.'

'I . . . I have found some accounting irregularities in the expenses for the gala and—'

'Tell me something I don't know.' The tycoon's voice was dry ice.

'It looks like the problem lies with the events company. I'm in the process of investigating further . . .' As Martina rambled, she heard tinny announcements in English and Mandarin from Peony's end.

'I'm boarding a flight for San Francisco. You have until I get back to straighten out your mess or I'll get the authorities involved.'

'There's no need to—'

'You are either corrupt or incompetent, Martina. You signed the cheques. As you Americans like to say, the buck stops with you.'

The line went dead.

Martina's teeth clacked together and a new wave of hives erupted beneath her linen trousers.

The taxi came to an abrupt halt outside Rockyda Manor.

Martina gave the driver an excessive tip, a slight tremble in her hand, pretending just for a moment that this was her home, revelling in the fantasy the driver might believe it. But as she rang the bell she knew she was far closer to a door-to-door salesman.

One of Elsie's fleet of helpers showed her to the terrace and its jaw-dropping view of Victoria Harbour below.

'Martina! Come and tell me all about Paris!'

Elsie waved as she poured herself tea from a celadon pot that likely belonged in the V&A. Martina waved back. She was glad to see her.

It's funny who steps up when the chips are down. Veronica's death had drawn them together. They hadn't been particularly close in the months leading up to the fateful gala, but over the last few years, Elsie had repeatedly come through for Martina. They'd grieved together and Elsie had become her most trusted confidante in Hong Kong. Partially because Elsie was as lonely as she was. Martina hadn't exaggerated her depiction of the bereft strawberry-blonde in her memoir and, thankfully, Elsie had never raised any objections.

Martina planted a peck on either of her cheeks and seated herself in one of the white, wrought-iron chairs.

'Tea?' asked Elsie.

'Do you have anything stronger?'

Elsie chuckled. 'You must be exhausted.' Catching the eye of someone hovering just inside the patio doors, she said, 'A pot of coffee, please.'

'Much appreciated.' Martina dropped her Birkin bag into the chair beside hers, undid the clasp and set an Eiffel Tower-shaped plush toy on the table.

'For me? You shouldn't have.'

With a snort, Martina said, 'Where's my goddaughter?'

'Oh, the pint-sized she-demon is around here somewhere,' Elsie told her, shrugging. 'No doubt terrorising Nanny with her older brother and sister.'

Martina had been beyond touched when Elsie had asked her to be godmother to little Fiona – whose existence she'd learned about on the night Veronica died. At first, she'd been hesitant, but Elsie wouldn't be dissuaded. She would have asked Veronica if she were alive, she'd said, and Veronica's best friend was the next best thing.

'Fifi is an angel and I won't hear a word against her!' Martina insisted with faux outrage. She was far better suited to the role of godmother. She had no regrets about the miscarriage, especially given how things had ended with Spencer. Her agent, however, had thought it might be better if Memoir Martina had a few.

'Do you have any photos of Fifi from the Easter recital I missed?' Martina said. 'Wasn't she playing a bunny?'

Elsie laughed. 'You didn't miss anything. And she was playing a rabbit – Fifi was very insistent she was a rabbit and *not* a bunny.'

'I'm so terribly sorry.'

Feigning the reluctance of a parent eager to share photos of their child, Elsie whipped out her iPhone. Martina gushed appropriately but it wasn't an act. She adored her goddaughter. She was merely ambivalent about having her own. What did Martina know about being a good mother? Hers liked to gripe about how clingy she'd been as a baby. Anette Torres also preferred dried flowers to fresh because they didn't require watering. Once Martina had become an asset, she was loved, rewarded.

Lifting her teacup, Elsie narrowed her pale blue eyes at Martina, saying, 'I didn't think we'd see you until you'd slept off the jetlag.' Even if Elsie didn't have the same sparkle as Veronica, she'd cared enough to learn Martina's quirks, to pay more than lip service to their friendship.

'Normally, you wouldn't,' Martina agreed. But there was nothing normal about these circumstances. 'You see, the thing is—'

A frail, lost-sounding voice interrupted Martina.

'Rupert? Rupert!'

Philippa Barron hurried out to the terrace, shuffling in a shaky manner. Her silver-blonde hair hung loose around her shoulders. She was garbed in an embroidered silk dressing gown. Her gaze, unfocused, swung from Martina to Elsie, confusion gripping her features.

'Elsie, where's your father?' she said, frustration plain. 'Is he out with Iain?'

Elsie clamped her lips together, a nerve ticking at one corner of her mouth.

'Yes, Mum. I think he went out with Iain a little while ago.'

'Bloody man never tells me where he's going.' She shook her head wildly. The once proud matriarch turned her attention towards Martina. 'You girls don't be late for school.'

'We won't,' Martina promised. At that moment a middle-aged Filipina woman in a nurse's uniform appeared and shepherded the elderly woman back inside.

Elsie dabbed at the tears leaking from her eyes in silence. She stared down at the city below, at the frothy wakes of ships rushing towards the South China Sea.

Martina doubted she was seeing any of it.

'It's been a rough couple of days,' Elsie said after a minute. 'It's getting worse. Sometimes Mum doesn't remember Daddy is dead – and I've stopped telling her.'

She blinked twice. 'The first time I did, and I had to watch her lose him all over again. I won't put her through that over and over. Why should I?' True bitterness crept into Elsie's voice. 'It's the worst kind of torture.'

'Of course not. You're doing the kindest thing,' Martina reassured her.

'You think so?'

'I do. Absolutely.'

'Thank you. You never expect to become your parent's parent. I don't think I'm doing anything right.' Elsie gave herself a shake. 'Now you know why Mum hasn't been to any big events lately.

The old Philippa couldn't stand to have anyone gossip about her. Certainly no pity.'

Gone was the grande dame she'd met at the FCC Ball what seemed like a lifetime ago. 'Nobody will hear it from me,' Martina promised, leaning towards her and giving her elbow a squeeze.

'I know I can trust you, Marty. More than anyone.' Elsie talked to her teacup. 'I should have told you why I moved back into Rockyda,' she said, releasing a long breath. 'Dex didn't want to live with his in-laws when we were married, but he's in Singapore all the time and I don't want to leave Mum alone with the nurses and helpers. Sometimes she forgets who they are and calls the police.'

Martina gave her elbow another pat. 'And what about Iain?' she prodded. 'Is he pitching in?'

Elsie's younger brother was Fifi's godfather and there had been chatter in the society pages that he and Martina were dating following the christening at St John's. He'd never shown Martina the slightest bit of romantic interest, however. Or anyone else, for that matter – not since Veronica died.

Elsie threw her hands in the air. 'He's a man.'

'Enough said.'

Nodding to herself, Elsie asked, 'What were you about to tell me when Mum came out?'

'Oh . . . I don't want to bother you . . . you have a lot on your plate . . .'

'Please, bother me. *Bother* me. I need some distraction.'

'If you're sure?'

Elsie canted her head. 'I'm not made of glass.'

Martina drew in a steadying breath, reached into her purse and whipped out the files Iris had compiled, handing them to Elsie. 'How about this for distraction?' she said.

Starting to sift through them, Elsie quirked her lips. 'What am I looking at?'

'Peony Huang thinks I've been embezzling from the foundation.'

'Excuse me?' Elsie gawked at her, shock filling her eyes. For a second, Martina panicked. Then she said, 'You would *never* do that. You don't have a dishonest bone in your body.'

Martina laughed and it was a tad hysterical. 'Maybe a pinkie – but I didn't commit fraud.'

'The very thought is outlandish,' Elsie agreed. 'So, what are these papers?'

'Iris found accounting irregularities in the expenses for the annual gala. It seems the events company has been overcharging us quite substantially.'

'Iris really is a gem.' Elsie's lips curved in a fond smile. 'I told you that you needed her.'

'And you were right. Do you know anything about this company?' Martina asked. 'Xtasy Events?'

'Hmm . . . that does sound familiar.' Elsie lounged back against her chair, cogitating. 'Oh! I know. It's the same company Cressida used for the Lifting Hope gala.'

'*The* gala?'

'Yes, *the* gala.'

Martina's tongue grew dry. Could there be some kind of connection between the embezzlement and the night Veronica went overboard?

It seemed preposterous. Life wasn't a murder mystery. Yes, Veronica had a lot of enemies, but Martina didn't believe someone had actually plotted an elaborate scheme to toss her overboard, not in reality. For some time now, Martina had been convinced that her extremely drunk friend had suffered a tragic accident. It being an accident made it worse – no rhyme or reason. At least murder would have been intentional. Purposeful. Given her loved ones some closure. Given Martina someone to blame . . . besides herself . . .

'Oh, Martina,' said Elsie. 'You look like someone walked over your grave.'

She shivered. 'I wonder if Xtasy Events overcharged Lifting Hope as well?' Was there a pattern or was someone just after Martina?

'I suppose you'll have to ask Cressida.'

'She'll be delighted.'

With a frown, Elsie offered, 'If you're not comfortable, I could talk to Cressida for you?'

'No, no. It's kind of you, but I'm a big girl.' *Incompetent or corrupt*, Peony had said. She wasn't wrong. But Martina would fix this.

She *had* to fix this.

Martina's fingers twitched involuntarily, jonesing for a hit of nicotine. 'What I don't understand,' she said, 'is who told Peony Huang?'

'Could be anyone.' Elsie's tone was unbothered. 'Peony has spies everywhere. How else did she become Peony Huang with a capital P?'

'I just don't know who would want to come after me like this,' said Martina, worrying her lip with her front tooth. 'I'm not important enough for anyone to target.'

Elsie took her hand, her grip firm, almost painfully so.

'You're important to me, Martina. Whatever you need, I'm here for you.'

Off to the Races

The wet, hot Hong Kong summer had started early this year. It had rained nonstop for the past few days as Martina tried in vain to reach Cressida Wong, who was clearly dodging her calls. At last she'd heard through a mutual friend that Cressida had returned yesterday from a duty visit to her mother-in-law in Chongqing and would be at the races tonight.

Barron Industries had a corporate membership to the Hong Kong Jockey Club and, as a Christmas present, Elsie had generously added Martina to their nominated members. Elsie was also an accomplished rider who stabled her horses with the club. Horses made Martina skittish – she pictured herself trampled under their hooves – but she'd never admit it.

Being Bitsy's only actual friend at Buxton, Martina had been a regular weekend sleepover guest at the Butterfield Estate in the Berkshires. She was viewed as something between playmate and hired help, but Bitsy insisted she be taught to ride with her at the family stables. Martina had mastered the trot, canter and gallop, sitting in her English saddle with surprising ease. Unfortunately, she was thrown quite badly going over her first proper jump, dislocating her shoulder.

Her parents would never dream of suing the Butterfields – oh no. Martina's mother had simply given her a few of her own Percocets and insisted she go to Bitsy's the following weekend. With no other choice, Martina got back on the horse. Yet the fear lingered.

The constant pitter-patter of rain began letting up as the taxi approached Happy Valley. Horns screeched as traffic slowed to a crawl. Rumour had it the wealthier residents of the ironically named valley didn't want an MTR stop because it would make it too easy for the wrong sort to swarm the neighbourhood on race night. As it was, Wednesday night meant gridlock and Martina was on her last nerve. She only half listened as the driver complained about the incompetent Hong Kong chief executive in English and Cantonese.

Just when she thought she would burst, the floodlights of the racecourse illuminated the sky, a beacon for those down on their luck. Growing up, from the window of her dollhouse-sized Manhattan kitchen, if Martina squinted, she could make out the lights of Yankee Stadium in the Bronx during home games. These lights were blinding in comparison. The hills that glowered above the racecourse were cast in shadow against the purpling horizon.

Martina paid the fare and hopped out into the throng of racing enthusiasts. Posters around the city urged responsible gambling but the Hong Kong Jockey Club was the biggest taxpayer in the Special Administrative Region despite being a non-profit organisation. Horse racing was the lifeblood of Hong Kong, something everyone could enjoy and agree on, and even Deng Xiaoping had promised not to interfere with the ponies after the Handover.

Electricity crackled around Martina as she made her way through the crowd. The atmosphere was charged, a combination of hope and despair, the sense that fortunes could change in under a minute. Racegoers squawked at their bookies on their cell phones, picking their horses through a strange alchemy of instinct, numerology and feng shui. Everyone had their formula and nobody shared. Martina passed by the grandstand, the ambience somewhere between glitzy and seedy. It was early enough in the evening that no one was too dead-eyed yet.

Martina placed her bets based on the horse's name, ignoring the odds, which her Hongkonger friends told her was all wrong. She'd won 10-1 on a horse named El Grande her first time at the track, however, so she kept to her system. She had her own alchemy too. But Martina had no interest in betting on the ponies tonight.

She was already gambling for much higher stakes.

The thunder of hooves resounded in her mind as she entered one of the Members Suites, on the hunt for Cressida Wong.

She found her quarry on a balcony overlooking the track, amidst a gaggle of society ladies in an array of brightly coloured frocks that reminded Martina of rainbow sherbet. She could hear the silk rustle, like the feathers of tropical birds, as they gossiped and tipped back champagne. Several heads cocked and eyes shuttered as Martina meandered toward them casually, purposefully.

'If it isn't the Bestseller. What are you doing here?'

She met Cressida's glare head on, forcing her shoulders not to curl forward.

'Hello, Cressida.' A thin smile on her lips, Martina shifted her gaze from Cressida to her companion. 'Evelyn.' To the third woman she only vaguely recognised, she said, 'I'm Martina.'

'I know who you are,' replied the woman in pistachio-green Pucci. She imbibed her champagne without introducing herself.

Martina flashed back to the Buxton school bus, when Tinsley Palmer told her all of her clothes were worthless because they didn't come from Bonpoint. A prickle travelled the length of Martina's spine. The crowd below roared as the winner crossed the finish line. Cressida's dark brown eyes continued to bore into hers.

Suppressing a gulp, Martina said, 'I've been seeing *Eight-Five-Two* magazine everywhere. It's the must-read for the jet set. Congratulations to both of you.'

'I am Editor Evelyn, aren't I?' Evelyn's smile was razor-sharp.

'Indeed you are,' Martina agreed with a laugh. No one laughed along. 'The app looks great too.'

'I'm surprised you've seen it. I thought my little publication was too far beneath you.' Cressida's tone was flat. After Martina had turned down the job, Cressida poached Evelyn and then bought the entire *HK City Chic* publishing group.

'Don't be silly. I love the rebranding you've done with *Eight-Five-Two*.'

'What a relief. Your opinion is so very important to me,' said Cressida. Evelyn and the woman in green sniggered. 'Well, this has been fun, but I need to find my husband in our box. Our *private* box.'

Cressida's minions took their cue to strut back inside. 'For the record,' said Evelyn over her shoulder, 'I'm #TeamCressida.'

As if she couldn't tell. Ignoring the barb, Martina placed a hand on Cressida's elbow as she started to walk away. 'Wait,' she said. 'I need to ask you about something.'

'You always need something, Martina.'

Lowering her voice, she said, 'It's about Xtasy Events.'

'Xtasy Events?' Confusion scrunched Cressida's features. 'What about them?'

'I think they've been overcharging the foundation for the annual gala,' Martina admitted, clenching the jade bangle around her wrist. 'I was wondering if you'd noticed any accounting irregularities for the Lifting Hope galas?'

She pursed her lips. 'We haven't held a gala since the junk trip – as you well know.'

'What about for *that* gala?'

Cressida held her gaze, her bravado faltering for a single moment, before retorting, 'I've never noticed anything. Besides, I'm not the one you should be talking to.' She scoffed. 'Go interrogate Quentin Turner. He was Veronica's great and good friend.'

Something clenched painfully in Martina's stomach. 'What does Quentin Turner have to do with anything?'

Cressida looked at her like she was an idiot. 'He owns Xtasy Events.'

'He does?' The question was a whisper.

A high-pitched laugh spilled from Cressida's lips. 'Veronica loved to collect followers and that's what you are, Martina.'

The uncomfortable burn of tears scratched at her eyes. Martina wasn't some hanger-on. She'd earned her place.

'But Veronica's gone,' Cressida continued, 'and you'll never be her. You'll never come close.'

'Neither will you,' Martina hissed as her chest tightened.

Cressida snarled a smile. '*I* wouldn't want to be Veronica. The old taipans are done. The sun has very much set on them.' She raised her champagne flute and drained it. 'This is not your world. You're nothing but a parasite.'

Cressida tilted her head towards the exit.

'Go home, *Marty*.'

Only one text message was required to discover Quentin's whereabouts. Martina didn't know why she hadn't deleted his number but she was glad of it now.

She took a long drag of her Gitanes cigarette, the second to last remaining from the pack she'd bought in Paris, inhaling the raw flavour – like licking fine leather. She watched the last embers flare, then threw the butt to the pavement and squelched it beneath her red-soled stiletto. Running a tongue over her teeth, Martina double-checked her reflection in a pocket mirror, the back covered with an enamel chrysanthemum – worthless tat she'd picked up in Stanley, but she liked it. She resisted the impulse to smash the mirror.

When she was thirteen, Martina had started swiping compacts from the purses of her mother's friends, women touching up their make-up in the ladies room at Saks Fifth Avenue, even a teacher or two. She would try on the shade then crack the mirror. When her mother discovered all the cracked compacts in her night-table drawer, she asked her why.

'I never look right,' Martina admitted.

'Such a drama queen. Must be your Latin side,' her mother tut-ted, and tossed them all in the trash.

Martina closed the compact gently and slid it back into her purse.

She'd high-tailed it from the Jockey Club to the Star Ferry pier, jumping on a green-and-white to Kowloon where the 118-storey International Commerce Centre had been constructed directly across the water from the 88-storey International Finance Centre. Talk about an architectural pissing contest. The elevator zoomed Martina straight to the top, her ears popping on the way, where the Ritz-Carlton's Ozone bar was located.

You're nothing but a parasite.

She forced Cressida's acid-tipped words from her mind. Cressida was jealous. She was nothing without her husband or her father despite all of her degrees. Martina understood the resentment that bred: she'd played second fiddle to Spencer too, and she almost felt sorry for Cressida – but not that sorry.

Preparing for another battle, Martina stepped from the elevator.

Up here, the thrum of the city mingled with the boom of air-planes and the hiss of trade winds. Touted as the highest bar in the world, the view was vertigo-inducing.

Don't look down.

Quentin had a table outside, a bottle of Chivas Regal and a char-cuterie board laid out before him. He looked up from his whisky, a satisfied grin spreading over his face. Reclining against the cush-ion of the loveseat, he looked every inch a princeling. His striped Oxford shirt had its top buttons undone to expose a tuft of chest hair.

'I hadn't expected to find you drinking alone,' Martina told him.

'I wasn't.' His grin turned enigmatic. 'But how could I desire anyone else's company when I could have yours?'

Quentin's gaze slid up her bare legs and form-fitting Roland Mouret dress, zipper down the front. She'd wanted to look her best to face down Cressida.

He raised one sardonic eyebrow and patted the cushion beside him.

With a snort, Martina borrowed a cabaret-style chair from a nearby table and sat down opposite him. Quentin polished off his whisky, then poured himself another.

'I understand,' he said in a conciliatory tone. 'You're afraid if you sit too close to me you won't be able to keep your hands to yourself.'

'I'm not the one with that problem.'

'Aren't you?'

Quentin stared at her from beneath cartoonishly long lashes, his messy brown curls screaming of tousled sheets. If Martina hadn't seen this act before, she might have been fooled. Motioning at the packed bar, he said, 'There are plenty of witnesses for our encounter – this time. In case you need to get your story straight.'

He filled a second glass and offered it to her.

'I'll have what you're having,' Martina told him and filched the glass he'd poured for himself.

Eyes sparking with mischief, 'It's almost as if you don't trust me,' Quentin said, throwing his head back in a chortle. 'Suit yourself.'

The whisky went down like velvety fire.

Quentin watched Martina's mouth, avidly. 'You've always appreciated the finer things.' His voice brimmed with approval. 'Your book had me riveted, by the way – my compliments. I considered introducing you to my lawyers after I finished reading but, in actual fact, my parties have never been more popular. So, thank you.'

He clinked his tumbler against hers.

'Just for your information,' he added, 'GHB isn't my style. If someone spiked Veronica's drink, it wasn't me.'

'As if you'd admit it. But I knew you wouldn't sue me,' Martina countered. 'You're a cockroach, Quentin. You don't want anyone shining a light into your dark corners.'

'And you're a feisty one.'

'Feisty is what men call women they can't control.'

'Ah, see, that right there. There's something about your smart mouth that makes me extend indecent proposals. I can't help myself.'

She snorted. 'You're not nearly the smooth operator you think you are.'

'You wound me.' Pinching a tranche of bresaola between his fingers, Quentin popped it into his mouth. 'While I can see the kink in being insulted by a beautiful woman,' he drawled, 'is there a reason you texted me?'

The urge to slap the smug expression off his face was nearly overwhelming.

'Yes.' Martina scooted her chair closer. 'I finally figured out your game.'

'Intriguing. And what game is that?'

'Xtasy Events.'

Quentin picked up his glass. 'One of my many lucrative ventures,' he said. 'We work with all the five-star hotels and big corporates.'

'And do you skim off the top from all your events? Or is the Lourdes Hawkins Foundation just special?' Martina demanded.

'Xtasy Events is a legitimate business.'

'I find that difficult to believe.'

'V hired us to do all of the Hawkins Pacific functions for years. We even fulfilled a couple contracts after her death. She trusted me.' Quentin made puppy-dog eyes again. 'Why won't you?'

The pang in Martina's stomach returned. She gazed into the amber liquid in her own glass, swirling it around, and indulged in another swallow. Martina hadn't invented Veronica's disgust with Quentin. She'd warned Martina off him and went out of her way to avoid him herself. When Martina had seen them fighting on the *Tin Hau 8*, she'd assumed Veronica was telling Quentin to go to hell. Yet again.

Had Veronica really still been doing business with him when she died?

Why would she do that? It made zero sense. He was lying, as usual.

'I can see the gears in your mind working,' Quentin teased. 'Maybe you didn't know V as well as you pretend.'

Her throat itched. She finished the whisky.

'Be that as it may,' Martina said, 'it's there in black and white — you overcharged the foundation from what the Lusitano has on their price list. You've been fleecing us and pocketing the difference.'

'I charged exactly what Vasco told us to charge. Not a farthing more. If you have a problem with the prices, take it up with him. But do be careful going in all Yank with guns blazing.' For a second, Quentin grew serious. 'There's a small list of people I wouldn't cross and he's right at the top.'

'Suppose I go see Ao Wing and tell him you've been stealing from Veronica's foundation. He's rich as Croesus. He doesn't need the money and — whatever he is — he cared about Veronica.'

Quentin resumed his unconcerned demeanour. 'I haven't been stealing from the foundation. And if I should meet an untimely demise, I have a — well, let's just call it an insurance policy. I won't be drinking tea like Neil Heywood. Not without a lot of fallout.'

Insurance policy. How sad that Quentin needed one, but she supposed he did. As if to emphasise his point, he told Martina, 'Vasco knows this.'

'Vasco is what his friends call him. I doubt you qualify.'

'Oh, I have a very loose definition of friendship.' He paused for a beat. 'As do you.'

'I don't know what you mean.'

'You made free with your hatchet. Not that I blame you. Most of the women in Hong Kong are simpering or tragic, like Elsie Barron.'

'Elsie is a friend. Shut your mouth about her.'

'What pretty claws you have.' Quentin snatched another piece of bresaola. 'I'd feel sorry for Spencer if I didn't know something you don't know.'

He was toying with her. Martina shouldn't take the bait. She shouldn't, and yet she couldn't stop herself from asking, 'And what is that?'

'What's it worth to you?' he purred.

'Forget it.'

'You twisted my arm.' Quentin set his tumbler down. 'Since you wanted to know, the night Spencer brought you to my house wasn't the first time he'd attended one of my gatherings.'

'What do I care?' Martina snapped. 'He's ancient history.'

'But you do care. I can see it.'

She held herself as still as possible. She would not let Quentin see that the wounds of her short marriage hadn't been fully cauterised.

'Fuck you, Quentin.'

'That's what I keep hoping.' He laughed with genuine amusement. 'A little friendly advice? If I were you, I'd sleep with one eye open.'

'You don't scare me.'

Having had enough, Martina started pushing to her feet.

'It's not me you should be afraid of.' Leaning across the table, Quentin touched a single finger to her knee. 'I would only hurt you if you asked me very, *very* nicely.' He flashed a tiger's smile. 'Not everyone in Hong Kong can say the same.'

Martina grabbed the bottle of Chivas by its neck and decanted it on to Quentin's crotch. 'Whoops,' she said, deadpan. She'd been wanting to chuck a drink at him for years.

'Oh, Martina. I do so love a golden shower.'

She slammed the bottle back on the table, summoning the attention of the patrons nearby.

'I'll have sweet dreams tonight,' Quentin called after her as she strode away.

'*Pervert*,' she said, garnering a few more sideways glances.

Unfortunately, Quentin was right. Martina had a powerful enemy, and she was running out of time to unmask them.

She wouldn't sleep a wink.

Luck Be a Lady

*M*artina's jaw ached as she walked into Ao Wing's office. This morning she woke to find she'd bitten clean through her mouth guard. She'd heard her teeth crumbling, disintegrating in her dreams. Discreetly, she rubbed the sore joint.

Before heading out from her apartment, she had pulled the plug from the bathtub and placed it in the trinket dish atop her dresser, a quotidian ritual. Iris used to replace it like clockwork when she cleaned, almost a tug of war, until Martina told her to stop.

Martina lived expecting the world to surge, overwhelm her when she wasn't looking. She anticipated a flood, always, and it had started long before Veronica drowned. Martina needed to control the inescapable sea inside her. Iris had taken to polishing the plug with her other jewellery instead, and left it where she found it.

Waiting for her audience with Ao Wing, she tossed back the espresso fetched by a primly dressed secretary. Her tongue still held the aroma of the Gitanes she'd smoked on the TurboJET from Hong Kong. Her last one.

Martina had made the journey many times over the past few years, yet her mind always travelled back to that first trip with Veronica. Especially today. She'd scarfed an egg tart as she paced in front of the Lusitano Palace, steeling herself for her appointment, picturing her dead friend beside her.

Quentin's taunts rattled around Martina's brain.

Maybe you didn't know V as well as you pretend.

Their friendship had been like a summer fling, burning brightly. A firefly in a jar. There was no time to learn all the details of Veronica's past that Jean-Pierre or Elsie knew, but Veronica had exposed her soft underbelly to Martina — that much was real. Staying up talking late into the night, they had shared what really mattered. Martina had confided childhood humiliations she'd never revealed to Bitsy or Spencer.

The hollow pain she'd felt when Grandma Olson proudly presented a photo album she'd crafted to bring with her on a trip back to Sweden that was devoid of any sign that Martina or her father existed. She was invisible. Erased.

Yet Veronica saw her, held her hand as she cried. Quentin was a malignant narcissist. Martina wouldn't let him gaslight her. She wouldn't.

Ao Wing's office was located on the floor above the gaming hall and Martina could hear the *ka-ching* of the slot machines distantly, persistently, which did nothing for her nerves. Crossing and uncrossing her legs, she scanned the gilded interior.

The décor was fit for a colonial governor. An oil painting of the Señado Square, with an air of Gainsborough about it, hung over the secretary's desk; carmine damask draperies lined the windows. The effect was more antechamber to a royal court than corporate waiting room.

But then, this was the Lusitano Palace and here Ao Wing was king.

When the secretary smiled placidly at Martina and said, 'He'll see you now,' she had to stop herself from running full tilt for the nearest fire escape.

Ao Wing was seated in a hunter-green leather chair behind an enormous antique desk that wouldn't have been out of place at Windsor Castle. A throne room, indeed. He stood as the secretary shut the door behind Martina.

'Come in, come in,' he said and she couldn't shift the sensation she'd been locked inside the lion enclosure.

'Thank you for seeing me on such short notice, Mr Ao.'

'Your timing is impeccable. I returned last night from checking on the construction of my new casino complex in Vietnam.' He gestured at a scale model of what seemed like a miniature city in a plastic case. 'The Lusitano Palace Mekong.'

Ao Wing strolled toward the mini-mega casino on the side table, not inviting Martina to sit, so she joined him. Wrinkles gathered at the corners of his eyes as he examined the diorama.

'It looks vast,' Martina said.

'It will be four times the size of the Cotai Strip, near the former imperial capital of Hue.' He peered at her sidelong. 'The Americans nearly bombed it out of existence but now . . .' Ao Wing shrugged. 'The communists are capitalists and everyone is friends again.'

Martina laughed weakly. Ao Wing's lips turned upwards but the semblance of a smile didn't reach his eyes.

'How is it that I can help you today?' he said, small talk over, cutting to the chase.

A lump formed in Martina's throat. She'd gone round and round in her head last night about the best way to suggest to a gangster that he was stealing from her. If Peony Huang didn't petrify Martina just as much, she never would have hopped on the hydrofoil at Shun Tak.

'Mr Ao, I'm hoping you can help me get to the bottom of something.'

'And that is?'

Martina tapped her index finger against the display case. At 3 a.m. she had decided the damsel-in-distress act was the best way to go. It was, after all, mostly the truth.

'I've become aware that some of the expenses for the foundation's annual gala don't add up.' Ao Wing lifted an eyebrow, expression neutral, and so she carried on. 'I'm concerned there could be damage to the foundation's reputation. We both know how much it meant to Veronica.'

'Lulu meant the world to Veronica,' he agreed. 'But I am unclear how it is that I can help you with your financial woes, Ms Torres.'

Martina's pulse rat-a-tat-tatted in her ears like the Little Drummer Boy.

'There seems to be a discrepancy between what Xtasy Events has charged the foundation and the standard rates the Lusitano Palace charges for room hire, food and beverage, floral design . . . the list goes on.'

'Then you have an issue with Xtasy Events.'

She cleared her throat. 'I spoke with Quentin Turner yesterday and he insists the fault is not with them. It was the Lusitano's corporate events manager who initially contracted Xtasy Events on behalf of the foundation . . .' Another cough. 'Mr Ao, I think . . . that is, I'm *afraid* someone at the hotel might be skimming off the top.'

Ao Wing's face remained relaxed.

'The Lusitano Palace has no need to cheat Veronica's foundation.'

'Oh, no, I know *you* wouldn't, Mr Ao. I'm just concerned that someone in middle management might have—'

He silenced her with his blank expression. 'I take full responsibility for my people. To cheat a guest would be to steal from me, and no one I employ is that foolish.'

Ao Wing spoke without malice, a simple statement of fact, which was all the more menacing. Martina had heard myriad rumours about Ao Wing's meteoric rise through the ranks of organised crime that she wasn't stupid enough to print in her memoir and she now believed every one of them. Why had Veronica trusted him so implicitly? It seemed out of character.

'I will have all of the relevant records sent to the foundation, of course, but you will find nothing out of order,' Ao Wing told her. 'After what you revealed about Quentin Turner in your book, I'm astonished you would take his word on anything.'

'You're right, Mr Ao.' Martina felt a flush scald her cheeks. He had read her book? 'I don't know what I was thinking.' And yet, despite the fact that she loathed the British bastard, she didn't think he was lying to her about this.

Which begged the question, why would Ao Wing lie? Was it merely that he couldn't brook the notion one of his employees might dare run a racket under his nose? Even if he found the culprit and dealt with them quietly, it wouldn't help Martina with her Peony Huang problem.

As if reading her thoughts, Ao Wing said, 'Panic and logic are not happy bedfellows, Ms Torres.'

She forced a laugh. 'I suppose not. Who said that? Samuel Johnson?'

He shook his head. 'My grandfather.' With a grim smile, Ao Wing said, 'I want to show you something before you leave.'

He walked to the corner of the room and turned a filigreed brass doorknob. Martina had expected a closet. Instead, the elderly Chinese man walked into another office. Could it be a panic room? Ao Wing was certainly the kind of person who needed one. Martina's survival instincts told her not to follow him into the confined space but she saw no alternative.

'This is where I do my real work,' he said. 'Not much to look at, is it?'

The secret room was entirely spartan. The walls were painted pigeon-grey. Both the desk and the chair were made from unadorned pine.

Ao Wing didn't wait for an answer.

'I have recreated my grandfather's study,' he explained. 'He was a devout Buddhist and a renowned professor of history at Fudan University.' Admiration underscored the statement. 'He raised me after my parents died. The universities were closed the year I would have started, of course. I fled Shanghai and came here, just before the 12-3 incident, but Grandfather wouldn't leave. The Red Guards came for him, sent him to a re-education camp for being a scholar.' The casino magnate blew out a breath. 'He died there. Starved to death.'

'I'm very sorry for your loss,' Martina said, weighting her words.

'My grandfather believed in the peace of simple things. The peace of a good book and a cup of tea. His books are what killed him.'

Ao Wing pointed to a painting over Martina's shoulder, hanging above the door, the only decoration in the room.

Against a deep plum canvas, a pot-bellied man dressed in imperial garb, a long beard touching the roulette wheel between his hands, gave the viewer a bemused smile.

'Caishen,' said Ao Wing. 'The god of wealth.'

There was something about the style of the painting that struck Martina as familiar, although she was certain she'd never seen it before. The aureole behind the Chinese god was reminiscent of a Christian icon, a blending of East and West that fitted Macau to a tee.

'I built this office to remind myself what it is to be poor and that there is no great nobility in poverty.' He frowned. 'Money is the only thing that buys peace, Ms Torres.' Ao Wing gestured for Martina to exit. 'Grandfather died for his principles and it was a waste.'

As Martina stepped across the threshold, she spied a signature in the corner of the painting, as faint as a spider's web.

Varenne '89.

Through the Looking Glass

*M*artina chased her Dramamine with a G&T on the ferry back from Macau, willing the sea to calm. Her stomach was a blender by the time she reached dry land and she was all sharp elbows in the taxi queue on her way to Gallery de Ladrones.

It wasn't surprising that Ao Wing should own a painting by Veronica's mother. Not at all. And yet, Martina distinctly remembered Veronica telling her the painting of Tin Hau at the gallery was Geneviève Varenne's only portrait, a gift to Veronica's father the year she was born. Martina couldn't recall the last time she'd seen the Tin Hau and she hadn't visited the gallery since it'd hosted the foundation's exhibition on protest art right after Thanksgiving.

She didn't know exactly what she was looking for when she told the taxi to take her to Duddell Street; she just wanted to look the goddess in the face.

An automated bell chimed as Martina entered the gallery. She heard Apple's voice coming from the mezzanine, switching between Cantonese and English. The wood floor creaked as Martina surveyed the latest exhibition, *Alice in Hong Kong* – a reimagining of the classic tale which was sure to sell well to both moneyed locals and expats.

Apple waved at Martina from above. She hadn't aged a day since Martina had first met her. Descending the spiral staircase, Apple said an abrupt goodbye to whomever she was talking to and ended the call.

'Martina!' she exclaimed. 'Always a pleasure to see you.'

'Likewise.' Martina eyed her Vivienne Westwood scarf. 'Love the orbs,' she said. 'Long live the Queen. Of fashion, I mean.' If it was a Shenzhen special it was exceptional work.

Apple twirled the end between her fingertips. 'Thank you.'

Glancing around, 'When did the new exhibition open?' Martina asked.

'Last week. Lots of red dots already.' A crease appeared on her baby-smooth brow. 'Didn't you get an invitation to the opening?'

'I'm sure I did. I was in Paris promoting my book.'

'How exciting for you.'

Apple stared at Martina expectantly. 'Listen, I have an out-of-the-blue question,' Martina said. 'Do you have a list of all the Geneviève Varenne works owned by the gallery?'

The crease on Apple's brow became a furrow. 'That is out of the blue.' She released a small laugh. 'I don't know if we have a record of all her artworks.' Apple tapped her chin. 'There is a catalogue from the retrospective exhibition the gallery did after her death, some-where around here. Let's see if I can find it.'

Martina trailed behind Apple as she climbed the stairs, trying to prevent her heel from getting caught in the iron grillwork.

'Is the Tin Hau painting up here too?' Martina asked. 'I haven't seen it in a while.'

'Oh no, we sold it ages ago.'

'*Sold it?*' A cold wave passed over Martina. 'Veronica loved that painting – I can't believe she'd allow it to be sold. Are you sure Jean-Pierre didn't take it?'

Apple cast a startled glance back at her. 'I can check,' she said sceptically. Although if Jean-Pierre had taken the painting, Martina supposed he'd be displaying it alongside his creepy Hall of Veronicas.

'Would you like tea? Coffee?' Apple said.

'No, no. Thank you.'

She surveyed the desk while Apple rifled through a bookshelf.

GALLERY DIRECTOR declared the plaque. Martina caught a glimpse of herself in its polished black glass. Her eyes were wild.

She counted her heartbeats. *One Mississippi . . . two Mississippi . . .*

'Here we are!'

Smiling perkily, Apple brandished a yellowing exhibition catalogue.

'You're a star,' Martina said. 'Could you look up the bill of sale for the Tin Hau?'

'It might take a minute. Why don't you make yourself comfortable downstairs?' she suggested. 'Would you like some warm water?' Warm water was what Hongkongers suggested to cure a variety of ills and Martina did look peaky.

Cantopop blared from Apple's cell phone. She frowned at it aggressively.

'*Aiya!* I keep telling this agent we're not interested even if his client is famous in the West. Dissidents are too hot to handle!'

'The best agents never give up.' Martina laughed. 'I'll leave you to it.'

She felt sorry for the person on the other end of the phone as Apple began to lay into him in Cantonese. No translation required. Ensconcing herself on the plush sofa beneath the mezzanine balcony, Martina regarded the catalogue cover, brushing away a thin film of dust.

Geneviève Varenne, 1949–1997 was printed across a black-and-white panorama of a fishing village that belonged to the Hong Kong of yesteryear. She started flipping through the thick pages, raking her eyes over temples in Chiang Mai and Siem Reap, slender alleys in Suzhou, snow monkeys in Hokkaido. Veronica's mother had switched to colour photography in the 1980s but there were no paintings included in the retrospective exhibition.

Was there a significance to the fact that Geneviève had painted a portrait for both her husband and Ao Wing? Or was Martina grasping at straws?

Her eye caught on a magnificent French colonial villa. The tiara-pointed roof gradually tapered, wings flaring like a phoenix about to take flight.

Chez grand-mère, Luang Prabang, 1974.

Grandmother's house – the same one Jean-Pierre had been sketching from an old snapshot of Veronica. He'd said it had been Geneviève's childhood summer home. Veronica had never spoken much about her mother's side of the family. When Martina was fact-checking her memoir, she'd been able to confirm the arrival of the Varennes in Hong Kong after the end of French colonial rule in Vietnam, but she hadn't had a reason to look into any branches of the family tree in Laos.

She traced the outline of the sweeping rooftop with her little finger.

'Martina?'

She looked up at Apple, who was clearly repeating her name.

'I was carried away by the photographs,' she lied. 'Such mastery of the lens.'

Apple humoured her with a smile. 'A rare talent.' Looking from the book to Martina, she told her, 'I found the bill of sale.'

'You did? And?'

Apple's lips compressed, glancing back at the open book on Martina's lap. 'What a coincidence.'

'Coincidence?'

One Mississippi . . .

Two Mississippi . . .

'The Tin Hau was sold to an anonymous buyer in Luang Prabang, Laos.'

Martina's throat grew dry. 'When?' she squeaked. '*When* was it sold?'

'Two weeks before Veronica died,' Apple said in a sombre tone.

But that didn't make any sense. Why would Veronica sell it *before* she died?

It couldn't be valuable enough to help with Hawkins Pacific's financial troubles. Did she do it to cover more of Jean-Pierre's gambling debts? No, why would she? Not when she was adamant she was leaving him.

Spinning the jade bangle on her arm, Martina's thoughts whorled. 'You're absolutely certain?' she demanded of Apple, a jagged edge to her voice.

'I can show you the file.'

'No, no.' Martina forced her features to soften. 'Do you still have the address of where it was sent?'

Apple lifted her eyebrows. 'Yes . . .'

'Great. I'll need that if you don't mind.'

'I don't know . . . the buyer must have wanted to remain anonymous for a reason.'

Martina snapped shut the book. The crack resounded in the empty gallery. 'It's important, Apple. I wish I could explain – just trust me that Veronica would want you to help me.'

Apple fiddled with the end of her scarf, considering. '*Hou dik.*' She sighed. 'Anything for Veronica.'

'You're the best, Apple. Simply the best.' Martina stood, clasping the catalogue to her chest. 'I'm just going to borrow this for a bit, OK?'

'OK. I'll email you the shipping address for the painting.'

'Oh, if it's not too much trouble, I'll wait while you print it out?'

Martina saw Apple strain not to roll her eyes. 'Whatever you prefer.'

'Thanks a million.'

She stared blankly in the direction of Apple's retreating size 0 form.

Unless Veronica's great-grandmother was a zombie, she was long dead, but a sneaking suspicion told Martina *someone* was living in that house. Could it be the same someone in Luang Prabang who had wanted the Tin Hau painting?

Could Ao Wing have bought the painting? Why would he go to the trouble of purchasing it anonymously and having it sent to Laos?

It didn't seem his style. The casino boss would hang it next to the god of wealth in his secret office where no one could hear you scream.

The bigger question, however, was why Veronica would have agreed to part with the painting in the first place?

Had she been in genuine fear for her life? If so, she'd given Martina no indication. Veronica laughed about all the angry messages failed businessmen with Napoleon complexes sent her. She'd downplayed the threatening texts so much that Martina had only included them in her memoir at the suggestion of her agent. They made for a better story.

Guilt made Martina itch. Unless, of course, Veronica hadn't planned to part with it – but that would mean . . . Goosepimples broke out across her chest. She refused to believe it.

Martina yelped as her cell phone announced the arrival of a text.

Just checking in. Drink at HH later?

A whoosh of air left her lungs. Only a text from Elsie. Not Veronica's ghost. Her jaw began to ache.

Yes!

Boy did Martina need a drink. And some answers.

But she'd start with a drink.

Twilight tinged the hills of Hong Kong Island an ethereal lavender, shafts of light shearing the clouds.

Martina tried to enjoy the view from her table on the veranda of Hullett House across the harbour. A couple of streets behind the boutique hotel, but a world away, lay the Chungking Mansions, the tightly packed rabbit-warren of low-rent shops immortalised in celluloid by Wong Kar-wai. Hong Kong was a city of stark contrasts and contradictions.

Martina had never been tempted to have her Tarot cards read

at any of the grim-looking basement shops between Lexington and Third Avenues, yet one evening after Veronica had vanished, she found herself taking the ferry to Kowloon and wandering the Temple Street night market aimlessly, remembering that first dinner at the Peninsula when their friendship was new and the possibilities seemed limitless.

Amidst the buzz of neon, tourists looking for bargains on Mao T-shirts and the scent of frizzling meat from the *dai pai dongs*, sat rows of fortune-tellers at rickety tables in the gardens of the temple to Tin Hau. Under the cover of divine shadows, the daring can choose to know their fate from their face, their hands, their ears. Or even from a small caged bird who will choose a card, any card, just for you.

Tin Hau. The girl goddess seemed to be the key to everything.

An agitated song had pierced the night air from the nearby Cantonese opera tents and Martina's pulse had sped up as she'd pulled out the stool opposite a skinny, grey-haired man. The poster behind him advertised his fortune-telling methods and that he spoke English.

He didn't smile at her. He studied her. He took her hand, the skin on the back of his own like gossamer. Then he stared at Martina's face so long she felt the flesh melting to reveal her bones. The tips of her ears burned.

That night she'd still been hoping that Veronica would be found alive. Somewhere. Somehow. She'd gone to the night market hoping for a beautiful lie.

Your heart is broken, the fortune-teller had pronounced. *You want to run away. It will do no good. Death will follow.*

He'd trailed his pinkie along the knife-thin scar on her forehead. *You must stay to change your luck.*

Martina sat down that night and started to write her memoir.

What if the beautiful lie was true?

Shaking her head, she ordered a second Negroni and withdrew

the exhibition catalogue from her handbag. She set it on the table and flicked to a highly saturated photograph of the Kuang Si waterfalls a short distance from Luang Prabang. Tourists waded in shallow aquamarine pools, old-fashioned Nikons around their necks. It was dated 1994.

Martina closed the book again, drumming her fingers on the cover.

Elsie arrived a few minutes later, all apologies: 'Mum was having another bad day and Rupes was having a tantrum . . .' Eyeing the Negroni cradled in Martina's hand, 'That seems like an inspired idea,' she noted and signalled the waiter for another.

Elsie pulled out the Qing dynasty-style chair, its back curved like a horseshoe, and settled against the rosewood. The breeze ruffled her chignon. She looked utterly in her element, heiress to a British *hong*. Cressida Wong might think they'd breathed their last gasp, but she'd never call Elsie a parasite.

'I remember when this place was still the Marine Police headquarters. Daddy sent the department a case of Scotch every Christmas,' she said. She looked back at the cascading stone staircase of the elegant Victorian building where a bride was having her wedding portrait shot. 'Everywhere left standing is bound to become a boutique hotel at this rate.' Elsie laugh-sighed. 'Have you seen the old jail cells inside the bar? Naughty patrons beware.'

'Gives new meaning to the term "drunk tank",' agreed Martina. 'I may be cooling my heels inside one of them soon enough.' She couldn't quite bring herself to laugh. 'Leg irons will be next season's must-have accessory.'

'Oh, darling. It won't come to that. How did you get on with Cressida?'

'Not very well.'

The waiter reappeared with Elsie's drink. 'Cheers.' She raised her glass at Martina and took a sip, closing her eyes briefly. 'Cressida's a crab apple. Don't take it personally.'

'Then why are you on her committee?' Martina retorted, knowing it sounded petulant, unable to pull Cressida's poisoned darts from beneath her skin.

'Why are any of us on *any* of these committees?' Elsie lifted an eyebrow. 'What did she say?'

'She insists Xtasy Events didn't overcharge Lifting Hope.'

'Too bad,' said Elsie. 'Not for the Cambodian orphans, of course.' She took a swallow of Negroni. 'I'm sorry it turned out to be a dead end for you, though.'

'Not an entirely dead end.'

'Oh?'

Martina sipped her own drink. Elsie tilted towards her. Watching her friend closely, Martina said, 'Did you know Quentin Turner owns Xtasy Events?'

Elsie's eyes widened. 'You're kidding?'

'You didn't know?'

'I would have told you, Martina.' Her voice held hurt, her gaze wounded.

'I'm sorry. It was a shitty thing to say.' Martina tapped the jade bangle, the cold burning her fingertips. 'I'm a shitty friend.'

'You're not. You're under a lot of stress.'

Martina smiled wanly. Elsie was always so forgiving – it was probably why she was still with her douchebag Texan of a husband. 'Quentin rattles my cage,' she grumbled.

Elsie made a sympathetic noise. 'I know he does. The rest of us are used to him, I guess. He's part of the woodwork.'

Martina decided not to tell Elsie that Quentin thought she was tragic.

'*Diseased* woodwork,' Martina said, clinking her glass against Elsie's.

Her friend's lips formed a dismayed O. 'Gosh, I hope not – for the sake of all the *tai tais* in Hong Kong.'

'He was drinking alone at Ozone last night.'

'You went to see him?'

Martina leaned back in her chair. 'Fat lot of good it did. He says he charged us what the Lusitano Palace told him to charge, and Ao Wing says the fault lies with Xtasy Events.'

Elsie paused mid-sip. 'You talked to Ao Wing too?'

'Got back from Macau this afternoon.'

'My, you *have* been busy.' She drained the dark cherry-coloured liquid from her glass and rattled the ice cubes. 'Another round?' she said, catching the server's eye. Martina nodded.

'What I don't understand is why Veronica would have hired Quentin's company for the Hawkins Pacific events. He said they were still under contract when she died. But she hated his guts.'

Elsie stared out at the waterfront. 'I don't know what happened between Veronica and Quentin. She never told me about Oxford. The first I heard of it was in your book.'

'Oh.' Martina bit her lip. She couldn't help but be a little glad Veronica had trusted her with her past above everyone else. 'Well,' she continued, 'if the hotel and the events company are pointing fingers at each other, it leaves me precisely nowhere. Peony Huang will still have my head on a platter.'

Happily, fresh drinks materialised and Elsie took another long pull.

'Peony is formidable, I grant you, but I don't see that you have any choice but to throw yourself on her mercy.'

Incompetent or corrupt. 'She's not the merciful type.'

'Worst case: you lose your job at the foundation. You still have your writing. Juggling both must be overwhelming.' A small shrug. 'Would it be so bad to step down?'

Martina gaped at her friend.

'If I'm charged with embezzlement it would be! And who would ever donate to the foundation again?' She couldn't keep her voice from growing shrill. 'Veronica trusted me with this. What would she think if she's looking down at me from the Great Beyond?'

The tumbler shook in Martina's grip.

'Of course you're right, and I'm sure she'd be grateful for how hard you've worked to secure her legacy.' Elsie placed a quelling hand on Martina's elbow. 'All I meant is that I think being honest with Peony is your least worst option. To err is human, after all.'

A car horn made Martina jump in her seat. She watched as the driver of the Phantom Rolls rolled down his window to yell at the octogenarian Chinese lady slowly pushing her cart of cardboard across Canton Road towards the nearest recycling centre, which would pay her less than a dime per kilo. He hurled abuse. She took her time. Hongkongers were more than equal to New Yorkers in true grit.

Martina did *not* want to leave. She tapped the gel nail of her index finger forcefully against the cover of the book. She did *not* want to fail.

Elsie squinted. 'What's that?' she asked.

'Oh, this? Apple was doing some reorganising at the Gallery de Ladrones. She thought I might be interested in seeing more of Veronica's mother's work,' Martina replied.

She couldn't say exactly why she was lying to her friend, only that Elsie's suggestion she step down from her position had rubbed her the wrong way, all the way against the grain. Elsie had been born to extraordinary privilege and she took it for granted.

Martina stroked the fishing boat in the foreground of the cover photo.

'There are some gorgeous photos of Laos in here. Do you know if Veronica still had any family in the country?' she asked, tone casual.

'I'm not sure,' said Elsie. 'Mum might have known, but these days . . .' Trailing off, she motioned with her Negroni in utter exhaustion.

'Not to worry. Just idle curiosity.'

Elsie pursed her lips. 'Huh. Now that you mention it . . .' She took a sip.

274 || KRISTINA PÉREZ

'Now that I mention it, what?' Martina urged.

'Oh, I was just thinking maybe that's why Veronica went to Laos shortly before she died?'

'What are you talking about?' The question was practically a bark.

Elsie stiffened at her tone. 'Teagan Sullivan – you know, the tennis ace from the American Club, killer backhand? – anyway, she happened to run into Veronica on a flight from Luang Prabang to Bangkok. She stayed at the Hôtel du Roi – said it was seventh heaven, by the way.' She canted her glass again at Martina. 'Teagan mentioned it to me when we played doubles not long after.'

'When exactly? *When* did she run into Veronica?'

'Let me think . . .' Elsie gazed into her glass.

One Mississippi . . .

Martina resumed her tapping.

Two Mississippi . . .

'It must have been two weekends before she died,' Elsie said after several eons. 'The whole thing totally slipped my mind.'

'Why wouldn't it?' Martina rearranged her face into what she hoped was a disinterested smile. 'I'm glad Veronica had one last jaunt. Teagan bumping into her . . . what a coincidence,' she said, echoing Apple from earlier.

'That's Expatdom,' said Elsie. 'Nowhere to run.'

Except that Martina no longer believed it was a coincidence.

Veronica had told Martina she'd been in Beijing that weekend. The same weekend that an anonymous art lover in Luang Prabang bought Veronica's prized painting.

She didn't know why Veronica would lie to her about the trip – or why she would fly commercial rather than taking her jet, but something was connecting Veronica's death, Ao Wing and the embezzlement to Luang Prabang . . .

Martina questioned her own sanity. It was the longest of long shots.

But, what did she have to lose?

'I'll have to check out Laos for myself,' Martina told Elsie. 'I have a feeling it will haunt me if I don't.'

Julie Cooke to direct missing Hong Kong Heiress biopic, *Hungry Ghosts* (exclusive)

Reel Insider Daily can exclusively report that arthouse darling Julie Cooke is set to direct the film adaptation of Martina Torres's internationally best-selling memoir, *Hungry Ghosts: Life and Death on the Peak*. Fresh off her slew of Best Director wins at Cannes, the Tribeca Film Festival and SXSW, *Hungry Ghosts* will be Cooke's first feature for a major studio. 'I was drawn to the Patricia Highsmith-worthy mystery at the heart of the story,' Cooke told this Reel Insider. 'Who was Veronica Hawkins really? A scion of industry? A vestige of colonialism? A cursed socialite? And, most of all, who wanted her dead?'

Filming on location in Hong Kong is set to begin this summer.

Your Fave Expat Auntie

@AuntiePeak

Send Auntie Peak all of your #overheardHK tips.
DMs open.

Your Fave Expat Auntie ✓ @AuntiePeak · Apr 6
Looks like Expatlandia's very own *New York Times* bestseller isn't cool enough to sit at the grown-ups' table. Or HKJC box. #overheardHK

Your Fave Expat Auntie ✓ @AuntiePeak · Apr 7
Another tip abt Expatlandia's bestseller. Spotted at Ozone shower-ing DB's most notorious swinger w/ malt whisky. Oh, what a night! #overheardHK

AsiaCapital Magazine sits down with Iain Barron

The first thing you notice about Iain Barron, CEO of Barron Industries, is his unassuming manner. He is the consummate gentleman, asking me twice if I'm comfortable and if I'd like another cup of Earl Grey (answer: yes). There is the slightest hint of a Scottish accent when he speaks, despite his being born in Hong Kong to one of its oldest British families. Self-effacingly, he blames it on boarding school in the Highlands.

While he wears his crown lightly, Iain took the reins of his family's century-old business in 2009 after the untimely death of his father, Rupert Barron, during a mugging in Guangzhou. Barron Industries was founded in the late nineteenth century by Hamish Barron who served in the British East India Company and was a close associate of Sir James Brooke, who is better known as the first White Rajah of Sarawak in Borneo.

Iain tells me that 'as a lad' he'd wanted to be a surgeon, but these days he seems to be using surgical precision in the careful expansion of Barron Industries into telecommunications with the recent acquisition of Hawkins Pacific.

It hasn't always been plain sailing for Barron Industries, however. The early 1990s saw the company's fortunes take a turn for the worse. Barron Industries was heavily invested in several Tokyo-based property firms that collapsed when the Japanese stock market crashed in 1992. It was Rupert Barron's shrewd investment in the Jing Iron Mining Corporation in northern China that reinvigorated Barron Industries, allowing it to become the equal to Jardine Matheson and Sun Hung Kai Properties that it is today.

'Dad liked to joke that gold is good, but iron is better,' Iain Barron recounts with a fond smile.

Land of Milk and Honey

*M*artina ran through Bangkok airport's labyrinthine terminals, her Fitbit congratulating her as she racked up more than her daily 10,000 steps, barely avoiding taking down a middle-aged Western woman in head-to-toe Jim Thompson, and making her connecting flight by the skin of her teeth. Thank God she'd packed light and had everything she needed in her rollaboard. When the flight attendant wasn't looking, she wiped the sheen of sweat from her forehead with the eucalyptus-scented towelette before handing it back.

Martina switched off her phone, grateful the older aircraft didn't have wifi. She'd made the mistake of checking Twitter – because her publisher insisted she be active and 'engage' with readers – only to discover @AuntiePeak had been documenting her Wednesday night. Martina generally found the gossip account amusing, she'd even sent in a tip of her own once or twice, and half hoped it was run by a PA or helper with a grudge, but she really, really didn't like anyone tattling on her.

Her agent would say any publicity was good publicity. True or not, rumours clung to you, a bitter aftertaste. Martina had whet her persona like the blade of a fine knife. It was why she couldn't admit her incompetence to Peony Huang. Something she wouldn't be able to make Elsie, who had grown up on the Peak, understand.

It was precisely why she'd booked the next flight to Laos.

The purple silk-clad flight attendant sashayed down the aisle with the drinks trolley, an orchid brooch on her shoulder, and Martina decided to be adventurous. The pristinely put together Thai woman poured reddish-black tea into a long glass over ice, followed by condensed milk, swirling them together until it turned orange and sweet as a Creamsicle. Martina sucked the concoction through a straw with indelicate speed. A sugar high impaired her judgement enough to wolf down several bags of chilli-flavoured rice balls.

The ride started to get bumpy as the plane descended through the clouds to reveal lush, green-carpeted mountains as far as the eye could see. She chewed her Nicorette gum viciously. Entirely landlocked, from above, Laos looked reluctant to give up its secrets. Martina could barely make out any signs of civilisation until the landing gear was being lowered. Her clapping was wholehearted when they touched down.

Disembarking directly on to the tarmac, Martina scanned the rinky-dink terminal, which sported the same peaked roofs as in the photo of Veronica's great-grandmother's house – albeit a more utilitarian variation. The mountains surrounding the airport glowed in the afternoon light, untamed and inviting. Her pulse began to accelerate. Immigration was a quick affair and soon a sedan was conveying Martina to the hotel.

What was she doing here?

Martina's saner side scolded her for pinning her hopes on this wild goose chase. Her perhaps-ex-friend Bitsy called a psychic in Sedona (who had her Centurion card on file) every week and used a rose quartz pendant to talk to her spirit guide, but Martina had never gone in for mystical hippy-dippy claptrap. And yet.

Her gut wouldn't relent. Martina's future was waiting for her in an old house in Laos. She just knew it. Besides, her goose was already cooked.

A friendly Laotian receptionist welcomed her to Luang Prabang. He checked Martina into her suite, which featured its own plunge pool and a California King bed draped with mosquito netting, and was surprised when Martina immediately asked for a car again. 'I need to go here,' she said, showing him the address Apple had printed out for her.

The young man's lips twisted as he examined the paper.

'Do you recognise the address?' she prompted. Martina slipped the exhibition catalogue into her YSL travel tote, ready to leave. Patience had never been her strong suit. Every moment that passed, she needed another Xanax.

In. Out. In. Out.

'Yes, Madame Torres, I know it. It's not far out of town.' Brow crinkled, the man said, 'But it's a private road. No hotels or restaurants. You're going to visit a friend?'

His tone was hopeful with a hint of caution, probably fearing an ignorant American was going to need rescuing within thirty minutes of arriving in the country.

Martina smiled too brightly. 'A friend? Yes, I'm going to visit a friend.'

She would soon find out if she was lying.

Martina rolled down the window and lit a cigarette. She didn't ask the driver's permission, preferring as a rule to ask forgiveness. He didn't say a word. She exhaled into the blisteringly hot air, sun on her face.

In the past week she'd been on planes, ferries and automobiles. Adrenaline warred with jetlag. She took another drag.

Driving through the centre of Luang Prabang, Martina passed by monks too young to shave cloaked in orange robes, schoolgirls on bicycles, and tuk-tuks sardined with backpackers. Golden temple spires pierced the sky. Star-shaped paper lanterns and red flags emblazoned with the hammer and sickle flapped in the breeze.

The road out of town was a free-for-all of mopeds transporting anything and everything: from an entire family including a babe-in-arms to a whole hog, lying belly up on the back of a bike, its snout still moist. As Martina's journey progressed, French-influenced two-storey villas gave way to more humble structures of corrugated tin topped with enormous satellite dishes.

The countryside was far more forested than Martina had antici-pated, dense green leaves of teak trees creeping up the ridges of the majestic mountains. Cattle meandered at their own pace beside the sedan, tired from their labours, eyes leery. A few minutes later, the car pulled off the main road into a tunnel of bamboo trees, loose stones and dirt grinding beneath its wheels. Martina had the strong-est sense of déjà vu, like reading a secondhand book and using the dog ears made by the previous owner, and she half expected to find Jean-Pierre in his chateau at the end of the tunnel.

She sucked on her cigarette. It was a truth universally acknowl-edged that the über-rich everywhere were in want of seclusion and long, windy driveways were an ubiquitous feature of their homes. The rush of flowing water filtered through the trees.

Martina took out the exhibition catalogue, opening it like a treasure map. X marked the spot. She strained her eyes, searching for the villa.

'I didn't think anyone still lived here,' the driver said, his words stilted. The Laotian man was in his fifties, the hotel uniform tight across his chest.

'Neither did I,' said Martina.

He met her eyes in the rear-view mirror. 'The king hunted here.'

That seemed pretty on brand for Veronica. The French side of her family must have been bigwigs in Laos before the fall of the monarchy.

They drove a few moments in silence. 'Mangoes,' said the driver, pointing up. Wild mangoes dangled from the branches above, plump and pink. The mango trees fanned out around a low wall that pro-tected Martina's destination.

Maybe this was what lucid dreaming was all about. The sublime villa from Geneviève Varenne's photograph came to life before her eyes. As a kid, Martina had watched *The Wizard of Oz* every Thanksgiving when they showed it on primetime. She'd count the minutes until the celluloid turned from sepia to Technicolor, desperate for a tornado to fling her somewhere – *anywhere*.

The black-and-white picture hadn't done the villa justice.

Gleaming gilded wood panels, carved with intricate scrolls and serpents, filled the space beneath the pitched roof. Aureate talons scratched the blue sky at the corners where its slope gentled. The stucco of the first and ground floors had recently been painted an understated goldenrod, the shutters a deep burgundy. Woven baskets overflowing with dawn-red plumeria blossoms hung from each of the rounded arches punctuating the veranda.

Martina definitely wasn't in Kansas any more.

She closed the book on her lap, shoving it back into her bag. The car came to a stop outside an ornate, slightly rusted gate. It made a nerve-jangling noise as its hinges swayed.

'I'll wait,' the driver said, more statement than question.

'Yes, thanks. I'm happy to pay you hourly. Charge it to my room.'

Stepping out of the sedan, Martina breathed in the fragrance of ripening fruit. Her mouth watered. Damn it was hot. Sweat trickled down her spine and between her thighs.

There was no sound but the droning of insects, bird calls and the incessant moan of a river. Gravel and twigs crunched beneath her Tod's loafers. She approached the gate with trepidation. She'd flown to another country and driven to the middle of nowhere to arrive at this squeaky gate.

'Moment of truth time, Piggy,' Martina goaded herself.

A brass doorbell glinted to one side of the gate. No intercom. Martina pressed the button, which was cool against her fingertip. She didn't hear a chime or a buzzing of any kind. She pressed again.

'Hello?' she called out.

Nothing.

Had she come all this way for *nothing*?

She peered through the gate, inspecting the grass, which looked recently trimmed, and saw several lotus flowers floating on the surface of ceramic pots. Someone was taking care of this place. She *had* to get inside.

Martina pressed the bell again, leaning her back into it. She waited. And she waited.

The driver stepped out of the vehicle. 'Your friend is expecting you?' he said.

'Not exactly.' She laughed nervously. 'It's supposed to be a surprise.'

He nodded, unconvinced.

Enough. Martina refused to accept defeat. She was getting into that house – one way or another.

Slinging her tote bag over her shoulder, she wedged her right loafer between one of the gate's iron curlicues. Using the upper-body strength she'd finely honed through years of hot yoga, Martina grabbed the gate and swung her left leg over the top. She dropped her tote on to the other side, recovering her balance.

'Madame?' said the panicked driver. 'Madame!' His expression was pure disbelief.

Still straddling the top of the gate, Martina reassured him, 'Wait here. I'll be back.'

She rounded her right leg over the gate, hoping she looked poised rather than deranged, and landed on both feet. Martina scored herself a ten for sticking the landing.

Picking up her bag, she followed a path of flagstones across the grass and around the side of the villa. Since she was already breaking and entering, she might as well maintain the element of surprise. Martina could fall back on the stupid lost tourist defence.

The flagstone path led her through well-tended gardens of frangipani, begonias and hibiscus until she spied a swimming pool. There were several lounge chairs positioned around it. And one of them was occupied.

The woman was sprawled in profile. Dark blonde bangs peeked out from her large straw sunhat, the pixie cut cropped behind her ears. Oversized black bumblebee shades covered her face. The blonde's legs were lithe and tanned, stretching out from leopard-print bikini bottoms.

If Martina had had a mirror, she knew her expression would match her mother's every time she rediscovered one of the pieces of jewellery Martina had hidden. The relief tinged with fear. The self-doubt. Her mother still hadn't guessed Martina was behind it – that her daughter had found a petty but effective form of revenge. Something she knew her mother wouldn't dare tell her father, something that would unsettle and panic the omnipotent Anette Torres.

A cocktail ring here, a pendant there. The Bulgari watch she prized more than her only child.

I'm so forgetful, she would say, and Martina would smile to herself.

Now Martina's breathing shallowed. The tables had turned. Her heart pounded painfully.

She stopped before the sun lounger, casting a shadow over the other woman's form.

'Dao, I'm just dying for a gin fizz.'

'I'm not Dao, and you're not dead.'

The woman whipped off her sunglasses and, suddenly, Martina was staring into a kaleidoscope of gold, green and umber, that vibrant gaze she'd never expected to see again.

Veronica smiled. 'You found me.'

The Great Beyond

'It's Isabella now, like the She-Wolf of France. Isabella Mortimer,' Veronica informed Martina. 'Pleased to meet you.'

'I don't give a shit what you're calling yourself. I went to your funeral!'

'Oh, I know. What was that poem you read? Never heard of it.'

'That's not the goddamn point!' Martina heard herself splutter. Her scalp began to tingle, her cheeks burned. She had fantasised about this moment since Veronica had disappeared, concocted hare-brained scenarios in which her friend was found alive on a desert island, but this . . . Veronica sitting on a lounge chair, the picture of cool . . . it was too much.

'I'm impressed you found me, Marty. It's rather inconvenient but still . . . impressive. Martina the Intrepid Reporter.'

The wonderment in Veronica's voice only infuriated Martina more.

'Inconvenient?' she spat. 'I'll tell you what's *inconvenient* – mourning your friend for years only to discover she's been alive the whole time. I don't know whether to be elated or punch you in the face.'

Martina's shoulders heaved. All of her grief and guilt became a red-hot alloy. She wanted to shake Veronica, strangle her. Her eyes stung with tears she refused to shed.

'It's too hot to get so agitated, darling.' Veronica said it cavalierly, but her fingers wound tighter around the stem of her sunglasses. 'Why don't you join me for a swim?'

Was she for real? 'I don't want to go swimming. I want to know why you look so good for a corpse.'

For a millisecond, Veronica's eyes lowered in something resembling shame.

Then she declared, 'Too bad. I feel like a dip,' and, languorously, stretched her arms above her head.

Veronica swung her legs toward Martina, forcing Martina to step back as she pushed to her feet.

'You can't just avoid me, Veronica.' Martina curled her hands into fists, cutting tiny crescents into the pads of her palms. 'I got myself all the way to Luang Prabang. I'm not going anywhere without answers.'

Veronica ignored her.

'Dao!' she called out. In the bat of an eye, a slim Laotian woman in a silk tube skirt and flipflops emerged from inside the house. 'Please find a swimsuit for my friend. And ask Keo for two gin fizzes.'

The maid concealed her alarm at the appearance of Martina with a shy smile.

'Don't tell me you object to a gin fizz,' Veronica said to Martina.

Acid sloshed in Martina's stomach, the unreality of the moment hitting her, as if time were unspooling like the tape of an old cassette fast-forwarded and rewound too many times.

'Right now I wouldn't object to an entire bottle of Jose Cuervo.'

Veronica's eyes crinkled as her lips curved – one of her elusive genuine smiles.

'Do you have a driver waiting?' she said to Martina. When she nodded, Veronica looked back toward Dao. 'Invite the man outside into the kitchen for some tea. See if he wants a snack.'

'Yes, Madame Mortimer.' The woman smiled again and disappeared.

Alone once more, Martina and Veronica locked gazes. She

could feel Veronica's pull like the tide, the force of her will, but she couldn't give in.

'Stop stalling, Veronica.'

'Relax, Marty. You'll put yourself in an early grave.'

She walked past Martina, gracefully arced her hands together and did a swan dive into the pool. Her laughter shimmered through the air.

Splash.

Maybe it was shock that led Martina to accept the canary-yellow one-piece proffered by Dao but, deep down, she knew it was something else. A spark reignited. A thrill she had lost. She changed while sipping her gin, then took a running start toward the deep end.

Whooping with abandon, Martina hurled herself into the air.

She closed her eyes.

For an instant she was seven years old again, enjoying every moment of Papi's undivided attention in the pool at Disney World while her mother smoked Winstons, thumbing through *Vogue*, piling the ashtray ever higher. Martina was seven, Martina was thirty-two. This was Florida, this was Laos.

Veronica was dead. Veronica was alive.

'Cannonball!' Martina squealed.

The water smacked her backside as she plunged to the tiled bottom. Bubbles rushed from her nose. Opening her eyes, she revelled in the sting of chlorine.

Stroke, stroke. Martina pulled her way through the water, sunlight sparkling as she reached Veronica in the shallow end. She tugged Veronica's ankle, unbalancing her where she sat perched on the mosaic-patterned steps leading into the pool.

Martina laughed as Veronica brushed away some of the gin she'd spilled on to her cleavage. She readjusted her bumblebee glasses.

Martina shook out her hair, letting it slap against her spine.

'Where are you staying?' Veronica said.

'The Hôtel du Roi.'

'The prison?'

'It bills itself as the French governor's mansion.'

'Everyone in town knows it as the prison. I suppose they don't advertise its afterlife in the brochure.'

Exhaling harshly, Martina said, 'I'm not here for hotel recommendations.'

'Testy, testy.' Veronica tutted. She gave her a long look. 'How *did* you find me?'

There was a quaver to the question, a chink in her armour. Veronica wasn't as unaffected by Martina's arrival as she pretended.

'Tin Hau,' she answered. Martina waited a beat, drawing out the moment. 'When I found out it had been sold, I knew something was up.' Her lips twitched. 'You would never part with that painting.'

Veronica released a chagrin-filled laugh. 'Sentiment will get you every time,' she said, licking the sugar from the rim of her glass. Her hazel eyes grew muted.

A heavy silence followed. Finally, 'You know me better than I realised,' said Veronica. 'Give the girl a Pulitzer.' Another laugh, more sour this time. 'But *why* did you start looking for me, Marty? Why *now*? You have everything you've ever wanted with me dead.'

Because it isn't true, Martina stopped herself from admitting. Current predicament aside, she hadn't slept well since Veronica died – or faked her own death, she should say.

Instead, 'I've missed you,' Martina said. 'I can't look at the Peak without thinking of you.'

Veronica inhaled a long breath through her nostrils. Her mouth formed a small moue.

'That's not why you're here.' She leaned closer.

'No, that's not why I'm here.' Martina circled her hands beneath the water, watched the ripples spiral outward. 'Peony Huang thinks I'm embezzling money from the foundation,' Martina explained. 'She's wrong.' She stared at Veronica head on. '*You* are.'

'Clever girl.'

A gasp escaped Martina's lips. Even though she knew she was right, she'd wanted Veronica to deny it. She swayed in the water, halfway between giddy and seasick.

'You have to tell Peony it's not me!'

'I have to do no such thing. I'm dead.'

The river roared in the distance. *Men are coming to slaughter you.*

Shaking her head, panic mounting, Martina said, 'I don't understand. Why would you steal from your own foundation?'

'Staying dead is expensive.'

'Surely you of all people have a slush fund.'

'My assets were all tied up with Hawkins Pacific.' Veronica gestured dismissively. 'I needed access to Lulu's trust.'

'Which is why you set up the foundation in the first place,' Martina realised. 'To disappear.'

'What's the fun of living in exile if you can't live in style?' Veronica raised her glass at Martina. 'You were the centrepiece of my getaway plan. I put you in charge because I knew you'd be too grateful to ask too many questions.'

The arrow struck true. Veronica was absolutely right, and Martina hated being so predictable. She hated that it'd been so easy to see through her veneer of sophistication and aspirational entitlement. Martina had *believed* Veronica had wanted to give her the chance to use her talents, to prove herself.

'I've been working my ass off to make the foundation a success for you, Veronica,' Martina shot back, voice grainy. 'To do you proud. To ensure your sister's legacy the way you would have wanted.'

'Oh, please, Marty. You've been making *yourself* a success.'

She slapped the water. 'Either way, you got greedy, Veronica. I can't hide the money trail. It's Ao Wing who's funnelling money to you, isn't it?'

'Skimming from the foundation is only temporary,' Veronica said unperturbed. 'I'm investing in one of his projects.'

'The Lusitano Palace Mekong.'

'It's fun to watch you connect all the dots, Marty.' She showed a teasing smile. 'It's why I chose you to chronicle my death.'

'You had no way of knowing I'd write a memoir,' Martina protested.

'Coy doesn't suit you.' Lifting her sunglasses, 'The day I met you I saw the hunger in your eyes,' Veronica said. 'I'm the biggest story that will ever happen to you.' She let the shades rest atop her head. 'All I had to do was drop hints that I was in danger, highlight shady characters – not hard in Hongkers – tantalise you with boarding-school drama . . . When I went tumbling overboard, I knew you'd do the rest. One way or the other, you'd put out the story I needed you to.'

Veronica dispatched her cocktail. 'You did do quite a number on poor Watercress. You should try your hand at a novel next. You're not very good at telling the truth.' She set down her glass by the edge of the pool with a *thunk*. 'I don't remember us discussing *Jane Eyre*, though. My house on Lamma is called Strawberry Hill? You do have Gothic sensibilities, Marty.' She let out a snort. '*Time is a River without Banks* – true enough, I suppose, but do you even like Chagall?'

'I do, actually.'

She licked her lips. 'Who do you think will play me in the movie?' Veronica continued musing. 'It'd better not be an American with a terrible accent.'

Martina twisted the jade bangle around her wrist, anger frothing. Tiny droplets sprayed against the surface of the water.

'You set me up,' she said, a growl in her voice. 'It was all a *set-up*? I thought we were friends.'

'*Best friends* – that's the story you sold the world.'

Veronica pierced Martina with her hazel eyes.

'I thought it was *true*.'

'Maybe it was. At first you were a means to an end, but then . . . I came to like you, Marty. Truly I did.'

But she didn't sound as if she liked Martina at all. The lump in Martina's throat grew until she could barely choke it down. Had she been nothing more than a patsy? A *joke* to Veronica? She'd pitied Quentin for his 'insurance policy' when, in fact, she'd been Veronica's all along.

Martina moved towards Veronica in a bolt, water breaking behind her. Veronica recoiled, showing the briefest flash of fear.

'Let's talk about why you're dead,' Martina demanded.

'That's rather old news, isn't it?' The corner of Veronica's mouth kicked up, yet it trembled slightly. 'I'd much rather hear about you.'

Crossing her arms, Martina said, 'You were never kidnapped.'

'Guilty as charged.' Veronica smirked. 'I wanted to give you another suspect for my tragic demise.'

And Martina had fallen for her long-suffering-wife performance hook, line and sinker. She was *such* an idiot. She'd wanted so much to believe that Veronica would confide in her above anyone else. It was nothing more than fool's gold.

Rage and disappointment exploded as Martina wheeled her hand through the water, dousing Veronica with a splash. Veronica wiped the water from her eyes.

'A model of maturity,' she sniped as she smoothed back her dyed bangs.

'Don't talk to me about maturity! Jean-Pierre is still tearing himself apart about it. He thinks *he's* the reason you're dead.'

A stronger wind rustled the palm trees that sheltered the pool. Martina watched the fronds dance for a few seconds, struggling to regain her composure.

'Why the hell did you do this to him?' Martina said in a low voice. 'To *me*?' Nearly a whisper.

'You always think everything is about you. You even managed to make my *death* all about you.'

'Then what was it about, Veronica? Tell me,' Martina said, gesturing at the garden, 'what *all of this* is about?'

Veronica retreated back towards the pool steps. She seated herself at the top, crossing her legs, and gave Martina a hard look. She wasn't used to being cornered.

'I can wait all day,' Martina prodded.

'Oh, Marty,' she said. 'No one's secrets stay secret forever. Your arrival being a case in point.'

Veronica slid her hand along the aluminium banister in the middle of the pool steps. White beams of sunlight bounced off it into Martina's eyes, forcing her to avert her gaze.

'What secrets could possibly be worth "dying" for when you're Veronica Hawkins?'

'You hit the nail on the head. I was Veronica *Hawkins*. My name was everything. My *family* name.'

'You're talking in riddles!' and Martina was losing her very last modicum of patience.

'Do I have to spell it out? Maybe you're not so intrepid, after all.' Veronica scoffed. 'I was being *blackmailed*, Marty.'

'I'm sure you could pay any price.'

She lifted a defiant chin. 'They didn't want money.'

'What, then?'

'To torture me. To watch me unravel. To *ruin* me – and my family's legacy. I couldn't let them win. I'd rather die. And so I did.'

Christmas Future

'What could they possibly have over you, Veronica?' Martina demanded.

Veronica looked at her a long moment. 'I'd better start from the beginning,' she said, as if she'd reached the conclusion of an internal debate. In the direction of the villa, she yelled, 'Another round of drinks, Dao!'

Veronica rose from the water, exiting the pool and grabbing a neatly folded beach towel that had been discreetly deposited on a lounge chair.

'Aren't you coming?' Veronica said to Martina. 'You'll catch a chill.'

'In this weather?' Martina sweltered even as the sun slouched lower on the horizon.

'Suit yourself.'

But Martina did get out, towelling herself off, the fibres thick and soft against her skin. She wrapped herself in the towel like it was chainmail, as if it could protect her from what was happening.

What the hell *was* happening?

'Thank you, Dao,' said Veronica as the woman laid two gin cocktails on a glass table between the lounge chairs.

Lowering herself on to the chair opposite Veronica, she picked up a drink. She listened to the gin fizz and she toyed with the dried lemon slice garnishing the rim.

Once the sliding glass door clicked shut, 'Grace period over,' Martina said. 'Tell me everything. *Now*.'

Veronica reclined sideways against the sun lounger, propping her head up with her elbow, an effortless Roman goddess.

'I said I'd start at the beginning, and I will.' Her ribcage expanded as she drew in a long breath. 'The last time I saw Lulu,' Veronica began, emotion seeping through her cool, 'I was fuming at her for stealing my lipstick. She refused to admit it but I knew she'd taken it. I was packing to go back to Oxford for Trinity term and I ransacked her bedroom looking for it. It was cheap, something I'd picked up from a stall in Mong Kok, but I wanted it back.' She traced the sun's steady descent with her eyes. 'I found it under Lulu's mattress after she died.' A few beats later, Veronica added, 'Lulu just wanted to be like me but I was nineteen and thought I was too important to spend time with her. The brand stopped making the shade soon after, so I commissioned my own.'

Martina knew the exact shade she meant. Cerise lip prints that were found on a glass laced with GHB. Veronica's signature. She hadn't been aware of its significance.

'I'm sorry about your sister, you know I am,' said Martina. 'But what does that have to do with anything?'

'It has to do with *everything*.' Pain roughened her words – abrasions nobody could see. Veronica faux-crossed herself. 'Bless me, Martina, for I have sinned. Now shut up and hear my confession.'

Despite her betrayal, Martina hated to see Veronica hurting. She dipped her forefingers into her glass and flicked the gin at Veronica like it was holy water. Veronica released a startled laugh.

'Fine,' said Martina. 'I'll shut up.' She drank her gin and waited.

'This was the end of April 1997,' Veronica resumed her story. 'I remember Arthur and Uncle Rupert arguing about a business deal while I was home for the Easter holiday. At the time, I didn't have any interest in Hawkins Pacific beyond my trust fund. If Arthur hadn't died, I don't think I'd ever have joined the family business.'

'What would you have done?' Martina couldn't help herself from asking.

'Who knows? I harboured illusions of being a singer, God help us all.'

Martina let that remark pass without comment.

'Anyhow, it was Uncle Rupert who taught me how to run a business. I was a natural, he said, but there was a lot to learn. I was green.' Veronica's fingernails clawed at her highball glass. 'Naive. The first deal he guided me through closing was for a mining corporation in the north of China.'

She plucked the lemon from the rim of her glass, steadying her breath.

'Arthur had agreed to go in with Uncle Rupert because Barron Industries couldn't provide the financing the Chinese wanted on its own. My family died on 22 May 1997 – Buddha's Birthday that year. I signed the paperwork to ink the deal two weeks later, wanting to carry out my father's final wishes.' A deep groove appeared on the bridge of Veronica's nose. 'We met with lawyers right after the joint funeral. Lulu's casket was so small.'

She bit down on the lemon rind too hard, teeth scraping together. Martina thought about the nightmares Jean-Pierre said had plagued her. Veronica was finally revealing their source.

'I moved into Rockyda Manor for a while,' she went on. 'I couldn't stand to rattle around my family home without them. I'm not much of a crier but Philippa lent me her shoulder when I needed it. Maman and I were like chalk and cheese . . . Philippa and I had always had an easy rapport.'

'Is that why you don't talk much about Geneviève?' Martina asked. She gestured around them with her glass. 'About this place? Her grandmother in Laos?'

Veronica's gaze turned owlish. 'How did you know this was her grandmother's house?'

Unable to resist a smug smile, Martina said, 'There's a photograph in the catalogue of the retrospective exhibition you held at the gallery.'

She sucked in a breath. 'I'd forgotten about that.' The gin frothed as she dunked the dried lemon back in the glass. 'Very good, Sherlock. Perhaps a Pulitzer isn't out of the question.'

'I suppose that makes you Moriarty.'

'How feminist.'

'On the ride over, the driver said the king hunted here?' Martina said leadingly.

'This used to be a tea plantation,' replied Veronica. 'But it was also part of the royal hunting grounds. Maman met the last king. He didn't lose his throne until the mid-seventies.'

Martina's gaze drifted toward the gardens where early evening whispered through the blossoms. 'You could pick a worse place to be dead.'

Veronica nodded dully.

As insects greeted the coming night, Veronica stared down at the ice clinking in her glass. Talking about the past seemed to be depleting her by the second. Martina felt compelled to share something of her own.

'When they were looking for you – for your body – I would take ferries to the outlying islands, no destination in mind,' she said. 'I was hoping to spot you, I think, like a mermaid.'

'You must be confusing me with the Veronica you created.'

Not acknowledging the gibe, 'Sometimes I still ferry hop,' Martina told her. 'When I want to feel close to you.'

'I never thought you were delusional, Marty.'

Martina bristled, the rejection prickling, hating how much she'd missed the way Veronica said her nickname. 'I'm still not seeing how this story ends in you faking your own death,' she said, trying to regain the upper hand.

'I'm getting to that.' Veronica inhaled as if it took great effort. 'Let's skip ahead to 2008, Beijing's coming-out party. The Olympics are in full swing, everyone's making money hand over fist and Vasco comes by some new information after a . . . let's call it a business merger.'

Rather than a bloodbath? Martina wondered, not wanting to think too hard about what Ao Wing was capable of. 'That information being?' she pressed.

'A well-placed source, as you journos would say, informed Vasco that he had been paid to sabotage my father's boat.'

Veronica paused, letting the statement hang in the air. 'Arthur usually took the boat out solo. He liked to be alone at sea, do a Hemingway, ponder the big questions. I don't think Maman and Lulu were intended targets. But . . . it was Buddha's Birthday.'

Martina touched a comforting hand to Veronica's shoulder, impulsive, before retracting it.

'I didn't want to believe it,' Veronica said. 'I'd only been able to move on with my life by becoming a fatalist. By believing it was an act of god. Unpreventable. Unavoidable. An earthquake. A bloody tsunami.'

She balled her right hand into a fist. 'It was the act of a man. A greedy, cowardly man.'

'Who was it?'

'If you've been paying attention, I think you know.'

Martina tensed, a squeezing sensation in her solar plexus.

'Rupert Barron,' she said on an exhale.

'*Ding, ding, ding.*' Venom oozed from Veronica's voice. Her pupils dilated.

'You're totally sure?'

'I wish I weren't.' She laughed caustically. 'There was proof. A wire transfer.' Veronica sat up straight. 'Vasco did his homework.'

Goosepimples pebbled Martina's skin. 'Why would Rupert want your father dead? What was his motive?'

'I thought you were paying attention.'

Combing through Veronica's soliloquy, Martina replied, 'Something to do with the mine in China.'

'We have another winner.' She gave Martina a weak round of applause, but the retort lacked bite. For once, Veronica was blinking back tears of her own. 'Arthur had been getting cold feet about financing Barron Industries, thought it might be throwing good money after bad.' Her jaw tightened. 'Before he could pull out, he was dead. And Barron Industries was saved. A stroke of luck, wasn't it?' She reached for her drink. 'I should have seen it sooner. I've raked myself over the coals, believe me. Uncle Rupert was my mentor, my fucking godfather. He told me once if Elsie had my instincts, he'd have let her take the mantle from him.' Veronica shook her head. 'I loved him, Marty, as much as Arthur. Maybe more . . . but not more than Lulu.'

Martina didn't dare interrupt. She remained quiet as Veronica collected herself.

'Vasco asked me what I wanted to do – it was my family. My decision,' she said. 'I gave Rupert every opportunity to come clean without asking him outright. I told myself if he confessed, if he *begged* for my mercy, I'd spare him. If I went through with it, I'd be no better than him. No worse, either. I looked at Uncle Rupert and saw my own Christmas Future.'

'Now who's being Dickensian?' said Martina.

Veronica ignored the dig. 'I saw him off on the train to Guangzhou. I thanked him for everything he'd taught me. Sometimes I wonder if he had any inkling what awaited him.'

Martina's brain whirred as she sucked in a breath. *Stabbed. A robbery in Mainland.* That was what Iris had told her, years ago now. But Rupert Barron hadn't been killed in a mugging gone wrong. He had been murdered.

'You sent him to his death,' she accused.

'I evened the score.' Veronica's words were granite hard.

'Does Jean-Pierre know?'

'He's an artist.' She shook her head. 'He looks for beauty in misery.' *Beauty in misery.* Was that what he saw when he looked at Martina?

Veronica ran a hand through her short blonde strands. 'But some-one knows. Someone who despises me. At first the demands seemed simple enough – bitcoin transfers, scuppering business deals. Then they became more outlandish: having my jockey throw a race, leav-ing a bag of uncut diamonds at the feet of Queen Victoria's statue in Causeway Bay. Almost as if the blackmailer had read too much John le Carré.'

Martina remained quiet as Veronica spoke. It did sound as if the blackmailer had been enjoying themselves.

'I liquidated everything I could, put Hawkins Pacific in the red – but it was never enough. They didn't want my money, they wanted me to twist in the wind.' Veronica laughed in a broken way. 'The last straw came right before our trip to Macau.'

'What happened?'

Martina had thought it was something about Macau that'd made Veronica more vulnerable, exposed the cracks in her facade, but she'd been wrong about that too.

'We went for Buddha's Birthday, if you recall?' Veronica said.

She did. Martina recalled every single detail.

'The blackmailer sent me a voicemail. A recording of my phone call with Vasco,' she elaborated. 'It might not have held up in court but it would have been enough to destroy everything my family rep-resented in Hong Kong.' The knuckles on her right hand had turned white. 'They stopped making any demands. They just kept sending me the same message. Every day. That's when I knew it would never stop. The blackmailer would torment me, waiting for the right day to make my world collapse around me.' Veronica gazed at Martina levelly. 'You probably think it's what I deserved.'

'Honestly, I have no idea what I'm thinking right now.' Her mind was whirring at a million miles an hour, the puzzle pieces fit-ting into place. Disbelief, mainly, but also a deep vein of sympathy.

'Fair enough,' Veronica said, laughing in her husky way. Martina had longed to hear that laugh again. So much.

'You never figured out who was behind the blackmail?'

'If I had, would I be *here*?' Veronica said in frustration. Martina didn't want to ask what Veronica would have done if she'd discovered the blackmailer's identity.

'So that's when you hatched your plan. In Macau.'

'I didn't see any other way out. There were moments I considered actually taking my own life, but I'm just not built that way.'

Martina savoured the slow burn of the gin, fingers twitching for a cigarette. 'You could have confided in me. I wouldn't have judged you.'

'Really, Marty?' Veronica lowered an eyebrow.

'Really. It's horrific what Rupert Barron did. I would have wanted revenge too,' insisted Martina. *Oh God. Poor Elsie*, she thought. Her father was a monster and she idolised him. She thought he'd died some version of a hero's death.

'You say you would have wanted revenge,' said Veronica, cutting into her thoughts. 'Taking it is a whole different matter.' Veronica looked Martina up and down. 'Would you have had the guts? A poisoned pen doesn't count.'

Martina swallowed audibly. *Would she have had the guts?* Part of her wanted to say yes; the same part that admired Veronica's Old Testament tactics. The other part felt ill.

'If I'd known you were in trouble, Veronica – *real* trouble, I would have helped. I swear I would have.'

'But you *did* help, Marty. Better than if I'd orchestrated it all myself,' Veronica told her. 'It was fate. Cressida's benefit gave me the perfect venue from which to escape. Overboard! Death on the high seas! The tabloids would eat it up.'

Veronica sneered but Martina could see the fear beneath it, the desperation that had driven her to the watery depths.

'Who would doubt I was dead? Veronica Hawkins reduced to fish food!'

Martina drew her legs into her chest, curling her arms protectively around her knees. 'The glass they found on the *Tin Hau 8* . . . the GHB,' she said. 'Did you plant it?'

Raising a shoulder, Veronica replied, 'A little misdirection goes a long way.'

So Quentin hadn't been lying about that, after all. 'How did you get off the junk?' Martina asked, pulling at all of the strands, needing to know the minutiae of Veronica's plan, needing to understand exactly how she'd been duped.

'I never left. I hid below decks – got a nasty crick in my neck. Took weeks of massages to get it out.' Veronica rubbed her shoulder. 'Lucky for me, Dao has magic fingers.'

Martina squeezed her knees tighter to her chest.

'And then?'

'A few well-placed bribes, a private speedboat to Macau, a new identity and Vasco's jet to Luang Prabang.'

'More misdirection,' Martina said, and Veronica curved her lips. 'What about the body that washed ashore?'

'Anything is possible in Macau.'

'You chose for it to be found at the Bauhinia Boat Club because Quentin's a member, didn't you?'

'It had to be found somewhere.' Veronica spoke lightly yet the pitch was too high, a sharply tuned string. 'I was sorry to see that dress go. Red has always been my colour. Especially now that I'm blonde.'

Martina knitted her hands together. 'But you made one big mistake.'

'Only one?'

'You should have flown private on your trip here before the gala,' Martina informed her. 'Teagan Sullivan from the American Club told Elsie she ran into you. It's how I found you.'

She infused the statement with as much triumph as she could muster, but she didn't feel particularly triumphant. Veronica had been pulling her strings from the start. Martina half wished Veronica had stayed dead – ghosts were easier to love.

'I'd figured the police would check the flight logs of my jet and I didn't want any link with Laos.' Shrugging, she said, 'Commercial was a minuscule risk.'

'Bad luck, I guess.'

Veronica ran her pinkie through the condensation on her glass.

'Arthur taught me to play chess before I could read,' she started, her eyes growing unfocused. 'We always played by tournament rules – touch move. If you touch a piece, you have to move it. My father didn't see a point in playing any other way.'

Her gaze fell towards the ground, a hush along with it. The golden hour cast the villa in an otherworldly hue, the pool burning orange.

A tendril of wind troubled the water. 'I didn't adhere to Arthur's rules when it came to you, Marty,' Veronica conceded. 'I put you into play before I knew exactly what I was going to do with you. That was my cardinal sin.'

Martina blew out a long breath. The scent of frangipani surrounded them, and Martina wished they could go back to the beginning, back to their Eden, before all the lies.

'I loved you, Veronica,' she said. 'I would have helped you if you'd trusted me – but I'm not taking the fall for you.'

Veronica looked up at her. 'Oh, I think you are.'

Martina swivelled on the lounge chair to face her no longer dead friend. She planted her feet firmly on the ground.

'Tell Peony Huang you're behind the skimming, Veronica, or I'll tell the world you're alive.'

'And here you were, trying to convince me I could trust you?' She clucked her tongue.

'My back's up against the wall. It's not what I want, I don't want to out you – but I'm not going to prison.'

'It's only white-collar crime, Marty.'

Martina gritted her teeth at Veronica's blithe tone. 'Fine, you're happy for me to go to Martha Stewart jail. But what will your black-mailer do when they know you're alive?'

Veronica shivered and Martina knew it wasn't feigned.

'By the time you tell anyone about me – about your *allegations* I'm alive – I'll be long gone.' She whirled toward Martina, their knees touching. 'They won't find a trace,' Veronica hissed. 'You'll be discredited. Who will buy your books then?'

'I don't care what you say – everything between us wasn't a lie,' Martina said, hurling the words at her, wanting them to be true. 'I can't believe you'd just hang me out to dry.'

Veronica took Martina's hand, twirling the bracelet.

'It's sweet you kept the bangle, Marty. I should be touched.' She gripped Martina tighter. 'I would be, I think, if you hadn't fucked my husband.'

'I . . .'

'Don't bother denying it.'

How could she possibly know? Was Veronica having Jean-Pierre watched? Was she having *Martina* watched?

The gin turned bitter in her throat. 'It was after you . . . I thought you were *dead*, Veronica. We were just comforting each other. The funeral was hard.' Martina sucked in a big breath, regret constricting her chest. 'It wasn't right, I know. I'm sorry. I was a mess, and so was he.'

Veronica threw her head back in an almost-cackle.

'You're something else. Jean-Pierre told me, Marty. It's why we were fighting the night I "died".' She cackled again. 'But by then I needed you too much.'

Martina felt herself go pale.

'I know all about Lamma. Almost makes me wonder what else my *best friend* left out of her memoir?'

She made a choking sound and Veronica winked.

'So, no, I don't owe you anything. You served your purpose. Go home, Marty.'

The words were a slap.

'You know it's true what they say,' said Veronica. 'Confession *is* good for the soul. I feel much lighter.'

Martina's heart pounded, fracturing, exploding into a thousand sharp slivers of glass. She had done this. She had found her friend only to lose her all over again.

'I never meant to hurt you, Veronica,' she rasped.

'And I never meant to hurt you. Doesn't change anything, does it?'

Veronica lifted her hand and the glass door slid open, Dao's silhouette emerging.

'Martina can see herself out.'

Voulez-Vous

The damp bathing suit squelched between Martina's breasts on the ride back to the hotel. She hadn't bothered to take it off before getting dressed.

'You had a nice time with your friend?' the driver asked, and Martina replied with a curt nod. She blew smoke out the window. Night had fallen on Luang Prabang as the sedan approached the hotel gates. Lanterns dangled above restaurant terraces, their warm glow at odds with the cold freezing Martina from the inside out.

The last hint of sunset evanesced on distant mountaintops. She just had to hold it together until she was in the privacy of her hotel room.

Go home.

Cressida wanted her gone.

Go home, Marty.

Veronica wanted her gone. Banished.

Where would she go? If Martina went back to Hong Kong without clearing her name, she had nothing. The life she'd built would be carried away like dust. And *she* had built it. It was *her* moxie and determination. Veronica couldn't take credit for everything.

Barely thanking her driver, Martina sprinted through the palm-lined courtyards towards her suite and hurled herself into the middle of the king-sized bed. She screamed into the heavenly soft pillows. She pounded her fists, kicked her feet. She let herself have a tantrum the magnitude of which she was never allowed as a child.

Go home, Go home, Go home. The command ricocheted around Martina's skull until it became meaningless. She buried her face further into the darkness.

Veronica was alive. Veronica was alive, and she hated her.

Veronica had betrayed her. Martina had betrayed Veronica too, and she knew it.

Like a twisted nursery rhyme the words repeated in Martina's mind. Had any of their time together been real? Could she even tell the difference between what was real and what wasn't?

She screamed until her throat was hoarse and all she could do was whimper.

Eventually her breathing slowed, her limbs grew heavy. The white noise of the air conditioner lulled her into a false sense of security, floating in the blackness. She had never felt this old. This tired.

A knock came at the door, rousing Martina from her stupor.

She couldn't say how much time had passed in her cocoon of pillows and mosquito netting. Peeling herself from the bed, she left behind watermarks on the linen duvet cover.

'Coming!' Martina called, her mouth cottonwool.

She staggered towards the door and finger-combed her hair. Air drying in the humidity brought out Martina's natural curl, which she'd been straightening since middle school. No one wanted to see a dark frizzy mess, her mother had said, as if her lack of blonde hair was a personal affront.

Rubbing her bleary eyes, Martina twisted the doorknob.

'Turn down?' asked a woman in the blue silk hotel uniform. Martina trailed her gaze towards the bed. She didn't want the maid wondering about her soggy clothes.

'No, thank you.' She shook her head.

'Chocolate?'

'Why the hell not.' Martina accepted a small box of truffles and started to close the door. The maid whipped out a plumeria blossom, extending it to Martina. She sighed a smile.

Popping two truffles in her mouth at once, salted caramel and chilli pepper melting on her tongue, Martina tucked the flower behind her ear as she padded towards the mini-bar and surveyed its contents. She decided to start with a neat Grey Goose, plucking the doll-sized bottle from its slot. For once she didn't bother looking at the price list. The foundation could foot the bill if Martina was already going down for misusing funds.

She tipped the contents into a tumbler. *Clink. Swirl. Mmm.* She stuffed another truffle into her face. Practically a chocolate Martini. It tasted like self-loathing.

With a hiccup, Martina grabbed the half-bottle of Laurent-Perrier Cuvée Rosé next. *Pop.* Everything was prettier in pink. She retrieved her iPhone from where she'd flung it, hearing Pavlov's silent bell, unable to resist checking her notifications.

Was anyone looking for Martina? Was anyone missing her?

The screen was ghostly bright in the dimly lit suite. One text from Iris asking if she'd checked in to the hotel safely.

Iris was the only person who knew where she was. What if Martina took a page from Veronica's book and simply ran away? Could she live a life in exile? But Veronica had had months to plan, to move Martina and all of the other pieces around the board.

Martina didn't have the contacts to forge a new identity and she had less than thirty grand in the bank – she'd been living to the very limit of her means, putting on the Famous Author show. She scratched at a hive that had appeared on her forearm. Even if she hid somewhere remote like Borneo she'd run through her funds in a year or two, and wind up teaching yoga to entitled divorcées or, worse, honeymooners.

Suddenly she was itchy all over.

Starting to tremble, Martina walked out on to the patio, flicked on the pool lights. The water glimmered aqua. The moon bounced atop the palm trees sheltering the plunge pool. She heard voices laughing nearby – a couple, no doubt having a romantic evening.

The night air was hot, pregnant with possibility.

She shucked off her sodden Tory Burch T-shirt and pedal push-ers. She swigged the champagne and snapped the strap of Veronica's bathing suit against her shoulder. She snapped it again, wanting it to leave a mark.

Veronica was right. A swimsuit proved nothing. Veronica undoubtedly had a crew of movers scrubbing her villa of any trace of her existence this very minute. Martina could call Peony Huang with a cockamamie story about Veronica coming back from the dead – but why would she believe her? She'd be branded a fantasist as well as a fraud.

Martina couldn't prove anything, and yet Ao Wing would know she knew the truth.

What would he do?

This was the end of the road. Once the news broke about the embezzlement, Martina's publisher would invoke the morality clause and cancel her book contract. Her agent would drop her. She'd have no career. No marriage.

Her thirty-two years on the planet would be for naught.

Martina could only imagine the delight Sybil Merton would take in her ex-daughter-in-law's downfall. *Good riddance to bad rubbish,* she'd tell her friends over a hand of bridge at the Colony Club.

Lowering herself into the plunge pool, she took another glug of champers. She spun the jade bangle around her wrist, faster, faster, the friction of a Catherine wheel against her skin.

She didn't blame Veronica for hating her. Veronica surely would have preferred for the missing funds to go unnoticed, but she must also be relishing this revenge on Martina.

Again, she couldn't blame her. Martina was so afraid to be alone, craved affection so much that she'd brought this on herself. When she'd been a little girl she'd invented an imaginary twin named Maria who always wanted to play with her, who held her hand in the dark until she fell asleep.

Tears streaked down Martina's face, her breaths ragged, coming in gulps.

Her friendship with Veronica and what had happened with Jean-Pierre occupied two completely different spaces in her mind, as if they belonged to two different Martinas. Martina the friend and Martina the adulteress were two separate people. The gates to hell had opened for one night only. After that night in Lamma, before Veronica disappeared, she and Jean-Pierre avoided each other.

Martina had considered coming clean to Veronica in Guangzhou, on their way back from the opera house, but she didn't want to make it real. If they never spoke of it, it would be like it never happened. Jean-Pierre must have thought he could close the distance between him and his wife with the truth.

He'd been wrong.

Martina let her toes drift along the tiles of the pool, sinking further, further, until she was fully submerged. The coral-pink blossom slid from behind her ear, petals fluttering beneath the water.

How many times had she imagined Veronica's final moments? How scared she must have been? Wishing she could have saved her?

All the while, Veronica must have been laughing at Martina. Or cursing her.

When had Jean-Pierre shrived himself to his wife? Did she leave him behind because of Martina? How many of Veronica's smiles had meant *fuck you*?

Water surged up Martina's nose. She surfaced, coughing, and reached for the champagne. She liked the weight in her hand.

It would be only too easy to wash down the new bottle of Xanax she'd purchased on Des Voeux Road without a prescription, let the hotel staff find her body – skin pruned from the water, become an expat cliché.

Martina's phone buzzed on the edge of the pool.

Elsie B.
How are you holding up?

Before she could respond, Elsie sent a follow-up.

> Fifi wants to see the dolphin show at Ocean Park tomorrow. Can I convince you?

Martina felt a twist in her gut. *Oh, Elsie.* She thought of Veronica like a sister and Veronica had ordered her father's death. But Rupert had killed Veronica's entire family.

Talk about a blood feud. It was all too surreal and Shakespearean. Now *that* was a story that would fly off the shelves.

She snorted, a rosé backwash rising in her throat. But it wasn't funny. It wasn't funny at all.

How would she face Elsie? Her friend deserved to know the truth but, at the same time, how would it make her life better? Veronica would still be gone. Elsie's father had died for his crimes. In this case, ignorance did seem like bliss.

Martina stared at the text, considering her reply.

She couldn't confide in Elsie where she was. She didn't know what Veronica would tell Ao Wing about Martina's discovery and she wouldn't put Elsie or her goddaughter in danger.

> **Me to Elsie B.**
> Can't tomorrow. Bad sushi from ParknShop.

> So sorry. Do you need anything?

> Iris has me covered. Speak soon xx

> Feel better. E

Martina scrolled through her text messages. The last half-dozen to Bitsy had gone unanswered. She hit the call button. She drank some more liquid courage as it rang.

Bitsy picked up on the sixth ring. She sounded out of breath. 'Hello?'

'Hi, it's me. Now a good time?'

'I'm on the treadmill.'

Martina heard the *thump, thump, thump* of sneakers on an endless track. It was Bitsy's favourite way to punish herself.

'Oh, right, that's great,' she said.

'I'm down to one-ten. No butterballs in sight.' *Thump, thump, thump.*

'You always look beautiful, Bitsy.'

A harsh exhale came down the line. 'Did you want something, Marty?'

'Just . . . to see how you're doing. It's been a while.'

'I'm fab. Went to St Barths for Easter.' Her tone was guarded, words clipped. She didn't sound like Martina's oldest friend at all.

'I saw the pics on Insta. Looked like a blast. I'm sorry I missed it . . . I . . . I missed you last time I was in New York. The book tour was such a circus, I wish we could have spent more time together. I've been thinking a lot about you,' Martina started to ramble. 'Everything has just been so much lately, sometimes I don't know which way is up . . .'

Thump, thump, thump.

'Are you drunk, Marty?'

'Tipsy. It's late here. But that's not the point. I wanted to make amends. I miss you, Bitsy.'

'You miss me so much you've never invited me to Hong Kong?'

'What?' Martina's voice hitched.

'I'm not cool enough for your new life. You don't need me any more.'

'Bitsy, you're wrong. I'm so sorry if I made you feel that way. You're always welcome. You don't need an invitation.'

Bitsy let out a long sigh. 'Whatever, Marty. I need to go. My heartrate is coming out of the target zone.'

'I mean it. I want you to come visit,' Martina pleaded. 'Why don't you come for your birthday in June?'

'I already have plans for my birthday.'

'Oh.' A pause. 'Then I'll come with you. Where are you going?'

'I don't think that's a good idea.'

'Why not?'

Thump, thump, thump. 'I'm going to Rome with Merritt Merton.' Bitsy let the revelation stretch the miles between them. 'Sleep it off, Marty.'

Click.

Martina slammed the phone down.

Merritt *fucking* Merton? Bitsy was going on vacation with Spencer's sister? Bitsy had never liked Merritt. When did they become such pals?

Had they burned her book together?

She started swilling the rest of the bottle. Somehow Martina had assumed Bitsy would always be there. They'd been friends for twenty years. She'd had no idea how badly she'd hurt Bitsy. It had never been her intention.

Doesn't change anything, does it?

Veronica's words from earlier echoed on the breeze. Martina tasted the dregs of the champagne on her tongue, floral and acidic. She leaned her head back on the edge of pool and stared up at the moon.

It wavered. She *was* drunk. She hadn't eaten anything besides truffles since Bangkok.

The phone trilled and Martina fumbled for it, heart leaping into her throat.

'Bitsy?' she said.

'This is your mother.'

Fuck.

She hadn't expected to hear from her until the mandatory birthday call in a couple weeks. 'Hi, Mom,' she slurred slightly.

'Did I wake you?'

Martina released a dramatic yawn. 'No, in bed. Long day. Stressful.'

'Mine too.'

'Sorry to hear that.' She effused empathy, navigating every conversation with her mother like a minefield. 'What time is it there?'

'Don't take that tone with me, young lady. It's almost one o'clock and my day has already been quite stressful.'

'I'm not taking any tone, Mom. What happened?'

'I was just informed that I won't be chairing the Thanksgiving Auction committee for Buxton, after all.'

'That's a sha—'

'Do you want to know why? Spencer's mother, of course. As one of Buxton's Gold Benefactors, Sybil decided she wanted to chair the committee – only when she heard I was chairing it this year. And we both know why that is.'

'Because she's a bitch.'

'Martina! This is your fault. You couldn't have a nice quiet divorce like everyone else, could you?'

A tension headache ignited on cue, pain thrumming behind her eyeballs.

Martina's wedding day had been the best day of her mother's life. The culmination of a decades-long campaign to infiltrate New York's elite. Martina's maternal grandmother, Grandma Olson, called her the 'half-breed' when she was out of earshot. In her mother's eyes, Martina Merton was a half-breed no more. It was the moment of acceptance, for both of them.

'I was supposed to stay married to Spencer so you could have your pick of fucking committees, is that it?' Martina burst out. Whoops, there went that landmine.

'Do not curse at me! I didn't say that!'

Martina jammed her eyes closed, willing away the pressure.

'I'm not having this fight again.' It would have killed her slowly, but Martina could still be Mrs Spencer Merton if she'd been prepared to commit to the programme.

'You embarrassed the Mertons, Martina, and they're not going to forget it anytime soon.'

'Mom, did it ever occur to you that Spencer was the one in the wrong?'

Beneath the water, Martina's legs began to itch. So what if she was a hypocrite? He cheated first. If Spencer had never cheated, Martina wouldn't have let herself be seduced by Jean-Pierre, and now Veronica might be willing to save Martina's skin.

She snapped the strap of her swimsuit. Again. And again.

'Was I supposed to look the other way? Suffer in silence so I could live in a co-op?' Martina demanded when her mother didn't reply. 'It's not the goddamn fifties.'

Drawing in a pained breath, her mother said, 'I'm sorry Spencer cheated on you, Martina. You still shouldn't have aired your dirty laundry in public. It's undignified.'

Her mother would never fight Martina's corner. Martina would always be at fault. She'd gotten off lightly when Martina created the memoir version of her childhood.

'You're on the other side of the world,' her mother pressed on, full steam ahead. 'You don't have to deal with the fallout. You never were one for consequences, little girl.'

'*I'm* your daughter. You should care more about me than being chair of some stupid committee!'

'I'm doing this for *you*, Martina. Don't you see that? Buxton wasn't thrilled about how you depicted your time there. I'm trying to salvage your relationship with the school in case you ever decide to have kids.' Exasperation bled through her mother's voice. She thought she was so Becky Sharp but she had nothing on Veronica Hawkins. She had no idea what Martina was dealing with.

'How did I raise such a short-sighted child?' lamented her mother.

Fury boiled over. 'I know I'll never be enough. Don't do anything more for me. I'm never coming home!' Martina shrieked with a violence that shocked her. 'There's nothing in New York for me!'

She hurled the phone into the water.

She watched it sink.

It drifted back and forth, gliding like a skate on ice, before hitting the bottom. It was as if she had watched all of Manhattan sink. She laughed.

The screen glowed up at her like a portal to another dimension. Oh no. What did she do?

You never were one for consequences, little girl.

Martina dove for the phone, rescuing it from its watery grave. She jumped out of the pool, clinging to the slippery metal case. Pulling on a bathrobe, she started jogging towards the main reception building.

Shit, shit, shit. She'd be stranded without her phone. Her entire life was contained in its ones and zeroes.

The hotel was eerily quiet. Martina heard only insects and her own footsteps. The sun umbrellas were folded, the lounge chairs bare around the pool. She followed the glowing hurricane lamps towards reception.

She dripped a trail of water in her wake.

Reaching an empty reception desk, Martina hated to be *that* demanding guest ringing the bell in the middle of the night. But this was an emergency. She flinched as it pierced the quiet.

The marble was cold against the soles of her feet.

Martina was about to ring again when a young man appeared from a narrow corridor and strolled towards her. He was white, early twenties, good looking in a wiry sort of way.

'*Bonsoir,*' he greeted her. 'I'm Jean-Luc, the night manager. How can I help you?'

Martina had to laugh. The universe had a sick sense of humour.

'Are all French men named Jean-something?' she said.

Jean-Luc smiled boyishly, his eyes crinkling at the edges. 'It's a popular name.' He came to a halt before her, gaze flicking to the water dripping on her feet. 'Although Jean Reno is just Jean, *tout court*. He's the most famous Jean.'

Martina held out her iPhone like it was a wounded baby bird.

'I, um, had a mishap in the plunge pool.'

'Ah. I see.' Jean-Luc stroked his chin, puckering his lips. His skin was baby smooth. His hair sandy brown. 'We have some rice in the kitchen.'

'Does that work?' Martina said with an arched brow.

'Sometimes.' He extended his hand for the phone. 'Shall we try?' His use of *shall* amused Martina and his expression could only be described as impish.

'Yes, we shall. I'm coming with you.'

The Frenchman frowned. 'I'll bring the rice to you. Why don't you wait by the pool?'

Martina pressed the phone to her chest, drying it with the terry-cloth bathrobe.

'OK, but hurry.'

She dripped her way back outside and took a seat at one of the café tables. A tremor in her hand, she removed the waterlogged Louis Vuitton case and smoothed the screen with the corner of her robe. She released a weary sigh. Today had not gone as planned. Not that she'd had a plan exactly. Her stomach complained. She was exhausted and hungry and she was about to become a social pariah.

Jean-Luc reappeared with a plastic bag of rice in one hand and a glass of Scotch in the other. He placed the Scotch on the table before Martina. The candle in the hurricane lamp flickered, orange shadows teasing his features.

'May I sit?' he asked.

'*Je vous en prie*,' replied Martina.

His eyes lit with surprise. 'You speak French?'

'A little.' Martina lifted the glass. '*Merci*.'

'Technology can be stressful.'

Mothers can be stressful, she thought. *Having your best friend fake her own death and frame you for embezzlement can be stressful.*

Jean-Luc smiled and a dimple appeared on his cheek. He must get away with murder with that smile. As soon the thought had crossed Martina's mind, she remembered that Veronica *had* gotten away with murder – just about.

How was anything about today reality?

'You should take the SIM card out first,' said Jean-Luc.

Martina glanced at him sideways. 'Shit. I don't have that stupid key thing.'

'Not to worry.' He withdrew a paperclip from the breast pocket of his uniform shirt – royal blue, which suited him.

'You're quite the boy scout,' Martina said. She was flirting. *Christ.* Her life was falling apart and she couldn't help herself. 'Could you do it? I'm terrible with these things.'

She handed him the phone, their fingers brushing briefly.

'My pleasure,' he said. Jean-Luc bit his lip as he jimmied open the phone and retrieved the SIM. 'You backed it up to the Cloud?' he asked as he worked.

'I don't know. Maybe?'

Iris had set it all up for her. Martina ran her fingers through her hair. She could feel it frizzing. She took a long, ill-advised drink of Scotch. She was sobering up enough to know this was a bad idea.

'I'm not the first stupid tourist to drop her phone in the pool, huh.'

Jean-Luc tilted his head at her. 'Accidents happen.' The Gallic shrug must be genetic.

'How long have you been night manager here?' asked Martina.

'A few months. Before that I was in Hanoi for a year. Langkawi the year before that.'

Raising the Scotch to her lips, 'You don't look old enough to have lived in so many places,' she said.

Jean-Luc laughed softly. 'I'm an old man of twenty-four.' He plopped the iPhone into the bag of rice, the grains shifting like sand.

'So old,' she mocked. Martina could no longer remember being twenty-four. It was a lifetime ago. She'd just started dating Spencer.

'I came out to Asia as soon I finished hotelier school. It was my dream to travel. There's always a new hotel opening in Asia, a new place to try.'

'Like the navy, but without the threat to life and limb.'

He chortled. 'If you like,' Jean-Luc agreed. 'And you, did you arrive today? Are you enjoying your stay?'

Martina swallowed. 'I was supposed to meet a friend here . . . it seems I'm on my own.' She swirled the liquid in the glass. 'I don't think I'll stay.'

Jean-Luc tied the plastic bag closed. 'There are many things to do here as a solo tourist. Don't leave so soon. America is a long flight.'

'I live in Hong Kong.'

'Even so.' He glanced around them. 'Tomorrow is my day off. I could show you around. It's a shame to be sad in such a beautiful place.'

Martina snorted. 'Sometimes you love the thing that hurts you worst most of all.' It felt like the universe was giving her a do-over, the chance to make another choice. She leaned back in her chair. 'How old do you think I am?' she asked him.

A comically panicked look crossed Jean-Luc's face. 'My age? Twenty-three? Twenty-four?'

'Thirty-two.'

'So old.' He used her words against her. 'But in France we appreciate older women,' he said with a wink. 'Catherine Deneuve. Isabelle Adjani.'

Martina grimaced at the name Veronica had chosen for her new life. She knocked back the rest of the Scotch.

'It's quiet here at night,' she said.

'The guests are sleeping.'

'But not us.'

'Not us.'

Martina wouldn't sleep tonight. She didn't want to be alone. Yearning scorched the inside of her chest. Boldly, she touch a hand to his cheek.

'Will you be missed?' she said.

Jean-Luc did another quick lap of the courtyard with his eyes.

'Not by anyone who matters.'

She smiled with her teeth.

'By the way, since you haven't asked, my name is Veronica.'

The name just slipped out. She couldn't say why. All she knew was that she needed to slip her skin.

Everyone had abandoned her. The firing squad awaited in Hong Kong. This could be her last night on earth. Why bother pulling herself together?

Why shouldn't Martina find some abandon for herself?

Queen Me

Martina's eyes opened on a damp patch on the ceiling. Her head pounded. The snuffling of a light snore tickled her earlobe. Early morning light bled across the walls, brightening a few sepia photographs of colonial Luang Prabang in cheap IKEA frames.

This was not Martina's luxurious suite. She groaned. Her muscles were stiff, aching, proving she was no longer in her twenties. She trailed her gaze along the sleeping form of her companion. He did have a nice ass. And what he'd lacked in skill he'd made up for with determination.

She needed to leave. This bed. The hotel. The entire country.

Careful not to wake him, Martina slipped out of the sheets and found her swimsuit. She could pass as some health nut awake for a morning swim, she told herself. She collected the bag containing her iPhone and scurried out of the staff accommodation. The phone bobbing in the rice reminded her of the goldfish she'd once received as a party favour at a classmate's birthday. *Who gives other people's children pets?* her mother had exclaimed as she flushed it down the toilet, telling Martina it would reach the sea. Little Martina knew it was a lie.

The resort was deserted. No witnesses to her walk of shame. She'd wanted an escape last night, knowing her skin would crawl in the daylight, knowing the weight of emptiness would return, swift and brutal. After Veronica's body was found, Martina had promised herself she wouldn't use sex to make herself feel less lonely. And she hadn't – for a while.

Since Veronica was alive, what did it matter? What did anything matter? Jean-Luc could swap stories about desperate cougars with his hotelier friends. What did she care?

Martina rubbed sleep and tears from the corners of her eyes as she packed. The phone was still dead. She wrung out Veronica's swimsuit and stuffed it into a side pocket.

She checked out at a near-silent reception, the wheels of her rollaboard echoing across the courtyard, and took a car back to the airport, chugging bottled water while keeping her eyes closed. A cleaner was still mopping the floor of the small terminal as Martina walked up to the Plumeria Airways counter.

'Good morning,' said a middle-aged Laotian woman with a yawn.

'I need a ticket for Hong Kong.' Where else could she go?

Tap, tap, tap. 'Flights are very full,' the ticketing agent cautioned. Martina gritted her teeth at the clacking and palmed another paracetamol.

'I'll pay for first.' *Tap, tap, tap.* When Martina couldn't take it any more, she demanded, 'What do you have?'

'There's a flight connecting through Hanoi. It's our only availability today.'

'I'll take it.'

Time to get the slaughter over with.

The woman behind the counter smiled apologetically. 'It's not until 4 p.m. this afternoon.'

Martina looked at her watch. It was 7.30 a.m. 'Can you put me on standby?'

'I wouldn't advise—'

'Put me on standby,' she cut her off. 'I'll take any route.' Martina handed over her passport and original ticket. *Tap, tap, tap.* 'Is there an electronics shop in the airport?' she asked.

'Not open yet.'

Of course not. Why should anything be going her way? 'I'm going to get some coffee. There is somewhere to get coffee, I assume? What time should I check back?'

'Yes, there's coffee. Try a café Lao. I should know more in an hour or two.'

Martina slunk away, defeat sinking into her bones. The airport café on this side of security was a fluorescent-light nightmare that did nothing for her hangover. The plastic chair was hard on her backside. She ordered a café Lao, roasted to put hair on your chest and lashed with condensed milk. She swirled the thick liquid with a teaspoon.

Despite the sugar and caffeine, Martina's eyelids drooped. She signalled the waiter for another. Airports were a hideous form of purgatory at the best of times. She wondered where Veronica was now. Wherever she was going, she was flying private. An hour passed. Still no news from the ticketing agent.

Martina returned to the café and dropped her head into her hands.

The waiter brought her another café Lao and a croissant without being asked. As Martina lifted the buttery, flaky perfection to her lips, she nearly gagged. She must be hallucinating.

Veronica strode directly towards her across the concourse, a vision in a red silk jumpsuit.

'You look like shit, Marty,' she said, sitting down at her table.

'And I'm seeing ghosts.' Martina folded her arms. 'I thought you'd be long gone.' A bead of sweat welled at the nape of her neck. 'Are you having me followed?'

'Don't be absurd.' Veronica picked up Martina's espresso cup and took a sip. 'I went to your hotel and they told me you'd checked out,' she said.

Martina rested her elbows on the table, leaning forward. 'But, why? You sent me packing yesterday.'

Veronica's chest rose and fell. Purple shadows ringed her eyes, her frown lines more pronounced. Up close, she looked as wrecked as Martina.

'You caught me off guard. I was angry, Marty.'

'I got the picture.'

She blew out a breath. 'I may have been a mite hasty. Maman nicknamed me Vesuvius because of my temper.' Veronica took Martina's hand and stroked the jade bracelet. 'I *am* glad you kept it,' she said, voice softening.

Martina swallowed. 'I never take it off.'

'You don't need to leave. Stay. Just for a couple days.' There was a beaten quality to Veronica's words that she didn't recognise. '*Please.*'

True, Martina wasn't in such a rush to put her head on Peony Huang's chopping block, but suspicion slithered down her spine.

'How do I know you're not planning to make me disappear?'

Veronica barked a shocked laugh. 'You think I'm that cold-blooded?' She worried her bottom lip between her teeth. When Martina didn't reply, 'Why wouldn't you?' she said, mostly to herself, almost forlorn. 'What a mess I've made.'

Martina continued to hold her tongue. She swayed in her seat, as if she were riding an old-fashioned carousel horse that was coming to a stop, bobbing up and down in slow motion.

'None of this has been easy for me, Marty.' Veronica squared her shoulders and looked at Martina straight on. 'People think I have an indomitable will because that's what I want them to think. I've been fighting to survive since I was nineteen. Sometimes I'm so tired all I want to do is sleep for the rest of time.'

She drained the remainder of the café Lao. The cup clanged as she replaced it shakily on its saucer.

'I still don't understand,' said Martina. 'You *hate* me. I betrayed you. Why would you want to spend any more time with me?'

Veronica shook her head, a melancholy laugh at the back of her throat.

'I wish I hated you, Marty. You were right. Not everything between us was a lie.'

It was exactly what she wanted to hear. Veronica was a dealer offering Martina a taste, just one more hit of what she truly craved. Forgiveness. Redemption. Acceptance.

Martina tapped the teaspoon against the table.

'Besides,' Veronica persisted, 'you're the only person other than Ao Wing who knows the truth. I didn't know how much I needed to hear my own name again. To be *me*. After you left, I realised how much I've missed you.'

Martina nodded, the pieces sliding into place. Veronica had spent too much time alone. She was exhausted. Edgy. Her control faltering. She needed a friend, and Martina wanted to be that friend. A fly being lured back into the spider's web.

'Does Ao Wing know I'm here?' Martina said. Veronica shook her head. She wanted to believe her. 'What would he do?'

'Nothing, Marty. *I swear.* You're no threat to him,' Veronica said, an urgency underscoring her words. 'When it comes right down to it, his involvement in my disappearance is untraceable. Nothing leads back to him.'

No, Martina reasoned, it wouldn't. 'Fine, you win. V for Victory,' she acquiesced. 'I'll stay. Just for a day or two.'

The corners of Veronica's mouth curved upward. A spider never considers a fly to be a threat.

'I know the perfect breakfast spot,' she enthused. Instantly, her energy changed to almost girlish excitement.

'Good,' said Martina. 'Because I am perfectly hungover.'

'Me too.' Veronica squeezed her hand and winked. 'Let's get out of here.'

Martina pushed out the rollaboard and stood.

'You wouldn't know where I can pick up a new phone? Mine ended up at the bottom of a pool.'

'Better the phone than me,' said Veronica with a dark laugh.

They shared a look. 'Just teasing. Yes, yes. We'll get you a new phone after breakfast.'

Veronica slid her arm through Martina's as they exited the airport. A genuine smile touched Martina's lips.

Last night, Martina had been sinking fast, flailing with the bends. Suddenly, unexpectedly, Veronica was throwing her a rope. She'd come back for her, invited her back into her world. Martina couldn't say no.

She couldn't say no to the chance to gather her own insurance policy. Martina the Intrepid Reporter. She'd forgotten her training. If she was going to play at Veronica's level, she could no longer afford to play fair.

This would be the interview of her life – proof of life. She'd gather incontrovertible evidence that Veronica Hawkins was alive and kicking.

Her days of being sidelined, discarded, relegated to second string were over. No more begging for scraps. No one would dare call her a parasite.

She would never need rescuing again.

Martina might have been Veronica's pawn, but pawns could become queens.

Honour Among Thieves

*M*artina's guestroom at Veronica's villa was as sumptuously appointed as the five-star resort. The frond-shaped blades of the ceiling fan sliced through the air in a hypnotic whirring. The next few days blurred together. Time dissolved.

One minute Martina and Veronica were on the patio of an authentic boulangerie in the Old Quarter, nibbling on *bánh mì* stuffed with lemongrass chicken; the next Veronica was rousing her before daybreak to offer alms to an endless procession of monks. Martina wouldn't have taken Veronica for an alms-giver. It wasn't clear she even wanted absolution.

Discreetly, secretly, Martina recorded their conversations with her new phone, uploading them to the omnipresent Cloud.

Sticky rice cooked in banana leaf became Martina's comfort food. Veronica's personal chef Keo was fattening her up like Hansel and Gretel. Peeling open the leaf one afternoon, the sweet steam coating her face, Martina asked Veronica, 'Why do you trust Ao Wing so much? Couldn't *he* be the blackmailer? Why would he be so loyal?'

Veronica set her chopsticks on the table. 'I think he was in love with Maman.'

Martina considered this. 'I saw her portrait of Caishen in his office.'

'He let you into his private office? Interesting.' Leaning toward Martina, she said, 'But Maman wasn't the only reason. Arthur saved his bacon after the 12–3 incident.'

Ao Wing had made a vague reference to the incident during Martina's visit. Rice caught between her teeth, chewy, almost caramelised.

'What happened?' she asked.

'During the Cultural Revolution, Mainlanders fleeing the Red Guards were taking refuge in Macau. Macau was divided between the Portuguese and the Macanese – racially, politically. It put the colonial authorities in quite a pickle.' Veronica gave a mirthless laugh.

'Ao Wing told me his grandfather refused to budge from Shanghai.'

Veronica nodded. 'When he first arrived, he got a job at the Hawkins Pacific office in Macau – as a janitor. On 3 December 1966 there was a protest against the Portuguese that became a riot. The colonial government declared martial law – total overreaction.' She threw a hand in the air. 'Anyhow, in an attempt to maintain control over Macau, they agreed to send Chinese refugees back to China, the Communists believing they were all pro-Kuomintang.'

'So Ao Wing was in danger of being sent back?' Martina surmised.

'Arthur took care of his people. Even a janitor. He ensured none of the Hawkins Pacific employees were deported.' Pride thrummed beneath her words. 'It's hard for outsiders to understand – for me, too, since I wasn't born – but those days were a crucible and no one came out the other side unchanged. Vasco had great respect for Arthur. He owed him his life.'

Martina couldn't empathise either, although she listened, rapt. She was stunned the old taipan cared one way or the other. Was Ao Wing as grateful to his white saviour as Veronica believed?

'In Vasco's case,' Veronica reflected, 'I think he was pro-KMT. The Triads mostly were. But that's another story . . . all of which is to say, he's not the man behind the curtain . . .'

Later that same day, watching the sunset together from atop nearby Mount Phusi, 'Christ, Martina,' Veronica said on an exhale. 'I've never been a big believer in honesty being the best policy but it's a relief – such a bloody relief that you know the truth. I don't have to pretend with you any more. I've been so fucking lonely.' And her loneliness had loosened her tongue.

The dying light glistened on Martina's jade bangle, still ice cold, resistant to the warmth of the sun.

One summer, when she was around four or five, her parents rented a beach house near the Hamptons. Her mother warned her only to touch the clear jellyfish because the magenta ones – the ones with spilled ink frozen inside – would sting. But Martina had no interest in the translucent jellyfish, in the creatures she could see through.

She was attracted to the dangerous, deceptively beautiful sea monsters. She wanted to feel them between her fingers despite their sting. Martina couldn't help but be entranced by Veronica, to reach out, even if she knew it would hurt.

Sometimes Martina forgot her own ulterior motive. She forgot she could sting too.

'Did you ever care about the foundation?' Martina asked Veronica. 'Or was it just a way to siphon Lulu's trust?'

Veronica sighed. 'At first? No. Art was Maman's passion. Not something we shared. I would have closed the gallery if it hadn't been so profitable.'

'What about the Polaroid camera she gave you? Those photos of the sea you took.' Martina kept her eyes trained on the sinking sun. 'Did you make that up too?'

'No, that was true. Maman didn't think much of my efforts. Too pedestrian. "Art is not for everyone, Veronica."' She laughed it off, but Martina could hear the wounded girl beneath.

'Motherhood is not for everyone,' Martina muttered.

Veronica touched her shoulder. 'Seeing how excited you got about the foundation, though, Marty,' she said, 'made me think differently. I started to think of it as something worthwhile to leave behind when I "died". A legacy I could be proud of.'

'I *did* want to make you proud.'

'And you succeeded. I've been keeping tabs, attending the virtual tours of the exhibitions,' said Veronica, giving Martina's shoulder a squeeze. 'You've done something substantial . . . more than I was expecting, to be honest.'

'Too bad Peony Huang is going to shut us down when I can't explain away your embezzlement.'

Veronica dropped her hand. 'Let's talk about something else.'

Tin Hau took pride of place in the villa's living room, looming, ever watchful.

The sea goddess passed no judgement as Veronica and Martina poured back lychee Martinis until 4 a.m. Martina lay sprawled on oversized throw cushions on the floor, wearing a thin silk nightdress she'd purchased at the Phusi market.

'He's still in love with you,' she slurred. 'Jean-Pierre. He's wallpapered the chateau with portraits he's painted of you.'

Veronica rolled on to her stomach, took another slurp of her Martini.

'When did you visit?' she asked.

'I was in Paris to promote my book. It was just lunch.'

'Just lunch.' Veronica went quiet a minute. 'Jean-Pierre is his own worst enemy,' she said, resigned. 'Loving him was like loving a drowning man – forgive the metaphor.' A bitter laugh. 'He's all yours.'

'It's not like . . . I'm . . . I'm not interested.'

'No, washed-up artist isn't your MO. Not long term. You like to hitch your wagon to a star.'

Martina met her gaze. 'Someone always does. Why shouldn't it be me?'

'Why shouldn't it be you, indeed?' Her eyes glittered. Veronica had been the brightest star, and they both knew it.

'Did you ever plan on taking Jean-Pierre with you when you faked your death?' Martina asked, face hot.

'No,' she said. 'I should have walked away sooner. The weak take the strong down with them.' Veronica released a dramatic sigh. 'After Rupert's death, I started pushing him away. Jean-Pierre lost himself in gambling – an old vice. There was a lie at the heart of our marriage and nothing could fix it.' She stared up at Tin Hau. 'I didn't want him to know the truth. I'd rather Jean-Pierre hate me than know I was a murderer.' Looking back at Martina, she added, 'Just because I was planning to leave him doesn't mean I wanted someone else to take him away. Especially not you, Marty. You were my friend.'

Martina's cheeks flushed further. 'I did it to hurt Spencer. To hurt *myself*. It sounds awful and selfish, but it wasn't about you.' She sat up, teetering slightly. 'You have to know it was the biggest mistake of my life.'

Veronica pressed her lips together. 'I think I believe you.'

'Can you ever forgive me?'

She didn't answer. 'Was your divorce very painful?' she asked instead.

'Not as much as it should have been.' Martina had felt scandalously little when it was all settled. Quentin's revelation about Spencer's exploits had rankled her the other night, but only because Martina couldn't stand to be humiliated.

'Still,' Veronica said in a soft voice. 'I wish I could have been there for you.'

'Do you?' Martina asked. 'Do you really?'

Veronica licked the lychee from her lips. 'You know, I do, Marty. I think I really do mean it.'

The next morning the Mekong river flowed beneath their slow boat, motoring upstream towards the Pak Ou caves. Veronica said Martina couldn't leave Laos without seeing them. Verdigris-coloured ripples lapped against the hull of the long, sleek wooden vessel.

Veronica had her own slow boat moored at the villa, of course, oddly rectangular as was the style, but lavishly decorated and painted a glossy turquoise. Like a puddle-jumper plane, the width of the hull only allowed for a single seat on either side of a splinter-like aisle. But these seats were upholstered in buttery leather. A flat roof covered the passenger deck and the window frames were expertly carved in a floral motif, left open to the elements. Thick curtains of *naga*-patterned silk billowed in the breeze.

Martina searched the water for the divine serpents who were meant to make the Mekong their home.

'What are you thinking?' Veronica asked, watching her from across the aisle.

'I'm thinking that I can't avoid Peony Huang forever. She'll be back in Hong Kong this weekend and my stay of execution will come to a swift end.'

'You could stay here.'

'Peony would let me off the hook if you asked her to,' said Martina.

Veronica laughed like it was the funniest thing she'd ever heard.

'I told you Hong Kong runs on favours and grudges – you got that part right in your book – but there's a limit to the favours Peony is willing to extend me. Or anyone. She certainly wouldn't take kindly to the notion I'd had her donate to the foundation so I could embezzle her money.'

'So where does that leave me?' Martina demanded.

'I didn't intend for you to get caught in Peony's crosshairs.'

Haze from the slash-and-burn farming along the riverbanks sheathed the rolling hills, heightening the surreal nature of Martina's present situation. Water buffalo bathed in the water, roamed the rocky banks. This was the girls' holiday Veronica had promised her. Cruising up the Mekong, Martina could believe the last few years had elided.

'When I read your book,' said Veronica, 'I wished it was all true. I've never had a friendship the way you described us. There was Lulu, but she was my little sister, it was different.' Her eyes were sad as they trained on Martina.

'I wanted it to be true too.'

Martina's dark strands fluttered as the boat increased its speed. Reaching into her bag, she retrieved a pack of Indonesian kreteks. Surreptitiously, she checked her phone was still recording. She lit the cigarette and blew out a plume of clove-scented smoke, watching it mingle with the hazy mountains.

'Quentin said you were doing business with him, using Xtasy Events for Hawkins Pacific up until you "died".' Martina turned to face Veronica. 'Why would you do that after warning me away from him? After Oxford. I don't get it. Were you lying about what he did?'

Veronica scowled. 'What I said about Quentin was true. Couldn't put my hand on a Bible and swear to the details. I was too drunk. I just knew I didn't want it to happen again.'

'Then why on earth would you work with him?'

'It's not that easy. He insinuated himself into my world. And he has his uses, shell companies and the like. The devil you know . . .'

She held her hand out for Martina's cigarette, and Martina passed it across the aisle. 'I grew hard, Marty. After my family. After Uncle Rupert. I'm not that nineteen-year-old any more.' Veronica took a long drag. 'Sometimes I'm glad Lulu never had to grow up.'

The caves teemed with tourists and pilgrims, hundreds of Buddha figurines lining every nook and cranny, and they kept their visit brief. On the return cruise, Veronica seemed subdued. She disappeared to the other end of the slow boat. Martina indulged her craving for another cigarette and watched the river in silence.

A while later, Veronica walked down the aisle carrying two glasses. 'Blue Ruin, my great-greats called it.' She held one up to the light before handing it to Martina.

'I never liked gin before I met you,' Martina confessed, and it was true.

'I never liked Americans.'

They clinked glasses.

'I've been thinking about Auntie Peony,' said Veronica, drinking deep. 'Instead of serving me up, why don't you try figuring out who served *you* up to her? Who has it in for you?'

'Besides you?'

'Ha ha. I'm serious. Who have you pissed off since I've been . . . gone?'

Martina sipped her gin. 'No one with a connection to Peony Huang. Other than Cressida, I guess.'

'No, it's not Watercress. Any scorned lovers?'

'Hardly. I've kept in constant motion the past couple years.'

Veronica raised an eyebrow. 'So there isn't anyone in Hong Kong missing you while you're with me?'

A shake of the head. 'The only person who knows where I am is my PA because she booked the flight.'

'*Now* you tell me? I should have dumped you in the caves.'

'I'd like to think Iris would rouse the troops.'

'Iris?' Veronica crinkled her forehead. 'Isn't she your helper?'

'She's my helper, PA and drill sergeant all rolled into one. She runs my life with military precision.'

Martina detected a hint of jealousy when Veronica said, 'Seems like you struck the jackpot.'

'Elsie recommended her.' Martina raised her glass. 'I'm indebted to you for introducing us at the FCC Ball. We've become close since your . . . since you've been gone,' she said and Veronica wriggled her nose. Veronica wasn't thrilled they'd become friends and Martina couldn't deny her gratification.

She enjoyed the burn of the gin. 'How did you stay friends with the Barrons after . . . Rupert?'

'Can't blame the whole family for his crimes,' said Veronica as if it were a totally reasonable thing to say. 'Although Elsie and I have never had much in common – despite having everything in common. I was closer to Iain. And Philippa . . . mostly Philippa.'

'Did you and Iain have a thing?' Martina needed to know.

334 || KRISTINA PÉREZ

'I may have taken the poor dear's virginity. If I'd known it'd result in a lifelong hang-up about me, I wouldn't have obliged. So tiresome.'

Martina covered her mouth to hide her guffaw. 'You're so bad.' Eyes stinging, she said, 'Iain and I are Fifi's godparents.'

'I saw that in the gossip rags.'

'You've been keeping up?' Martina dabbed at her eyes. 'Why?'

'Morbid curiosity. Filling the hours. I tried making my way through the classics but the Russians broke me.' Veronica gritted her teeth. 'Anyhow, Fifi is just as likely to be Quentin's as Dex the Texan's.'

Martina's heart came to an abrupt stop.

'What do you mean?' she said.

'What do you mean what do I mean?' Veronica parroted back. 'If you and Elsie have grown *so close*, you must know she and Quentin are fuckbuddies. On and off for years now.' She said it as if she were telling Martina that water was wet. 'I bet Fifi's eyes are blue – like Elsie and Quentin,' she went on. They were. 'Dex's are brown.'

Small mercy that she was sitting down because Martina couldn't feel her legs. She clutched at her chest, her breaths becoming needles. The world became unfocused. She was underwater, starved for oxygen.

'Marty?' Veronica snapped her fingers in front of her face. 'Marty?'

'Di-did she know Quentin owns Xtasy Events?'

'Of course she knows. They cater all of the functions at Rockyda Manor.'

Which meant everything Martina thought she knew about Elsie Barron was a lie. Elsie had lied to her face.

Elsie was setting her up.

Martina couldn't feel her lips. Her cheeks tingled. Her legs itched.

Had Elsie spent *years* ingratiating herself with Martina with the sole intention of framing her? All the lunches and spa days, trips with

Fifi to Disneyland, summer nights in the Barrons' gin palace . . . Had it all been another fucking set-up?

'Elsie's the one framing me,' she told Veronica. 'Elsie pretended she had no idea Quentin owns Xtasy Events. She's only ever presented him as a passing acquaintance. And she told me to throw myself on Peony's mercy.'

'But how would Elsie know about the skimming?'

'From Quentin. Loose lips sink ships.' They must have laughed so much at her expense during their pillow talk.

Veronica wagged a finger. 'They're fuckbuddies, Martina. Quentin's not in love with her – not that he's capable, and he wouldn't risk Vasco's wrath for her.'

'He did call her tragic,' she acknowledged, but maybe that was playacting. Theatrics for Martina's benefit.

'Ouch,' said Veronica. 'Sounds about right, though.'

'How could I be so blind?' Martina said numbly. Looking at Veronica, she added, 'Again.'

Veronica sucked in her cheeks. 'Fine – let's say, for argument's sake, Quentin told Elsie there's skimming going on at the foundation, *why* would Elsie expose you?' She raised her brows. 'Especially if you're such close friends?'

The jigsaw pieces started to arrange themselves in Martina's mind. *Oh God.*

There was only one reason why Elsie would betray Martina to Peony Huang. Only one reason that made sense.

'To destroy *you*, Veronica. Don't you see? It's clear as day. She *knows*.'

Elsie had made Martina her pawn too. Elsie had reached out when Martina was floundering, made her godmother to her own child, ensured that Martina would never doubt her motives. Martina's nerves zinged like livewires.

'No, Marty. No, I don't see.' Veronica shook her head several times, more violently with each gesture.

'*You* killed her father,' said Martina in a furious whisper. 'You're gone, but she can't let it go. She's going after your legacy.'

Elsie had played Martina for a fool. Martina had wanted to *protect* Elsie from the circumstances of her father's death, she'd wanted to shield her from the ugly truth. She shook her head. Elsie had known all along.

'Elsie is your blackmailer and now she's hanging me out to dry.'

Veronica reached across the table and took a firm hold of Martina's arm. 'Elsie doesn't have the stomach for blackmail.' Martina felt Veronica's nails dig into her skin. 'When we were kids she would sob at the drop of a hat. She's just a sad little waif.' But even as Veronica protested, her bottom lip quivered.

'Think about it.' Martina pried Veronica's talons from her skin. 'Barron Industries has taken over Hawkins Pacific. You're "dead". The foundation is the only thing standing between Elsie and total annihilation of the Hawkins legacy.'

'Total annihilation,' repeated Veronica.

She collapsed back against her chair, downing her gin. The boat passed another group of water buffalo and this time their moans took on a foreboding quality.

'Elsie . . . Elsie,' Veronica said, still stunned. 'How did she find out about Rupert? She seemed neck-deep in diapers and not much else.'

'We both underestimated her,' said Martina. Elsie presented herself as a fragile flower when in fact she was as deadly as nightshade.

Shaking her head, 'It's too late now,' Veronica said. 'She's won. I've had my Waterloo.'

'Well, *I* haven't.' Martina was ready to scorch the earth. Righteous anger coursed through her and it felt good. 'I'm not letting her get away with this. This is not how my story ends.'

'I love your can-do American spirit.'

'Fuck you, Veronica.'

Veronica grabbed the glass from Martina's hand. 'I'm already royally fucked, Marty. Nothing more you can do to me.'

'Then why don't we fight?' said Martina.

'Are you forgetting that, if Elsie is the blackmailer, she has the recording of me talking to Vasco about Rupert?'

Martina pursed her lips. 'How did she get it?'

'Beats me. It's not out of the realm of possibility that an intelligence agency was listening in on Vasco, or Hawkins Pacific, in the lead-up to Rupert's death.' Another defeated sigh.

'You can't be so apathetic,' insisted Martina. 'Elsie drove you out of Hong Kong. Are you willing to hide out in Laos for the next fifty years?'

'I'm not apathetic, Marty. I want Elsie's guts for garters.' The muscles in Veronica's neck grew taut. 'But we don't always get what we want.'

'Not if we don't try!' Martina threw up a hand.

Veronica gulped down another swallow. She looked at Martina steadily.

'Why would you want to help me? I betrayed you as badly as Elsie.'

Martina licked her lips. 'It's not the same. You – you were running scared, searching for a lifeboat. You didn't set out to hurt me.'

'No,' Veronica said in a sombre tone. 'I didn't intend to hurt you.'

'But Elsie . . . as far as she knows you're dead. This is just the cherry on top. She knows destroying the foundation means destroying me and she doesn't care! Intent *does* matter.'

Martina's breathing shallowed as another surge of anger overwhelmed her. She struck the side of the boat with a closed fist. 'We can do this, Veronica. We can take the bitch down. *Together.* Elsie doesn't know we know she's the blackmailer and she doesn't know you're alive. We have a tactical advantage.'

'I don't see how, Marty.'

'We just need to get the recording back. Destroy it.'

'The enemy of my enemy?' Veronica teased.

Martina extended her hand.

'Come on, Veronica. I could tell Elsie you're alive – but I don't want to. I want *you* to.'

Martina had gathered enough proof to expose Veronica to Peony Huang, to the world, but it wasn't what she wanted. Veronica might be a schemer and a murderer but Martina didn't want to lose her from her life again. She didn't want to be alone.

Veronica stared at Martina's hand, lips pinched. Her gaze was vacant. Martina held her breath.

'I'm sorry, Marty. I can't risk it.' Her chin trembled. 'I want to help you – I do, even if you don't believe me. But I'm just not that brave.'

Martina dropped her hand to her lap. Her throat grew scratchy. Veronica's admission touched a chord. Cradling her empty gin glass, shoulders curled forward, she looked battle-worn.

But Martina wasn't prepared to cede Hong Kong to Elsie, to turn tail and run.

She still had too much to lose.

Dead Man Walking

Veronica sulked on the day of Martina's departure.

While Veronica was doing her daily laps in the pool, Martina slinked into her bedroom. She snapped a photo of Isabella Mortimer's Australian passport and stored it with the recordings on the Cloud. She also stole Veronica's hairbrush like a weirdo, thinking the DNA would bolster Martina's claim she was alive – if it should come to it.

Not that Martina wanted to use her evidence. It was strictly for a break-glass-in-case-of-emergency situation. Martina was determined to remake reality the way she wanted it – with Veronica back from the dead and Elsie begging for mercy. She wouldn't rest until she'd found the recording. But just in case . . .

'You're leaving,' said Veronica, towelling herself off.

Martina wheeled her suitcase on to the patio. 'And you're staying . . . put.' She pushed down the fear that Veronica would leave her high and dry, take a powder, and vanish into the wide blue yonder.

'Where would I go?' Veronica flicked her wrist. 'I'm like Sleeping Beauty, waiting for you to break my curse.'

Martina laughed. 'That makes me your faithful knight?'

'Something like that.' Then, more seriously, she told her, 'Be careful. Take care of yourself, Marty.'

As the wheels of the Plumeria Airways plane touched down at Hong Kong International Airport, Martina felt a pang. Laos was already beginning to feel farther than the goddess in the moon. There were a million things that could go wrong. She still had no idea how she'd get Elsie to lead her to the recording. While waiting to board her plane in Luang Prabang, Martina had purchased a toy tuk-tuk made from hot pink plastic for her goddaughter. She hated to use Fifi in her schemes but Elsie had started it. Poor kid. She'd be in therapy for the rest of her life.

Armed with a triple espresso from San Marco's, Martina unlocked the door to her apartment in Starscape. The 31 rue Cambon keychain glittered on the table in the entry hall. Iris was home. The strains of Lea Salonga belting out showtunes from the other end of the apartment confirmed it.

Martina nursed the strong black coffee and rifled through the mail that had been left on the table. An invitation to a charity boxing match at Hong Kong Disneyland promised 'an evening of blood, sweat . . . and a sprinkling of fairy dust'. Behind that was a flier for a new gated community development in the PRD which would 'Give you luxury of between lips and teeth'.

Pass, and pass, thought Martina.

She unzipped her rollaboard and pulled out two silk scarves. Inhaling deeply, she walked down the corridor and knocked on Iris's door.

The music stopped.

A startled expression gripped Iris's features as the door creaked open. 'Oh, Martina!' she said. 'You scared me.'

'Sorry about that.'

'I didn't know you were coming home today,' said Iris. 'You didn't ask me to book your flight?'

Martina raised her eyebrows. 'I do know how to book a flight myself.'

'Of course.' Her tone was dubious.

'I got you a present.' Martina held out the scarves. 'And one for Angelica – so you don't have to send her yours.' She gave Iris a wink.

Iris plucked her Fendi glasses from the bedside table. Pushing them up the bridge of her nose, she examined the finely woven scarves.

'Thank you. You don't always have to get me presents, Martina.'

'It's nothing. I bought too many.'

She looked from the scarf to Martina, a line deepening on her brow. 'You had a good trip to Laos? I was starting to get worried.'

'No need to worry. I just needed some time to . . . think.'

'Your phone is working again?' asked Iris who had patiently talked Martina through reconnecting to the Cloud.

'Just like magic.'

Iris laughed. 'Have you had lunch?' she asked. 'I made macaroni salad.'

'I shouldn't,' said Martina. 'But you know how much I like it. Unless I'm interrupting?'

Shaking her head, Iris told her, 'I was just practising. My church choir is singing "A Whole New World".'

'Indeed it is.'

Martina followed Iris down the hallway towards the kitchen. An overcast sky illuminated the hills behind Starscape in a silvery haze. She sipped her espresso as Iris retrieved the Tupperware container from the fridge and started preparing a plate for Martina.

The macaroni made a plopping sound as it landed on Martina's wedding china. She'd considered ritually smashing the plates the day she signed her divorce papers, but it was Royal Doulton and she liked the gold lace pattern. At least her marriage had lasted long enough that she didn't need to return the gift registry.

Grabbing a fork, Martina tucked eagerly into the sweet Filipino-style salad. Her stomach growled and Iris chided, 'You need to eat more.'

'I ate plenty in Laos.' She'd stopped counting calories and would need to live in the hot yoga studio in between her scheming.

'I'm glad,' Iris said as she popped the lid back onto the container. 'Ms Elsie said you had food poisoning.'

Martina's fork hovered in mid-air. 'When did you talk to Elsie?'

Iris stepped past her in the small kitchen and put the Tupperware back in the fridge. 'I don't know,' she said, uneasy, talking into the refrigerator. 'A few days ago. She dropped by to see how you were feeling.'

A needle of panic stabbed behind Martina's eye.

'And what did you tell her? Did you tell her I wasn't here?' Martina said, tugging on her shoulder until Iris spun around to face her.

'I . . . I didn't know what to say. I didn't know the trip to Laos was a secret.'

Iris's jaw tightened. She tapped the frames of her glasses.

Iris was lying to her. Why was Iris lying?

Martina set the plate of macaroni down on the countertop. 'What exactly did you tell Elsie, Iris?'

'Just that you were away. Ms Elsie was concerned about you, that's all.'

Her mind started reeling. Elsie hadn't texted Martina since she'd fobbed her off with the food-poisoning excuse. She must be wondering why Martina had left town without telling her. Would she put it together that Martina had gone to Laos following a lead on the embezzlement? Martina swallowed, the too-sweet macaroni lingering on her tongue.

No, she'd never mentioned the Tin Hau painting to Elsie. She wouldn't make the connection. She couldn't possibly suspect Veronica was alive.

Iris fidgeted her hands. She coughed. Martina narrowed her eyes. She was missing something . . . something else was going on here.

Picking up the plate, Iris offered it to Martina. 'You should eat.'

'Join me.' She accepted the plate and strolled into the living room, seating herself in one corner of the L-shaped sofa. A light rain started mulling the hillside.

Martina gestured for Iris to sit opposite her. 'We've been living together for going on five years soon,' she began. 'If you're unhappy with me, I hope you'd tell me.'

Iris interlaced her fingers. 'I'm not unhappy.'

'That's a relief.' Martina skewered another forkful of macaroni. 'I'm curious. Why did Elsie recommend you come work for me?'

'She told me you needed a helper, that you were new to Hong Kong and could use help getting settled.' Iris raised a shoulder. 'I would see her sometimes at Rockyda.'

Martina turned the fork over on the plate several times, doing some quick math.

'When did you work at Rockyda?' she said, trying to sound casual. 'I thought you'd worked for the Barrons at their house in Shek O.'

'I did for years. After Mr Rupert died, Ms Philippa shut up the house and we moved to Rockyda.'

'Hmm. So you helped with all of the events and parties at Rockyda Manor, I guess.'

Iris's brow furrowed in a quizzical expression. 'Yes?'

Martina's heart started to race. She forced herself to eat a few more mouthfuls. She gazed out at the hill, lifting her eyes toward the Peak.

Snapping her gaze back to Iris, she said, 'Then you must have known Xtasy Events caters all of the functions at Rockyda Manor. Why didn't you tell me?'

'I—' Iris faltered before Martina interrupted.

'Did you know Quentin Turner owns it?' She set the fork on the plate with a *clink* that bounced off the walls. Iris jammed her lips together.

Martina set the plate on the coffee table and slid closer to Iris along the sofa.

'Did you know Elsie and Quentin are lovers?' she hissed.

Iris's eyes went wide behind her glasses. 'No,' she said, shaking her head. 'I didn't know that.'

'When did you first notice the accounting irregularities with the foundation gala?'

'I . . . when you were in Paris. When you asked me to look into it . . .'

'And I was in awe at how fast you did your audit, at lightning speed. But the strange thing is,' Martina continued, 'when I spoke to Elsie, she wasn't surprised. She knew all about it.'

Iris visibly swallowed. 'She did?'

The look on her face confirmed Iris's lie. Martina was going to be sick.

Someone had to bring the embezzlement to Elsie's attention. And Veronica was right, it wasn't Quentin. He valued his neck and his relationship with Ao Wing too much.

'You figured out the fraud on your own and told Elsie, didn't you?' Martina demanded. Iris had access to the foundation's records because Martina had given her access.

The whir of the air conditioner filled the space between them. Iris buried her face in her hands. A long way off, a jackhammer pummelled the earth.

'*Answer me.* Did Elsie ask you to spy on me right from the start?'

'It wasn't like that,' Iris protested, talking to her hands. She released a shuddering breath.

'So what was it fucking like?' Martina vibrated with rage. Elsie had planted a spy in her *fucking house.* 'I *trusted* you, Iris,' Martina spat. 'We live together, eat together – spend holidays together! I paid for your diploma . . . and all this time, you've been *spying* on me?'

Martina wanted to jump out of her skin. She'd given Iris the keys to her own destruction.

'No, Martina. No.' As Iris lifted her face, Martina saw that her eyes were wet, yet unyielding. 'I would see Elsie sometimes at Rockyda when I visit Ms Philippa – poor lady. Elsie would ask how you were doing, who you were seeing . . . it didn't seem strange.'

'She wanted to know about Veronica Hawkins, didn't she?'

Iris nodded. Elsie had been watching Martina because of her friendship with Veronica for far longer than she'd suspected.

'When I was first working for Ms Philippa and Mr Rupert, Veronica saw them a lot,' Iris said. 'She stopped visiting so much when Mr Rupert was murdered and Ms Philippa had her stroke.' She paused. 'The very next day. Poor lady,' she repeated.

That was new information. Elsie had never mentioned to Martina that her mother had had a stroke when her father died. Elsie was a master manipulator, clearly, better than even Veronica.

'Right,' said Martina. 'When did Elsie ask you to start snooping into the foundation accounts?'

Iris touched the simple gold cross that dangled from a thin chain around her neck.

'A couple months ago, Ms Elsie invited me to lunch. You were in New York for your book,' she said. 'She told me I needed to find dirt on you or the foundation. Something that would close it down.'

Martina's blood boiled as the other woman spoke. 'And you went along with it?' she burst out. 'Why the hell would you do that?' Her booming voice echoed around the living room.

'My husband is dead,' Iris said.

Martina inhaled sharply. 'Since when? You never told me.'

'*Legally* dead.'

'I don't understand.'

'No divorce in the Philippines.' Clutching the cross, Iris said, 'I needed another solution.'

Martina drummed her fingers on the back of the sofa. 'I can see your dilemma. What does this have to do with me?'

Iris threw her shoulders back, resolve straightening her spine. 'There were two options: hitman or bribing a judge.'

Martina barked an awkward laugh.

'My daughter deserved better than a drunkard for a father. I wanted university for Angelica.' Iris's hand curved tighter around her cross. 'I'm a Catholic. I couldn't kill him. But I couldn't afford the bribe. Mr Rupert knew many prominent men in the Philippines. As a favour, a judge in Manila had my husband declared legally dead.' The story rushed out of her. 'Our marriage was dissolved. My daughter didn't suffer because I married the wrong man.'

'So now he's a dead man walking around Manila?'

Iris shrugged. 'I don't know where he is. When I asked the Barrons to pull strings, they did. I owed them.'

'Well, that's quite the tall tale.'

'I didn't want to hurt you, Martina. I'm sorry – I didn't want to get you in trouble, I swear I didn't. Not you, just the foundation. I told Ms Elsie I won't help her any more.'

'But you already did! You sealed my fate!'

'She threatened me.' Iris's shoulders heaved. 'You don't understand.'

'Then make me understand, Iris. Please make me understand how you could betray me like this. I thought we were *friends*. I saw you like an older sister.'

'*Sister?*' Iris spluttered. The hands in her lap curled into loose fists. 'We're not *sisters*, Martina. We're only friends on your terms. When it suits *you*. It's always the same – you, Elsie, Philippa, all of the *tai tais* – I'm your friend when you need a friend, but you pay my salary. Buying me trinkets to make yourself feel better about having a maid doesn't change anything.' An exasperated laugh escaped Iris. 'You didn't even know my husband was dead. You never asked! That's not a real friendship.' She gave a small shake of the head. 'I won't risk my daughter's welfare for you, Martina. I just won't.'

Martina stared at Iris, stunned. She tasted the resentment in the words that had been smothered for too long – years, decades . . . She wrapped her arms around her middle, the wind knocked out of her.

'I didn't realise you felt that way.' Martina stifled the urge to cry. Iris took several steadying breaths. 'I haven't thought of you as an employee for a long time. Maybe I'm just a shitty friend.'

Iris wet her lips, frustration pinching her forehead. 'But I *am* your employee – I depend on you for my visa. I've lived in Hong Kong for twenty years but I don't qualify for permanent residence. They want me here to do jobs Hongkongers won't do but they don't want me to belong.' She flung a hand to the side. 'You worry so much about what the people in New York think of you that you don't see how lucky you are. You can get residency here like all the other expats and I can't. We're not equal. It's not the same at all.'

Bile rushed up Martina's throat. She'd hated being dependent on Spencer. It had never crossed her mind that Iris might feel the same way about her.

'The rules here are unfair. Terrible. I get that.' Martina inhaled through her teeth. 'But what does it have to do with Elsie and your daughter? Did she threaten to have you deported?'

'No.' Iris leaned back against the sofa. 'Angelica thinks her father is dead. In the ground. It was better that way. I didn't want him in my daughter's life.' Her voice rang with finality. Martina had known she was no pushover. She hadn't scratched the surface. 'Elsie threatened to tell her the truth and I couldn't let that happen.' Iris gave Martina a penetrating stare. 'Angelica is everything to me. I didn't want to betray you, Martina, but she comes first. Always.'

As the truth sank in, regret washed over Martina that her own mother would never protect her in this way. Iris was a lioness beneath her cheerful smiles, and she couldn't help but envy Angelica.

'Hard fucking lines,' muttered Martina. Elsie had been playing for keeps. 'What a bitch.'

'Yes, what a *bitch*.'

Martina had never heard Iris curse before and despite everything it made her chuckle. Her gaze drifted to the plate of half-eaten macaroni. She didn't ask Iris to cook for her; food just appeared in the kitchen. She expected it, relied on it. She'd thought Iris liked cooking to unwind.

'I appreciate everything you do for me, Iris. I do. I'm sorry if I don't show it.'

Iris's face softened. 'I'm sorry too. I didn't see any other choice.'

Their eyes met. 'It shouldn't take me long to find another position.'

Martina nodded, part of her not wanting Iris to go. 'Do you really want to work for another *tai tai*?'

'It's not about what I want.' She snorted. 'I'm saving money for Angelica's restaurant. She wants to open a place on the beach in Boracay for the tourists. I want her to own her own business – not to depend on anyone. Then everything will have been worth it.'

Martina scooted another inch closer to Iris on the sofa. Their knees touched. The seed of an idea had been planted. Lightly, she dropped a hand to the other woman's elbow.

'If you're truly sorry, I know a way you can make it up to me,' Martina told her.

Eyes wary, 'What is it?' Iris asked.

'Elsie is living at Rockyda Manor again. If she had something extremely valuable, do you know where she would keep it? Somewhere in the manor she would hide it?'

Iris's eyes fell to her lap. Her gaze remained pinned there for several moments.

'There's a safe in Ms Philippa's bedroom.'

Time to spin the wheel of fortune. 'It's Friday,' said Martina. 'Elsie gets her weekly mani-pedi and blowout at the Mandarin. She'll be out all afternoon. Get your purse.'

'Why? Where are we going?'

'We're going to visit Ms Philippa.'

'No, I can't. *I can't.*'

'Iris, if you do this for me, I can make sure you can retire to the Philippines in style. Be with your daughter. Angelica can open a *chain* of restaurants – do whatever she wants!'

Iris canted her head, lips twisted. 'You don't have that kind of money. Or power. Nothing like the Barrons. I'm sorry, Martina.' She folded her hands. 'I can't help you.'

Martina gritted her teeth. Iris had certainly put her in her place. Everyone understood the pecking order in Hong Kong.

'You're right,' said Martina. 'But I know how we can both get what we want.'

Iris sat very still.

'I'm not doing this for me,' Martina continued. 'I have a powerful backer. Someone who is very interested in what might be contained in that safe.'

Reaching for her cross, Iris said, 'I want an apartment in the Makati district of Manila and capital for Angelica's restaurant.' After a moment, she added, 'And an investor visa for Hong Kong – one on residency track.'

Martina's lips ripened into a smile. Veronica could make all that happen once she was back.

'Done,' she agreed.

'How?'

'Ao Wing is a much better friend than an enemy.'

Iris stood. 'I'll get my purse.'

South China Daily classifieds

Xanadu 97 yacht for sale. Classic offshore cruiser with good sailing performance in all conditions. Designed and built in 1979 by Tin Hau Yachts. Asking price: HKD 888,888. Ashore on Lamma Island. Contact xanadu97@netvigator.hk for details.

Touch Move

+852 XXXX XXXX to Elsie Barron
Meet me at Skye Villa
Bring the recording.
I know everything.

Read 12:07am

*M*artina tinkled the ivories. Her fingers slid over the keys in the grand reception room, Veronica's ancestors staring down at her with disapproval, her joints bending nimbly in an arpeggio. Skye Villa – Martina liked the name she'd given it in her memoir better – had been bequeathed to the foundation and it was used for rotating artists' residences. Fortunately, it lay empty at the moment.

Twilight descended as she waited, dangling herself as bait. She kept her hands busy. Iris had delivered more than Martina had bargained for – but not what she was expecting to find. She'd revised her strategy accordingly and set the pieces in motion. Tournament rules.

The clock was ticking.

Martina exhaled as she came close to exhausting her Cole Porter repertoire. *Middle C, D, E.* The wire of the lavaliere microphone itched against her bra. She'd made a quick trip to the Wan Chai Computer Centre and bought the top of the line.

Just as she was beginning the beguine, she heard footsteps progressing toward her, the clicking of pointy heels resounding off the tiled corridor.

'What am I doing here, Martina?'

Elsie's question had a serrated edge. Martina continued to play.

'You got my message,' she said, aloof, hoping Elsie couldn't hear the thundering of her heart, a toxic brew of sorrow and shame swirling inside her. *Fool me twice.*

'From a burner phone – *really*?' Elsie raised her brows toward the ceiling.

Martina channelled her nerves into the bass notes, pinkie and thumb trembling. C, G, G. 'You still came,' she reminded her. C, G, G. C, G, G.

'Can you stop that?' Elsie spluttered. 'It's doing my head in.'

'Not a Cole Porter fan?' said Martina mildly.

'Not especially.'

'Your loss.'

Elsie thrust her hands on to her hips, chest rising in agitation. She wore a lightweight silvery-lavender raincoat, hanging open atop an understated sheath dress. The shade flattered her strawberry-blonde colouring. A Dior saddle bag was slung over one shoulder.

Martina lifted her hands from the keys and gently closed the lid. It made a *thwuck* as it shut. Outside, the sea rushed against the shore.

She plucked the pink toy tuk-tuk from the music stand and held it out to Elsie. 'For Fifi,' Martina told her. 'A souvenir from Laos.'

Elsie frowned. 'You're acting very strangely, Marty. I think the pressure of the embezzlement is getting to you.' Her tone grew solicitous, a true Machiavelli. Martina refrained from giving her a round of applause.

'Did you bring the recording?' she asked instead.

'I don't know what you're talking about.'

'Then why did you come?'

Elsie's blue eyes darkened, burning cold. 'Because you visited Mum yesterday, apparently, and she's been inconsolable ever since. What did you say to her? *Why* did you go to see her?'

'I thought she could use the company.'

Martina shoved the piano bench backwards and pushed to her feet, unhurried. She pressed the plastic tuk-tuk into Elsie's hand.

'Mum doesn't know you – she scarcely knows me. You upset her. I can't believe the staff let you in alone.' A muscle in Elsie's jaw ticked. 'That won't be happening again.'

The other helpers at Rockyda Manor had promised Iris they'd keep her visit a secret. Seemed like they were true to their word.

'I'm sorry if I upset her,' Martina said. 'It wasn't my intent.' Walking towards the sideboard where several crystal decanters radiated deepening shades of amber, she asked Elsie if she'd like a drink.

'I don't have time for a drink, Marty. I didn't have time to come to bloody Lamma. Maggie and Rupes will have tied Nanny up by now.'

Martina decanted a cognac that was older than she was. 'Your kids do act out a lot, Elsie,' she agreed. 'Do you think it's because they never see their father?'

'Fuck you.'

Pouring the caramel liquid into a tumbler, Martina said, 'Do they even know who their father is?' A sideways glance. 'Do you?'

'I'm leaving.'

They watched each other, equally matched predators. Elsie didn't make a move towards the door.

'It's funny what you can learn when you put your ear to the ground,' Martina told her. 'Like the fact your good friend has been having an affair with a notorious sociopath for years. The same sociopath skimming money from your foundation.'

Elsie sucked in her cheeks, accentuating her birdlike features and the bruise-coloured rings beneath her eyes.

'Quentin called you tragic when he was trying to get into my pants last week. I can't think why you'd trust him to keep his mouth shut.' Martina raised the cognac to her lips. 'You sure you don't want something to steady your nerves?'

'My nerves are fucking fine.' Elsie twisted the tuk-tuk between her hands.

'If you say so.' Martina savoured the fire on her tongue. *Boom, boom, boom.* 'Just give me the recording and you can go home to rescue Nanny.'

'I'm not in the mood for guessing games, Marty. What is this recording you think I have? And why the hell were you bothering Mum about it?'

Martina scanned Elsie head-to-toe, doubting herself for several seconds. Elsie clasped her purse tighter to her body.

'Philippa was on good form yesterday. Very lucid,' she informed Elsie. 'I couldn't believe it when she told me the combination to her safe.'

Elsie's nostrils flared. 'You're lying. It's been locked for years. Mum doesn't know the code – I've asked her a million times. There can't be anything valuable inside.'

'Depends what you consider valuable.'

'Aren't you the philosopher?'

Martina ignored her scathing tone. 'Two, two, five, one, nine, nine, seven,' she said, emotionless. 'More precisely: 22 May 1997. British date style, of course.'

Elsie scoffed. 'Is that supposed to mean something to me?'

'Huh. I think I will pour you that drink,' said Martina, all hostess with the mostest. She selected another glass. 'It took me longer than it should have to put it all together.' Martina lanced Elsie with her gaze. 'But I don't have the best judgement when it comes to my friends.'

She walked towards Elsie, forcing the tumbler into her hand and clinking it with her own. 'To your health,' Martina said. Taking another sip, she said, 'It was something Ao Wing told me that finally made me see the bigger picture. I do so hate being a sacrificial lamb.'

A look of fear passed over Elsie before she smoothed it from her face. She shoved the tuk-tuk into her coat pocket. 'Bottoms up,' she said, tipping back half the glass.

Martina grinned. 'Now we're getting somewhere.'

Raindrops tapped louder against the floor-to-ceiling windows. This was the Hong Kong weather Martina liked best, florid sun setting through the rain.

'You're going to tell Peony Huang that Quentin was working solo to embezzle from the foundation,' said Martina, as coolly as she could manage. 'And you're going to give me the recording – the one with incriminating evidence against my new best friend, Ao Wing.'

Elsie's hand tightened around the cut-glass crystal.

'This was never about you, Marty,' she said.

'No, I get that. I'm a minnow.' Martina sighed at the dusk. 'I've spent my life swimming with sharks.'

'If you knew why I did it, you'd understand why I can't do what you're asking.'

'I'm all ears.'

Discreetly, Martina touched her blouse. The microphone rested safely in the crevice between her breasts.

Elsie's shoulders curled forward and she blew out an enormous breath. She stared into her cognac. Shaking her head, she fought an internal battle.

'Ao Wing didn't tell you what was on the recording,' Elsie presumed, and Martina didn't correct her. Agony streaked her face, raw and difficult to look at. 'He had my father killed – on Veronica's orders.'

Martina widened her eyes in an exaggerated manner.

'Mr Ao doesn't strike me as someone who takes orders.'

'You don't believe me?' Elsie inhaled shortly. 'Of course you don't. You were still buying what Veronica was selling when she went overboard.' A half-moon smile lit her lips. 'Fucking morning sickness! I can't believe I missed it. Best night of my life and I was home hugging a toilet bowl.'

'You don't mean that.'

'Bloody hell I don't. I thought about killing her but . . . I couldn't.' Elsie's hand shook on the tumbler. 'I'm not Veronica. I'm not a *murderer.*'

Martina took a dramatic step backward. 'I want to believe you, I do. But *why* would Veronica have wanted your father dead?'

'I don't know! Because she's psycho? Because he got in her way somehow?' Elsie sliced a hand viciously upward through the air. 'When we were girls, before Lulu was born, Veronica would get unceremoniously dumped with us for the summer, her parents gallivanting around the globe together. Mum would tell me to make her feel welcome but one summer I woke up to find her cutting off my hair while I slept.' She downed what remained of her drink. 'I slept with my door locked after that.'

Martina suppressed a laugh at the image. What was becoming evident was that Elsie genuinely had no idea what might have motivated Veronica to order Rupert's death.

She squashed a pang of sympathy.

'But she's dead, Elsie,' Martina pleaded. 'Why go after the foundation? Why frame *me* to do it?'

'Like I said, it wasn't about you. I just can't let Veronica's legacy stand. She doesn't deserve it.' Elsie ground her teeth together. 'Mum had her first stroke after Daddy died. I blame Veronica for that too.'

'How can you be sure Veronica was behind it?'

'I found the recording. Or Mum did.' When Martina prompted Elsie with an eyebrow, she continued, 'Mum didn't believe Daddy had been in the wrong place at the wrong time. She hired an old friend, a senior officer from the Royal Hong Kong Police Force days, to look into it. He's still very well connected.'

Elsie tipped back her now empty glass, tongue straining for a taste. 'She never told me about any of it. Or Iain. I don't know why. It was only after her vascular dementia started to interfere with her daily life that I started going through her papers, found the evidence Mackay had amassed.'

'You're certain this Mackay fellow didn't get it wrong?' Martina said.

'He didn't get it wrong. Veronica deserved to have everything she loved taken away from her the way she took Daddy from me.'

There was no remorse in Elsie's eyes.

'Why not expose Veronica, then?' said Martina. 'Why drag *me* into it?'

'The evidence is circumstantial. The Mainland police consider my father's case closed. They're not interested in reopening it – and Ao Wing probably has them in his pocket.' Elsie ran her tongue along her bottom lip. 'My revenge was watching Veronica squirm while she was alive. There's no satisfaction with her dead.'

'Then just give me the recording and save yourself from Ao Wing's wrath.'

Elsie slammed the tumbler down on the lid of the grand piano. 'No.' She shook her head. 'I'm sorry, Marty. I can't – I *won't*. I'd rather go down with the ship.'

'Rather on the nose.' Martina's laugh was hollow.

A ray of scarlet light bisected Elsie's face. 'Thanks for the drink. I'm afraid I must be going.' Her heels clicked on the teak as she took two steps toward the door.

'I can't let you leave with the recording. I know you have it with you.' Martina's eyes strayed toward the Dior saddle bag.

'Unless you're prepared to kill me, I'll be on my way.'

'Nothing as uncouth as that. I'll just ring Ao Wing and tell him that Iain has the evidence against him.'

Elsie did an about face and strode toward Martina. Grabbing Martina's arm, she said, 'Iain doesn't know *anything*. He's an innocent in all of this.'

'Too bad for him. I doubt Ao Wing will believe it.'

'You really are a bitch. No wonder you and Veronica got on like a house on fire.'

'Who are you to throw stones, Elsie? I thought *we* were friends. You made me Fifi's *godmother* and for what? All so you could get to Veronica?' Martina couldn't keep the hurt from infecting her accusations. 'You need help. What chance does Fifi have with you as a mother?'

Elsie bared her teeth and for a split second Martina expected a slap.

'Stay away from my daughter,' she said, low and harsh.

Martina chopped her free hand between them. 'Flash drive. *Now.*' She showed an open palm.

Elsie took a step back, releasing her hold on Martina.

One Mississippi . . .

Two Mississippi . . .

The sea covered the sand. Lips screwed to the side, Elsie reached into her purse. As if it caused her physical pain, she plucked a USB key from inside it.

Martina waited for Elsie to come to her. Reluctantly, the other woman dropped it in her outstretched palm.

'I presume this is the only copy,' said Martina.

'You *hope* this is the only copy.'

'Shall I give Ao Wing a ring?' she suggested. 'Or Iain? He's still pining for Veronica, it's obvious. What would he think about what you did?'

'I was *protecting* Iain,' Elsie said angrily. 'He's my baby brother. I've spent my life protecting him.'

Martina's fist closed around the small piece of plastic. Something so insignificant worth more than its weight in gold.

'Don't you think Veronica felt the same about Lulu?' she charged.

'I don't think Veronica ever cared about anyone but herself.'

'There's only one person who can answer that question.' Glancing over her shoulder at a crack in the wall undiscernible unless you knew precisely where to look, Martina said, 'I believe this belongs to you?'

Certified letter to Philippa Barron c/o Lloyd, Mak,
and Ruttonjee Solicitors

To: Philippa Barron
From: Rupert Barron, OBE

1 January 2000

My Dearest Pippi,

I am writing this letter while I watch you sleep. It is the first day of a new millennium and I wonder what it will hold for us, for our children, and future grandchildren. It is perhaps the remnants of drink from our celebrations last night that has urged me to put pen to paper, but I think not.

You are as beautiful to me this morning as the first time I saw you at the Hong Kong Club in 1964, sent to stay with your doddering aunt and uncle to atone for mischievous acts of a varied nature in London. You were twenty-two and I was a wizened old man of thirty but I took one look at you and decided to make it my life's work convincing you to stay with me in Hong Kong forever.

You are the greatest marvel of my life. When we came so close to losing you, I put on a brave face for Elsie and Iain but I did not know how I would continue on without you. Somehow, unreasonably, unfairly, my prayers were answered. I tick every day in my diary that you are cancer free. You tease me for the check mark but to me it is a miracle. It has been two years, three months, and sixteen days since you went into remission.

I do not know how many more years we will have together but I hope they are numerous. I am, however, a weaker man than you, Pippi. I don't want to live without you and so I hope that I am first to depart this earth. If I am granted this wish, then you will be reading this letter now, which I will instruct our solicitors only to deliver in the event of my death.

You are the most wonderful wife and mother that a husband could hope for and you embraced my family, my legacy, from the start. You helped me rebuild the crumbling empire left to me by my father, never asking for recognition or accolades.

There is a weight that presses on you, my darling. I see it in your eyes. If I were less of a coward, we would have this conversation while I'm living. I know that you saved Barron Industries when I could not. I found the wire transfer to White Horse Holdings. You sank the Hawkins's ship so that we might survive to fight another day. I am resolved to show you every day of my life how grateful I am.

This burden should not have been yours. You expected to die in those months and wanted our children to have their legacy. I understand completely. You do not need my forgiveness, but you have it. Please have no regrets. I have no regrets with you by my side.

With all my adoration, always, Rupert

Endgame

'My dear adoptive sister, you look like you've seen a ghost.' Stepping out from the shadows, red sunbeams illuminated Veronica.

Ao Wing's hidden office had been inspired by the listening room at Skye Villa. Veronica's great-greats had eavesdropped on unsuspecting guests, stealing trade secrets, making and breaking political careers. Empire Building 101.

Elsie stumbled backwards, heels skittering on the teak, flinging an arm at the grand piano for support. Her fingernails dug into the wood.

'It can't be . . .'

'What is it they say? Reports of my death have been greatly exaggerated.' Veronica winked at Martina. She took the flash drive from her hand. 'Cheers, darling.'

Triumph shot through Martina. She'd placed the classified in the *South China Daily* as they'd agreed, a coded message only Veronica would understand, but Martina hadn't known whether she would come back for her. Veronica had crossed the Rubicon now. Relief made Martina dizzy.

'But how . . .' Martina watched as Elsie turned a putrid shade of green. 'They found your body,' Elsie insisted.

'They found *a* body,' Veronica corrected her. 'An important distinction.'

She sauntered towards the sideboard and placed the USB on the veiny marble top. Choosing one of the decanters, Veronica lifted the crystal and smashed it down on the drive. Elsie emitted a yelp, a strangled squeal, as if Veronica were crushing her bones instead.

Swivelling her shoulders in Martina's direction, 'Would you like a go?' Veronica asked her, offering the decanter. 'It's really very cathartic.'

Her lips parted in a gleeful smile.

Considering it, Martina said, 'You know what? I don't mind if I do.'

Crossing towards the sideboard, she slid her fingers around the neck of the bottle. She planted her feet and slammed it down on the plastic shards of the drive. And again. The metal inner casing remained stubbornly whole.

'*Hmm.*' Martina scoured the room for something heavier. 'I have an idea.'

Elsie watched them with horror, chin trembling. Spotting a solid bronze statuette of a clipper ship on the coffee table, Martina measured its heft.

'This should do nicely,' she said, carrying it back towards the sideboard. This was also precisely why all of Martina's recordings were being sent directly into the ether, including this evening's dramatic turn of events.

'You two *disgust* me,' Elsie sneered.

Veronica laughed. 'I think we make a rather marvellous team, Marty and me.'

Crunch.

The metal of the drive twisted under the weight of the clipper ship. Martina brought it down once more. A fissure appeared in the marble.

'Oops,' said Martina.

'Not to worry.' Veronica regarded the antique sideboard indifferently. Picking up the contorted scrap of metal, 'For good measure,' she said, and dropped it into a full decanter of whisky.

'How can you *help* her, Martina?' Elsie burst out. 'You may be a shameless social climber but I thought you had a conscience!'

'I've been called worse. Mostly by my ex-mother-in-law.'

'Don't pick on Martina,' Veronica told Elsie. 'I'm the one you want – the one you've always wanted. Is it because you wanted to *be* me? I wonder. Uncle Rupert spent more time with me than with his own daughter. That had to burn.'

Pure ferocity shone from Elsie's eyes. 'You don't deserve to say his bloody name!'

'On reflection, Uncle Rupert underestimated you. He didn't think you had what it would take to helm his dynasty,' Veronica continued. 'Neither did I. Seems I was wrong. I never would have pegged you as my blackmailer in a million years. Well done.'

'I don't want your congratulations.'

Elsie's shoulders started to heave. A prickle of dread zipped down Martina's spine. The other woman looked to be re-evaluating her position on bodily harm.

'It was Marty here,' said Veronica. 'She's the one who read between the lines – realised we had a common enemy.'

'The most dangerous thing in the world is underestimating a smart woman,' Martina agreed. She tipped a grin at Veronica.

Elsie rounded on Martina. 'But you thought she was dead. You didn't fake that. *No one* is that convincing.'

'You're right, Elsie. I believed she'd drowned that night. If you hadn't tried to feed me to the wolves, I never would have sought out the clues.'

'Laos,' said Elsie, oddly quiet. 'Veronica was in Laos.' Her face contorted with fresh anger. 'Bully for you, Miss Marple. It doesn't explain why you're siding with a murderer!'

'Because she knows something you don't,' Veronica answered for Martina.

The muscle above Elsie's right eye vibrated rapidly, her breathing growing shallower, her demeanour more unhinged by the second.

'And what the hell is that?'

'Why.'

'There's no excuse for what you did!'

Veronica inhaled. 'Why would I want Uncle Rupert dead? Think for a minute, Elsie. He took me in, trained me up. I adored him.'

'That's why you're a *monster*,' Elsie replied hoarsely.

'Maybe. But so was he.' Veronica shifted her gaze from Elsie to the waves crashing on the beach. 'Yes, I had Rupert killed – but only because he had my family killed first.'

Elsie erupted in a frenzied laugh. 'You'd say anything, Veronica! You'd stoop to any low. Daddy wasn't capable of malice and you know it. *Kill* Uncle Arthur? Don't be absurd. He loved him like a brother.'

Martina saw Veronica's expression grow mournful. 'As it turns out, you're right, Elsie. Uncle Rupert was merely a coward.'

'Don't you *dare* call him a coward.'

'It was Philippa.'

Elsie stared at Veronica, uncomprehending. Or maybe wilfully obtuse.

Martina took a step closer to Elsie. 'Your mother paid to have the Hawkins's boat sabotaged,' she told her.

'You're both out of your minds!'

'I went to Rockyda yesterday looking for the recording,' Martina explained, 'but I found something else. A letter from your father to your mother. He knew what she did. He was complicit.'

'All those Christmases I spent with Uncle Rupert and Auntie Philippa, grateful at least to have them – it makes me *sick*,' said Veronica with a shudder. 'When I think about how Philippa dressed me for their funerals, brushed my hair . . . Your mother was deranged long before she got dementia.'

Elsie's shoulders started to quake. 'I don't believe you. I don't believe *either* of you!'

Martina reached a hand into her trouser pocket and retrieved her iPhone.

'The original is safely stored,' she said to Elsie. 'I took a photo.' Martina held it up so Elsie could see. 'Your father wrote the letter by hand.'

'You could have had this forged,' Elsie protested.

'It's Uncle Rupert's handwriting,' said Veronica. 'A graphologist can prove it, if need be. But that's not what I want.'

'This should be good. What *do* you want, Veronica?'

'I want you out of my city. If you leave, your mother won't spend her final years enduring the stress of a trial. Or worse. Your children never have to know what their grandmother did.'

Veronica bored her eyes into Elsie's. 'Philippa took away my whole family. Her body count is still higher than mine. But even I can't have a senile old lady killed. *That* would be demented.'

A disconsolate wheeze escaped from Elsie.

Martina did pity her for a moment. She looked pitiful. Her entire world had broken apart at the seams. She'd convinced herself she was the hero of this story.

'Where am I supposed to go?' Elsie retorted miserably.

'You have a husband in Singapore if I'm not mistaken?' Veronica reminded her. 'Take your mother and your brood and get thee to the Lion City.'

Veronica's laughter was wicked. Hongkongers regarded the city-state in the same way a New Yorker would the lovechild of Palm Beach and New Jersey. For Elsie, being exiled there was a fate worse than death.

'Oh, and one more thing, before you go,' said Veronica. 'You're going to solve Marty's Peony Huang problem. Granted, betraying the father of at least one of your children will be awkward.'

She made a sympathetic noise. 'The choice is yours. Your lover, or your mother.'

'Fine,' said Elsie. 'But what do I tell Iain?'

'Tell him whatever you want.'

'You won't tell him about Mum?' There was a quaver to Elsie's voice.

Veronica gave her head one shake. Elsie let out a tremulous breath. 'Iain should have become a doctor. Life's short, after all.' Glancing at Martina, 'Does that cover it?' Veronica asked.

'I think so.' She slipped the iPhone back into her pocket.

Veronica jerked her chin at Elsie. 'We're done here. You can leave.'

Elsie stepped into Martina, leaning in until their noses were almost touching.

'Siding with Veronica is going to be the biggest mistake of your life,' she hissed.

'She's not the one who tried to put me in prison. We're all villains here. I'm loyal to the villain who's loyal to me.'

'Truer words.'

Veronica and Martina watched Elsie storm out of the room, out of the villa, and out of their lives.

'Was that true about cutting off her hair?' Martina asked.

'What can I say? I thought she'd look better with a bob.' Martina laughed as Veronica slipped her hand into hers. 'You did it, Marty. You slew the dragon and broke my curse. I'll never forget it.'

'I wanted you back.'

'Me too. Thank you.' Veronica gave Martina's hand a squeeze. 'Now it's time for my second coming.'

Triad member confesses to kidnapping Veronica Hawkins

A mid-level member of the 14K Triad organisation in Macau, known to the Hong Kong Police Force as Ghost Boy Cao, has been charged with intimidation, extortion and kidnapping in connection with the Veronica Hawkins case. The heiress shocked the world last month when she revealed she had faked her own death. 'I give my profound apologies to all those who I hurt and deceived,' stated Ms Hawkins, 39, in her police press conference. 'My only defence is that I feared for my life. The past few years have been a torturous state of limbo. I am so happy to be home again.'

The 27-year-old suspect, surnamed Cao, admitted under interrogation to extorting the heiress. Cao confessed to holding Ms Hawkins against her will and forcing her to transfer funds to cover the gambling losses at various Macau casinos of her then-husband, Jean-Pierre Renard, 58.

In light of Cao's confession, Hong Kong Police Commissioner Raymond Kwan has declined to charge Veronica Hawkins with misleading a police investigation or wasting police resources. Ms Hawkins has agreed to repay the cost of the search-and-rescue mission carried out by the Government Flying Service. She will also voluntarily perform 100 hours of community service.

Mr Renard, a French national, could not be reached for comment. Lawyers for Mr Renard would only confirm that Ms Hawkins filed for divorce, citing irreconcilable differences.

Your Fave Expat Auntie
@AuntiePeak

Send Auntie Peak all of your #overheardHK tips. DMs open.

Your Fave Expat Auntie ✓ @AuntiePeak · May 13

Spotted at HKIA, Elsie BJ with a one-way ticket to SIN, slinging back cocktails in the Marco Polo Club. Why would she leave? @me your best guess.

Turner Private Wealth under investigation

HKFinanceJournal.com
49 minutes ago

Quentin Turner, 40, the founder and principal of Turner Private Wealth, has been barred by the Hong Kong Securities and Futures Commission from working in the financial services industry. Turner has been charged with using his events management company, Xtasy Events, to embezzle funds from several charities in Hong Kong and around the region. A wider probe has been launched into the activities of Turner Private Wealth, which is based in Chater House, Central. Turner denies all wrongdoing.

Eight-Five-Two

Culture Fix: Through the Lens

Eight-Five-Two's don't-miss exhibition of the week is *Through the Lens* at the Gallery de Ladrones (Duddell Street, Hong Kong). Hosted in conjunction with the Lourdes Hawkins Foundation, the photography retrospective creates a dialogue between the past and present. Martina Torres, the foundation's executive director, personally selected twenty photographs by Geneviève Varenne – mother of Lourdes Hawkins and founder of Gallery de Ladrones – and invited twenty young Asian artists to respond to the works.

'I've always been fascinated by the concept of call and response,' said Torres. 'Especially in the artistic process. We are all of us building upon our pasts. We can't escape our legacies and yet we can reframe our futures, create something new, simply by changing the focus of the lens.'

Barron Industries sells mine stake to Park Lane China following scandal

ain Barron is stepping down as the CEO of Barron Industries in what is being hailed in Hong Kong as the end of an era. Barron Industries has been a family-run business since 1867 when the first office was opened in George Town, Malaysia.

Earlier this summer, leaked footage surfaced online that appeared to show striking miners at the Jing Iron Mining Corporation facility in Inner Mongolia being shot dead by security guards. Chinese netizens were outraged and an investigation by the local government revealed that the security firm was directly contracted by and under the supervision of Barron Industries, a partner of Jing Iron Mining Corporation.

The *South China Daily* obtained proof that Barron Industries was aware of the incident that took place in November 2015 and had facilitated a cover-up. Protests erupted at Pacific Star mobile phone branches and Barron's Minimarts throughout the Pearl River Delta.

The mining operation, which drove Barron Industries' profitability, has been sold to Park Lane China together with its telecoms division for an undisclosed sum.

Peony Huang, founder and CEO of Park Lane China, is widely seen as a steadying hand by the Chinese central government, having been awarded numerous contracts as part of the Belt and Road Initiative.

In his resignation speech, Iain Barron told reporters, 'I am deeply grieved by the loss of life. This happened on my watch and I must assume responsibility for it.'

TravelAsia

Hot Table: Boracay edition

The hottest restaurant opening of the autumn is a mother–daughter venture. Situated on the pristine white sand beaches for which the island is renowned, Dos Angeles is a chic contemporary fish and tapas bar.

The menu features a tempting array of Filipino, Asian and Spanish seafood dishes that rivals the fine-dining resort restaurants for quality without the eye-watering price tag. Packed to the gills every night since opening its doors, former tour guide Angelica Aguilar manages the front of house while her mother, Iris, oversees the kitchen. 'We're already considering opening a branch in Hong Kong,' says Angelica, grinning from ear to ear.

Dishiest dish: Spicy Philippine Ceviche

Retired detective found dead in Wan Chai

etired Detective Senior Inspector Graham Mackay, 59, formerly of the Royal Hong Kong Police Force, was found dead this morning at the Dorchester Wan Chai in a suspected suicide.

Originally from Glasgow, Scotland, DSI Mackay was posted to Hong Kong in 1987. After retiring from the force, he specialised in security and corporate risk management throughout the Asia region for global investment firms and high-net-worth individuals. The long-time resident will be especially missed by members of the Hong Kong Football Club where he served as chairman. Friends were shocked to hear the news, saying Mr Mackay was always quick with a smile and a joke.

You're the Top

'Snow in Macau?' Martina said to Veronica. 'Hell must actually be freezing over.'

'It couldn't hold me.'

Veronica grinned at Martina, eyes crinkling, as fake-snow machines blew gold and opaline confetti around the Lusitano Palace lobby. The corridor leading to the Dom Pedro V ballroom had been transformed into a winter wonderland. Anyone who was anyone had scrambled to get on to the guest list for the Lourdes Hawkins Foundation's Christmas Ball. Veronica had been keeping a low profile since coming back to life and a rare glimpse of the heiress was more than worth the price of admission.

Picking a piece of confetti from her still-blonde hair, Veronica said, 'Deck the bloody halls.'

Martina rolled her eyes. 'Oh, bah humbug. It's for a good cause.'

'Yes – mine.'

'Ours.'

'*Ours*,' Veronica agreed with a laugh.

The doyens and doyennes of Hong Kong, PRD, and much further afield descended on them the instant they reached the ballroom. Martina blinked at the spotlight trained on the entrance. Too bright. Too bright, and yet she basked in it.

Veronica was swathed in Titian-hued velvet – no doubt, red was her colour, and so Martina had chosen green. They made a fine pair.

Her parents had been marginally disappointed she wasn't coming home for Christmas but there was nowhere Martina would rather be on Christmas Eve.

This is my home, she'd told them. The one she'd made for herself.

Martina took a break from the initial round of glad-handing to make a survey of the ballroom, ensuring that the evening's running order was going to plan. No matter where she was in the room, she felt the tug of Veronica's presence. Everyone did. She was a meteor. She could decimate life on earth. But she needed Martina in her own way. Martina understood that now.

Veronica turned herself into the police as soon as Elsie had decamped to Singapore. The night of her press conference, Martina had thrown out Veronica's hairbrush. Keeping it at Starscape had made her feel like a whacko stalker. All of the recordings Martina had made in Laos and that night in Lamma, along with a copy of Isabella Mortimer's passport and Rupert Barron's confession, were stored in multiple accounts in the sky. If the circumstances of her death were ever to be deemed suspicious, Martina's lawyer would disseminate the passwords to all the papers of record. She hoped it would never come to that.

Martina had the Sword of Damocles swinging over Veronica's head but she didn't need to know it. They were equals now. That was all that mattered. Martina was quick on her feet and she was determined to survive in this world – to play for keeps.

She strolled around the edge of the ballroom, smile plastered on her face. Martina had decided to keep the event management in-house from now on and promoted Priscilla Yip from assistant fundraising peon to head of donor relations. The promising young woman hadn't said a word to anyone else at the foundation about her conversation with Peony Huang and was overjoyed when the accusations against Martina were proved to be false.

She found Priscilla, clipboard in hand, beside the shellfish bar.

Kissing her on the cheek, Martina said, 'Everything looks great, Priscilla. And so do you.'

'Thank you, Martina. The auction items are all set to go,' she said, nerves showing. 'I just had to try some of the chilli prawns.' Priscilla blushed.

'Don't fret, Priscilla. Live a little. The prawns are delicious,' said Martina. 'Straight from Boracay.' She pointed to the DOS ANGELES FISH BAR banner. 'The owner used to be my helper.'

'No! Really?'

'I believe in promoting women.' Martina smiled. 'I see a brilliant career ahead of you at the Lourdes Hawkins Foundation. Merry Christmas.'

'Merry Christmas,' echoed Priscilla as Martina walked away.

Snagging a glass of champagne from a passing waiter, Martina waved at Apple across the dancefloor. If she wasn't mistaken, Apple was wearing a gorgeous paisley Etro gown. She'd put two and two together as soon as Veronica reappeared, and Veronica rewarded the gallerist's discretion by financing Apple's own gallery on Hollywood Road.

'Martina!'

She found herself waylaid by an all-smiles Cressida Wong. 'Happy Christmas, Cressida,' she greeted her.

'What a wonderful event.'

'That's kind of you to say.'

Quarter-sized diamonds dangled from Cressida's ears. 'The last few months must have been a whirlwind for you,' she said. 'Did you visit the set when they were filming? SinoTop provided all of the security for the A-listers while they were in town, did you know?'

'No, I didn't know.'

Martina had assumed that when Veronica was found to be very much alive the movie about her death would be cancelled. Nope. The Burbank money men just slapped a 'Based on True Events' disclaimer on the film and were excited to capitalise on the worldwide notoriety. If it did well at the box office, they were set to greenlight a sequel where Veronica comes back from the dead.

Fancy that.

'Listen, Martina,' said Cressida, lowering her voice. 'Last time we saw each other, I was in a bad place. I said things I regret.'

Martina sipped her champagne. 'I don't think you do, Cressida. But I don't blame you. I wasn't fair to you in my book.'

Cressida stared at her a moment. 'No, you weren't.'

'Clean slate?'

'Clean slate,' she said with a cautious smile.

'Excellent. I'll count on you at the auction later.'

Martina wandered away before the other woman could reply. Cressida undoubtedly still considered Martina a parasite, but now she was a parasite she didn't want to piss off. It was Christmas, Martina could afford to be charitable.

She stopped by the dim sum buffet table, helping herself to a *xiaolongbao*, when she heard a voice at her ear. 'So you're incompetent but not corrupt.'

Martina pivoted on the spot.

Peony Huang's expression was blank. She wore a red silk gown and a finely embroidered bolero jacket.

'Veronica wants to keep you heading the foundation and she says she has you to thank for coming back to life – but I'll be monitoring my investment closely.'

Martina tried hard not to choke on the soup dumpling. 'We have new safeguards in place. I'd be happy for you to audit us whenever suits you.'

Peony didn't acknowledge her offer. 'You were close with the Barrons, weren't you?' She spoke of them as if they were dead.

'I suppose it's all relative.' Martina shrugged. 'I hear Iain's returned to Edinburgh to study medicine. For the best. The business with the mine was shocking.'

'Yes, shocking.'

'Would you like some dim sum?' Martina said, a bead of sweat sluicing down her neck.

'Too greasy. Not like in Guangzhou.'

Veronica saved her from more terrifyingly awkward small talk. 'Auntie Peony, Happy Christmas!'

The two women exchanged kisses. 'Are you enjoying yourself?' asked Veronica.

'I came straight from Beijing,' said Peony.

'It means so much to me.'

'It's cold. You still plan to move there after new year?'

Veronica looked from Martina to Peony. 'I'll fly back and forth, but yes. I signed the lease for an office on Financial Street. Cixi Consulting has a nice ring to it, don't you think?'

The older woman chuckled at last. '*Hao*. Arthur would be proud.'

'I want to foster Sino-Anglo relations,' said Veronica. 'Strike out on my own. Make my mark like my great-greats.'

'Didn't your great-greats start the Opium War?' said Martina.

Peony Huang pierced her with a glance. 'Maybe you are not so stupid.' To Veronica she said, 'Happy Christmas. We'll go to Liqun for duck when I come north.'

And then she walked away.

Veronica guffawed. Martina finished her drink. 'She's starting to like you,' she said.

'You're joking.'

'Not at all, darling.'

The auction made a stupefyingly large amount of money before the band struck up a rendition of 'Santa Claus Is Coming To Town'.

Martina spied Ao Wing standing on his own near the stage, observing his kingdom.

'Merry Christmas, Mr Ao,' Martina said, coming to stand beside him.

'Merry Christmas. I like the way Americans say it,' he told her. 'But you must call me Vasco. We are friends now, I'd like to think.'

Martina swallowed. 'Me too.'

'Friends do each other favours.'

'They do.'

'I have been thinking much about my grandfather recently. About my life.' Ao Wing gazed out at the drunken revellers. 'I want people to hear my story in my own words. You are a good writer, I am told,' he said. 'You could help me do this.'

'Be your ghostwriter?' Martina said.

'Funny word.' It was the first real smile she'd ever seen on his lips. 'I like it. Yes, you will write about my ghosts.'

'It would be my honour.'

He turned to go. Martina touched a hand to his shoulder. Ao Wing looked at her askance. 'Mr Ao – Vasco. I had been wondering . . . I've just received a sizable payment for my books that I'd like to invest.' *Now or never, Piggy.* 'Are you still accepting investments in the Lusitano Palace Mekong?'

'No.'

'Oh, well never mind . . .'

'I have a new project in need of investors, however. In Myanmar.'

'Isn't there . . . isn't there a war going on?' asked Martina.

'It will pass.' Ao Wing seized her gaze. 'The Lusitano Palace Mandalay. On the banks of the Irrawaddy. Magnificent.'

Martina counted the beats of her heart in her throat. She looked at the money splashing around the ballroom. She thought of Spencer's family. She thought of the reprobates at The Buxton School. *This* was why she didn't want to antagonise Ao Wing or Veronica with knowledge of the recordings. She wanted them on her side. She wanted to do business with them. She no longer cared about passing moral judgement. Hell, even the Kennedys had been bootleggers.

No one ever made a fortune in a generation playing by the rules.

'*Yes,*' Martina breathed. 'It sounds like a fantastic opportunity. Thank you, Vasco.'

'Come by my office next week. You'll give me your money, and I'll repay you with my ghosts.'

'Ho, ho, ho!' A roly-poly Santa burst on to the stage, distracting Martina. A minute later, Ao Wing was gone.

Veronica danced with the Santa before he traversed the ballroom, handing out party favours, cheap freshwater pearl bracelets.

Sidling next to her, Martina said, 'Yes, Veronica. There is a Santa Claus.'

Veronica snorted. A fresh round of snow fell from the ceiling.

Looking around them, Martina said, 'Is this the Christmas Future you envisioned?'

Veronica raised her champagne flute aloft.

'God bless us, every one, Marty! Every bloody one.'

Best Friends Forever

Martina Torres

Camden Press

Uncorrected proof. First edition: Fall 2017

I Will Survive

Conventional wisdom holds that everyone has one great love. I am not a conventional girl. A material one? Yes, guilty. But no devotee of orthodoxy.

My first – and, so far, only – husband was not my soulmate. Not by a long shot.

Life has taught me that the greatest love you can have is someone who sees you as you really are. This might be the person who shares your bed, or it might not.

For me, my greatest love was my best friend. The first person to see me as a survivor. Fierce as an alley cat, a chipped china teacup, used but serviceable. More than anything else, the last few years have shown me I can survive anything. As my great-grandmother who hailed from the land of the Northern Lights would say, *When it snows, you walk in the snow.*

I lost my best friend when I was twenty-eight years old. I mourned her with a grief that was almost unbearable because she was the only person in my life to recognise what I was truly capable of – it took her death for me to figure it out for myself.

When I was thirty-two going on thirty-three, I got her back.

And it was just the beginning. The beginning of me . . .

Author's Note

*I*dentity is mutable. Who we want to be, who we were, who we convince ourselves we are, how we want to be perceived – especially the desire to control how we are classified by other people – is at the heart of *The Many Lies of Veronica Hawkins*. Veronica is willing to 'die' to protect her family's legacy, and Martina will go to extraordinary, even criminal, lengths to maintain the fictitious self that she's willed into being.

The strands that would weave themselves into this novel first began swirling around the back of my mind in the spring of 2020, during the bizarrely balmy weather of London Lockdown 1.0. When news of a virus spreading in China first emerged, I was transported back to being quarantined in my apartment in Beijing with swine flu for a whole week, which seemed like an eternity at the time. Naively, I assumed Covid would be contained like swine flu and SARS before it.

In my day job as a literary agent, I was pitching a non-fiction proposal about the 2019 Hong Kong protests by a veteran journalist as the virus took hold and dramatically changed the story. By the end of June 2020, a new national security law had been passed by Beijing, giving sweeping powers to the central government to shape life in Hong Kong as never before. I'd left shortly before the first Occupy Central, or Umbrella Movement, began in response to a decision by the Standing Committee of the National People's

Congress regarding who could stand for Chief Executive. This move was widely seen as reneging on a key part of 'one country, two systems' and its promise of eventual universal suffrage. It is, of course, important to note that, as a crown colony, Hong Kong never benefitted from true democracy. Nevertheless, the city did have a vibrant, rowdy, free press of which I'd been a part, and it was hard to imagine that ever coming to a crashing halt.

Yet the Hong Kong I recognised was vanishing before my eyes. Nostalgia, perhaps, but also something more urgent propelled me to write the city I had experienced, the city I loved and which had given me so much, on to the page. There are places that seep into your bones, and Hongkers is one of those places for me. At the end of my very first trip, a decade after the Handover, as the skyscrapers peppering the hills faded in the rearview mirror of the taxi, I felt an ache, a knowing that Hong Kong wasn't done with me yet. By the time I finished writing my first draft of *Veronica*, the book had become historical fiction.

While I was drafting, I also had to run the gauntlet known as the Life in the UK Test. To remain on this soggy isle, I diligently learned all manner of sundry facts, from who was the first person to run a mile in under four minutes (Roger Bannister) to what is the national flower of Wales (daffodil). I forced my Cornish husband – who didn't know the answers – to drill me every night. Being prone to rumination, I wondered how it would feel to finally gain British citizenship more than two decades after I first came to study in the UK. Would I ever actually feel British (and what did that *mean* exactly?) or would my accent ensure that I'd forever be a Yank?

Like Martina, I was born in a city of immigrants – the Big Apple – to first- and second-generation immigrants from Europe and South America. Living in China, Hong Kong and Singapore as a pale-skinned Westerner, I was labelled an expat rather than an immigrant – sometimes with not unjustified contempt, as I was also attributed a correspondingly higher social status than immigrants from elsewhere in the region working in construction or as domestic servants. If I had stayed in Hong Kong, unlike Iris, I would have received my permanent residence with little fanfare. No tests required.

My identity as a Latina, in addition to American, is something that was elided in Asia, as it always has been in the UK. Back in the 1990s, when I was filling out registration forms at the GP's office, I remember my surprise that there were no Hispanic or Latino boxes to tick. Especially since my first real contact with British culture came via Argentina, the country of my father's birth.

I was too young for the war over Las Malvinas to have made much of an impression, but I do remember going to the only other Harrods in the world, which had been established in Buenos Aires in the early twentieth century. My Argentine cousins played rugby, football and polo. I delighted in having afternoon tea with them every day after school, although we ate *medialunas* and *dulce de leche* instead of scones and clotted cream. Although Argentina never officially comprised part of the British empire, it was arguably financially colonised.

After two failed invasions of Buenos Aires, the British merchants succeeded where the Navy had failed in becoming an integral part of the fledgling state when what became Argentina gained independence from Spain. The Anglo-Argentine families of Scottish, English and Welsh descent financed and controlled the critical infrastructure and industries throughout the nineteenth century, during which Britain was the largest market for Argentina's exports and its biggest investor.

The commercial underpinnings of the development of both Argentina and Hong Kong therefore have some striking similarities. When Veronica tells Martina that Hawkins Pacific invested in Argentine railways, it is a subtle reminder that her family was on top there too. The British influence in Hong Kong was, of course, much more pronounced, yet as I explored the city, I had this strange sensation, almost akin to déjà vu. It was as if the same veneer had been painted on to a city that lay continents away from Buenos Aires.

The hybrid identity of Hong Kong is, of course, so much richer and more complex than just its colonial legacy. It's an amalgam of all the peoples and cultures who have made the city their home. What the recent protests brought to the fore was the strength and singularity of the Hongkonger identity.

Working as a journalist, I met people from a cross-section of society. I was energised by profiling the people I encountered but, at the same time, I was also wary of falling into the trap of 'worlding the world', as articulated by postcolonial critic Gayatri Chakravorty Spivak. 'Worlding' is Spivak's term for the imperialist project that presumed that the territory it colonised was uninscribed; it refers not only to the colonial conquest itself but the way in which it is narrated, in which the historical record is produced.

My father taught me to love antique maps as much as he did the day he told me that the boundary lines could change – that I should study who changed them and why, who were the winners and who were the losers. He embodied the so-called American Dream: the immigrant whose high school history teacher called him a 'taco twirler', who went on to get a PhD in history from Stanford University funded by the US Defense Department. I first learned about 'worlding' from him.

Spivak also critiques the innate colonialism with which 'metropolitan' (white/First World) feminists can often regard non-Western women. There is a tendency towards essentialism that leads metropolitan feminists to view non-Western women as a collective mirror through which they perceive themselves. This projection is therefore inherently narcissistic. Spivak famously explores the dangers of this attitude in her critique of Julia Kristeva's *On Chinese Women* and the resulting attempt by Western women to intervene on behalf of non-Western women with superior benevolence.

What I have attempted instead – and the road to Hell is paved with authorial intentions – is an act of anamorphosis. Perhaps the most well-known example of anamorphosis is *The Ambassadors* (1533) by Hans Holbein the Younger, which currently hangs in the National Gallery, London. The painting depicts two French ambassadors to the English court of Henry VIII standing before a table decorated with books, navigational instruments and red-lined globes. In the foreground is what at first appears to be a stain or smear but which when viewed from the right angle is revealed to be a skull.

This process of resolving the distorted object is called anamorphosis. French psychoanalyst Jacques Lacan employs the concept of anamorphosis as illustrated by *The Ambassadors* to describe the unconscious, applying it to both our deepest fears and desires – those which we're afraid to acknowledge. He uses anamorphosis to explain how a person or thing might represent to our unconscious mind something completely different from what first appears to be the case.

The Ambassadors' skull has been interpreted by art critics as a memento mori: a reminder that no matter how young and powerful you are, death is always waiting. But given the other details Holbein the Younger included in the portrait, it could also be read as the pain and suffering behind the glorious lie of empire. We can see how Spivak's 'worlding' and the Othering of non-Western peoples as part of the imperialist project was an attempt *not* to see the skull, to make colonised peoples the container of Western fear-fantasies.

You must shift your perspective to see the truth behind the object. Sometimes we must also be taken completely out of context, to have our perspective turned on its head, in order to see the uncomfortable truths contained within our lives, within ourselves. The truths we have been hiding from and yet which have been hiding in plain sight all along.

My reference to Jane Eyre's red room in the book was intentional – not for the reason Martina gives – but because it is Bertha Mason (the first Mrs Rochester), a Creole woman from Jamaica, whose wealth is directly responsible for the affluent life which Jane enjoys upon her marriage to Rochester (after her predecessor has conveniently died in a fire she set). It is the spectre of imperialism that truly haunts the beloved classic. Similarly, Martina chooses to look away from her reality by siding with Veronica time and time again. Like identity, there are many forms of empire and Martina allies herself with whichever power she sees as in the ascendant.

Martina claims at the beginning of her memoir to have written a love story, but it is an *amour fou*, a love that requires disavowal. You won't believe me, but I wrote Veronica as Martina's courtly lady without realising it. My academic training as a medievalist is evidently deep-seated. The courtly love ballads that delighted audiences in twelfth-century France portrayed an impossible relationship – usually between a knight and a married lady, like Tristan and Isolde. It is a love that cannot be consummated without dire consequences.

The courtly lady is put on a pedestal by the male poet, and she becomes the idealised object of his desire and a mirror for his fantasies. Because the courtly lady is emptied of substance, becoming a vessel for the knight's desires, it is impossible to form an emotional bond with her. Like I said, you won't believe me that it wasn't a conscious decision. Martina idolises Veronica, writes her a love letter in the form of a memoir, is desperate for her resurrection.

And yet when she gets Veronica back there is a lingering sense of dread, of denial and potential cruelty. Veronica is everything Martina is not: she is the trauma of the impossibility of Martina's desires. She longs to be Jane, but the night Martina pretends to be Veronica in Laos, she catches a glimpse of herself as Bertha and immediately runs away. She sees the skull but she denies it.

Having lived outside the country of my birth since the age of seventeen, going on thirty years, I know that every time you're taken out of context, your biases are thrown into sharper relief. You are forced to reconsider whether your views and beliefs are truly your own.

You gain the opportunity to ask what you really want. To see who you really are.

The trick, the challenge, is to not be afraid of the answers.

In writing this book, I hope I've asked the right questions. It's up to you to decide.

Reading Group
Discussion Questions

1. Martina states several times in her memoir that her book is a love story. Having finished the novel, do you think that's true? How did your perception change as you read?

2. Martina feels that she changes fundamentally as a person by leaving New York, meeting Veronica and experiencing a world that has different rules and expectations to the one in which she grew up. Have you ever experienced growth or change by moving to a new place?

3. The reader first meets Martina in her memoir where she is presenting a curated version of herself. In Part II, Martina says that people prefer Memoir Martina to who she really is. Did you find the Martina in Parts I and II to be different?

4. Similarly, how is Veronica different in Parts I and II? Why do you think she casts such a spell on Martina?

5. Martina has a difficult relationship with Cressida Wong, in part because she relates to her too much. They were both outsiders at their elite high schools because neither of them was considered white. Why do you think Martina chose to side with Veronica over Cressida time and time again? What does that tell you about Martina?

6. How do the different characters feel their Otherness? How does this interact with the postcolonial context? Which characters still hold Orientalist views and what purpose does the tension inherent in the colonial legacy serve in the narrative?

7. What was your impression of Martina's marriage with Spencer? Do you think she portrayed him fairly? Do you agree with her assessment that Spencer married her as an act of rebellion against his parents?

8. Martina's relationship with her mother features prominently in the narrative. What influence do you think Martina's mother had in the choices that Martina ultimately makes?

9. Veronica and Martina have had an arguably toxic friendship throughout the book. Do you believe that either of them can ever be the friend to the other that they say they want to be?

10. The book ends with Martina making the decision to do business with Ao Wing whom she knows is involved with organised crime. Did this surprise you? What do you think this means for Martina's future? What would you have done?

Acknowledgements

*B*ook people really are the best people and there are so many who deserve a hearty round of applause. Top of the list is Joelle Hobeika, who encouraged me to write something that drew on my time in Asia and became the most wonderful friend and collaborator. Thank you also to Josh Bank, Matt Bloomgarden, Sara Shandler and Romy Golan for believing in Veronica and Martina from the start. My editor Krystyna Green is an absolute star and understood exactly the story I wanted to tell. Thank you to the whole Constable team, especially Christopher Sturtivant and Hannah Wann.

I suspect that many readers will have picked up this book because of the stunning cover and I must thank Ellen Rockell for hitting it out of the park. Huge appreciation also goes to the terrific rights team – Rebecca Folland, Jessica Purdue, Helena Dorée and Louise Henderson – for all they do. Likewise, Brionee Fenlon and Henry Lord are the masters of buzz and getting the word out. Thanks also to Rebecca Sheppard, Howard Watson, Amber Burlinson and Amanda Keats for your eagle eyes.

Pandemic aside, writing can be a lonely pursuit and I want to thank all my early readers and supporters for their advice, suggestions, corrections and cheerleading which continues to keep me sane: Lokkei Li, Carlie Sorosiak, Diana Chu, Nisha Sharma, Olivia Abtahi, Sarah Kay, Karen McManus, Natasha Ngan, Kelly deVos,

Elizabeth Lim, Andrea Ledoux Richards, Annie Stone and Kamilla Benko. As always, a shout out to my Trinity girls (you know who you are). Without the fabulous colleagues and friends I made across China and SE Asia, this book would not exist and, in particular, I am grateful for Winnie Chen, Sandy Zhang, Terence Leung and Ying Chan for her mentorship.

Launching a literary agency and a debut novel in close proximity to one another is perhaps not to be advised and a massive debt of gratitude goes to Isabel Lineberry, my right-hand woman at Pérez Literary & Entertainment, for too many things to list. Thank you, also, to my talented and generous clients for their support.

To Jack Mozley, my partner in all things: *Ne vus sanz mei, ne mei sanz vus.*

And last, but certainly not least, I want to thank you, the reader, for coming on this journey with me – I hope you've enjoyed it!